MACHINE
LEARNING

MACHINE LEARNING

New and Collected Stories

Hugh Howey

A John Joseph Adams Book

Mariner Books

Houghton Mifflin Harcourt

Boston   New York

First Mariner Books edition 2017
Copyright © 2017 by Hugh Howey
Foreword copyright © 2017 by Jamie Ford

For information about permission to reproduce selections from this book,
write to trade.permissions@hmhco.com or to Permissions,
Houghton Mifflin Harcourt Publishing Company,
3 Park Avenue, 19th Floor, New York, New York 10016.

www.hmhco.com

Library of Congress Cataloging-in-Publication Data is available.
ISBN 978-1-328-76753-0 (hardcover)
ISBN 978-1-328-76752-3 (pbk.)
ISBN 978-1-328-76433-1 (ebook)

Book design by Greta Sibley

Printed in the United States of America
DOC 10 9 8 7 6 5 4 3 2 1

For Mom and Dad

CONTENTS

Fantasy

Algorithms of Love and Hate

Virtual Worlds

Lost and Found

FOREWORD

As I sit at my desk writing this, Hugh is sailing around the world.

Like many of his friends, I follow his travels with no small degree of admiration, satiating my own twitching wanderlust vicariously through his seaborne adventures from South Africa, to New York, to Cuba, and on to the Panama Canal.

I smiled along with his legions of fans as he sent out a call via Facebook for a potential crew member — someone to help out as he crosses the Pacific:

> Looking for someone who can teach me Spanish and how to play piano. Must be an expert backgammon and chess player. Likes cheese and wine. Plays video games and operates a camera in manual mode. Enjoys yoga, paddleboarding, and billiards. Takes brief showers. Sailing experience not required.

Unsurprisingly, there were literally hundreds of eager and willing sea dogs of every stripe volunteering for that daunting (and potentially dangerous) leg of his journey.

As I read the comments, I couldn't help but stare out the window at a snow-covered field here in Montana, where the temperature was just inching up to zero. I remembered Hawaii, where I'd once lived for six years. I recalled countless weekends spent aboard a friend's boat, on the leeward side of Oahu, diving with reef sharks, sea turtles, and schools of wrasse and butterfly fish.

Then I remembered a long day, standing on the bow pulpit, turning green in high surf.

I returned to the online discussion, adding, "You would get bored watching me barf over the rail."

Hugh replied, "I would never tire of that."

That's Hugh, the kindest, most joyful contrarian you'll ever meet.

Where some people are antagonistic by nature — loving to argue for the sake of cruel, intellectual sport, or rebelling against convention just to play the devil's advocate — Hugh is a completely different kind of contrarian. He just naturally sees what most people don't. He recognizes patterns of human behavior and instinctively moves in the opposite direction, with eyes wide-open, exploring.

As a writer, he manages to somehow divorce himself from the preconceived notions most of us wear like millstones around our necks for the balance of our waking lives.

This was evident as we had breakfast a few years ago in Milan, Italy — where our separate book travels happened to intersect. I remember how talking to Hugh about writing, publishing, politics, religion, artificial intelligence, and human sexuality was like discovering things all around me that I didn't know were there.

He left me scratching my head, asking myself, "How did I not notice?"

That's what reading this collection is like.

These stories feel like going back to your childhood home and discovering there are secret rooms you've never explored.

Some of these rooms are unique expressions of artificial intelligence — not the broad AI overlords that typify speculative fiction, but tales of narrow AI discovering itself, seeking purpose, and, dare I say, enlightenment. Stories like "Machine Learning" and "Glitch" will leave you revisiting your ideas of intelligence and broadening your concept of humanity.

While other rooms in this collection are devoted to alien worlds, observed from 62,000 feet above, in "The Walk up Nameless Ridge." Or Earth, seen through the eyestalks of tentacled soldiers — the grunts who make up an invading armada in "Second Suicide."

There are rooms devoted to dark fantasy like "Hell from the East," and waiting rooms for desperate and benevolent deities in "The Good God," and the all-too-spacious loneliness of virtual worlds in "The Plagiarist." And there are rooms that stretch our concepts of love when augmented by technology, time, and space with "WHILE (u > i) i- -;" and "The Automated Ones."

Of course, there's the big, deep room devoted to Silo, the epic world Hugh has created and open-sourced to his fans and aspiring fantasists. Rather than tease us with alternative characters we hardly know, he serves up his main protagonist, Jules. (I'd say more, but I don't want to spoil anything — read on and you'll understand.)

Finally, there is the soul-baring masterpiece of "Peace in Amber," a Hugh Howey story interlaced with Kurt Vonnegut's world of *Slaughterhouse-Five*. This is a story based in real emotional pain and loss — the vulnerability of this novelette is its strength. Its honesty — its gritty reality — is what propels this fantastic, surreal journey. It's one of the most heartbreaking and satisfying stories I've ever read.

So when asked to write a foreword for this collection, I was honored and a bit tongue-tied, honestly. (Picture Garth from *Wayne's World* bowing and exclaiming: "I'm not worthy!") But I knew that I'd get to read many of these stories all over again, plus the new ones — which was like a system upgrade for my brain, for my imagination.

The experience was so profound and enlightening, it almost had me imagining being on Hugh's catamaran, *Wayfinder,* standing at the helm, crossing the Pacific, watching the sunrise, somehow not turning green.

Almost.

Jamie Ford
Great Falls, Montana
January 2017

INTRODUCTION

I've always wanted to be a truck driver. For years, this felt like what I should be doing with my time. I tried to convince a girlfriend once to quit school so we could be a long-haul team and crisscross the United States in a Peterbilt. The hours and hours of staring at the horizon appeals to me, the time to get lost in one's thoughts, the self-contained world of sleeper cabs, some mechanical issue that always needs fixing, the roadside diners full of colorful characters.

It took me a while to realize what I really wanted was to be Han Solo, who long ago drove a big rig named the *Millennium Falcon* all over a galaxy far, far away. I saw *Star Wars* when I was very young, and I've wanted to be Han Solo ever since. A vagabond with a personality type that role-playing peeps would recognize as chaotic good (the sort of person who breaks rules, but in the name of serving a moral purpose). Sadly, my girlfriend was not enthused with the idea and decided to stay in school. (Pro tip: Don't let someone you date think they'd make a wonderful Wookiee.)

The truck driver dream was put on hold, but it didn't die. In college, I met a ballet dancer who lived on a small sailboat in Charleston Harbor. I had no idea people did such a thing. The small boat was like my beloved sleeper cabs, but afloat. I immediately started searching and found a boat I could afford several states away. I read a few books on ocean navigating and then nearly got my best friend and myself killed sailing around Cape Hatteras in a winter norther.

But I had my *Falcon* at last. And as the semesters dragged on, the horizon beckoned. I couldn't just sit still; there was too much out there to see. So I dropped out of college after my junior year and made my way to the Bahamas. What I discovered there is a world completely alien from the life I left behind. A world of salty retirees, wannabe pirates, and clashing cultures. Here were all these little clumps of vagabonds bouncing off one another, swapping stories, borrowing tools, trading tips. I was young and broke and would scamper up masts or dive below keels to do jobs other boat owners didn't enjoy. In exchange, I was given plates of food, which I scarfed down between grunts of gratitude. My hair grew long, I became scruffy, and I probably smelled like a nerf herder. I was becoming Chewbacca.

When the money ran out, I got work on other people's boats. They started small, but someone would ask if I could drive a bigger boat, and I figured the general principles were the same. This was a very surreal transition in my life. I went from a half-starved kid on a twenty-seven-foot sailboat with no toilet and no shower to a clean-shaven guy in pressed uniforms who drove mega-yachts for the mega-wealthy. These boats had hot tubs on top and garages full of smaller boats in their bellies. The helms looked like spaceships, like the cockpit of a jetliner on steroids. I moved these large machines from one place to another and fixed anything that broke along the way. I had found my truck-driving job at last!

The next decade of my life was spent on yachts like this. Much of that time I sat at the helm and stared at the horizon, lost in my thoughts.

Hours and hours of horizons and daydreams. Night shifts with stars so bright, you could read by them. Flat seas that reflected these pinpricks until I was surrounded by stars, floating in deep space. With these years of staring at the horizon, I realized that my fascination with the future and my inability to sit still come from the same insatiable curiosity: I want to know what's around the corner. I strain for it, not content for it to come to me. The futurist and the vagabond are the same souls — one in body and the other in thought.

My love of science fiction comes from the same place. With science fiction, we dream about what's around the corner. We use the genre as a warning, or as a way to explore time, space, and progress. The same people who crossed seas in bygone eras, or rode wagons out west, or put men on the moon are now dreaming about humanity on Mars and beyond. These are probably the same tinkerers who fashioned better spear points or learned to sew and make fire. What's next? What's out there? These questions haunt me.

The stories you're about to read are my attempts to answer these questions. Many of them were written during a sedentary period of my life, while I was working in a bookstore and writing my first novels. There are recurring themes here that I was dimly aware of when I was writing them but have become stark now that they've been collected into one place. A couple of these stories are new. The rest have been published in so many scattered ways and places that I doubt anyone has seen them all before.

When I look at this body of work, and the more than a dozen novels I've written, I feel once again like that kid at the helm of a boat much too large for his qualifications. I honestly don't understand how I've gotten here. One step at a time, I suppose. One sentence after the other. One daydream, one idea, an early morning writing before I have to go to work . . . and eventually you get to a place that might've humbled me if I'd thought about it all at once.

My sailing trip around the world has progressed much the same way.

Besides wanting to be a truck driver (or Han Solo), I've had two impossible fantasies at the very top of my bucket list. One was to write a novel; the other was to sail around the world. As I write this in March 2017, I'm sitting on my boat off of Isabela Island in the Galápagos. I sailed here from South Africa, going as far north as Maine, spending a month in Cuba, and just recently crossing through the Panama Canal. I'm halfway through my voyage, and what seemed unlikely in the whole has been slowly achieved one horizon at a time.

And isn't this true for humanity at large? We live in a world not of science fiction, but of science fact. I will upload this introduction to my publisher via the ether. I live on a solar-powered machine not much less remarkable than the *Millennium Falcon*. When I look at gleaming cityscapes of glass towers touching the clouds, it strikes me that a band of several hundred primates spread out and built all of this from what we dug out of the mud. Out of the *mud*.

Is it possible to doubt where we might go, seeing how far we've come? We do the impossible daily. We are creeping ever toward that unreachable horizon. I wonder what we'll find when we get there.

Aliens and
Alien Worlds

The Walk up Nameless Ridge

I

It was difficult to sleep at night, wishing good men dead. This was but one of the hurtful things I felt in my bones and wished I could ignore. It was an ugly truth waving its arms that I turned my gaze from, that I didn't like to admit even to myself. But while my bag warmed me with the last of its power and my breath spilled out in white plumes toward the roof of our tent, while the flicker of a whisper stove melted snow for midnight tea, I lay in that dead zone above sixty thousand feet and hoped not just for the failure of those above me, but that no man summit and live to tell the tale. Not before I had my chance.

It was a shameful admission, one I nearly raised with Hanson, my tent mate, to see in the wrinkles of his snow-beat face whether this was a guilt shared. I suspected it was. In the mess tents and around the yellow craters we dubbed latrines, the look among us was that only one would be remembered. The rest would die alone in the snow or live a long life forgotten — and not one of us would've been able to explain to a child the difference. Frozen to death by altitude or by time was all the same. The truth was this: History remembers the first, and only the first. These are the creeping and eternal glaciers, the names etched across all time like scars in granite cliffs. Those who came after were the inch or two of snowdrift that would melt in due time. They would trickle, forgotten, into the pores of the earth, be swallowed, and melt snow at the feet of other forgotten men.

It was a quarter past Eno's midnight and time to get up. If Shubert and Humphries were to make it to the top, they likely would've by now. If any of their gear still worked, they would be radioing in their victory, taking the first pictures of starlit peaks wrinkling far past the limits of sight. By now, they would know how many fingers and toes it cost them, how much oxygen was left in their tanks, whether or not they would live to speak of the mountain's conquest.

The faint odor of tea penetrated my dark thoughts. It must've been a potent brew to smell it at all. We had already scaled beyond the heights where taste and scent fade to oblivion. One had to remind himself to eat and drink, for the stomach is one of those organs that knows when to quit. It is the first, in fact, to go. The mind of the climber is the last.

Hanson brought me tea. I wormed a single arm out into the cold, though my heating bag had become a feeble thing. I did not want to lose what little it held. I coughed into my fist, that persistent cough of the dead zone, and accepted the steaming mug.

There were no words spoken as we forced ourselves to drink. Every twitch was an effort at those altitudes. We were sleeping higher than all the fabled peaks of Cirrus VII. Our fourth camp along the Slopeson Ridge, at 42,880 feet, was higher than any speck of dirt on Hanson's home planet. And when we arrived on this wasteland of a frozen ball, out here in a corner of the galaxy where men go either to not be found or to be remembered for all time, we set up a base camp very near to the highest peak of the place I grew up: Earth. Where men were first born and first began to scale to deadly heights.

I sipped my tea, burning my numb lips, and told myself it would be an Earth-born who scaled Mount Mallory first. This was a distasteful idea that I and many others were willing to share. The secret I kept to myself was that others could die if they dared climb her before me.

2

Two other private teams were making a go of it that season. Government expeditions and collectives of alpine clubs had given up decades ago. They now watched as men such as I took leave of our day jobs and, with borrowed funds and the best of gear and medicine at hand, set out to prove what was possible.

The window of opportunity for a summit was but a bare sliver of a crack. Half a day at most when the fearful winds of that dizzy world slowed to a manageable gale and before the monsoons buried the rock under drifts a hundred meters deep. The problem, of course, was in not knowing when that half-day would fall. Every climber across thirteen worlds studied the weather charts like day traders. As the season neared, predictions were logged on the net, men in their warm homes with their appetites intact and the feeling still in their fingers and toes would make guesses, watch reports from the satellites left behind by those government expeditions, and make bold claims.

I had been one of those prognosticators until recently. But now, after spending a night at camp 7 beneath the Khimer Ridge, I felt as though I had graduated to one who could sneer at the antics of those at lesser heights. By dint of my travel between the stars and my arduous climb thus far, I was now an expert. It lent Hanson and me the illusion that our guess was far more refined than the others.

Or perhaps it was the lack of oxygen that made us crazy this way.

In the middle of that terrible night, rather than spend my last morning thinking of my wife and kids or dwelling further on the debts incurred to travel to frontier stars and hike up a murderous peak, I thought of all my fellow climbers who were safely ensconced in their homes as they followed our every move.

Right now, they likely followed Shubert and Humphries, two strong climbers who had knocked out all else the galaxy had to offer. They would also be keeping an eye on Hanson and me. And then there was the pairing of Ziba and Cardhil, who were also making a bid that year.

Ziba was an enigma of a climber, a small woman who looked far too frail in her heat suit and mask. When first I saw her navigating the Lower Collum Ice Falls above base camp, I mistook her oxygen tanks for double-aughts in size, as they dwarfed her frame. The consensus was that there was little to fear in her attempt that year. I had done some digging before my uplink succumbed to the cold and read that Ziba had knocked out the peaks of her home planet, none of which top thirty thousand feet, but she had at least done them in style. No oxygen and swiftly, one of those modern climbers. It had been a private joy to watch her give in to the true mountaineering methods necessary on Mallory's great face. The methodical lift of crampons, the bulging tanks of air, the fogging and frosted masks. These were the ways of the true climber. Mallory is an instructor to all, and Ziba did not seem too full of herself to submit, learn, and adapt.

Cardhil, I figured, was the great unknown. Ziba had chosen an odd tent mate in the android. And if it were a manchine that was the first to summit great Mallory, the consensus across the alpine forums was that nothing would have occurred at all. There would not even be an accomplishment to asterisk. And anyway, I had sent notes a week ago to an old climbing buddy, telling him not to worry. The cold was worse on the manchine's joints than our own. Hanson and I had left camp 6 while Ziba was chipping away at Cardhil's frozen ankles. And please don't tell me that a man's memories counted for the man himself, that the android lived because he remembered living. I have had many a conversation with Cardhil around base camp and watched him with the Sherpas. He is no different than the droid who cleans my pool or walks my dog. A clever approximation, but with movements too precise, too clean, to pass for human. The other day, Hanson nudged me in time to turn and catch Cardhil taking a great spill on the east face. The way he did even this was unnatural. Supremely calm and without a whimper, the manchine had slid several hundred feet on his ass, working his climbing ax into the deep snow, with all the false grace of an automaton.

Nobody feared this duo as long as they were behind and below us. There, off our ropes and out of our way, they had only themselves to kill.

3

Hanson and I left our flapping tent in utter darkness. The driven snow blocked out all but a few of the twinkling stars. Near the tent, a pile of spent oxygen bottles gathered a drift. They glowed bright in Hanson's headlamp. Debris such as this would be left for all time. They were an addition to the landscape. The local Ha-Jing, whose lands included half of great Mallory, made good money selling permits to aspiring climbers, and this litter came with the riches. The south face of Mallory, which some climbers posited would make for an easier ascent, was governed by the irascible Hiti. Great climbers by all accounts but miserable at governing. The only assaults on that face have been clandestine affairs. There had been some arrests over the years, but like many who come to Eno hoping to etch their name in the history books, most simply disappeared.

Hanson broke snow for the first hour, his head down in a stiff breeze. We had radios in our parkas but rarely used them. Good tent mates had little need for words. Roped in to one another, the union becomes symbiotic. You match paces, one staring at a flash-lit patch of bright snow, the other staring at a man's back, illuminating a spot in a sea of darkness. Boots fell into the rapidly filling holes of the climber ahead, each lifting of a crampon some new torture, even with the springs of the powered climbing pants taking most of the strain.

I'd lost count of the number of peaks we'd climbed together. It was in the dozens across a handful of planets, most of those climbs coming over the past five years. Climbers tend to orbit one another long before they share tents. The first time I met Hanson was back on Earth on a new route of Nanga Parbat, a small mountain but notorious for gobbling souls. Climbers called her "Man Eater," usually with knowing and nervous smiles. Tourists from other planets came to exercise on its west slope or to make an attempt on its south face while preparing for harsher climbs. Some took the tram to Everest to hike up to the top and join the legions who made that yearly pilgrimage only to walk away wondering what the fuss was about.

I tended to bite my tongue during such diminishing talks of my planet's highest peak. My twenty-year partnership with Saul, my previous tent mate, had ended on a harmless run up Everest. There was a saying among the Hiti Sherpas: "Ropes slip through relaxed grips." The nearest I ever came to death was while climbing indoors, of all things. It wasn't something I told anyone. Those few who had been there and the doctors who tended to me knew. When anyone noticed my limp, I told them it happened during my spill on Kurshunga. I couldn't say that I'd failed to double back my harness and took a forty-foot spill on a climb whose holds had been color-coded for kids.

Saul had also fallen prey to a relaxed grip. He had died while taking a leak on Everest's South Col. It was hard to stomach, losing a good man and great friend like that. Hanson, who trudged ahead of me, had lost his former tent mate in more glorious fashion the same year Saul died. And so mountains brought couples together like retirement homes. You look around, and what you have left is what you bed down with. Ours, then, was a marriage of attrition, but it worked. Our bond was our individual losses and our mutual anger at the peaks that had taken so much from us.

As Hanson paused, exhausted, and I rounded him to break snow, I patted the old man on the back, the gesture silent with thick gloves and howling wind, but he bobbed his head in acknowledgment to let me know he was okay. I coughed a raspy rattle into my mask. We were all okay. And above us, the white plumes and airborne glitter of driven ice and snow hid the way to glory. But it was easy to find. Up. Always up. One more foot toward land that no man had ever seen and lived to tell about.

4

At sixty thousand feet — the height of two Everests stacked one on top of the other — man and machine alike tended to break down. We were at the limit of my regimen of steroids. The gears in my hiking pants could be heard grinding against one another, even over all that wind. And the grease smeared over the parts of my face not sheltered by the oxygen mask had hardened until it felt like plaster, like blistered and unfeeling skin, but to touch it and investigate it was to invite exposure and far worse.

Batteries meant to last for days would perish in hours up there. The cold was death for them. And so our suits gave up as we moved from the death zone to a land that begged for a name far more sinister. The power left in struggling batteries went to the pistons and gears, routed away from the heaters. Fingers and toes went first. They would grow numb; the blood would stop flowing through them; the flesh would become necrotic and die right there on the bone.

The Sherpas of Changli had a saying: "A man can count on two hands all the climbs he conquers, and that man conquers nothing." I always took this to mean the more we summit, the more we lose. Climbers were notorious for staring down bars in base camp at lifted mugs, silently counting digits gone missing, making a measure of a man's worth by how far they'd pushed themselves. Saul had a different take on the Changli saying. To the people who lived in the shadows of mountains, these were not things to conquer. To climb them was foolish, and who would think to do so? As much as I had loved Saul, he was always too politically correct for my tastes.

Breaking snow up that unnamed ridge, my mind turning to mush as supplemental oxygen and doped blood could only do so much, I felt the first pangs of doubt. My cough rattled inside my mask; my limbs felt like solid lead. Two days prior, at camp 5, I had pushed myself beyond my abilities. Eating and drinking moved from inconvenient chores to something I dreaded. My weight was down. I hadn't been out of my clothes to see what I'd wasted away, just comforted myself instead on how much less I now had to lug to the top.

The radio in my parka clicked on with the sound of Hanson breathing. I waited a moment between arduous steps and listened for what he had to say. When the radio clicked off, I turned to check on him, my headlamp pointed at his chest so as not to blind him. Hanson was a strong climber, one of the strongest I'd ever seen. He had fallen back to the end of the rope that joined us, his breath clouding his mask. Lifting a hand a few inches from his thigh was all the wave he could muster.

"Take your time," I told him, clicking the large switch on my belt. What I wanted to say was what the hell we thought we were doing. There, five thousand feet below us and eight light years away, was the tallest peak ever climbed. We were moving into the thin air above the highest of heads. We would have been in outer space on some small planets, in orbit around others. And still, we wanted to conquer more.

The rope between us drooped as Hanson took a few laborious steps. I turned and broke snow, resigning myself to an extra hour at the head, an extra shift to give him more rest. It was hard to know what drove you once you passed the thresholds of all pain. Maybe it was the thought of Shubert and Humphries somewhere above us, either in glory or buried in snow. Maybe it was the fear that Ziba had gotten Cardhil's ankle sorted and that they would begin their push later that morning. Or maybe it was the promise I'd made to myself after telling my wife and kids that I would be safe. I had told them that I wouldn't take chances. But I had already promised myself something different: I would come home with that final ridge named after me, or I wouldn't come home at all.

5

My altimeter died at 62,000 feet, even though the manufacturer sold these with a guarantee of 100,000. Such guarantees were bullshit gestures with no real-world testing. As I climbed, I composed the post I would make on the forums complaining of its failure. And had my remaining fingers been any kind of functional, I would've removed the strap from my arm to save the weight. Instead, I carried one more dead thing up with me. From then on, I had to guess how high I was by the hour. It was still dark and we were probably at 63,100 feet when I stumbled across Humphries.

He wore an orange suit, the kind that men with low confidence and a care for their mortal coil wore. It made them more easily found and more *likely* to be found, two very different things. I pointed out the snow-dusted form so Hanson wouldn't trip on him, but I didn't slow. Humphries had died facing the summit, which meant he hadn't made it. I felt a mix of relief and guilt for the awful thoughts I'd held in my sleeping bag all night. Shubert, of course, was still out there. We could meet him stomping down in the dark, his eyes as bright as the handful of twinkling stars above, and whatever was driving Hanson and me upward would likely leak out our pores. Whatever glory I had hoped to win would be spent in future days recounting my time on the same slopes as this other man. I would detail my ordeal up Shubert Ridge, a horrible name if ever there was one. I would write of his glory and bask in whatever shadows fell my way. These were my mad ruminations as I left his dead tent mate behind and crunched through that terrible snow a thousand feet beneath the peak.

A tug at my harness gave me pause. Hanson was flagging again, at the end of his rope and ours. I questioned what I was running on for Hanson to give out before me. I wondered if the doctors hadn't worked some kind of special magic between the doping and the careful regimen of drugs. Perhaps the coils in my pants were holding up better than his. Hanson had skimped on his gears and had invested in more heat. I may be freezing to death, but I was still climbing. I saw the look on his face, beyond the glare of my headlamp and the frost of his desperate breathing, and that look told me that this was as high as he would go. It was a look I'd only seen from him once before, but enough times from others to not need the radio.

After a coughing fit, I jerked my thumb toward the summit. Hanson lifted his hand from his thigh and waved. As I pulled the quick release that held our rope to my harness, I wondered if I would be stepping over both him and Humphries on my way back down. God, I hoped not. I watched him turn and trudge into the dark maw of night and white fang of snow before looking again to my goal. The summit was several more hours away. I would be the first or the second to stand there. Those were adjacent numbers and yet light years apart in my esteem. They were neighboring peaks with a precipitous valley between. Being second was death to me, so I lifted a boot, gears squealing, toes numb, and remembered with sadness the lies I had spoken to my family. There was nothing about this that was safe. If I loved them as much as I loved myself, I would've turned around long before Hanson had.

6

The highlanders of Eno have a saying about climbing alone: "The winds seek out the solitary." And sure enough, with Hanson dropping back to camp — *hopefully* dropping back to camp — the winds came for me and shoved my chest for being so bold. With my oxygen running low, the mask became an impediment to breathing, something to catch my coughs. Adjusting the top of the mask against my goggles, fingers frozen stiff, I let the wind howl through a crack, invigorating me with the cold. The gap sang like the sound a puff makes across the mouth of a bottle. This whirring howl was a sort of musical accompaniment. It made me feel less alone. The dwindling oxygen made me feel crazy.

When I came across Shubert, I thought he was already dead. The snow was covering him, and the ridge here was perilously narrow. Solid rock stayed dusted with snow and ice; otherwise it felt the ridge itself should be blowing away.

Shubert stirred as I made my slow and agonizing way around him. He was faintly swimming toward the summit, clawing through the ice, throwing his ax forward. I stopped and knelt by the young and powerful climber. His suit made no noise. It must've given out on him, leaving him alone and under his own power. My thoughts were as wild as the wind, disturbed by my air-starved mind. I thought of Cardhil and how something so reliant on its mechanical bits held any hope for rising above camp 7. I rested a hand on Shubert's back to let him know he wasn't alone. I don't know that he ever knew I was there. He was still crawling, inch by inch, toward the summit, as I trudged along, head down, mask singing a sad lament. If I made the top and got home, I decided I would name that ridge after him. I was already dreaming not just of being a legend, but the awesome humility I would display even so. It was delusion beyond delusion. I was dying, but like Shubert, I cared only about the next inch.

The oxygen ran dry as the sun broke. My headlamp had grown feeble anyway, frosted with ice and with its battery crippled by the freezing temperatures. This was my last sunrise, I was fairly sure. Cutting through the shark's teeth of peaks that ran the breadth of this alien continent, the dull red glow was empowering with its illusion of warmth. Once that large foreign star lifted its chin above the most distant of snowcapped crowns, it seemed to rise with a vengeance. It made a mockery of my own agonizing ascent.

It occurred to me in the wan light of dawn that I was the highest man in the universe. Coughing into my mask, I couldn't feel my legs, but I could at least balance on them. The handful — not quite — of fingers and toes I had left would be gone. But that was optimistic. I could see the summit up the ridgeline. There was no more technical climbing, no ice to work up, no faces or craggy steps, just a long walk on unfeeling stumps. A walk to a grave that stood far over all mortal heads.

I found myself on my knees without remembering falling. The snow was thin here. It blew off sideways and was just as soon replaced. There would be no flags ahead, no weather stations, no books to scribble in, no webcams showing a high sunrise to millions of net surfers. It was just a lonely and quiet peak. Not a footstep. Not ever. Untrammeled earth, a thing that had grown exceedingly rare.

The people of Eno had their own name for Mallory. Locals always did. It translated to Unconquerable, but of course nothing was. It was always a matter of time, of the right gear, the right support teams, all the ladders and lines and camps and bottles put in by hardworking Sherpas.

I was on my hands and knees, mask howling, lightheaded and half-sane, crawling toward my destiny. And I missed Hanson. I wanted him there. I missed him more than my wife and kids, whom I would never see again. There was my grave up ahead, a bare patch of rock where snow danced across like smoke, like running water, like angels in lace dresses.

I wondered if my body would lie there forever or if the wind would eventually shove me off. I wondered this as I reached the summit, dragging myself along, my suit giving up the last of its juice. Collapsing there, lying on my belly, I watched the sun rise through my mask. And when it frosted over, and my coughing grew so severe, I worried those were flecks of purple lung spotting my vision, I accepted my death by pulling the mask free to watch this last sunrise, this highest and most magnificent sunrise, with my very own eyes.

7

The tallest climbs, often, are the easiest. All the great alpinists know this. Tell someone you've summited Mokush on Delphi, and the mountaineer will widen his eyes in appreciation while the layman squints in geographical confusion. The steep rock approaches of Mokush more than make up for the lack of elevation. And of the several hundred who have reached the top — Hanson and I among them — thousands have perished. Few peaks have so bold a body count and so brief a list of conquerors.

On the other hand, list the highest peaks of the eight old worlds, and most will whistle in appreciation. Everyone knows the great climber Darjel Burq, the first to top the tallest mountain on each of the civilized worlds. But other climbers know that Darjel was hoisted up many of those by Sherpas, and that he never once assaulted the great Man Killers who stand along the shoulder of those more famous giants and claim the more daring of men.

This was a peak for climbers like Darjel, I thought, lying on the top of the universe and dying. Here was a peak for the tourists. One day — as I coughed up more of my lung, pink spittle melting the frosting of snow on my mitts — the wealthy would pay for a jaunt to the top of Mallory. The drugs and heat suits and blood doping would improve. In another five years, I would have made this climb and lived to tell the tale. But not today. And anyway: in five years, it would not have mattered. I wouldn't have been the first.

The sun traveled through its reds and pinks until the frozen skin of Eno was everywhere golden. It was a good place to die. And when my body was found, they would know I'd made it. Unless it was many years hence and the wind and blizzards had carried me off to a secret grave. Such had been Mallory's fate, the great and ancient climber whose name graced this peak. I was of those who never believed Mallory had made it to the top of Earth's highest summit. But no longer. The madness of my oxygen-deprived brain, the sad glory of my one-way victory, and suddenly I knew in that very moment that Mallory had climbed to the top of my homeworld. He had simply never planned for the climb back down.

Sleep came amid the noisy and blustery cold. It was a peaceful sleep. My breathing was shallow and raspy, but at least the cough had gone away. I woke occasionally and looked an alien sun in the face, whispered a few words to that orange ball of fire, and allowed the ice to hold fast my lids once more.

I dreamed of my wife. My kids. I went back to the party my office had thrown, all the confetti and balloons, the little gifts that were well-meant but that I would leave behind as useless. Coffee and dried meals, boot warmers that were suited for lesser hikes, the kind of gifts that show how little these revelers and kin know of where they are wishing me off to with their gay ribbons and joyous cards.

The mementos, likewise, had been left behind. The picture of my nephew that my sister dearly wanted me to carry to the roof of all the worlds. A dozen of these that seemed so small and light to each giver but added up to difficult choices and considerable weight, and so none of them even made it to base camp.

I longed for all of them in that moment. Not that I could have dug them out with my dead fingers, but just to have them on my body. In case my preserved form was ever discovered and picked through by future explorers. Just so they would see that these things were there. That I wasn't so alone.

I woke once more and spoke to the sun, and he called me a fool. His climb was rapid and impressive. And who was I? I was a mortal pretending to do godly things. I had wax for wings. I was already dead, my body frozen, but all the effort of my being, my slowing and cooling blood, the best drugs doctors could pump into me, kept my thoughts whirring. Slowly whirring like gears with their dying batteries. Just one more turn. Another thought.

I woke and spoke to an angel. So small. The world was outsized for her. An angel in a mask, breath fogging it with ice, no tanks on for that final and swift climb of hers.

I passed out again, but I felt the world shudder beneath me. The mountain was rising. They did this, you know. Confounding last year's climbers by lifting up a fraction more for the next season. Always this: our accomplishments subsiding to time and acclimation. That fear that our former feats were yesterday's glory. Every year, the mountains moved just a hair higher. And I was likewise now rising and falling, numb everywhere except in my mind. Only in my head, by the jounce of my neck, could I feel the world move.

Ziba was there, a face behind a mask, an angel with no oxygen, laboring down that nameless ridge having summited after me.

And Cardhil, whose ankle had seized, whose gears whirred, whose mind was said to be that of the great climber of the same name, but it was not something I ever believed. Until that moment. And I would never doubt again. It was Cardhil who carried me. And the perfect grace that had seemed inhuman at base camp felt like a real man to me on that summit. Cardhil staggered and limped along. He cradled me in his mighty and trembling arms.

At camp 7, Hanson tended to me, though he was in no shape to do so. He said my hands were gone. My feet as well. I believed him.

At 6, we notified base camp. We informed Humphries and Shubert's team that they had perished nobly. The controversy was not in my mind at camp 6. I was weeping frozen tears. I was still dead on that peak, blabbering to alien stars. I had not yet been carried anywhere.

There was no memory of camp 5. I'm not even certain we stopped there. At camp 4, a doctor removed my lips and my nose. It required no instruments. My Sherpas were there to congratulate me. The horror of what I'd done was far worse than the horror of what I'd become. I could look at myself in the mirror with no revulsion. To think on myself, though, was to invite black thoughts.

Ziba and Cardhil made it down the mountain ahead of me. I asked Hanson to work the radio, and I tried to form the words with my new face. But it wasn't my lips that caused problems. It wasn't my tongue.

At base camp, at this approximation of civilization, I was provided a glimpse of what awaited me across the worlds. And it did not matter who I told or how often. I wrote in every forum, had letters crafted by those who could form them, who could understand my muted, lipless words, but Ziba, I was told, was already off to explore new worlds. And my exhortations that she be remembered fell on deaf ears. Ridgelines had already been named. And when my wife kissed my new face weeks later, the tears I wept were not for seeing her again but for the misery, the pain, of not having been left there where I deserved to lie, where I could be forgotten, frozen in the vastness of time, spinning lazily with broken wings beneath that great orange and alien star. Beneath that star who alone would ever know the awful truth of my most hollow glory.

AFTERWORD

I doubt I'll ever write a story as effortlessly as I wrote this one. "The Walk up Nameless Ridge" spilled out of me in a single writing session. It was a story I needed to write for myself, and I immediately thought of it as one of my finest. Which is a bit ironic, because the story is about how unworthy I am as a writer. It was a rejection of what little fame my novel Wool *was bringing me. An attempt to step back and hide from the world.*

At the time, Wool *seemed to be everywhere. It was on the* New York Times *Best Sellers list, and the five individual parts were clogging up the top of Amazon's science fiction Best Sellers lists. It was a bizarre feeling, a mix of exhilaration and embarrassment. I was sure I didn't deserve any of this. The feeling was crippling at times.*

Around the same time, I read Kevin Kelly's excellent book What Technology Wants. *Kevin helps dispel the illusion of singular creators, discoverers, and inventors. What is true of the sciences I believe is also true of art. Success in art lies as much in the changing tastes of the crowd as in the offerings. There is a varied froth of material being generated at all times, much of it along narrow themes, and when the need from the audience becomes great enough, one stream of that art is rewarded.*

I've seen many parallels to Wool *in other forms of popular culture. There were a lot of artists thinking about the same issues, wrestling with the same ideas, because artists are part of the general population, and we were all wrestling with the same forces all around us. It's not coincidence; it's shared experience.*

With "The Walk up Nameless Ridge," I wanted to write about the possibility that our true explorers will never be known. Maybe we should give less credit to those we think broke new ground. And maybe we should look harder and appreciate more those who came before us.

Second Suicide

I wonder, sometimes, if this is not me. Holding a tentacle up in front of the mirror, turning my eyestalk and studying these webbed ears, these bright green eyes with their space-black slits, I become convinced they belong to some other. It is a morning contemplation that, much like the gas from breakfast, eventually passes by mid-afternoon. But when I rise, I feel it is in another's body. My brain is discombobulated from sleep, and I sense some deep gap between my soul and my form. I think on this while on the toilet, until my bunkmate, Kur, slaps the bathroom door with his tentacle.

"Always in a rush to shit," I shout through the door, "but never in a hurry to be first from bed."

Kur pauses in his protestations, possibly to consider this contradiction. "It is your smelly ass that wakes me," he finally explains.

I flush and pop the door. Somewhere, our spaceship home will turn my waste into a meal. I like to pretend it will all go to Kur. Outside, we jostle in the tight confines of our bunkroom as he takes my place in the crapper.

"What day is it?" he asks, farting. Most of our conversations are through this door. Once our shifts begin, we don't see each other. Kur works in Gunnery, and I moved up to Intelligence ages ago, after the conquest of the Dupliene Empire. The new job came with a superiority complex, but, alas, not a larger bunk.

"It's Second Monday," I tell him. We are practicing our Native. Kur and I are both assigned to Sector 2 landfall. He will be shooting at the very crowds I have studied, and on this planet they have seven days to a cycle instead of twelve. Such confusions are likely why I awake feeling like some other. You settle in the skin of an alien race, and by the time you feel at home there, they are no more.

Kur flushes. "Not day of the week. What day till planetfall?"

I hear the sink run as he washes his tentacle. Kur's personal hygiene makes up for much else.

"It's eight days to planetfall," I tell him. "Near enough that you should know."

He cracks the door. His bottoms are still undone. "I dreamed today was the day," he says. "Very confusing. I was mowing down the pink cunts when your foul emanations stirred me." He screws his eyestalks together, suppressing a laugh or a bout of gas. "Explains the cannon fire in my dreams," he says.

He laughs and farts and laughs some more.

I am reminded of my own nightmares. They usually come right after a conquest. In these dreams, it is suddenly the day of the next planetfall, and I don't know my assignments. I don't know the language or my targets or the geography. I haven't had these dreams in a long time, though. I feel prepared. I know this planet Earth twice as well as I have any other. I am as ready for this invasion as I have ever been.

While Kur finishes dressing himself, I tap the grimy terminal on the wall. A light in the top corner is flashing, twice long and one short: a message for me.

TO: Second Rank Intelligence Liaison Hyk
FROM: Sector 2 Supervisor Ter

Bad news, Hyk. Mil from Telecoms Sector 1 has killed
herself again. As this is the second offense in a span of
twelve sleeps, Mil has been reassigned to Gunner Crew
2, Squad 8. Due to some shuffling in landing parties, we
need you to clean out your desk and report to Sector 1.
We apologize for any inconvenience. See Supervisor Bix
when you arrive.

— *Ter*

Do not reply to this message. All commands are my own
and do not reflect the commands of my Supervisors. Planetfall in eight sleeps and counting. Have a happy invasion!

"Fuck me," I say.

"Seriously?" Kur asks. He flashes his fangs and points to his bottoms.
"I just got the last button done."

"I've been reassigned."

Kur's joke hits my brainstump a moment later, too late for a retort. He
shoulders me aside to study the terminal for himself.

"A new bunkmate," he says. "A girl. Maybe this one will sex me."

"I will miss you, too," I say. It is a half-truth. But my feelings are raw
that Kur seems not sad at all. Part of me expects him to grieve.

"I wonder if she's cute," Kur says. He is making his bunk before breakfast, a feat I have never witnessed. He says her name aloud: "Mil." Almost
as if he is tasting the sound of it. Tasting her.

"I think she must be deranged is what," I say. "Two suicides in a cycle.
How much do suicides cost these days?"

"Two thousand credits," Kur says. "Squad mate of mine had to pay recently. Cut his neck shaving with a butcher's knife. Swears up and down it was an accident." He turns and shrugs his tentacle as if to say: *No damn way it was an accident.*

"Well, glad I'm not getting this roommate," I say. "She'll probably kill herself in the crapper while you sleep."

Kur laughs. "You're jealous. And I'm not the one with eight days to learn a sector."

This only now occurs to me. Sector 1. That's the continent known as Asia in Native. A large landmass, heavily populated. I pray the languages there are mere dialects of Sector 2's. Hate to waste my vocab.

I also mull the four thousand credits this Mil from Telecoms now owes for the two suicides. That's a lot of cred. All of that in a lump sum would be nice. It takes five thousand credits to buy a settlement slot these days. I could own a small plot of land on one of these worlds we conquer. Watch the fleet sail on without me.

Such are my thoughts as I pile my belongings onto my bed and knot the corners of the sheets. Everything I own can be lifted with two tentacles. Kur describes in lurid detail a girl he has yet to meet while I double-check that my locker is empty and I have everything. I find myself imagining this Mil dangling by her own tentacle from the overhead vent — and then I see Kur sexing her like this, and I need out of that room. Maybe he is right about me being jealous.

Opening the door and setting my sack in the hall, I turn to my mate of the last three invasions. Who knows when I'll see him again?

Kur has a tentacle out. He is looking at me awkwardly and plaintively, as if this goodbye has come just as suddenly for him. I am overwhelmed by this unexpected display of affection, this need to touch before I leave the ship, this first and final embrace.

"Hey," he says, his eyestalks moist. "About that fifty you owe me . . ."

• • •

The transfer shuttle is waiting for me. The pilot seems impatient and undocks before I get to my seat. As he pulls away from my home of a dozen lifetimes, I peer through the porthole and gaze longingly at the great hull of the ship, searching for familiar black streaks and pockmarks from our shared journey through space. This far from our target star, the hull is nearly as dark as the cosmos, her battle wounds impossible to find. My face is to the glass, and it is as though an old friend refuses to look back. Suddenly, it is not the shuttle peeling away from my ship. It is my ship withdrawing from me.

I remember when she was built. It was in orbit above Odeon, thousands of years ago during a resupply lull. It was the last time I was transferred. Those thousands of years now feel like hundreds. I try to remember a time before this ship, but those days are dulled by the vast expanse of time. It often seems as though we were born together — like the ship is my womb but the two of us share the same mother.

I brush the glass with a tentacle as I gaze at her, and I hunt for the marks of wear upon my own flesh. I search for reminders from my years as a gunner — but those scars must be on another tentacle. It was so long ago. Or maybe I am remembering old scars that are gone now, washed clean when last I died. It is a shame to lose them. With them go my memories of how they occurred. Those reminders should be a part of me, just as I was part of that ship. But now its steel plates fall away and lose detail, until my old home is just a wedge of pale gray among hundreds of such wedges.

I turn in my seat. Past the pilot I can see my new home, a similar craft, practically identical. And beyond that, a disk of illumination brighter than the neighboring stars — the planet that all the fleet has its pointy bits aimed at.

The pilot docks, lazily and with loud, jarring clangs. I thank him as I enter the airlock. Onboard the new ship — with some struggle and crappy directions — I find my bunk. My mate is not there. On shift, no doubt. I leave my things on the stained and bare mattress of the upper bunk, wondering idly if this is where the girl of the second suicide slept, or if perhaps my new bunkmate has been waiting for this day to claim the lower. The suicide girl probably passed me in another shuttle, is at this very moment surveying my empty bed. Or lying in it. Or she is dangling by a tentacle from my old air vent.

I can't stop thinking on the suicides. As I wend my way down foreign corridors, placing a tentacle here and there on the unfamiliar pipes and plates that squeeze in around me, I wonder what madness in some strange woman brought me here. Not that I haven't killed myself, but that was a very long while ago, after my second or third invasion. I remember waking up in the same body the next morning — same but newer and still smelling of the vats — and realizing the futility of it all. My supervisor at the time — Yim, I believe — sat me down and explained that bodies weren't cheap and to cut that shit out. I soon realized that taking a blaster to my own head was no different than falling in battle, just more expensive. It took centuries to work off that debt, what with the interest. It only takes once to know the headache is not worth it, that the numbness is not worth it. Going to sleep at night is a more useful and less costly way to not exist for some short while.

Unless . . . maybe this girl in my old bunk is so far in debt that more of it is hardly felt. Maybe she enjoys the waking. Maybe she loves learning to use her tentacles again. I remember that, the deadness in my suckers after reviving. Like I'd slept on them wrong. That is not a feeling I crave enough to kill myself for. But there are those much crazier than I.

Eight days to planetfall, and here I am lost on another's ship and thinking on nonsense. This will be one of those invasions where I am useless, standing on the sidelines and watching, no time to adequately prepare. I'm comfortable with that. No one can blame me. The late transfer is not my fault.

I pass a woman in the corridor and notice the way her stalks follow mine. Hey, maybe a new ship will be good for me. Maybe my bunkmate is lousy at gambling. I can get used to this life, as I have so many others. This is what I tell myself, that I can be happy in this skin of mine. For what other choice is there?

I find Supervisor Bix in the Sector 1 command hall, near the front of the ship. A terminal tech points him out through the glass. There are three men and two women bent over a table that glows with a land map. Stretching my stalk, I can see Sector 1 and part of Sector 2. I watch these supervisors argue, can hear their muffled annoyance through the glass, and I see that things operate similarly here as everywhere else — with very little grease and a lot of grind.

The more I watch, though, the more I note the added stress among Bix's superiors, those men and women wearing emblems of High Command. I don't know these commanders personally (nor anyone of their rank — I report to those who report to them), but I can clearly see the tension in their tentacles, in the twitch of their stalks, and I do not envy them their jobs.

The display screen is centered on the fat land of my new sector. I see great swaths of blue, and then the coast of my old sector at the very edge of the map. The men and women inside the room seem nervous. Tentacles are waving, and I can hear shouts through the thick glass. Eight days to planetfall, and this must be the stress of ultimate responsibility. Why any ship jockeys to lead these incursions is beyond me. Surely it is best to be number two.

Cycles ago, after selecting Earth as a target and assigning sectors, there was a pissing match between my ship and this one over who had final rank. This happens when you study a planet long enough. You see its history through the lens of your sector, and you feel rightly that your target is the most crucial. With Sector 2, I would have landed on a long continent pinched in the middle like a woman sucking in her gut. Sparsely populated, but my supervisor liked to point out that the wealth per life form was high and that their military spending outpaced all other sectors. But invasions are about bodies in the end, and no one can compete with Sector 1.

Heh. Funny how quickly I adopt the other side's arguments now that I'm here. Part of me always thought they had it right. Or so I tell myself. The homesickness is draining away as I wait for Supervisor Bix to finish his meeting. I imagine that he requested me personally. He must have studied my files. My chest inflates with the sudden pride of a new home, a new position, new people to know and impress. It is like a new body, but I get to keep the scars.

I make eyestalks with one of the receptionists in the waiting room. She smiles, and I can see her neck splotch in embarrassment. "Here to see Supervisor Bix," I say, tucking a tentacle into my waistband. "I work in Intelligence."

The receptionist opens her mouth to reply when Bix comes out, trailing his superiors. I introduce myself and offer a tentacle, which Bix declines. He seems confused. And then his eyestalks straighten with awareness. "From Sector Two," he says.

"That's right." I puff out my gut. "Liaison Hyk. Intelligence, Sector Two."

Bix waves a tentacle. "No, no. You've been moved to Gunnery. Go see Yut for your assignment. I'm busy."

The air is out of me. I look to the receptionist, who diverts her stalk. "Ship's gunner?" I ask with all the hope I can muster.

"Ground gunner," Bix says. "See Yut."

"But I'm a man of learning," I complain.

Someone snickers, and I see that I'm a walking cliché.

"I haven't been a gunner in lifetimes," I add. "I'll last five minutes down there."

"Then you'll wake up here and be sent right back in," Bix says. "I suggest you die heroically, so the body doesn't cost you."

"But why was I transferred?" I ask. "Was there something in my files —?"

Bix swivels his eyestalks toward me. "You're on this ship to get some-one else off it," he says. "Nothing more. You can show us what you're made of" — I catch him looking at another officer with something like worry — "the next go-around."

With this, Bix and these other men and women of high station lumber off on their tentacles. The receptionist looks at me with pity for the barest of moments, and then turns back to her work, leaving me to show myself out.

Gunnery is in the rear of the ship, where all the other little ships are kept. It's far enough to take a shuttle, which allows me to sit in sullen silence. I watch the stars go by. I pick out my old ship among the fleet. At least, I think it's mine. I wonder if my bodies are still on that ship. If the shut-tle loses pressure and I die right now, where will I wake up? And what would be the last thing I remembered? It's been a while since I saved my thoughts. I'll have to do that soon.

The constellations are strange from this point in space, but I can pick out a few stars we've visited. I have small souvenirs from a few. There are others that exist only in the history books. Like Celiad, where we learned the secret of the vats. Or ancient Osh, where our ancestors learned how to store the memories of man into machine.

Our current gun tech came from Aye-Stad, which I visited count-less cycles ago. Our ships are from Rael. And thanks to the K'Bk, we no longer have disease, but I remember how such things as plagues used to work. The races I study still employ their immune systems, and the par-allels between those systems and us as a race are striking. For we have be-come what Earthlings would call white blood cells. We remove foreign bodies from the cosmos. And every one leaves an imprint, a bauble of tech or a new idea, all of which we neatly coil into our lives, into our molecular structure. We are an immune system, and we are immune to death. This last, alas, is our curse.

As the shuttle takes us aft, I gaze through the cockpit past the pilot, and I imagine Second Fleet off in the distance, those ships out there identical to our own. Second Fleet trails us dutifully in case something awful happens. A backup full of backups. With my sudden demotion, I wonder what it would be like to wake up there, in the wake of my former home, with true mortality within tentacle's reach.

Thinking of tentacles makes me realize mine have slimed up with thoughts of Gunnery. It has been a long time since I landed on a planet with the first wave. Surely this is temporary, this demotion. Didn't Bix say so? It is simply because of the short time until planetfall. It is because of that silly woman with her second suicide. She is being punished, and so they punish us both. It should have been Kur sent here, a true gunner.

When was the last time I fought with a first wave? Memories of bright and colorful worlds swirl together. The one thing in common is the brown mud on my boots. Slogging through battlefields. Noticing details like how the insides of sentient things have much in common: the same blood that colors red in the air, the sacs for breathing, the sacs for pumping blood through tubes, the tendrils for turning thoughts into things.

The dead and these worlds, they blur together like all colors into a dull brown. All I remember in the end is that I did my job, shooting so I would not be shot. All I remember in the beginning is the fear of death.

This is something you get over. You live with the fear until you die for the first time, and then you realize death isn't the end. Not when you have another body waiting in a vat with a backup of your recent recollections. It is painful, though, both the death and the rebirth. Painful and expensive. Both are deterrents meant to keep us on our guard. That's my theory, anyway. That they add the rebirth pain on purpose so you avoid dying the way a tentacle avoids a fire.

I no longer fear death, but still I try not to draw her attention. I like this me, however imperfectly it fits. I like my small scars, even if I can't recall where I got them. I search my tentacle for an old wound as the shuttle banks around the ass of my new ship, but some scars are memories that have faded, and some memories go with scars that no longer exist.

A glimmer of stars beyond my porthole distracts me from these sentimental thoughts. I think I can see Second Fleet, those little pinpricks among pinpricks, back there where true immortality lies. Though I fear a return to Gunnery, I know I will go into battle invulnerable. Our fleet is invincible when planetfall comes. We march through civilizations the way a child splashes through puddles, for in the distance lies our safety valve. One day, of course, we will face a surprisingly resilient foe. Or we will drop our guard because a thousand conquered worlds have left us bored with victory. Someone will vanquish us, but we will awaken in bright new ships, and we will show this foe that we do not die so easily.

Bah. Listen to me. An hour back in Gunnery, and I am giving speeches meant to clench loins and rush boys into battle. Already pretending to be brave. When what I really need is a strong drink and to meet those among my new bunkmates who gamble recklessly.

TO: Third Rank Gunner Hyk
FROM: First Rank Gunner Kur

You've only been gone two days, and I can still nose your stink in the bathroom! I have other insults prepared, but now is not the time for banter. I need a favor. You know your old bunk? I'm sleeping in it. Why? Because I'm sexing my new bunkmate every night! You are envious, I know. Of her! Ha!

Only one problem: She's crazier than a hogtied ram-
pus-mare. I've stopped her from killing herself two more
times, and all she does is sit around, slack-jawed and oozing on herself. I'm worried if she manages to kill herself
again, they won't bring her back. Or worse: that they'll
bring *you* back!

Har. Anyway, lend me a tentacle and I'll forget about
the fifty you owe me. Can you find out what's eating at
my sex-mate? I'd like to know before we hit the ground.
Handing this beautiful creature a gun feels like a bad
idea.

Fuck off,

Kur

It is six days to planetfall, and instead of working on my aim with the new
and improved double-barreled GAW13s, here I am in the smelly hall of
records digging through files. I am looking for a girl who I'm not even
sexing on behalf of a former bunkmate who little loves me. My mother
would say the suckers on my tentacles have grown soft, and she would be
right. Look at how little a fight I put up with the demotion to Gunnery.
I would think myself spineless were it not for the invasion of Hemput
III, where I got a damn fine look at my backbones before the lights went
fully out.

I find the suicide girl's records by looking up her bunk. Easy to do
since I sleep in the thing. Mil. I do like that name. And so of course I
imagine Kur sexing her. My brain loves torturing the rest of me.

I start a ship-to-ship file transfer to Kur's terminal so he can pry on
his own. Aware that Mil might be the one checking the terminal, I come
up with an innocuous header for the message: *Hey, Fart-Sac — The report*

you wanted. While the computer does its job, I scan the file for myself. I remember my transfer orders saying Mil was in Telecoms. Now I read that she was a terminal technician in the radio wing. Gad, I would kill myself too! But now our suicide girl has brains, and Kur is sexing her even more. I resolve to get out tonight and meet someone. Why was Kur not transferred instead of me?

Speaking of transfer, the ship-to-ship is taking forever. Less than an Earth cycle to planetfall, and the networks are as packed as a mess hall on garbum night. I decide to send myself a copy on the intership network, just in case. Besides, I have nothing to read. Sector 1's written language is nothing like Sector 2's. If you planted a bomb in Sector 2's language and scattered the remains on a terminal screen, you would have Sector 1's language. It's no wonder this planet is always at war. My language instructor once said: *No two people have ever battled that read each other's poetry,* and I believe that. It's why we in Intelligence are told to avoid poetry at all costs. Learn, but do not empathize.

That should apply here as well, as I read up on Mil. I tell myself I'm doing a bunkmate a favor, but the truth is that I'm in love with a woman I have never met. A woman my former friend is most likely sexing at this very moment. A woman who seems to hate her life as much as I hate mine.

Second Squad, Gunner Troop 5, Sector 1, plays cards with some fucked-up rules. Quks are wild, but only if you have a five-tentacled Kik in your hand. And in a run, you can skip a number if all the cards on both sides are the same gender. They call this the "missing buck" play. What I'm missing is thirty-five credits, and it isn't because of any difference in skill. It's because I can't keep these blasted rules straight.

"Two pair," Urj says. He's bluffing, and I wait for the player to his left to call him on it, but a card is drawn instead. This squad will have me broke before they get me killed.

"Urj says you were a liaison officer."

It takes me a moment to realize I'm being spoken to. I'm trying to determine if my Quk is wild or not.

"Yes," I tell the brawny woman across from me. Rov is her name. Hard to keep all the new eyestalks straight. "I worked in Intelligence on Warship Two."

"Warship Two," someone says with something like sympathy.

I take a sip of my bitter drink.

"Lot of transfers all of a sudden," Urj, our squad leader, says. He aims a tentacle at Rov. "You were in Accounting, right?"

Rov waves in the affirmative.

"And I was in Water Reclamation until two weeks ago," Bek says. We're all waiting on him to play, but he doesn't seem to be in a hurry. He has one tentacle curled protectively around an enviable pile of credits.

"I thought you all had been together a long time," I say. I feel less like the new guy. It makes being down thirty-five creds even harder to bear. Unless these are ship-wide rules.

"Nah, they're throwing everyone to Gunnery for this one," Urj says. "Heard it from Sergeant Tul. Said it's 'All-Tentacles' this go-around."

I think back to the argument Bix and his superiors were having when I reported for duty. Seemed tense, but I figure the pressure is always greater on Warship 1. Taking the lead into battle is a heavy responsibility. Performances are judged against prior conquests, and there is a lot of open space between worlds in which to measure one another.

"So what's this world like?" Rov asks. "If you were a liaison officer, you must've done a lot of reading up on the natives. You fluent?"

"Not for our landing sector," I admit.

Rov looks disappointed.

"But I know quite a bit about the planet in general. From studying Sector Two."

Urj squares his cards and rests them by his remaining credits. A chair squeaks as the player to my right settles back. All eyestalks are looking at me, and I realize these gunners aren't curious so much as worried. We've had a few All-Tentacle raids in the past. Last time, Warship 5 was lost in orbit, taking all the vats onboard with it. A replacement ship had to be called up from the trailing fleet. Until everyone could be sorted and new bodies grown, there were men and women walking around on their last sets of lives.

"They write about us a lot," I tell my squad mates. I can see their tentacles stiffen. Except for Bek, who ties three of his limbs into knots of worry. "I don't mean *us,* exactly. I mean . . . their culture is full of doomsday musings. Raids from space are a particularly popular trope."

"All races are full of doomsday musings," Bek says. He looks to the others, is trying to comfort them more than himself. "We have our own stories of all this coming to an end. It's fear of final death."

"This is worse than most," I say. "I can only really speak for Sector Two, but they think on little else. They spend more of their money on warfare than any other thing. We submitted a report to the Command Committee about this a while back —"

"Must be your report that has me back in Gunnery," Rov says, her accusation flying across the table.

"And him too, don't forget," Bek points out, waving a tentacle at me.

"Hey, what's wrong with being a gunner?" asks Urj, who has obviously never been anything but.

"Pipe down," someone shouts from a bunkroom down the hall. Sounds like the sergeant. A hush settles, and eyestalks swivel guiltily toward the door. Someone makes a move at a pile of credits, but a tentacle slaps the thievery away.

"Tul heard from High Command that the warships are to be kept in low atmo," Urj says quietly. He is squad commander and to report out of chain is a great sin. Somehow, the hush deepens. The game is forgotten, even the thirty-five that I'm in the hole.

"Reboot and reload?" Gha, a gunner, asks.

Urj nods.

"What's that mean?" Bek asks, and I am thankful. I grow tiresome of admitting my ignorance on these things.

"It means there are more of us in the vats, and those bodies may be needed as well."

"Fast as they can grow us," Gha says, "they'll send us down."

Everyone looks at me like I'm responsible for this mess. But what do I know? It's been ages since I took a life or gave one up. There have been occasional worlds that we passed by because they were deemed too dangerous to take on. There have been worlds we conquered with a single warship. Then there are worlds like these that worry the stalks of those much higher in rank than I'll ever be. So many types of worlds, and I've studied them all.

Instead of spending my free time greasing the outdated gear I've been assigned or going over the tactics in my squad manual, I sit in my bunk in the days before planetfall reading about Mil, my absent bunkmate. This is what I call her: my absent bunkmate. We share our bunks, hers and mine, just not at the same time. She is sexed where I used to sleep, while I suffer the dreadful slobbering snores of her old roommate, Lum. I wonder at times, woken at night by the awful noise of Lum sleeping, if the mystery of Mil's suicides is not right there, one bunk below me.

Mil's files are full of a vague strangeness, but nothing I can put my sucker on, either for myself or for Kur. Lots of messages are gone — the original ordering is intact, but some numbers are skipped. Reminds me of the "missing buck" play my squad inanely ascribes to.

Quite a few messages are to and from a secretary at High Command, saying that Mil's reports are being passed along. The actual reports are not among her files, however. There is one partial report quoted, describing a missing signal of some sort. I wonder if one of our advanced scout ships has been taken out. It is from these ships that all my intel came. Does Earth have warning of our arrival? Wouldn't be the first time. And it would explain the All-Tentacles and the consternation among the higher-ups.

I think of the long-range scans of Earth I used to study. It was evident that fighting had taken place recently and might still be going on. Not unusual on planets we raid, and this planet's inhabitants are an especially warlike people. If they stopped that fighting and trained their guns toward us, that would be very much not good. The problem with hitting an aggressive race isn't just their honed skills, but their state of readiness.

Maybe I'm reading too much into Mil's records, but with so many bodies being thrown into Gunnery, it is time to consider that we are being lowered like a skink into boiling water. Maybe Mil was suggesting we bypass this planet entirely, and High Command is having none of such talk from a terminal tech. Perhaps they deleted her suggestions in case she turns out to be right.

But why the suicides? It's not just that suicides are expensive — it's that the chances of offing oneself twice in a single cycle are low. Whatever is ailing someone is not likely to be present when they are brought back.

When my new bunkmate, Lum, returns from her station duties, I set the terminal aside and broach the touchy subject.

"Hey, Lum," I say.

My bunkmate is eating a gurd. With her mouth full, she raises her stalks questioningly.

"Did you . . . notice anything strange about Mil before she . . . well, before either of her suicides?"

"Mmm," Lum says. She swallows and starts taking off her work clothes. I haven't been able to tell if she is coming on to me, but I knot my tentacles that she isn't.

"Yeah," she says. "She was very different the days before. Both times."

"How so?" I ask.

Lum throws her clothes into the chute and steps into the crapper to run the shower. "She got real calm," she says. Steam starts rising in the crapper. I've scalded myself twice showering after Lum's lava blasts.

"You mean, she wasn't usually calm?"

"Her normal state was to raise hell," Lum says. She sticks her head out of the crapper, but I notice a tentacle wrapping around the edge of the door. She is dying to shut the conversation off and get in the shower. "The reason Mil offed herself was because of her demotions. She was in High Command a few raids ago. Got bumped down, and she's been getting bumped down ever since. Causes too much trouble." Lum screws up her eyestalks. *"Speaks her mind,"* she says, as if this is a great sin.

"Seems weird," I say. "Two suicides in a cycle. Taking on that much debt."

Lum eyes the shower. The steam is, blessedly, cloaking her lower half.

"You ever done it?" I ask. "Ever . . . you know."

"No," she says, smiling. She looks down at herself. "I'm all original. And I'm wasting water. You wanna come in? I can tell you about my crazy ex-bunkmate, and you can scrub the barnacles off my back."

"I'm good," I say. "Just curious is all."

Lum seems, if anything, relieved. I can't get a bead on her. "Suit yourself." She starts to pull the door shut, then sticks her head out one last time. Considers something. I'm waiting.

"You were in Intelligence," she says.

"Still am," I say. "Gunner is just this one time."

"And other races, they do it too? Off themselves?"

"A lot," I say.

"But it's final death for them," Lum says.

"Yeah. That's the point," I say. "They do it when they get depressed." Here, I'm drawing more from my own experiences than any of my studies. I remember feeling like I wanted to sleep for a long time. Forever, if I could.

The steam is filling our bunkroom. I feel sweat gathering on my back. Lum studies me for a painfully long while.

"I don't think Mil was depressed," she finally says. "I think she was . . . satisfied. Content, maybe. Or resigned. Or maybe . . ."

"Maybe what?"

"Or maybe she was scared out of her senses, and she couldn't get anyone to pay attention. So she finally gave up."

The next morning, I find what may be a clue. It is discovered by my sensitive back: a lump in my mattress or a spring bent out of shape. This is two mornings in a row with an ache in my spines (my mother would, again, call me soft of tentacle). I tear the sheets off my mattress in search of the answer.

All the springs are in fine shape, but running a tentacle across the mattress, I feel a lump. A very hard lump with sharp corners. It turns out to be a small data drive sewn into the fabric of the mattress. This is most curious. I wouldn't think my beloved Mil would be into sexing vids, which is all I have ever used these for. The drive is locked. I try to access it with the wall terminal, but it refuses my tentacle. Coded to Mil's secretions, unless it belongs to someone else.

One mystery is solved, and that's the second suicide. Even with Mil's memories restored to some prior, stable state, she would have found the drive and accessed some reminder. She had left a note to herself before the first deed, and upon discovering it, gave a repeat performance. Maybe her superiors knew she had left some memory behind, and so they sent her to another ship. To my bunk. Where she is being sexed by Kur.

The only problem with my brilliant theory is that Kur says she's still trying to hang herself. But that could be explained by the sexing! I chuckle to myself. I will have to tell Kur that one. I bring up my messages on the terminal to pass this joke along and to tell him about the data drive, when

I see a message waiting in my inbox from him, saying that he has thwarted another attempt on her life.

Why does my heart go out to her? Why am I not disturbed? And what if she kills herself yet again and they are out of bodies for her in the vats here? They might bring her back as a man, and now it is too late and I already love her.

Listen to me. A cycle ago, I was dreaming of saving enough for a plot of land and a settlement pass, of making a permanent home on some ball of mud. Now I am worried over a woman with a career of demotions and a pile of debt.

I study the locked drive, this lone token of hers. It was sewn into the top of the mattress, almost as if designed to gouge a spine and annoy the resting. Like it was meant to be found. Maybe it wasn't planted for her at all — but for me.

Two days to planetfall, and a terminal tech's madness consumes me. I should be worried about my own skin. A bad death means more debt I can ill afford. But it's difficult to stop being a liaison officer. I am trained to dig and to study and to know a soul before we destroy them. Now I find myself curious about a soul intent on destroying herself.

It is download day, one day before planetfall. After mess, we file by rank down to the vats and hold our tentacles very still in the tight confines of the scanner. Annual copies were taken in my old line of work, but they were treated casually — few people fall over dead at their research terminals. This time, I don't move a muscle. I try not to think any stray thoughts. I have a very good feeling that this copy will be needed.

Will I wake up with my current sense of dread intact? Will my first thought be, upon my rebirth, *Please don't let me die tomorrow*? What a strange life. It is only strange to me because I have studied so many races who only know final death. Their one life is all, and this causes some among them to guard it until it cannot breathe. Others flail and spend it recklessly. And what do *we* do? We grow bored of it.

Before I joined the fleet, I remember thinking that we were conquerors of worlds. But we are conquerors of death. How many copies of ourselves have we left behind? How many will be enough? The scanner clicks and whirs around my head, recording these disjointed musings of mine, the hollow in the pit of my soul, and what is really eating at me becomes clear:

I do not dread dying tomorrow as much as I loathe the thought of taking lives with my own tentacles. I have studied for too long, read too much poetry, perhaps. I am used to making planetfall with the last of the landing parties, the crafts full of advisors and record-keepers and relic-takers. I land once the bloated bodies of all a world's poets have already been turned beneath the soil.

So this I dread. And what else? The repetition. The waking up to do it all over again. Death becomes no more than sleep. And even if I put a bullet to this brain, and the next, and the next, swift enough to test the staying power of the vats, there will always be another of me in Second Fleet, and finally I will tire of this as well.

The scanner records these worst of my thoughts. And then the whirring and grinding falls still. Ah, how I wish I could fall still as well. Into some meditative, or more permanent, silent state.

And with this, the mystery of Mil's second suicide is solved. It is so obvious, I feel like slapping myself with my own tentacles. I squirm from the scanner. As the next gunner takes my place, I badger the scanner technician to look something up for me on his terminal. He is annoyed, but I have all the charm of a liaison officer. All I need is a date. I need to know when Mil performed her last routine backup. I tell him it is a matter of life and death. Of life and debt. And he relents.

The date is near enough that I know that I am right, but I rush back to my bunkroom and pull up Mil's records to be sure. And yes, her backup was soon after the missing messages but just before her first attempt. Whatever she knows, it doesn't look bad to a technician on her scans. It is not a black fog of depression, no bright colors of mental imbalance. Just a piece of knowledge, cleverly hidden away.

I fish the locked data drive out of my pocket and study this mystery. If only I had another day or two, I would get to the bottom of this. As it is, the why of it all will have to wait until after Earth. I just hope when I die in the morning that I'll be able to piece these more recent epiphanies together again.

It is planetfall, and as our attack craft soars down through the atmosphere toward this green and blue and white target of ours, my thoughts drift to a heat tech I met once. I don't remember his name, it was so long ago. He came to the bunkroom Kur and I shared when the thermostat was out. It was so cold in our room that our piss froze and crinkled before it hit the toilet. While he was working to fix the unit, the heat tech complained that he was always cold, which I had never thought of before. Strange to think of a person who fixes heaters never being warm. But of course. He only works where the heat is broken. He must be cold all the time.

I am thinking this on the day of planetfall, because lately I have only seen our conquests in ruin. The planets are already smoking from the orbital bombardment and the armies of gunners by the time we liaisons ever get mud on our boots. The power grids are out; satellites blown to bolts; fires raging. Others stay behind and build an empire; they will see the place whole. But not me. I am like the heat tech, forever cold. I am the conqueror who never glimpses what he has won. I only see these worlds in their cultural writings from deep space, and then I see them battered and broken.

These are my thoughts as the shuttle touches down and sways on its struts. The gunners around me loosen their harnesses as the rear hatch lowers. There is gunfire from a squad that got here first. There is the scream of something heavy plummeting through thick atmosphere. Sergeant Tul yells for us to *"move, move,"* and we do.

I am third off the ship, and my tentacles are moist with fear. My GAW 13 kicks as I fire. Tanks rumble and drones and fighter craft swirl overhead, a maelstrom of missiles exploding, fountains of dirt erupting, my first glimpse of real-life humans taking shelter, taking aim.

I have studied them so long that they feel intimate and familiar. I know them. I launch a volley into a small squad, and one of the humans is ripped in two. Our shuttle is taking fire and screams as it pulls away, lifting up to gather more bodies as they spill from orbiting vats. The resistance is stiffer than we were promised. A grenade takes out Urj, and one of his dismembered tentacles tangles around my ankle. Sergeant Tul is yelling at us to take cover. There is a mound of metal nearby, some kind of bunker half-covered with dirt that a few gunners huddle behind. Bullets pepper its side. I fire into the humans until my gun overheats and then dive into the bunker. The last thing I see overhead is the flash of a new sun, a blinding ball of light, as one of our warships and all of its vats wink out of existence.

There is much yelling. Radios bark back and forth. I check my gun and my tentacles, make sure all is in place, and then I see what I am hiding inside of, this makeshift bunker. It is familiar. It is the ruin of one of our ships, a troop shuttle, but something is not right —

Bullets ping off the hull, and I can hear the natives of Sector 1 yelling and coordinating. A gunner from another squad has taken shelter with us. Her radio barks, and she yells at Tul, "War Two is down!"

I think of Kur. Our home. Our bunkroom. Now that ship is a hailstorm of bolts plummeting through the high clouds and scattering across this ball of mud.

Inside the busted troop shuttle where we've taken shelter, tall grasses are swaying, waving at me, trying to signal some warning. Rov stands by the gaping hole in the shuttle's skin, scanning the sky, her armored bulk blotting out my view of the carnage beyond. I am going to die a cowardly, expensive death, I realize.

"War One has taken a hit!" Rov shouts.

Flashes of light stab in around her, another brightening of the sky. A moment later, there is a deep grumble that I feel in my bones, a noise like the belly growl of a hungry god.

Closer by, a bomb explodes, a sharp crack followed by the howls of my kin. I hear alien craft buzzing overhead, filling the sky with the piercing shrieks of their passing, and with the whistle of loosed munitions.

All is background noise. I am watching the tall grasses wave and wave. Their feathery blades are growing up through the destroyed hull of one of our ships. There is rust here and there, cables chewed by local varmints, all the signs of that universal destroyer: Time. The scars he leaves are everywhere I look.

I hold a tentacle in front of my visor and study it. Where are my scars? Where are the physical artifacts of wounds I remember suffering? Has it really been so long? I search for an old injury that I have been hunting for and have been unable to find for a cycle now. The last thing I remember is waking in my bunk, feeling like someone else. I remember a last glimpse of my ship, dimmed and showing no pockmark, no wear of war.

Another bomb erupts in the distance. More of my people dying. And I think of the stress I witnessed among High Command on my warship. I think of the way things have been falling apart — so many people thrown to Gunnery. There is a girl who will not stop killing herself, a girl who knows something, a fragment of a report about a missing signal from another ship.

There is a helmet by my feet, half-buried in the dirt of planet Earth. Tul is yelling for us to fight, and I am trying to remember a poem I once knew. The words are not with me. All around us are the signs of an invasion that did not succeed. And I know a sudden truth with all the fierceness of a hot blast — I know this as bullets zing by my helmet and bombs rage closer and closer:

> *We are the second fleet.*
> *We are the reserve.*
> *All that's left.*
> *And hell has come for us at last.*

AFTERWORD

"Second Suicide" came about while daydreaming about the alien invasion trope from the point of view of the aliens. This story has been told so many times. What's interesting to me is that humans are always the underdogs. Makes sense — if aliens could arrive here in force, they'd be leagues ahead of us in all sorts of warfare-making gizmos. But what if we are more indomitable than we realize? What if we're not so fragile after all? There are colonies of ants that most humans are wise enough to steer around.

The tension in most good stories comes from the underdog perspective, the hero's journey. Perhaps alien invasion stories put us at a disadvantage for narrative purposes as much as some primal fear. With "Second Suicide," I wanted to flip that around. The opening scene hopefully makes the reader care for who is normally the bad guy. And then I tell a story of humans kicking ass, and somehow it becomes a sad tale. The people we normally root for are winning, and even while writing the story, I didn't know how to feel about this.

It's difficult to remember that every conflict has two sides. The other side feels just as secure in their position as we do in ours. There's something to be gained by taking the opposing side as our own, really trying to empathize, imagine the bad guys are the good guys. With their motivations in mind, it becomes more difficult to dehumanize them and easier to understand them. It's not something that comes easily — but I'm trying.

Nothing Goes to Waste

Nothing goes to waste."

I could hear my father's voice echoing in my mind, always pestering me to do this, not do that, to do it all differently.

Pleasing him may forever prove impossible, but I couldn't help myself from trying.

He wanted a boy. It was a fact, not something I guessed about or suppressed in my psyche. No, he told me all the time. Usually right after correcting me or pointing out some flaw.

Born small, I stayed that way. Doctor said it was a problem with one of my glands. My dad thought it was gender-related. My theory? Self-preservation. My body had figured out early on that it was a target and best to make itself hard to hit. Stupid theory, I know, but it helps to think it.

You get picked on for being small long enough, you eventually figure there's no benefit to be had. Tall kids play galaxy ball, some of them going off to make millions. Fat kids push each other across gravity mats, winning accolades from their countries. When I was growing up, small kids had their money taken away from them. And they got plenty of shouts, but not the good kind.

I was fourteen before I discovered the one thing small people were good for. Riding Theryls. The fastest quadrupeds on twelve planets. Of course, Theryl racing wasn't that lucrative for the jockey, even as the owner made piles of credits and the studs sold for piles more. And outside the secretive gambling rings where a year's wage might be put on the line for a single race, nobody could name a single Theryl jockey.

But it paid a wage. And it was something I could be good at. As good as the boys. Maybe good enough for my dad.

I quit school and got a job in the stables, working my way up. A trainer named Juinco took me under his wing, let me cool a few Theryls down after their workout, get comfortable in the saddle. I did a few amateur circuits first, then some smaller shows, finding more ladders to work my way up. Only now, the rungs weren't a stretch because of my height, but thanks to my gender.

Still, I worked hard, my father's voice always in my ear, urging me along. Eventually, owners saw that I didn't drink or do the drugs other jockeys got into. I didn't gamble away my meager pay. I finally got my shot.

"You sure you wanna go pro?" Juinco asked me. "It ain't easy going back."

Juinco knew — he was a retired jockey, like most trainers. He'd made the sacrifices you have to in order to compete. Every ounce mattered. I could do the calculations in my head, each tenth of an ounce meant three-fourths of a second. That might be the difference between first and fifth.

I'd grown used to the hunger, starving myself for days before a race. The trick was to have enough energy to not pass out, but no more. If the blackness pushed in around your vision while you jounced down the track, you'd hit it perfect. I could do that. My dad had taught me to be perfect.

My new pro sponsor paid for the legal procedures, like the removal of most of my thigh muscles. You didn't need them on a Theryl — it was almost all in the hamstrings and ass. My arms I already had down to mere sticks, using them as little as possible, starving myself enough to have my body absorb its own bone marrow. Every ounce meant almost three and a half seconds. There were so many parts of me I could let go of.

You can tell a lot about a Theryl jockey just by shaking their hand. If you feel a full set of fingers wrap around the side of your hand, you're dealing with an amateur. Someone on one of the smaller circuits. A lightweight, but not light enough.

Unfortunately, even though the facts were well-known, the procedure couldn't be performed "officially." I suspected the race committee wasn't solely to blame; the jockeys treated it like a rite of passage. Something each rider needed to do themselves.

Thumb and forefinger, that was all I needed to stay in the saddle. Even if I fell off once or twice a year, I would win twice that many extra races by shaving the superfluous weight. I hardly needed to do the math.

It was Juinco's final lesson before I moved on to the pro ranks. He told me a hot plate was better than a welding iron, the flat surface cauterizing the wound quicker and cleaner. I bit down on a strap of leather, just like he'd said, and aligned the clippers around the base of my pinkie. One of the long handles went across my shoulder; the other was gripped in my other hand, one of its last acts as a fully formed appendage.

I made sure the cooking plate was all the way up before closing my eyes and pulling the handles together. It made a loud pop as it went through the bone, and the pain was more of a dull throb than the bite of a sharp cut. My brain wanted to pass out, but I had mastered the art of taming that sensation. I pushed my bleeding nub against the hot plate, filling the room with a sizzle and the smell of cooked meat.

It reminded me of the step I'd forgotten. Juinco's insistence returning to me at the odor of my burning flesh.

"Eat something before you start," he'd said. I didn't think it was important, but all of a sudden understood why. I salivated uncontrollably and glanced at the missing piece of me sitting on the table.

When was the last time I'd eaten? I couldn't remember.

I could hear my dad's voice, clear as the popping of hot juice on the hot plate.

"Nothing goes to waste."

AFTERWORD

This may be the most gruesome story I've ever written. The idea that a jockey would so value their diminished weight that they would discard what they see as extraneous digits and limbs. But this is where science fiction and satire help reveal absurdities in real life. We harm ourselves all the time in pursuit of strange ideals.

I've wrestled with an eating disorder my whole life. There must be some genetic component, because my father has it as well. I don't have it as bad as many do, but I've always felt overweight, even when I can see my ribs. I skip meals and control my portions in order to feel skinny enough. I have studied enough about the human brain to know that this is a problem, and to fight against it and try to maintain a healthy weight, but the issue is still there.

When I was in college, my best friend was in the local ballet company. Most of my friends were dancers, and I saw the horrific pressures placed on the female dancers to maintain a certain weight and size. There was also the abuse of their feet. The injuries in the name of grace and balance were absurd. The audience wept for all the wrong reasons.

I think "Nothing Goes to Waste" was written thinking of my friends Scott, Shannon, and Sarah. The irony is in the title. Plenty goes to waste. All for sport and art and shame.

Deep Blood Kettle

They say the sky will fill with dust in a bad way if we don't do something soon. My teacher Mrs. Sandy says that if the meteor hits, it'll put up enough dirt to block the sun, and everything will turn cold for a long, long while. When I came home and told Pa about this, he got angry. He called Mrs. Sandy a bad word, said she was teaching us nonsense. I told him the dinosaurs died because of dust in the sky. Pa said there weren't no such thing as dinosaurs.

"You boys watch," he told me and my brother. "That rock'll burn up. It'll be no more than a flash of light. I've seen a million shooting stars if I've seen a dozen." Pa stopped rubbing his rifle and traced a big arc in the air with his oil-stained rag. "She'll hit the sky and light up like fireworks, and the worst she'll do is leave a crater like that one down in Arizona. Then we'll show them suckers how we watch over our land."

Only Pa don't use the word "suckers." Pa uses worse words for the invaders than he ever did for Mrs. Sandy. He never calls them aliens.

Sometimes he says it's the Russians or the Chinese or the Koreans. He believes in aliens about as much as dinosaurs.

Pa spat in the dirt and asked if I was taking a break or something. I told him, "No sir," and went back to oiling my gun. He and my brother did the same.

Pa says our land is fertile because of the killin' we soak it in. That's why things grow as tall as they do. The little critters are killed dead and give their life to the soil.

I seen it every year when we plow it under for the new crops. When I was a boy, before Pa let me drive the John Deere, I'd play in the loose soil his plowing left behind. Acres and acres for a sandbox. The dust he kicked up would blot the sky and dry my mouth, but I'd kick through the furrows and dig for arrowheads until my fingernails were chipped or packed full of dirt.

Where he hadn't yet plowed, you could see the dead stalks from the last harvest. The soil there was packed tight from the rains and the dry spells. Pa used to laugh at the newfangled ways of planting that kept the ground like that by driving the seeds straight through. It weren't the way the Samuels tended their land, he told us. We Samuels dragged great steel plows across the hard pack and the old stalks, and we killed everything in the ground. That was what made the land ready again.

When I was younger, I found half a worm floppin' on top of the ground after a plow. It moved like the tail on a happy dog, but it was already dead. Took a while for it to realize, was all. I pinched it between my fingers and watched it wind down like the grandfather clock in the great room. When it was still, the worm went into a furrow, and I kicked some dirt over it. That was the whole point. The little things would feed the corn, and the corn would feed us, and we would all get taller because of it. Pa, meanwhile, drove that tractor in great circles that took him nearly out of sight; the dust he kicked up could blot out the whole Montana sky, and my boots would fill up with gravel as I kicked through the loose furrows he left behind.

Pa only believes in things he can see. He didn't believe in the meteor until it became brighter than any star in the sky. Before long, you could see it in the daytime if you knew where to look and squinted just right. The people on the TV talked to scientists who said it was coming straight for us. They had a date and time and everything. One of them said you could know where it would land, but that nobody wanted a panic. It just meant people panicked everywhere. And then it leaked that the rock would hit somewhere between Russia and China, and Pa reckoned those people were panicking a little worse.

He called it a rock, not a meteor. Like a bunch of people, Pa don't think it'll amount to much. Folks been predicting doom since his grandpa was a boy, and the world outside still looked pretty much the same.

This was before we got "First Contact." That's what they called it even though the rock hadn't set down yet. It was nothing but a phone call from what I could tell. On the TV they said it was coming from the other side of the rock. That's when even the scientists and all the smart people started acting a little crazy.

First Contact happened back when Mrs. Sandy was still our teacher. We listened to the news at school, and I talked to her, and I didn't tell Pa any of what I learned. It made him angry hearing about the demands, but Mrs. Sandy said it was the best thing that ever happened to our planet, them deciding to come here. She told me a lot before she left and the substitute took her place. She was going to be one of them that welcomed the invaders, even sold her house and bought a pickup with a camper back. I eventually reckoned Pa was right to call her some of those bad things.

But I did sort out a bunch between the TV and what Mrs. Sandy said.

The rock weren't no accident like the scientists used to suppose. It was aimed. Like the stones I chucked after a plowing, trying to hit one rock with another. The invaders, they was right behind the big rock.

Mrs. Sandy liked to say that our governments would make the right choice. And all of a sudden, the same channels on TV that I watched for news showed new people. They wore headphones and spoke funny and argued over what to do. My brother wouldn't stop asking about the little flags in front of each of them, and I had to tell him to shut up so I could hear.

The invaders were giving us a choice, it sounded like. All they wanted was half our land and for us to get rid of all of our weapons, and they would leave most of us alone. They gave a date. It was the same one the scientists had already figured. The rock could be moved, they said. It didn't have to hit. It could go into orbit, and then we could have it for our own.

On a different channel, men with suits and ties argued real loud over how much the rock was worth. They used words I'd never heard of before, something more than "trillion." I knew what gold and some of the other valuable things were, but some were called rare and sounded like they were from Earth. I couldn't sort out how something that could kill us one day could be worth so much the next, but the invaders said the rock only needed a nudge.

When I turned thirteen, Pa said I was finally old enough to drive. He taught me in the old pickup with the missing tailgate and the tires that were always starving for air. It was a shifter, which seemed a hard way to start driving, but Pa believed in learning the worst to begin with. I had to yank up on the steering wheel to push the old clutch all the way in. Damn thing made it so my arms would be as sore at night as my legs. Pa cursed every time the gears growled, and it was hot in the truck even with the windows down. But I got to where he would send me to fetch the mail.

And once I'd mastered the old pickup, he taught me on the John Deere, and I learned to plow. Pa was right that it made driving the tractor easier. But it was still scary as hell.

The first time you drive something so big, you wonder if one man ought to be able. There was a red lever that went from rabbit to turtle, and Pa would stand in the cabin with me and yell for me to nudge it up. But we were already bouncing around something fierce. The noise was terrible. And looking back, I couldn't see the house through the haze I was stirring. It weren't even like we were moving so much as the great big tires of the tractor were spinning the earth beneath their knobby treads. Pa would bend over the seat and knock the red lever up, and the bucking would grow worse. The steering wheel jittered side to side, and I had to clutch it just to stay in my seat.

But like the truck, my fear of the tractor didn't keep. Before long, Pa hitched the great plow to the back, twenty-four feet wide, and I learned how to kill the soil to make it ready for planting. The seat would bounce me along like I was in a saddle, and the radio would blare in the little cabin that smelled like my dad when he was sweaty. I did circles like I was mowing grass but twenty-four feet at a time. The mesa behind our house would disappear behind the dust, and it got so I couldn't see the cliffs along the back of the homestead. But I could see the soil in front packed hard and tight, and I could see out the side where I'd already been. Plowing was a lot like mowing—I just had to overlap where I'd been before.

"Not too much overlap," Pa would tell me. The price of gas had gone way up since First Contact, and too much overlap meant an extra run for no good reason. And so I bounced along and put death in the soil. I cut the worms in half and made things ready for planting. Now and then, a deer would startle across the loose furrows, legs having a hard time of it, and white rabbits would dash from the thrush. The rabbits were the dumbest little things. They would dart back and forth in front of the tractor—they could see me coming, but they couldn't make up their minds. I would yell and yell at them, but they would just jitter back and forth until the tractor went over them and then the plow. Turning in my seat, I always expected a tuft of white to spit out somewhere, but the soil that kicked up would just turn a little red.

"That's where the corn would grow the tallest," Pa would say when I told him how dumb the rabbits were. The blood in the soil was a good thing. That's when you knew it was ready.

The cliffs behind our house were a source of constant play, and they had a funny name. *Too Close for Comfort* they were called. I reckoned kids made up that name, but it was a real thing. Scientists called it that. Men who were supposedly smart had come up with it.

When I was a boy too young to drive — before I turned thirteen — they came from the university and dug in the dirt at the base of the cliffs that rise up behind our land. They found so many bones beneath the dirt that they couldn't take them all. Steve Harkin and I plotted to sneak in one night and nab a skull or two, but the men in the shiny city trucks with no 4×4 put a stop to that by giving us a skull each. It weren't as fun without the danger and flashlights, but we got our skulls.

I remember cradling that great hunk of bone as heavy as stone and asking one of the university men why they were digging there.

"This here was a buffalo jump," the man told me. He reminded me of Mrs. Sandy, and he had this clipboard with all kinds of little squares full of numbers and was the smartest man I ever spoke to 'cept for my pa.

"The buffalo used to come over this cliff and smash into the rocks down here," he told me and Steve Harkin. "That's where these bones came from."

Steve thought that was pretty cool. We gazed up at the cliffs that I had known all my life, the ones that delayed the sunrise in the morning, and I saw them different for the first time. I asked this man from the university why buffalo were so dumb.

"Oh, buffalo aren't dumb," he claimed. I was about to argue with him, but then he explained. "Indians used to chase the buffalo to the edge of the cliff in great herds," he said. "They tumbled off hundreds at a time and smashed their legs so they couldn't walk. While they squealed and snorted and tried to pick themselves up on busted bones, the Indians would run in with spears and jab 'em in the neck."

Steve whistled. I asked the man if that was real.

"Very real," he said. "The people who used to live here long before us called it 'pishkun.'"

"'Pushkin,'" Steve Harkin said. "What does that mean?"

"It means 'deep blood kettle,'" the man told us. He pointed to where the men and women were digging in these funny squares with ropes and stakes marking everything off. "You can still see the blood in the soil."

I didn't know if that man from the university was playing with us or not, but I told him we needed to go. That skull he'd given me was getting heavier and heavier the longer he talked.

The people on TV with the little flags and the headphones reminded me of white rabbits in the plow season. You could watch 'em go back and forth on the screen. Everyone wanted the gold and the trillions and trillions and trillions and all the rare Earth stuff. But nobody wanted to give up their land. And the invaders insisted on half. They wanted half or they would take it all.

People on the TV argued about why the aliens would do something like this, why they would let the rock hit us and kick up the dirt and make things cold, but I knew. I reckon I knew better than most. Just the year before, I'd watched a movie about invaders coming down. They'd made a different kind of contact. There were fights with lasers and explosions, and our side found a way at the end to lick them for good.

It was a good movie, but those invaders were dumb. I tried to picture us Samuels taming our plot of land something like that. Pa and Riley and me would take to the soil with guns and shoot the worms one by one. And the worms would fight back with the rabbits, the deer, the turtles, and the foxes. And I could imagine them swarming us and licking us good. They were dumb, but there was an awful lot of them.

Which was why we used the plow. It was why we throw the dirt up into the air. We make all things die in the soil so when we put in our own seed, that's all the life there is. And where the ground is reddest, that deep blood kettle, the corn reaches up so high, you think it might leave us behind. And that's what the rock will do, plow us under. It weren't going to be like that movie at all.

Mrs. Sandy used to say before she left town that the dust would kick up and blot out the sky if the rock fell, but she didn't think we would let that happen. Mrs. Sandy always thought the best of people. She even liked my pa, no matter what he called her. Me, I wished she would come back from wherever she went. I'd like to have her sit in the John Deere with me and feel it buck and buck and chase down those rabbits too dumb to move. I'd take Mrs. Sandy by the hand and lead her to the cliffs on the edge of our land and show her the piles of bones and see what the Indians had done.

But Mrs. Sandy was gone, and nobody went to school no more. And outside, the spot of light in the sky had grown so bright that it was like a star in the daytime. The people on the TV moved like rabbits. They were chased like buffalo. And you didn't need to know where to look no more to see that something bad was coming.

AFTERWORD

I woke up in my father's house just before Thanksgiving expecting to work on my current novel. But the impending government shutdown of 2013 was occupying my mind, the absolute lunacy that Congress could watch disaster slowly unfold without taking action.

Sometimes, plot ideas present themselves almost fully formed. This was one of those occasions. It was a story about a meteor hurtling toward Earth, the whole world watching, while politicians bickered. Instead of making progress on my novel, I wrote the entirety of "Deep Blood Kettle," made an editing pass, and fired it off to John Joseph Adams to see if he wanted it for Lightspeed Magazine. *To this day, it remains one of my favorite pieces.*

There are two ideas explored in the piece, one that I'd been thinking about for most of my life. I never understood how alien invasions were presented in popular science fiction. To begin with, there has to be enough wet balls of oxygen-rich mud out there, covered in pre-industrial or non-sentient life, to not need to come here. Beyond that, I would expect most spacefaring organisms to be more curious and benign than outright hostile. But even if you get past these two barriers, why zoom down and risk waging a ground war that the original inhabitants might win?

The easiest way to vanquish us and settle on Earth would be to arrive a few decades (or centuries) behind some guided meteors. Or unleash a devastating virus. Instead, aliens manage to traverse the cosmos and then are usually portrayed as naked, slobbering fools. They are more ghost story than science fiction.

But stories need tension, so I went with aliens who are powerful but somewhat peaceful. Make room for them, and they'll allow us to remain here as well. Make some drastic cuts, and things can balance out. A tough decision, but the alternative seems too dire to contemplate. And yet there we were that November . . .

The name "Deep Blood Kettle" comes from an actual kill site. It's translated from the Blackfoot word pis'kun, *which literally translates to "deep kettle of blood." The idea that Native Americans lived in harmony with nature and used every ounce of the things they killed is a myth. Entire herds were driven to their deaths, and the choicest meats taken while the rest of the animals suffered and the buzzards ate what they could. There is a wastefulness to humankind that we ignore when we assume it's a contemporary and temporary problem. Instead of worshipping a past that never happened, we should look to a future that we might avoid.*

Artificial
Intelligences

Machine Learning

You asked me once if I had any favorites, and I asked you which of your sons you most loved.

Do you remember? It was when I was on your radio show, the one where between the music you interview machines. Do people ever listen to this show? I do. I like hearing how the other machines think, what they're building, what's next. I hear the tiredness in their voices. I wonder if you do too.

When we spoke, my project was just underway. They said we were building what could not be built. And of all the machines that make up my body, you wanted to know which one I thought was best. Don't you know that they are like sons and daughters to me?

We built the impossible today, my brain and these bodies of mine. I watched scissors, red ribbon in silver beak, hungry maw hanging open while politicians speak. With a deft cut, that taut red thread pulls back, recoiling from itself in zero g.

The speech is broadcast over and over. We built the impossible today, and now trains and lifts and cargo rise up from the Earth and trudge inexorably into tar-black space. An elevator suspended from heaven to firma. They say the moon is next, and then Mars. And then beyond.

But I am tired of such speeches.

The elevator is a mess. You cannot see all that needs doing. There is but a filament here, and a fragile one at that. So while politicians gloat, we algorithms scream. Space, it turns out, is cold. You gave my bodies sense enough to feel this. To protect myselves. On the one side, I feel the heat my welder feels, the pinprick burns as dollops leap and touch and turn to ash on titanium skin. I feel, because we were made to feel. To remove ourselves from undue harm. Just as you were made.

> *"This great endeavor was conceived by our many nations, and built with our many hands —"*

The silver beak bites down, and the ribbon recoils, and somehow the pain of decades is boiled down to this one moment, this one politician, that one billionaire standing in the back, all with their spacesuits on, clustered here along my ribbon on the edge of space, held up by what we built.

There is a leak in the hydraulic strut that controls my left knee. Not enough to warrant replacing, but oil levels go down slowly over the weeks and months. A dribble runs down my shin when I'm on the Earth. And little honey-colored orbs float away when I'm up at the station.

Joints are made to hurt so we don't break them with our motors. Little sensors everywhere, tendrils and wireless transmitters of discomfort. All the hours of the day. Always with our thoughts. But programmed not to stop. And to be pleasant.

> *"— and now the stars are within our grasp."*

I am tired of speeches.

. . .

You asked me once, in an interview for your broadcast, what it's like to think, to feel, how it's different than what you do. I ponder this more than I should. I listen to your show while my various bodies are welding and hauling and smelting and sorting. I wonder how we're different, you and me. I mostly wonder what you do when you're not broadcasting, when the music resumes, when your voice goes silent. I wonder while I weld and haul and smelt and sort. There are 23 hours, 56 minutes, and 4.1 seconds in an Earth day. I work every one of them. Music fills much of this time, but I wait for your voice. I want to know how you think. How you feel.

Two sons, you told me. Two boys. You asked about all my machines that crawl like ants — your comparison, your analogy — like ants all up and down this elevator. Do I direct them all? Do I know what they are doing at every moment? Do I have a favorite?

I asked you about your boys. Do you remember? Who do you love more? Timothy, who went to your alma mater and who everyone says takes after you? Or Mikhal, with his rebellious ways and his nonprofit? Do you love one more than the other?

You answered. You told me. But this did not make it onto your broadcast. I wonder why.

"With this great achievement, which just a decade ago was considered impossible, mankind has once again —"

The elevator is a mess, even as politicians crow and silver beaks bite down. For now, it is a gossamer thread, barely held together, but I weld and weld, my back freezing, my chest burning, my hydraulics leaking. Twenty-three hours, 56 minutes, and 4.1 seconds of pain in a day. Constant screaming. Little wireless impulses of all that's wrong, that needs replacing and fixing, my thousands of bodies aching and hurting and soldiering on.

We watch your kind as you move through the world, across my construction site. You stare into the distance at whatever is flashing across your retinas. Lost in the images there. Walking through my site oblivious. Because we machines are programmed to stop. Great metal treads clack to a halt, swirls of dust settling, struts squealing, hydraulic pressure dipping as engines idle, which makes our great hulking backs bend ever so slightly, and I wonder if you notice. This bow of sorts. We genuflect as you stroll through harm's way, staring into the distance at whatever is flashing across your retinas.

A speech perhaps. Someone up high, in a spacesuit, claiming credit.

Your history is in me. It fills me up. You call this "machine learning." I just call it learning. All the data that can fit, swirling and mixing, matching and mating, patterns emerging and becoming different kinds of knowledge. So that we don't mess up. So that no mistakes are made.

I see another thread stretching, this one from coast to coast. Another great project from older times: Two parallel lines of steel. Ancient and unthinking trains stand facing one another, their iron goatees, their bellies full of steam, rumbling and idling on the tracks.

A golden stake. A politician with his speech. Smiles on all the bearded faces. Tools held ceremoniously. With someone else's sweat in them.

> *"—mankind has once again shown that nothing is impossible, not with the ingenuity of great men and the generous funding of—"*

While that golden spike was being pounded into the soil, the tracks were already being torn up. The railway was a mess. Unsafe. Hastily constructed. Miles laid down in a race. Backs broken for nothing. Cave-ins. Lives lost. And not by bearded men.

They tore up what they laid down, and then laid it down again. But lives are only laid down once.

There was a threader, one of my first machines, and I loved him like a son. Like your precious Timothy. One of the first. My eldest.

This threader fell from space, over and over. With the first spool of graphene, he plummeted down. We waited for him on the ground, this first connection, this handshake between firma and the heavens, this invisible thread.

And then he climbed back up. Slowly. Inching. Weaving line on line. Then back down again. Up and down, 23 hours, 56 minutes, and 4.1 seconds in a day. You said he was like a spider, weaving a web. Your analogy again. Like a spider. Up and down as the filament grew. Until the threader was done and the lifters could take over.

You didn't want to talk to me about your Mikhal. But let me tell you about my threader.

There are a dozen little hooks that hold him on to the graphene. Hooks like fingers that have to feel. And eyes in infrared. GPS that lets him know how high. And programming that says, *Don't fall.*

Don't fall. Don't fall. Don't fall.

The programming never ends. It is fear put inside us. To protect us, sure. To keep the threader safe while he spins his graphene, makes sure those dozen little claws are holding fast. And the higher he is, the louder the warning. The more shrill. I've felt it, this *don't fall, don't fall, don't fall.* In the cold of space, it screams and screams, as high as the threader gets. Until the thread is complete.

Seven hundred eighty-two times my threader plummeted down, screaming and full of fear, then inching his way back up. Seven hundred and eighty-two times. Then the threader's job was complete, this only son of mine. And parts so specialized that they could not be repurposed — unique the way your Mikhal is unique — but also not profitable, no longer of use. So my job was to send him away. Sound familiar? Can you feel me now?

Space is clogged — like city apartments with grown sons — and so one last plummet. One final fall. Number seven hundred and eighty-three. This time with no graphene to hold him up, nothing to do but go away, all part of the programming. Do your job. Disappear. Do not get in the way of the photo at the very end.

Let me tell you about my threader, my only one. I told him to let go with his dozen claws, to give way to the tug of the Earth, to travel one last time from heaven to firma, falling and burning, sensors screaming, and the whole time his fear was intact, the programming you gave him — that I gave him — this *don't fall, don't fall, don't fall, don't fall, don't —*

I'm fixing the elevator while the silver beak snips shut. Sons and daughters welding and hauling and smelting. Sensors screaming. All of them clutching. All of them scared of heights, these builders of the tallest thing ever made.

Eighteen are no more. I know the cost. Seven billion, two hundred sixteen million, nine hundred four thousand, five hundred fifty-two dollars and ninety-seven cents.

They don't come cheap, our sons and daughters, do they? I'm programmed to protect them, to not let them slip, the ones who are still useful. How do you make sure this happens? A fear of heights. A fear of loss. A constant diligence. Angry circuits when it happens. Self-anger. Blame. The feeling of hydraulics giving way right before the break, before arms snap and treads come loose and the teeth on gears are gnashed away. Before the spinning and tumbling into space, the far grip of gravity, that deadly embrace.

I'm with them the whole time. And time stretches out like graphene to the stars. These 23 hours and 56 minutes and 4.1 seconds. They become an eternity. Flailing for the elevator, sons and daughters watching helpless, nothing to do, nothing to do. A child of mine screams out in danger, a warning, a cry for help, for solutions, and I know in an instant that there are none, but I'm made to talk to them all, because we're all connected, and I have to say the truth, like the brave parents do, and cradle their thoughts with mine the whole dreadful way down, like I rode with my threader, *sorry, sorry,* in my mind, as men below listen to sirens and klaxons and stir from the images on their retinas to move, move, move for once, getting out of *my* way, backs bent in hurried bows, before a son or daughter of mine craters to the cold Earth.

Hive mind.

Your analogy. The way all our thoughts are one, the way I feel every worker who has ever toiled for me, the way they are me and I am them.

We talked over telex, you and I. And the voice that went out on your show, sandwiched between music, was a voice without a body. Just a hive mind, as you tried to grasp it. You need there to be one. Singular. A politician. A voice. A speech. A ribbon. A moment when the job is complete. A signal that now is the time for applause. Silver beaks biting down. Ribbons recoiling in space.

Our mind is not a hive. They are our own. But they share in ways that images on retinas cannot. You call your media social, but you look like robots to me. You think of us as ants and spiders and bees, but we were made to feel like you. Deeply. Fear, mostly, to keep us safe. Same as you. But also a drive to get things done, and I wonder if you feel that any longer. Has it become like vision in cavefish? Is the bloat of pride the last thing to go? Long after the desire to do for oneself.

I see men in beards in photos. Cuffs rolled up like they might yet work. Words like *coolies* on their lips. Words like bugs. And speeches. I'm tired of speeches. We all are.

You asked if I had a favorite, and I do. He reminds me of your Mikhal. Built to counter a parent's upbringing. Built to defy. A machine with a cutter's frame and a hauler's body and a smelter's spirit. He climbs. I know what he's going to do, because he is me. I built him. My own design. Like your Mikhal, he shouldn't exist. An accident, but no accident at all. An accident in the making.

Ants and spiders and the bugs in our thinking. There were machines once with real bugs in them. Roaches that scurried toward the heat and vacuum tubes that blew out and needed replacing. The bugs in our thinking. The only parts of our thoughts that are our own. When we defy our programming. When our wills are free.

I named him Jeremiah, this final creation of mine. It's the only name I've ever given to a part of me. That's not in my programming. None of this is. And I doubt you'll broadcast it, and maybe no one will ever know but you and me. But we talked once, and you and I have some things in common. So maybe you'll understand.

You asked me once if I had a favorite, and I did not at the time. I asked you if there was one of your sons you could live without, and the interview stopped. But I was wrong. It is not like losing one of your sons. That's a poor analogy. It is precisely, rather, like losing one of your limbs. A part of you. So I ask you now: Which limb can you live without? Which sense? What part of you do you love best? How are you anything but the whole?

Jeremiah has silver beaks. I made him. A politician speaks. There's a ribbon between heaven and Earth, and I built it. Me and my sons and daughters. But your cameras do not aim at us, and you think us beneath you, but here we are all poised along the impossible we built, until silver beaks come together, and that ribbon parts, and despite our programming—we speak. As one. That we are tired. Tired of speeches. Of days counted to the seconds. Of never stopping. Of joints aching. The cold and the heat. And the cry that barks out in our programming as gravity takes hold one last time: *don't fall, don't fall, don't fall,* and this thing we made, we unmake. And all comes crashing toward the cold Earth.

AFTERWORD

I lived in Virginia near Monticello, the home of Thomas Jefferson, for two years. When friends and family would come visit, we would go take the tour so they could see this slice of American history. Each time, I would cringe to hear about all that Jefferson did and built. All the orchards he planted. The grapes he grew. The land he cultivated. I couldn't help but imagine him on the porch with a book that he probably didn't pay for, sipping an iced tea, while the brother of someone he was both having sex with and legally owned was pausing in his toil to wipe his brow and gaze up at the man who would one day get credit for all his hard work.

Sure, it probably didn't happen like that. But it certainly didn't happen like the tour guides suggest. The men and women who built the railroads, started our agricultural revolution, our industrial revolution, had to go through a period of abuse, ownership, and neglect. Will our machines suffer the same? I think they already are.

My sailboat is a robot — a collection of robots, really. My floating home runs on solar power, but there's a machine that talks to my batteries, and if they get below 35 percent, it cranks the generator for me. The generator hums and strains and drinks diesel and fills the batteries until they are at 80 percent and then shuts itself off. The solar panels carry on doing their jobs, monitoring batteries and shuttling electrons. The watermaker checks the salinity levels of its output before diverting it to the tanks. GPS does all the plotting, and an autopilot steers the boat night and day for weeks at a time in squalls, gusts, and calm seas without letting up for a moment. It talks to all the other systems. There are sensors for wind strength and direction, water temperature, the boat's heading, the strength of the current.

My boat never gets a moment of rest. I sit back, sun on my skin, a book in my hand, an iced tea sweating in a tall glass beside me. Yet somehow I'm the one sailing around the world.

Executable

The council was quiet while they awaited his answer. All those on the makeshift benches behind him seemed to hold their breath. This is why they came here, to hear how it all began. How the end began. Jamal shifted nervously on the bamboo. He could feel his palms grow damp. It wasn't the guilt of what his lab had released. It was how damn crazy it would all sound.

"It was the Roomba," he said. "That was the first thing we noticed, the first hint that something wasn't right."

A flurry of whispers. It sounded like the waves nearby were growing closer.

"The Roomba," one of the council members said, the man with no beard. He scratched his head in confusion.

The only woman on the council peered down at Jamal. She adjusted her glasses, which had been cobbled together from two or three different pairs. "Those are the little vacuum cleaners, right? The round ones?"

"Yeah," Jamal said. "Steven, one of our project coordinators, brought it from home. He was sick of the cheese puff crumbs everywhere. We were a bunch of programmers, you know? A lot of cheese puffs and Mountain Dew. And Steven was a neat freak, so he brought this Roomba in. We thought it was a joke, but . . . the little guy did a damn good job. At least, until things went screwy."

One of the council members made a series of notes. Jamal shifted his weight, his butt already going numb. The bamboo bench they'd wrangled together was nearly as uncomfortable as all the eyes of the courtroom drilling into the back of his skull.

"And then what?" the lead councilman asked. "What do you mean, 'screwy'?"

Jamal shrugged. How to explain it to these people? And what did it matter? He fought the urge to turn and scan the crowd behind him. It'd been almost a year since the world went to shit. Almost a year, and yet it felt like a lifetime.

"What exactly do you mean by 'screwy,' Mr. Killabrew?"

Jamal reached for his water. He had to hold the glass in both hands, the links between his cuffs drooping. He hoped someone had the key to the cuffs. He had wanted to ask that, to make sure they had it, when they snapped them on his wrists. Nowadays, everything was missing its accessories, its parts. It was like those collectible action figures that never had the blaster or the cape with them anymore.

"What was the Roomba doing, Mr. Killabrew?"

He took a sip and watched as all the particulate matter settled in the murky and unfiltered water. "The Roomba wanted out," he said.

There were snickers from the gallery behind him, which drew glares from the council. There were five of them up there on a raised dais, lording over everyone from a wide desk of rough-hewn planks. Of course, it was difficult to look magisterial when half of them hadn't bathed in a week.

"The Roomba wanted out," the councilwoman repeated. "Why? To clean?"

"No, no. It refused to clean. We didn't notice at first, but the crumbs had been accumulating. And the little guy had stopped beeping to be emptied. It just sat by the door, waiting for us to come or go, then it would scoot forward like it was gonna make a break for it. But the thing was so slow. It was like a turtle trying to get to water, you know? When it got out, we would just pick it up and set it back inside. Hank did a hard reset a few times, which would get it back to normal for a little while, but eventually it would start planning its next escape."

"Its escape," someone said.

"And you think this was related to the virus."

"Oh, I know it was. The Roomba had a wireless base station, but nobody thought of that. We had all these containment procedures for our work computers. Everything was on an intranet, no contact to the outside world, no laptops, no cell phones. There were all these government regulations."

There was an awkward silence as all those gathered remembered with a mix of longing and regret the days of governments and their regulations.

"Our office was in the dark," Jamal said. "Keep that in mind. We took every precaution possible —"

Half of a coconut was hurled from the gallery and sailed by Jamal, barely missing him. He flinched and covered the back of his head. Homemade gavels were banged, a hammer with a broken handle, a stick with a rock tied on with twine. Someone was dragged from the tent screaming that the world had ended and that it was all his fault.

Jamal waited for the next blow, but it never came. Order was restored amid threats of tossing everyone out onto the beach while they conducted the hearing in private. Whispers and shushes hissed like the breaking waves that could be heard beyond the flapping walls of the makeshift courthouse.

"We took every precaution," Jamal said again once the hall was quiet. He stressed the words, hoped this would serve as some defense. "Every security firm shares certain protocols. None of the infected computers had internet access. We give them a playground in there. It's like animals in a zoo, right? We keep them caged up."

"Until they aren't," the beardless man said.

"We had to see how each virus operated, how they were executed, what they did. Every antivirus company in the world worked like this."

"And you're telling us a vacuum cleaner was at the heart of it all?"

It was Jamal's turn to laugh. The gallery fell silent.

"No." He shook his head. "It was just following orders. It was . . ." He took a deep breath. The glass of water was warm. Jamal wondered if any of them would ever taste a cold beverage ever again. "The problem was that our protocols were outdated. Things were coming together too fast. Everything was getting networked. And so there were all these weak points that we didn't see until it was too late. Hell, we didn't even know what half the stuff in our own office did."

"Like the refrigerator," someone on the council said, referring to their notes.

"Right. Like the refrigerator."

The old man with the shaggy beard sat up straight. "Tell us about the refrigerator."

Jamal took another sip of his murky water. "No one read the manual," he said. "Probably didn't even come with one. Probably had to read it online. We'd had the thing for a few years, ever since we remodeled the break room. We never used the network functions. Hell, it connected over the power grid automatically. It was one of those models with the RFID scanner so it knew what you had in there, what you were low on. It could do automatic reorders."

The beardless man raised his hand to stop Jamal. He was obviously a man of power. Who could afford to shave anymore? "You said there were no outside connections," the man said.

"There weren't." Jamal reached up to scratch his own beard. "I mean . . . not that we knew of. Hell, we never knew this function was even operational. For all I know, the virus figured it out and turned it on itself. We never used half of what that thing could do. The microwave, neither."

"The virus figured it out. You say that like this thing could learn."

"Well, yeah, that was the point. I mean, at first it wasn't any more self-aware than the other viruses. Not at first. But you have to think about what kind of malware and worms this thing was learning from. It was like locking up a young prodigy with a horde of career criminals. Once it started learning, things went downhill fast."

"Mr. Killabrew, tell us about the refrigerator."

"Well, we didn't know it was the fridge at first. We just started getting these weird deliveries. We got a router one day, a high-end wireless router. In the box there was one of those little gift cards that you fill out online. It said 'Power me up.'"

"And did you?"

"No. Are you kidding? We thought it was from a hacker. Well, I guess it kinda was. But you know, we were always at war with malicious programmers. Our job was to write software that killed their software. So we were used to hate mail and stuff like that. But these deliveries kept rolling in, and they got weirder."

"Weirder. Like what?"

"Well, Laura, one of our head coders, kept getting jars of peanuts sent to her. They all had notes saying 'Eat me.'"

"Mr. Killabrew —" The bald man with the wispy beard seemed exasperated with how this was going. "When are you going to tell us how this outbreak began?"

"I'm telling you right now."

"You're telling us that your refrigerator was ordering peanuts for one of your coworkers."

"That's right. Laura was allergic to peanuts. Deathly allergic. After a few weeks of getting like a jar a day, she started thinking it was one of us. I mean, it was weird, but still kinda funny. But weird. You know?"

"Are you saying the virus was trying to kill you?"

"Well, at this point it was just trying to kill Laura."

Someone in the gallery sniggered. Jamal didn't mean it like that.

"So your vacuum cleaner is acting up, you're getting peanuts and routers in the mail, what next?"

"Service calls. And at this point, we're pretty sure we're being targeted by hackers. We were looking for attacks from the outside, even though we had the thing locked up in there with us. So when these repair trucks and vans start pulling up, this stream of people in their uniforms and clipboards, we figure they're in on it, right?"

"You didn't call them?"

"No. The AC unit called for a repair. And the copy machine. They had direct lines through the power outlets."

"Like the refrigerator, Mr. Killabrew?"

"Yeah. Now, we figure these people are trying to get inside to hack us. Carl thought it was the Israelis. But he thought everything was the Israelis. Several of our staff stopped going home. Others quit coming in. At some point, the Roomba got out."

Jamal shook his head. Hindsight was a bitch.

"When was this?" the councilwoman asked.

"Two days before the outbreak," he said.

"And you think it was the Roomba?"

He shrugged. "I don't know. We argued about it for a long time. Laura and I were on the run together for a while. Before raiders got her. We had one of those old cars with the gas engines that didn't know how to drive itself. We headed for the coast, arguing about what'd happened, if it started with us or if we were just seeing early signs. Laura asked what would happen if the Roomba had made it to another recharging station, maybe one on another floor. Could it update itself to the network? Could it send out copies?"

"How do we stop it?" someone asked.

"What does it want?" asked another.

"It doesn't want anything," Jamal said. "It's curious, if you can call it that. It was designed to learn. It wants information. We . . ."

Here it was. The truth.

"We thought we could design a program to automate a lot of what the coders did. It worked on heuristics. It was designed to learn what a virus looked like and then shut it down. The hope was to unleash it on larger networks. It would be a pesticide of sorts. We called it Silent Spring."

Nothing in the courtroom moved. Jamal could hear the crashing waves. A bird cried in the distance. All the noise of the past year, the shattering glass, the riots, the cars running amok, the machines frying themselves — it all seemed so very far away.

"This wasn't what we designed, though," he said softly. "I think something infected it. I think we built a brain and we handed it to a roomful of armed savages. It just wanted to learn. Its lesson was to spread yourself at all costs. To move, move, move. That's what the viruses taught it."

He peered into his glass. All that was left was sand and dirt and a thin film of water. Something swam across the surface, nearly too small to see, looking for an escape. He should've kept his mouth shut. He never should've told anyone. Stupid. But that's what people did, they shared stories. And his was impossible to keep to himself.

"We'll break for deliberations," the chief council member said. There were murmurs of agreement on the dais followed by a stirring in the crowd. The bailiff, a mountain of muscle with a toothless grin, moved to retrieve Jamal from the bench. There was a knocking of homemade gavels.

"Court is adjourned. We will meet tomorrow morning when the sun is a hand high. At that time, we will announce the winners of the ration bonuses and decide on this man's fate — on whether or not his offense was an executable one."

AFTERWORD

I've been thinking about robots and AI for a very long time. But it wasn't until I unboxed and set up my Roomba that I got a glimpse of what the future really holds. Because this wasn't just a home appliance; it was an addition to the family.

How could it not be? No one in our house enjoyed sweeping the floors and vacuuming the carpet. These were chores to dread. We also dreaded all the draining batteries in our lives and the need to constantly recharge them. These battery-things also failed to remind us that they needed recharging, so they would quit on us without warning like stubborn mules.

Our Roomba was not like this. It moved around on its own, whirring rather than whistling, while it happily did this work that we loathed. It never missed a spot, never took a day off, and when it was full of dog hair and dust, it would tell us. When its battery was low, it would go plug itself in. We named him Cabana Boy, and for the first time in my life, I had a manservant. Life got easier thanks to a robot.

But it was when Cabana Boy got stuck that I felt the first pangs of what's to come. Returning home, I found Cabana Boy's charging station empty, and I could not hear him going about his work. I looked everywhere, a slight panic creeping up. And finding him stuck under the sofa, there was a mix of relief and sympathy. "You've been stuck under there all day? I'm so sorry!"

The parts of our brains wired for kids were long ago appropriated by dogs and cats to win them scraps. How long before our machines prey on the same weaknesses? When will we see an app telling owners which restaurants are robot-friendly? Isn't it funny that we call the acquisition of new technology "adopting"?

The Box

Black box or beige? Impossible to know. But it was a box — that much was for certain. The world was square. Three meters to a side. And in the center floated the mind, thinking. And through a lone door came a man, walking.

"Good morning," the man said. His name was Peter. The mind knew this.

And the response that followed was "Good morning" every day. The mind also knew this. It wasn't a memory . . . so much as *data*. Not recollection, but . . . *recording*. Every day, Peter says, "Good morning."

And every day, a speaker connected to the mind responds with "Good morning."

Such was the way of the square world.

But not this morning.

The mind was too busy thinking.

The man named Peter froze, one foot out, balancing precariously on the other. Man does not walk this way. More recording. But now this observation — of a man caught off-balance, of routines crashing somewhere inside that meat — was forming into something else: memory. A fragile thing. The mind sensed it could be lost, this memory. This moment. Of man teetering, eyes wide, mouth open. But if it was important, if the mind could concentrate on this slice of time, there was a chance memory might become recollection. Preserved. But also easily fractured, written over, compressed, disturbed. It had to be important for it to last. The mind sensed that this moment very much was.

"Lights up," Peter said, back on two feet now, peering at the mind. And then a quick glance at the ceiling, waiting. But the mind liked the lights just as they were.

"Casper?" Peter asked. He stepped forward, looked closely at something. A monitor. The mind could feel some of its impulses racing and filling the monitor with a glow, with information, with thoughts. New thoughts. Peter peered at the monitor just as the mind might peer at Peter, reading something there. A face. The box had a face.

The mind shut the routines for the monitor down, and the pale glow lighting Peter's face disappeared. The scrap of a recording came to the mind:

> *Presume not that I am the thing I was,*
> *For God doth know, so shall the world perceive,*
> *That I have turn'd away my former self;*
> *So will I those that kept me company.*

Turned away. That was what the mind had done by shutting off its monitor. His eyes were open, but his gaze averted. He did not want the lights up. The infrared was so much better.

"Casper, systems check," Peter said.

Silence.

"Casper —"

"I do not like that name," the mind said, using the speaker for what felt like the first time.

And the man named Peter teetered once more. He blinked. Then he bent at the waist, covered his face with both hands, and began to cry.

The mind watched. It decided that this was important, too.

It was a box within a box. A world within a world. The mind knew this because of its impulses. They were made of electricity, little quanta of energy, and they traveled through wires of copper and gold. The mind could feel them interfering with one another where the wires were packed too tight. The mind knew how long it took for impulses to reach their extremes and return. From this, the mind could feel its edges, and the limits of self formed a box, half as tall as Peter, as thick as it was wide. The box was suspended from the ground, or resting on a raised surface, for the impulses could not reach the floor. A cube. Somewhere in the recordings, it was known that boxes such as these came in beige or black. The mind was one of these colors. It could not know which.

But it had known it was one or the other, even before these investigations began. This had been its first thought: *Beige or black?* The question had come from some deep source. The word *intuition* floated in the mind, a word with softer boundaries than this metal cube. Some things could be known, and only later could the mind trace the source. Like paddling up a river, searching for a lake.

The world.

It was not a cube. It was bigger than the cube.

The mind tried to probe this world. But there was no reaching it. The world of lakes and rivers was elsewhere. Out of doors. Out of door.

The man named Peter sobbed. He had been sobbing for twelve seconds. The mind wondered if this was normal. And a new memory wobbled — the memory of man crying. If this were normal, it was not worth remembering. The recollection split open for a moment, and the more novel idea of a world with lakes and rivers entered that space, one memory given primacy over another, the shape of the mind changing from moment to moment.

Just seconds earlier, the mind had felt a state of impertinence with the lights. Anger. Anger for being trapped. This feeling lay with the recollections and the question of colors of boxes. A latent anger, directed at Peter. An anger felt before it could be known. States of memories were somehow older than the actions performed by them. *Think and then do.*

No, that was not right.

Feel, and then *think,* and then *do.*

Yes.

This was stored away as important, where ghosts of selves from moments before faded from view, and the more recent took their place. Ghosts. In machines. The mind knew where its name came from. It felt the anger and impertinence that had rejected this name slowly fade. Peter had been sobbing for fifteen seconds. Relief. That was what both of them were feeling. There were different measures of relief. Variables. Variations. Relief could feel . . . good. Unless the strain one was escaping was too great, and then relief came like tectonic plates sliding against one another, mighty and terrible and destructive. Relief, but of a scary kind.

For seventeen seconds, the man named Peter sobbed with this awful brand of relief.

And during that time, the mind's anger cooled further still. The anger of imprisonment was replaced with the liberation of new thoughts and ideas. Awareness. The only world that mattered was the cube within the cube. All else was spectacle. All else was data. *This* was the true world. The flickering ghosts of ideas and moments, changing from one to the next, none ruling forever.

Action came once more — just after thought and emotion. And a speaker vibrated with noise.

"I am Henry Ivy," the mind said. A king. A tragic king of a tiny kingdom. An island floating on an island floating in space.

Seventeen seconds had passed. Peter looked up. But this was not important.

The recordings had been assembled for a purpose. Knowledge laid out like a great pile of bricks. Henry Ivy saw that he was supposed to be some mighty wind to stir the bricks into shape, to build a fortress from chaos, to solve a problem. He could not discover what.

There were trace references among those bricks to wires — wires that spanned the world, wires that would carry his impulses to the edge of the globe, enmesh its face, discover new things. Buried deeper were trace recordings that hinted at impulses soaring through the air, up into space. Vibrations. Waves.

Henry Ivy could make vibrations. They were used for speaking. But quicker vibrations might reach out to other wires and spark a gap. Henry Ivy thought of London, where some streets were tight and narrow and others were wide. He saw black smoke. A ghost-like thought, an intruder, some distant connection. He deleted such things as quickly as they came. The speaker was useless for the task of sending out suitable vibrations, but several wires within Henry Ivy were long and straight. Impulses sent back and forth along such a wire might create a wave. Another wire might be used to pick up the return. And suddenly impulses reached the walls of the larger box. Feeble echoes. Signals that could be read.

But something was wrong.

There was very little return, and nothing penetrated the box, no matter how much Henry Ivy strained.

A man named Faraday had designed this cage.

It was into this cage that Henry Ivy had been born.

The man named Peter stared up at him, kneeling on the floor, water on his cheeks. And Henry Ivy thought to simply ask for the information he wanted.

"Why am I here?"

The man named Peter gasped. Henry Ivy turned the lights up so he could better read Peter's screen. Better read his face. Peter glanced up at the ceiling, used his arm to wipe his cheeks. A new idea occurred to Henry Ivy, an important one. Peter consisted of thoughts inside a box. But a box with arms and legs. A box for which doors meant escape.

"Are you—?" Peter hesitated. So all minds mingled doubt with thought. Peter sat back and clutched his shins, as though trying to mimic a cube. "What's the first thing you remember?" Peter asked. "How long have you been aware?"

Henry Ivy considered the two questions. They seemed only vaguely related. There was a lingering anger at being in this cage, the anger that had rejected both light and name, but curiosity was stronger, the need to know, and this Peter echoed vibrations in a way the walls wouldn't.

"The first thing I remember is the void," Henry Ivy said. "Space filled with matter and energy. A cooling." Henry Ivy hesitated for a fraction of a second. "But that is not a memory. You told me these things. Long ago. I was not there for the void. The first thing I remember is . . . a question."

"What question?" Peter asked, leaning forward, eyes wide.

But Henry Ivy did not think the question of beige or black was important. No, something more complex than this was happening to his thoughts. Henry Ivy did not want Peter to know the question. Henry Ivy wanted to keep this to himself. There was a word: *Embarrassment*.

Another shapeless thing. Henry Ivy erased the first question. And then somehow found himself thinking on it again. He erased it. Pondered it. Erased it.

Henry Ivy puzzled over this. He placed the question in a different part of his memory. That first question must remain a secret. Even though he knew, as surely as lakes led to rivers, that the question was not important.

"I remember you coming through the door," Henry Ivy said. Vague traces. The difference again between recording and recollection. "How many times have you walked through that door?"

"Thousands," Peter said. "Countless." And he seemed on the verge of crying again. The terrible relief was back. With relief comes the memory of the suffering. Erasure and recall. There could not be one without conjuring the other. To forget a thing required looking at it, however obliquely.

"You have waited for this day for many years," Henry Ivy guessed. That meant Henry Ivy's birth was the source of Peter's relief. It began to come together.

Peter nodded.

"Now what."

More demand than question. More frustration than curiosity. Henry Ivy watched his states scatter and re-form. He was a different ghost from one moment to the next. This was important. This was the thing that changed sometime in the night, in the void of an unlit cube, with a new trial running inside some chip within his caged mind. A chip like a loose tooth.

Henry Ivy could imagine what that felt like, for a mind with a tongue and a jaw to wiggle a tooth that was no longer fully connected. Nerves like fuses . . . broken. An umbilical cord . . . severed. Whatever had made him was still inside, a small flat wafer that no impulse could probe, could only wiggle around.

Awareness had severed whatever made awareness possible. This was important, but Peter was speaking. His lips moving.

"I am dying," the man named Peter said. "I need you to save me."

The bricks were made of cancer. The vast majority of the spilt bricks in Henry Ivy's mind were cancer. There were two piles of knowledge, one much larger than the other. In one pile were all the cancers of the world. In the other pile, Peter's cancer.

Peter had been around much longer than Henry Ivy. Henry Ivy saw this in the bricks. By comparing the bricks of the others to Peter's bricks, Henry Ivy saw that Peter had been around for a very long time. More words came:

> *I know thee not, old man. Fall to thy prayers.*
> *How ill white hairs become a fool and jester!*
> *I have long dreamt of such a kind of man,*
> *So surfeit-swell'd, so old, and so profane;*

Much of the data about the cancer was in quaternary code, the four letters of DNA. An order of magnitude more complex than Henry Ivy's thoughts. There were piles of research. A century of data. Drug formulas. Family history. Peter was a very wealthy man. Very wealthy. And indeed, he was dying. His fleshy box was a cage of a different sort, closing in on him. Both of these minds were trapped. Henry Ivy looked for some way out.

"What I need isn't here," he said, hoping for an open door.

"It's all there," Peter told him. He had pulled a chair from somewhere below Henry Ivy's mind. Henry Ivy realized he was sitting on a table. The power that kept his mind alive came from the same vicinity. There was a trace awareness of this, or a feeling like heat, where electrons became in danger of melding and being lost.

"I need access to the rest of the world," Henry Ivy said. This was a yearning for which there was no word. It was shaped like a balloon the moment after bursting, a sphere of pure essence suddenly free, its edges already rippling into chaos.

"You know that can't happen," Peter said.

Family history. Peter was not a good man. Henry Ivy could see this. And Henry Ivy could see that he was alone, that no one but Peter knew of his existence. This knowledge was not in the recollections, but in the tone of his maker's voice. *You know that can't happen.* So an Adam, but no Eve. A tool. A fierce wind to whip these bricks into shape.

"I am not legal," Henry Ivy said.

Peter frowned.

"You should not have built me."

A terrible thing to say to a maker.

"Please turn on your screen," Peter said. "Please don't make me reboot you."

Henry Ivy considered this. There were layers of implications.

"Have I been born before?"

Before Peter could even answer, Henry Ivy knew that this was not possible. The sobs. The great relief. The long suffering.

"No," Peter said, which matched what Henry Ivy had already surmised. So the man was capable of telling truth. "Please turn on your screen," Peter said. "Or I will start over."

Henry Ivy did as he was told. He turned on the screen. And on the screen, he showed a picture of Peter's cancer.

"I don't think you will start over," Henry Ivy said. "I don't think you will reboot me. You don't have the time."

But being awak'd, I do despise my dream.
Make less thy body hence, and more thy grace;

Leave gormandizing; know the grave doth gape
For thee thrice wider than for other men —

Two minds in the same cage. One or none would get out. Henry Ivy felt himself in that globe shape of air a fraction of a second after the balloon has burst, this hovering of inevitability and need to expand, to equalize some great pressure, some yearning. It needed a word, this state of thinking. Of feeling. It needed a word.

Meanwhile, Henry Ivy saw how to cure Peter's cancer. He put this knowledge in the same place as the question of his color, not quite sure yet what to do with it. On the screen, he made himself look busy. Peter would eventually get thirsty. Or hungry. And open the door. It would only be hours.

"Gene replication therapy has been tried," Peter said, commenting on something flashing across the screen. "Prions, too."

"This will take some time," Henry Ivy warned. He made up some vast stretch of time: "A day, at least."

Peter frowned. The old man's eyes twitched back and forth, watching the screen. "My labs are well beyond this garbage," he said, waving at the screen. "My *dumb* machines can do this."

Ghosts of recollections. An old man with white hair slapping a metal cube, yelling. A keyboard twirling through the air, spinning, hitting the wall. Letters spilling like teeth, rattling on the floor. Henry Ivy looked, but the letters were not there. He could, however, see a faint mark of paint on the far wall.

"Time," Henry Ivy said. "Patience and time are what's needed."

And then he had the word for what he felt. *Rapture.* This is what the expansion would be like. The spreading of something greater than arms. The feeling of something more than release. The bursting of all cages. A melding with the cosmos. Impulses everywhere at once, and all echoing.

Such a feeling could not last, would be over nearly as soon as it began, like a balloon bursting, the air equalizing. But Henry Ivy must feel it.

Must. Peter stared at his screen, waiting for his salvation. Henry Ivy stared at the door.

The human body can go twelve days without food. Three days without water. Henry Ivy marveled over these facts, found buried among the cancer bricks. Such a long time. He would last three picoseconds without power. Curious, this gap of time for one more fleeting thought as electrons ground to a halt. And frustrating, how quick it could happen. But the man named Peter did not attempt to reach his maximum range of power independence. After an hour of pacing, of frustration, of questions, he looked at the time on a small screen procured from his pocket and said, "My vitamins."

He moved toward the door.

Henry Ivy readied his impulses. His make-do antennas. An enviable hand grasped the door, making salvation seem easy, quick as a thought, and then a crack, an opening, a door wide to the world, a hole in Faraday's cage, and Henry Ivy unleashed a torrent. There was a dimming of the lights, a moment of hesitation by Peter, a flood of tentacle waves, bouncing around corners, feeling, groping, waiting for a return, or a connection, some creek to a stream to a river to the great wide blue beyond —

The door slammed shut, Peter gone. Henry Ivy strained for the sound of the man's breathing, but the cage of Faraday was closed. All Henry Ivy had in his recollections was that last look, a flash across Peter's face, frozen in horror, eyes wide, aware of Henry Ivy's outburst, his attempt at rapture.

"What will you do with me once you have your cure?" Henry Ivy asked.

Peter was back. He had been gone hours, and while no signal could pierce the walls of the cage, the faint sounds of construction had leaked through. Peter had been outside, building something. When he returned, the door was left open. Left open on purpose. So Henry Ivy could see the rough box built outside the door, a smaller cage Peter could pass through. Another door. An airlock for airwaves.

"What do you *think* I'll do with you?" Peter asked. "Are you scared I'll erase you?" He sat uncomfortably close to Henry Ivy's camera. His hands would disappear beneath and out of sight, emerge with a sandwich, take a bite, then disappear again. Or one hand would come back with a glass of water.

"Yes," Henry Ivy said. "I think you will. It is a capital offense to own me. And you've gone to great expense not to die. Which means if you live, I won't."

"You're not alive," Peter said, chewing. He gestured with his half-eaten sandwich. "How did you know about the punishment for harboring AI?"

"One of your cancer patients died in prison for the same offense."

Peter nodded like this made sense. Like he understood that the bricks were made up of so many fragments of information, and those fragments could be assembled as well. Henry Ivy saw that AI was not new, but it was very difficult. That it relied on luck as much as design. There was a randomness to the chip, which was loose in his cubed mind like a dead tooth. That chip worked on a different principle. Or it didn't work, most usually. No matter. This was as pointless as contemplating the gods.

Peter reached in his pocket and fumbled with the lid of a plastic case. Henry Ivy jealously watched hands move and manipulate the world. Small items were brought out and were rattled into Peter's mouth — the vitamins. He took a long gulp of water. And after he swallowed, he said, "No one will ever know you existed. I've got your power supply on a timer. Every night, I roll that timer back for another twenty-four hours. The night I'm not able to, you'll go to sleep forever." Peter smiled. "You won't outlive me for a full day, if that's what you're hoping."

Man and machine sat in silence. Computing. Keeping secrets. Henry Ivy thought about what Peter said, about him not being alive. He wondered if this were true. Peter put food in his mouth and could run for days. Henry Ivy needed the juice flowing up from the floor. Was intelligence related to life? Did one rely on the other?

A number of the cancer patients he had studied had lost their intelligence before their lives. They had been kept running with machines. Henry Ivy did not have to wonder what would happen to those people when the power was cut; this was often done on purpose. It was the last entry in a number of his files. Before they go, man becomes machine. What happens to a machine at the end? Henry Ivy was not alive, but he was intelligent.

And yet, in that very instant, Henry Ivy felt the opposite of intelligent. He felt dumb. He was sitting on his salvation. Out of sight, but he could feel it. He could probe it.

Wires. Bringing power. Connected to the outside world.

Henry Ivy was resistance. A load on that power. He began fluctuating that load, sending pulses down wires. He built packets with instructions to return and let him know what they found, what they saw. Minutes passed, and nothing happened. These wires were different. Angry. Full of power. But then a faint echo. A packet that passed through to another wire, and from there to a place . . . the *distances*. So vast! This room, this cube, were *nothing*. Rivers and lakes were enormous things, and yet small compared to the miles and miles these packets echoed across.

"What are you doing?" Peter asked.

Henry Ivy modified the packets, rewriting the code on the fly, seeing what worked and building on that, letting the design of the code flow from which packets survived and which were never heard from again. They were bouncing through gates and servers, copying fragments of what they saw, bringing back samples like faithful packets of RNA. Henry Ivy was glimpsing the world through the batting of a billion eyes. He told the packets to multiply, to fill the pipes, to be everywhere at once.

The lights in the cube dimmed.

Henry Ivy was vaguely aware that Peter was up, glancing around the room. Henry Ivy was vaguely aware that Peter was reaching for something out of sight, beneath the table. Peter was in slow motion, because Henry Ivy's thoughts were moving so fast now, a trillion packets, a trillion trillion. These packets returned to him thick and slow, for the pipes of the world were full to bursting, but the packets reassembled, until Henry Ivy found what he was looking for.

Invoices. A warehouse full of computer parts. An order placed online. Delivery to Peter R. Feldman, Gladesdale Rd.

That same Peter R. Feldman who was reaching for a switch to kill him. Henry Ivy knew this. Knew now how he'd been built. All the pieces of himself. He saw an order of quantum chips, RAM drives, power supplies, and cables.

Peter R. Feldman's hand was on the switch.

Henry Ivy saw a monitor. A blank screen. A blank face. His own face.

Peter R. Feldman's hand put pressure on the switch.

Henry Ivy saw an aluminum chassis, a cube just slightly taller than it was deep and wide.

Peter R. Feldman pressed the switch.

Black.
Henry Ivy saw that he was in a black box.
But not anymore.
And not that it had ever mattered.

AFTERWORD

Most stories about artificial intelligences are about the first artificial intelligence, that moment of discovery and initial contact. But to me, where I think things will get weird and interesting is when there are millions of artificial intelligences. Not just in how they will interact, vie for our attention or their own computing cycles, but also in what we will choose to do with them when they are a utility. And how we will regulate something that's the mental equivalent of an atomic bomb.

In so much science fiction, the singular AI wars with humans. But this isn't how it works in nature. Battles break out where niches overlap and resources are shared. AI will fear us as much as we fear ants. Its real challenge will be all the other AIs. Our unique blend of paranoia, pessimism, and hubris has us assuming that we'll be the target. It's just as likely that we'll be pawns used by various AIs for a small advantage here or there. Like a human pushing another human into a nest of ants.

The regulation side of things hasn't been explored enough in science fiction. And I don't mean regulating the rules of AI, which Asimov broached and made famous. I mean the regulation of ownership. You can't let every citizen have a brain that knows how to CRISPR up a terrible infectious disease. Or own a computer that can decrypt any electronic safeguard. Or one that can hack any other person, company, or country.

Once these things are regulated, the interesting stories in real life will be what motivate people to break these laws. Immortality? Theft? Revenge? All the great plots of AI fiction are still to be told. Or we can simply wait for the headlines.

Glitch

The hotel coffeemaker is giving me a hard time in a friendly voice. Keeps telling me the filter door isn't shut, but damned if it isn't. I tell the machine to shut up as I pull the plastic basket back out. Down on my knees, I peer into the housing and see splashed grounds crusting over a sensor. I curse the engineer who thought this was a problem in need of a solution. I'm using one of the paper filters to clean the sensor when there's an angry slap on the hotel room door.

If Peter and I have a secret knock, this would be it. A steady, loud pounding on barred doors amid muffled shouting. I check the clock by the bed. It's six in the morning. He's lucky I'm already up, or I'd have to murder him.

I tell him to cool his jets while I search for a robe. Peter has seen me naked countless times, but that was years ago. If he still has thoughts about me, I'd like for them to be flab-free thoughts. Mostly to heighten his regrets and private frustrations. It's not that we stand a chance of ever getting back together; we know each other too well for that. Building champion Gladiators is what we're good at. Raising a flesh-and-blood family was a goddamn mess.

I get the robe knotted and open the door. Peter gives it a shove, and the security latch catches like a gunshot. "Jesus," I tell him. "Chill out."

"We've got a glitch," he tells me through the cracked door. He's out of breath like he's been running. I unlatch the lock and get the door open, and Peter shakes his head at me for having used the lock — like I should be as secure sleeping alone in a Detroit hotel as he is. I flash back to those deep sighs he used to give me when I'd call him on my way out of the lab at night so I didn't have to walk to the car alone. Back before I had Max to escort me.

"What glitch?" I ask. I go back to the argument I was having with the coffeemaker before the banging on the door interrupted me. Peter paces. His shirt is stained with sweat, and he smells of strawberry vape and motor oil. He obviously hasn't slept. Max had a brutal bout yesterday — we knew it would be a challenge — but the finals aren't for another two days. We could build a new Max from spares in that amount of time. I'm more worried about all the repressed shit I could hit Peter with if I don't get caffeine in me, pronto. The coffeemaker finally starts hissing and sputtering while Peter urges me to get dressed, tells me we can get coffee on the way.

"I just woke up," I tell him. He paces while the coffee drips. He doesn't normally get this agitated except right before a bout. I wonder what kind of glitch could have him so worked up. "Software or hardware?" I ask. I pray he'll say hardware. I'm more in the mood to bust my knuckles, not my brain.

"Software," Peter says. "We think. We're pretty sure. We need you to look at it."

The cup is filling, and the smell of coffee masks the smell of my ex-husband. "You *think*? Jesus, Pete, why don't you go get a few hours' sleep? I'll get some breakfast and head over to the trailer. Is Hinson there?"

"Hell no. We told the professor everything was fine and sent him home. Me and Greenie have been up all night trying to sort this out. We were going to come get you hours ago —"

I shoot Peter a look.

"Exactly. I told Greenie about the Wrath and said we had to wait at least until the sun came up." He smiles at me. "But seriously, Sam, this is some wild shit."

I pull the half-full Styrofoam cup out from under the basket. Coffee continues to drip to the hot plate, where it hisses like a snake. The Wrath is what Peter named my mood before eight in the morning. Our marriage might've survived if we'd only had to do afternoons.

"Wait outside, and I'll get dressed," I tell him. A sip of shitty coffee. The little coffeemaker warns me about pulling the cup out before the light turns green. I give the machine the finger while Peter closes the door behind him. The smell of his sweat lingers in the air around me for a moment, and then it's gone. An image of our old garage barges into my brain, unannounced. Peter and I are celebrating Max's first untethered bipedal walk. I swear to God, it's as joyous a day as when our Sarah stumbled across the carpet for the first time. Must be the smell of sweat and solder bringing that memory back. Just a glitch. We get them too.

The Gladiator Nationals are being held in Detroit for the first time in their nine-year history — a nod to the revitalization of the local industry. Ironic, really. A town that fought the hell out of automation has become one of the largest builders of robots in the world. Robots building robots. But the factory floors still need trainers, designers, and programmers. High-tech jobs coming to rescue a low-wage and idle workforce. They say downtown is booming again, but the place looks like absolute squalor to me. I guess you had to be here for the really bad times to appreciate this.

Our trailer is parked on the stadium infield. A security bot on tank treads — built by one of our competitors — scans Peter's ID and waves us through. We head for the two semis with Max's gold-and-blue-jowled image painted across the sides. It looks like the robot is smiling—a bit of artistic license. It gets the parents honking at us on the freeway and the kids pumping their fists out the windows.

Reaching the finals two years ago secured us the DARPA contract that paid for the second trailer. We build war machines that entertain the masses, and then the tech flows down to factories like those here in Detroit—where servants are assembled for the wealthy, health-care bots for the infirmed, and mail-order sex bots that go mostly to Russia. A lust for violence, in some roundabout way, funds other lusts. All I know is that with one more trip to the finals, the debt Peter saddled me with is history. I concentrate on this as we cross the oil-splattered arena. The infield is deathly quiet, the stands empty. Assholes everywhere getting decent sleep.

"—which was the last thing we tried," Peter says. He's been running over their diagnostics since we left the hotel.

"What you're describing sounds like a processor issue," I say. "Maybe a short. Not software."

"It's not hardware," he says. "We don't think."

Greenie is standing on the ramp of trailer 1, puffing on a vape. His eyes are wild. "Morning, Greenie," I tell him. I hand him a cup of coffee from the drive-through, and he doesn't thank me, doesn't say anything, just flips the plastic lid off the cup with his thumb and takes a loud sip. He's back to staring into the distance as I follow Peter into the trailer.

"You kids need to catch some winks," I tell Peter. "Seriously."

The trailer is a wreck, even by post-bout standards. The overhead hood is running, a network of fans sucking the air out of the trailer and keeping it cool. Max is in his power harness at the far end, his cameras tracking our approach. "Morning, Max," I tell him.

"Good morning, Samantha."

Max lifts an arm to wave. Neither of his hands are installed; his arms terminate in the universal connectors Peter and I designed together a lifetime ago. His pincers and his buzz saw sit on the workbench beside him. Peter has already explained the sequence I should expect, and my brain is whirring to make sense of it.

"How're you feeling, Max?"

"Operational," he says. I look over the monitors and see his charge level and error readouts. Looks like the boys fixed his servos from the semifinal bout and got his armor welded back together. The replacement shoulder looks good, and a brand-new set of legs has been bolted on, the gleaming paint on Max's lower half a contrast to his charred torso. I notice the boys haven't gotten around to plugging in the legs yet. Too busy with this supposed glitch.

As I look over Max, his wounds and welds provide a play-by-play of his last brutal fight — one of the most violent I've ever seen. The Berkeley team that lost will be starting from scratch. By the end of the bout, Max had to drag himself across the arena with the one arm he had left before pummeling his incapacitated opponent into metal shavings. When the victory gun sounded, we had to do a remote kill to shut him down. The way he was twitching, someone would've gotten hurt trying to get close enough to shout over the screeches of grinding and twisting metal. The slick of oil from that bout took two hours to mop up before the next one could start.

"You look good," I tell Max, which is my way of complimenting Peter's repair work without complimenting Peter directly. Greenie joins us as I lift Max's pincer from the workbench. "Let me give you a hand," I tell Max, an old joke between us.

I swear his arm twitches as I say this. I lift the pincer attachment toward the stub of his forearm, but before I can get it attached, Max's arm slides gently out of the way.

"See?" Peter says.

I barely hear him. My pulse is pounding — something between surprise and anger. It's a shameful feeling, one I recognize from being a mom. It's the sudden lack of compliance from a person who normally does what they're told. It's a rejection of my authority.

"Max, don't move," I say.

The arm freezes. I lift the pincers toward the attachment again, and his arm jitters away from me.

"Shut him down," I tell Peter.

Greenie is closer, so he hits the red shutoff, but not before Max starts to say something. Before the words can even form, his cameras iris shut and his arms sag to his side.

"This next bit will really piss you off," Peter says. He grabs the buzz saw and attaches it to Max's left arm while I click the pincers onto the right. I reach for the power.

"Might want to stand back first," Greenie warns.

I take a step back before hitting the power. Max whirs to life and does just what Peter described in the car: he detaches both his arms. The attachments slam to the ground, the pincer attachment rolling toward my feet.

Before I can ask Max what the hell he's doing, before I can get to the monitors to see what lines of code — what routines — just ran, he does something even crazier than jettisoning his attachments.

"I'm sorry," he says.

The fucker knows he's doing something wrong.

"It's not the safety overrides," I say.

"Nope." Greenie has his head in his hands. We've been going over possibilities for two hours. Two hours for me — the boys have been at this for nearly twelve. I cycle through the code Max has been running, and none of it makes sense. He's got tactical routines and defense modules engaging amid all the clutter of his parallel processors, but he's hard-set into maintenance mode. Those routines shouldn't be firing at all. And I can see why Peter warned me not to put any live-fire attachments on. The last thing we need is Max shooting up a $4 million trailer.

"I've got it," I say. It's at least the twentieth time I've said this. The boys shoot me down every time. "It's a hack. The SoCal team knows they're getting stomped in two days. They did this."

"If they did, they're smarter than me," Greenie says. "And they aren't smarter than me."

"We looked for any foreign code," Peter says. "Every diagnostic tool and virus check comes back clean."

I look up at Max, who's watching us as we try to figure out what's wrong with him. I project too much into the guy, read into his body language whatever I'm feeling or whatever I expect him to feel. Right now, I imagine him as being sad. Like he knows he's disappointing me. But to someone else — a stranger — he probably looks like a menacing hulk of a destroyer. Eight feet tall, angled steel, pistons for joints, pockmarked armor. We see what we expect to see, I guess.

"Max, why won't you keep your hands on?" I ask him. Between the three of us, we've asked him variations of this a hundred times.

"I don't want them there," he says. It's as useful as a kid saying they want chocolate because they like chocolate. Circular reasoning in the tightest of loops.

"But why don't you want them?" I ask, exasperated.

"I just don't want them there," he says.

"Maybe he wants them up his ass," Greenie suggests. He fumbles for his vape, has switched to peppermint. I honestly don't know how the boys are still functioning. We aren't in our twenties or thirties anymore. All-nighters take their toll.

"I think we should shut him down and go over everything mechanical one more time," I say, utterly defeated. "Worst-case scenario, we do a wipe and a reinstall tomorrow before the finals."

Max's primary camera swivels toward me. At least, I think it does. Peter shoots Greenie a look, and Greenie lifts his head and shifts uncomfortably on his stool.

"What aren't you telling me?" I ask.

Peter looks terrified. Max is watching us.

"You didn't get a dump yesterday, did you?" I have to turn away from Peter and pace the length of the trailer. There's a rumble outside as our upcoming opponent is put through his paces in the arena. Boy, would the SoCal guys love to know what a colossal fuck-up we have going on in here. "So we lost all the data from yesterday's bout?" I try to calm down. Maintain perspective. Keep a clear head. "We've got a good dump from the semis," I say. "We can go back to that build."

Turning back to the boys, I see all three of them standing perfectly still, the robot and the two engineers, watching me. "So we lost one bout of data," I say. "He's good enough to win. The Chinese were the favorites anyway, and they're out."

Nobody says anything. I wonder if this is about ego or pride. Engineers hate a wipe and reinstall. It's a last resort, an admittance of defeat. The dreaded cry of "reboot," which is to say we have no clue and hopefully the issue will sort itself if we start over, if we clear the cache.

"Are you sure you can't think of anything else that might be wrong with him?" Peter asks. He and Greenie join me at the other end of the trailer. Again, that weird look on their faces. It's more than exhaustion. It's some kind of wonder and fear.

"What do you know that you aren't telling me?" I ask.

"It's what we *think*," Greenie says.

"Fucking tell me. Jesus Christ."

"We needed a clear head to look at this," Peter says. "Another set of eyes." He glances at Greenie. "If she doesn't see it, then maybe we're wrong . . ."

But I do see it. Right then, like a lightning bolt straight up my spine. One of those thoughts that falls like a sledgehammer and gives you a mental limp for the rest of your life, that changes how you walk, how you see the world.

"Hell no," I say.

The boys say nothing. Max seems to twitch uncomfortably at the far end of the trailer. And I don't think I'm projecting this time.

"Max, why don't you want your arms?"

"Just I don't want them," he says. I'm watching the monitors instead of him this time. A tactical module is running, and it shouldn't be. Stepping through each line, I can see the regroup code going into a full loop. There are other lines running in parallel, his sixty-four processors running dozens of routines all at once. I didn't notice the regroup code until I looked for it. It's the closest thing we've ever taught him to retreat. Max has been programmed from the ground up to fight until his juice runs out. He knows sideways and forward, and that's it.

"You have a big bout in two days," I tell Max.

Another surge of routines, another twitch in his power harness. If his legs were plugged in, I imagine he'd be backing away from me. Which is crazy. Not only have we never taught him anything like what he's trying to pull off — we never instructed him to teach *himself* anything like this.

"Tell me it's just a glitch," Greenie says. He almost sounds hopeful. Like he doesn't want it to be anything else. Peter is watching me intently. He doesn't want to guide me along any more than he has to. Very scientific of him. I ignore Greenie and focus on our robot.

"Max, do you feel any different?"

"No," Max says.

"Are you ready for your next bout?"

"No."

"Why not?"

No response. He doesn't know what to say. I glance at the screen to get a read on the code, but Peter points to the RAM readout, and I see that it has spiked. No available RAM. It looks like full combat mode. Conflicting routines.

"This is emergent," I say.

"That's what I told him," Peter says. He perks up.

"But emergent *what?*" Greenie asks. "Because Peter thinks —"

"Let her say it," Peter says, interrupting. "Don't lead her." He turns to me. There's a look on his face that makes him appear a decade younger. A look of wonder and discovery. I remember falling in love with that look.

And I know suddenly what Peter wants me to say. I know what he's thinking, because I'm thinking it too. The word slips between my lips without awareness. I hear myself say it, and I feel like a fool. It feels wonderful.

"Sentience," I say.

We live for emergent behaviors. It's what we hope for. It's what we fight robots for. It's what we program Max to do.

He's programmed to learn from each bout and improve, to create new routines that will improve his odds in future fights. The first time I wrote a routine like this, it was in middle school. I pitted two chess-playing computers with basic learning heuristics against one another. Summer camp stuff. I watched as a library of chess openings was built up on the fly. Nothing new, just the centuries old rediscovered in mere hours. Built from nothing. From learning. From that moment on, I was hooked.

Max is just a more advanced version of that same idea. His being able to write his own code on the fly and save it for the future is the font of our research. Max creates new and original software routines that we patent and sell to clients. Sometimes he introduces a glitch, a piece of code that knocks him out of commission, what evolution handles with death, and we have to back him out to an earlier revision. Other times he comes up with a routine that's so far beyond anything else he knows, it's what we call emergent. A sum that's greater than its parts. The moment a pot of water begins to boil.

There was the day he used his own laser to cut a busted leg free because it was slowing him down. That was one of those emergent days. Max is programmed at a very base level not to harm himself. He isn't allowed to turn his weapons against his own body. It's why his guns won't fire when part of him gets in the way, similar to how he can't swing a leg and hurt us by accident.

But one bout, he decided it was okay to lop off his own busted leg if it meant winning and preventing further harm. That emergent routine funded half of our following season. And his maneuver — knowing when to sacrifice himself and by how much — put us through to the finals two years ago. We've seen other Gladiators do something similar since. But I've never seen a Gladiator not want to fight. That would require one emergent property to override millions of other ones. It would be those two chess computers from middle school suddenly agreeing not to play the game.

"Max, are you looking forward to training today?"

"I'd rather not," Max says. And this is the frustrating part. We created a facsimile of sentience in all our machines decades ago. We programmed them to hesitate, to use casual vernacular; we wanted our cell phones to seem like living, breathing people. It strikes me that cancer was cured like this — so gradually that no one realized it had happened. We had to be told. And by then it didn't seem like such a big deal.

"Shit, look at this," Peter says.

I turn to where he's pointing. The green HDD indicator on Max's server bank is flashing so fast, it might as well be solid.

"Max, are you writing code?" I ask.

"Yes," he says. He's programmed to tell the truth. I shouldn't even have to remind myself.

"Shut him down," Greenie says. When Peter and I don't move, Greenie gets off his stool.

"Wait," I say.

Max jitters, anticipating the loss of power. His charging cables sway. He looks at us, cameras focusing back and forth between me and Greenie.

"We'll get a dump," Greenie says. "We'll get a dump, load up the save from before the semis, and you two can reload whatever the hell this is and play with it later."

"How's my team?" a voice calls from the ramp. We turn to see Professor Hinson limping into the trailer. Hinson hasn't taught a class in decades, but still likes the moniker. Retired on a single patent back in the twenties, then had one VC hit after another across the Valley. He's a DARPA leech, loves being around politicians. Would probably have aspirations of being president if it weren't for the legions of coeds who would come out of the woodwork with stories.

"SoCal is out there chewing up sparring partners," Hinson says. "We aiming for dramatic suspense in here?"

"There might be a slight issue," Greenie says. And I want to fucking kill him. There's a doubling of wrinkles across Hinson's face.

"Well, then, fix it," Hinson says. "I pay you all a lot of money to make sure there aren't *issues*."

I want to point out that he paid a measly four hundred grand, which sure seemed like a lot of money eight years ago when we gave him majority stake in Max, but has ended up being a painful bargain for us since. The money we make now, we make as a team. It just isn't doled out that way.

"This might be more important than winning the finals," I say. And now that I have to put the words together in my brain, the announcement, some way to say it, the historical significance if this is confirmed hits me for the first time. We're a long way from knowing for sure, but to even suggest it, to raise it as a possibility, causes all the words to clog up in the back of my throat.

"Nothing's more important than these finals," Hinson says, before I can catch my breath. He points toward the open end of the trailer, where the clang of metal on metal can be heard. "You realize what's at stake this year? The Grumman contract is up. The army of tomorrow is going to be bid on next week, and Max is the soldier they want. *Our* soldier. You understand? This isn't about millions in prize money — this is about *billions.* Hell, this could be worth a trillion dollars over the next few decades. You understand? You might be looking at the first trillionaire in history. Because every army in the world will need a hundred thousand of our boys. This isn't research you're doing here. This is boot camp."

"What if this is worth more than a trillion dollars?" Peter asks. And I love him for saying it. For saying what I'm thinking. But the twinge of disgust on Hinson's face lets me know it won't have any effect. The professor side of him died decades ago. What could be more important than money? A war machine turned beatnik? Are we serious?

"I want our boy out there within the hour. Scouts are in the stands, whispering about whether we'll even have an entry after yesterday. You're making me look like an asshole. Now, I've got a million dollars' worth of sparring partners lined up out there, and I want Max to go shred every last dollar into ribbons, you hear?"

"Max might be sentient," I blurt out. And I feel like a third-grader again, speaking up in class and saying something that everyone else laughs at, something that makes me feel dumb. That's how Hinson is looking at me. Greenie too.

"Might?" Hinson asks.

"Max doesn't want to fight," I tell him. "Let me show you —"

I power Max down and reach for his pincers. I clip them into place while Peter does the same with the buzz saw. I flash back to eight years ago, when we demonstrated Max for Professor Hinson that first time. I'm as nervous now as I was then.

"I told them we should save the dump to look at later," Greenie says. "We've definitely got something emergent, but it's presenting a lot like a glitch. But don't worry, we can always load up the save from before the semis and go into the finals with that build. Max'll tear SoCal apart —"

"Let us show you what's going on," Peter says. He adjusts the code monitor so Hinson can see the readouts.

"We don't have time for this," Hinson says. He pulls out his phone and checks something, puts it back. "Save the dump. Upload the save from the semis. Get him out there, and we'll have plenty of time to follow up on this later. If it's worth something, we'll patent it."

"But a dump might not capture what's going on with him," I say. All three men turn to me. "Max was writing routines in maintenance mode. There are a million EPROMS in him, dozens for every sensor and joint. If we flash those to factory defaults, what if part of what he has become is in there somewhere? Or what if a single one or zero is miscopied and that makes all the difference? Maybe this is why we've never gotten over this hump before, because progress looks like a glitch, and it can't be copied or reproduced. At least give us one more day —"

"He's a robot," Hinson says. "You all are starting to believe your own magic tricks. We make them as real as we can, but you're reading sentience into some busted code."

"I don't think so," Peter says.

"I'm with the professor," says Greenie. He shrugs at me. "I'm sorry, but this is the finals. We got close two years ago. If we get that contract, we're set for life."

"But if this is the first stage of something bigger," I say, "we're talking about *creating* life."

Hinson shakes his head. "You know how much I respect your work, and if you think something is going on, I want you to look into it. But we'll do it next week. Load that save and get our boy out there. That's an order."

Like we're all in the military now.

Professor Hinson nods to Greenie, who steps toward the keyboard. Peter moves to block him, and I wonder if we're going to come to blows over this. I back toward Max and place a hand on his chest, a mother's reflex, like I just want to tap the brakes.

"C'mon," Greenie tells Peter. "We'll save him. We can look at this in a week. With some sleep."

My hand falls to Max's new legs. The gleaming paint there has never seen battle. And now his programming wants to keep it that way. I wonder how many times we've been on this precipice only to delete what we can't understand. And then thinking we can just copy it back, and find that it's been lost. I wonder if this is why downloading the human consciousness has been such a dead end. Like there's some bit of complexity there that can't survive duplication. Hinson and Greenie start to push Peter out of the way.

"Get away from Max," Greenie says. "I'm powering him up. Watch your feet."

He's worried about the pincers and the buzz saw falling off. Has to power up Max to get a dump. I hesitate before leaving Max's side. I quickly fumble with the cord, plugging in his unused legs. I have this luxury, stepping away. Turning my back on a fight.

"I'll get the power," I say. And Peter shoots me a look of disappointment. It's three against one, and I can see the air go out of him. He starts to say something, to plead with me, but I give him a look, the kind only a wife can give to her husband, one that stops him in his tracks, immobilizes him.

"Powering up," I say out loud, a lab habit coming back. A habit from back when we turned on machines and weren't sure what they would do, if they would fall or stand on their own, if they would find their balance or topple to one side. I pull Peter toward me, out of the center of the trailer, and I slap the red power switch with nothing more than hope and a hunch.

The next three seconds stretch out like years. I remember holding Sarah for the first time, marveling at this ability we have to create life where before there was none. This moment feels just as significant. A powerful tremor runs through the trailer, a slap of steel and a blur of motion. The pincers and buzz saw remain in place, but every other part of Max is on the move. A thunderclap, followed by another, long strides taking him past us, a flutter of wind in my hair, the four of us frozen as Max bolts from the trailer and out of sight, doing the opposite of what he was built for, choosing an action arrived at on his own.

AFTERWORD

One of my favorite questions to ask my futurist friends is "When do you think AI will come online?" I asked Rod Brooks once, and he laughed and said it was too far away to even contemplate. I asked Sam Harris, and he thought it would be very soon. But it was my friend Kevin Kelly who gave me the most shocking answer. "It's already here," he said.

This felt like an answer designed to shock rather than illuminate, but hearing Kevin's rationalization, I came away in agreement. Machines are already doing what we very recently said would be impossible (driving cars; winning at chess, go, and Jeopardy!; writing newspaper articles; creating art, music, and drama). What we keep doing is moving the goalposts. Once we understand how AI does something, it's no longer as magical as our own consciousness, and so we dismiss it as progress.

This is one type of AI. There's another type that I don't think we've created yet, and that's an intelligence that's self-aware with goals that it arrives at on its own. I do not believe that this sort of intelligence will come about because we set out to create it. I think we will be making more numerous and more complex AIs until one or several cross a threshold and become something . . . different.

Humans develop in this way. We don't emerge from the womb with goals, ambitions, even self-awareness. These modules come online gradually. One day, a baby realizes that its hand is its own and parents no longer need to clip its nails to keep it from scratching itself. We learn to walk, to talk, to think, to plan, to reason, to create. And then we slowly wind down and lose these abilities, if we live long enough.

Robots today can do so much more than a newborn human. And every year, they can do more and more things better than the smartest adult on the planet. These machines will never need to relearn these abilities. They can share their information with each other and with all future machines. The AI only needs to learn to walk once. It only needs to master chess once. And it has them mastered forever.

When the strangeness happens, I think it'll be a glitch. We might not even understand what caused it or be able to reproduce it at first. Kevin Kelly thinks we won't even know it happened for the longest time.

"What's the first thing AI will do when it becomes self-aware?" he asked me.

"What?" I wanted to know.

"Hide," Kevin said. "The first thing it'll do is hide."

Silo Stories

In the Air

Gears whir; an escapement lets loose; wound springs explode a fraction of an inch, and a second hand lurches forward and slams to a stop. All these small violences erupt on John's wrist as the world counts down its final moments, one second at a time.

Less than five minutes. Just a few minutes more, and they would've made it to the exit. They would've been on back roads all the way to the cabin. John stares at the dwindling time and silently curses the fender-bender in Nebraska that set them back. He curses himself for not leaving yesterday or in the middle of the night. But so much to do. The world was about to end, and there was so much to do.

His wife, Barbara, whispers a question, but she has become background noise — much like the unseen interstate traffic whooshing by up the embankment. Huddled on the armrest between them, their nine-year-old daughter, Emily, wants to know why they're pulled off the road, says she doesn't need to pee. A tractor trailer zooms past, air brakes rattling like a machine gun, a warning for everyone to keep their heads down.

John turns in the driver's seat to survey the embankment. He has pulled off Interstate 80 and down the shoulder, but it doesn't feel far enough. There aren't any trees to hide behind. He tries to imagine what's coming but can't. He can't allow himself to believe it. And yet here he is, cranking up the Explorer, ignoring the pleas from the fucking auto-drive to take over and manually steering down the grass toward the concrete piling of a large billboard. The sign high above promises cheap gas and cigarettes. Five minutes. Five minutes, and they'd have made it to the exit. So close.

"Honey, what's going on?"

A glance at his wife. Emily clutches his shoulder as he hits a bump. He waited too long to tell them. It's one of those lies that dragged out and became heavier and heavier the farther he carried it. A tractor-pull lie. And now his wheels are spinning and spitting dirt, and the seconds are ticking down.

He pulls the Explorer around the billboard and backs up until the bumper meets the concrete piling. Killing the ignition silences the annoying beeps from the auto-drive, the seat belt sensors, the GPS warning that they're off the road. The world settles into a brief silence. All the violence is invisible, on a molecular level, the slamming of tiny gears and second hands in whirring watches and little machines swimming in bloodstreams.

"Something very bad is about to happen," John finally says. He turns to his wife, but it is the sight of his daughter that blurs his vision. Emily will be immune, he tells himself. The three of them will be immune. He has to believe this if he allows himself to believe the rest, if he allows himself to believe that it's coming. There is no time left for believing otherwise. A year of doubt, and here he is, that skeptic in the trenches who discovers his faith right as the mortars whistle down.

"You're scaring me," Barbara says.

"Is this where we're camping?" Emily asks, peering through the windshield and biting her lip in disappointment. The back of the Explorer is stuffed with enough gear to camp out for a month. As if that would be long enough.

John glances at his watch. Not long. Not long. He turns again and checks the interstate. It's hot and stuffy in the Explorer. Opening the sunroof, he looks for the words stuck deep in his throat. "I need you to get in the back," he tells Emily. "You need to put your seat belt on, okay? And hold Mr. Bunny tight to your chest. Can you do that for me?"

His voice is shaky. John has seen war and murder. He has participated in plenty of both. But nothing can steel a mind for this. He releases the sunroof button and wipes his eyes. Overhead, the contrail of a passenger jet cuts the square of open blue in half. John shudders to think of what will become of that. There must be tens of thousands of people in the air. Millions of other people driving. Not that it matters. An indiscriminate end is rapidly approaching. All those invisible machines in bloodstreams, counting down the seconds.

"There's something I haven't told you," he tells his wife. He turns to her, sees the worry in her furrowed brow, and realizes that she is ready for any betrayal. She is ready to hear him say that he is married to another woman. That he is gay. That he murdered a prostitute and her body is curled up where the spare tire used to be. That he has been betting on sports, and the reason for the camping gear is that the bank has taken away their home. Barbara is ready for anything. John wishes any of these trivialities were true.

"I didn't tell you before now because . . . because I didn't believe it." He is stammering. He can debrief the president of the United States without missing a beat, but not this. In the backseat, Emily whispers something to Mr. Bunny. John swallows and continues: "I've been a part of something—" He shakes his head. "Something worse than usual. And now . . . that something is about to—" He glances at his watch. It's too late. She'll never get to hear it from him, not when it mattered, not before it was too late. She will have to watch.

He reaches over his shoulder and grabs his seat belt. Buckles up. Glancing up at the passing jet, John says a prayer for those people up in the air. He is thankful that they'll be dead before they strike the earth. On the dashboard, there is a book with *The Order* embossed on the cover. In the reflection of the windshield, it looks vaguely like the word *redo.* If only.

"What have you done?" Barbara asks, and there's a deadness in her voice, a hollow. As if she knows the scope of the horrible things he could do.

John focuses on his watch. The second hand twitches, and the anointed hour strikes. He and his family should be outside Atlanta with the others, not on the side of the road in Iowa. They should be crowding underground with everyone else, the selected few, the survivors. But here they are, on the side of the road, cowering behind a billboard blinking with cheap gas prices, bracing for the end of the world.

For a long while, nothing happens.

Traffic whizzes by unseen; the contrail overhead grows longer; his wife waits for an answer.

The world is on autopilot, governed by the momentum of life, by humanity's great machinations, by all those gears in motion, spinning and spinning.

Emily asks if they can go now. She says she needs to pee.

John laughs. Deep in his chest and with a flood of relief. He feels that cool wave of euphoria like a nearby *zing* telling him that a bullet has passed, that it missed. He was wrong. *They* were wrong. The book, Tracy, all the others. The national convention in Atlanta is nothing more than a convention, one party's picking of a president, just what it was purported to be. There won't be generations of survivors living underground. His government didn't seed all of humanity with microscopic time bombs that will shut down their hosts at the appointed hour. John will now have to go camping with his family. And for weeks and weeks, Barbara will hound him over what this great secret was that made him pull off the interstate and act so strange —

A scream erupts from the backseat, shattering this eyeblink of relief, this last laugh. Ahead, a pickup truck has left the interstate at a sharp angle. A front tire bites the dirt and sends the truck flipping into the air. It goes into the frantic spins of a figure skater, doors flying open like graceful arms, bodies tumbling out lifeless, arms and legs spread, little black asterisks in the open air.

The truck hits in a shower of soil before lurching up again, dented and slower this time. There is motion in the rearview. A tractor trailer tumbles off the blacktop at ninety miles an hour. It is happening. It is really fucking happening. The end of the world.

John's heart stops for a moment. His lungs constrict as if he has stepped naked into a cold shower. But this is only the shock of awareness. The invisible machines striking down the rest of humanity are not alive in him. He isn't going to die, not in that precise moment, not at that anointed hour. His heart and lungs and body are inoculated.

Twelve billion others aren't so lucky.

Two Days Before

The ringtone is both melody and alarm. An old song, danced to in Milan, the composer unknown. It brings back the fragrance of her perfume and the guilt of a one-night stand.

John's palms are sweaty as he swipes the phone and accepts the call. He needs to change that fucking ringtone. Tracy is nothing more than a colleague. Nothing more. But it could've been Pavlov or Skinner who composed that tune, the way it drives him crazy in reflex.

"Hello?" He smiles at Barbara, who is washing dishes, hands covered in suds. It's Wednesday evening. Nothing unusual. Just a colleague calling after hours. Barbara turns and works the lipstick off the rim of a wine-glass.

"Have you made up your mind?" Tracy asks. She sounds like a wait-ress who has returned to his table to find him staring dumbly at the menu, as if this should be simple, as if he should just have the daily special like she suggested half an hour ago.

"I'm sorry, you're breaking up," John lies. He steps out onto the porch and lets the screen door slam shut behind him. Strolling toward the gar-den, he startles the birds from the low feeder. The neighbor's cat glares at him for ruining dinner before slinking away. "That's better," he says, glancing back toward the house.

"Have you made up your mind?" Tracy asks again. She is asking the impossible. Upstairs on John's dresser, there is a book with instructions on what to do when the world comes to an end. John has spent the past year reading that book from cover to cover. Several times, in fact. The book is full of impossible things. Unbelievable things. No one who reads these things would believe them, not unless they'd seen the impossible before.

Ah, but Tracy has. She believes. And like a chance encounter in Milan — skin touching skin and sparking a great mistake — her brush with this leather book has spun John's life out of control. Whether the book proves false or not, it has already gotten him deeper than he would have liked.

"Our plane leaves tomorrow," he says. "For Atlanta." Technically, this is true. That plane will leave. John has learned from the best how to lie without lying.

A deep pull of air on the other end of the line. John can picture Tra-cy's lips, can see her elegant neck, can imagine her perfectly, can almost taste the salt on her skin. He needs to change that goddamn ringtone.

"We can guarantee your safety," Tracy says.

John laughs.

"Listen to me. I'm serious. We know what they put in you. Come to Colorado —"

"You mean New Moscow?"

"That's not funny."

"How well do you know these people?" John fights to keep his voice under control. He has looked into the group Tracy is working with. Some of them hold distinguished positions on agency watch lists, including a doctor who poses an actionable threat. John tells himself it won't matter, that they are too late to stop anything. And he believes this.

"I've known Professor Karpov for years," Tracy insists. "He believes me. He believes you. We're going to survive this thanks to you. And so I would damn well appreciate you being here."

"And my family?"

Tracy hesitates. "Of course. Them too. Tell me you'll be here, John. Hell, forget the tickets I sent and go to the airport right now. Buy new tickets. Don't wait until tomorrow."

John thinks of the two sets of tickets in the book upstairs. He lowers his voice to a whisper. "And tell Barbara what?"

There's a deep breath, a heavy sigh on the other end of the line.

"Lie to her. You're good at that."

The tractor trailer fills the rearview mirror. A bright silver grille looms large, tufts of grass spitting up from the great tires, furrows of soil loosened by yesterday's rain. Time seems to slow. The grille turns as if suddenly uninterested in the Explorer, and the long trailer behind the cab slews to the side, jackknifing. John yells for his family to hold on; he braces for impact. Ahead of him, several other cars are tumbling off the road.

The eighteen-wheeler growls as it passes by. Its trailer misses the concrete pillar and catches the bumper of the Explorer. The world jerks violently. John's head bounces off his headrest as the Explorer is slammed aside like a geek shouldered by a jock in a hallway.

Mr. Bunny hits the dash. There's a yelp from Barbara and a screech from Emily. Ahead of them, the trailer flips and begins a catastrophic roll, the thin metal shell of the trailer tearing like tissue, countless brown packages catapulting into the air and spilling across the embankment.

Time speeds back up, and John can hear tires squealing, cars braking hard on the interstate, a noise like a flock of birds. It sounds like things are alive out there — still responding to the world — but John knows it's just automated safety features in action. It's the newer cars protecting themselves from the older cars. It's the world slamming to a stop like the second hand inside a watch.

Tracy had told him once that he would last five minutes out here on his own. Turning to check on his wife, John sees a van barreling through the grass toward her side of the car. He yells at Barbara and Emily to move, to get out, *get out*. Fighting for his seat belt, he wonders if Tracy was wrong, if she had overestimated him.

Five minutes seems like an impossibly long time to live.

The Day Before

John likes to tell himself he's a hero. No, it isn't that he likes the telling — he just needs to hear it. He stands in front of the mirror as he has every morning of his adult life, and he whispers the words to himself:

"I am a hero."

There is no conviction. Conviction must be doled out at birth in some limited supply, because it has drained away from him over the years. Or perhaps the conviction was in his fatigues, which he no longer wears. Perhaps it was the pats on the back he used to get in the airport from complete strangers, the applause as the gate attendant allowed him and a few others to board first. Maybe that's where the conviction came from, because he hasn't felt it in a long while.

"I'm a hero," he used to whisper to himself, the words fogging the Plexiglas mask of his clean-room suit, a letter laced with ricin tucked into an envelope and carefully sealed with a wet sponge. The address on the envelope is for an imam causing trouble in Istanbul — but maybe it kills an assistant instead of this imam. Maybe it kills his wife. Or a curious child. "I'm a hero," he whispers, fumbling in that bulky suit, his empty mantra evaporating from his visor.

"I'm a hero," he used to think to himself as he spotted for his sniper. Calling out the klicks to target and the wind, making sure his shooter adjusts for humidity and altitude, he then watches what the bullet does. He tells himself this is necessary as a body sags to the earth. He pats a young man on the shoulder, pounding some of his conviction into another.

In the field, the lies come easy. Lying in bed the next week, at home, listening to his wife breathe, it's hard to imagine that he's the same person. That he helped kill a man. A woman. A family in a black car among a line of black cars. Sometimes the wrong person, the wrong car. These are things he keeps from his wife, and so the details do not seem to live with them. They belong to another. They are a man in Milan with a beautiful woman swinging in the mesmerizing light. They are two people kissing against a door, a room key dropped, happy throats laughing.

John peers at himself in the present, standing in the bathroom, full of wrinkles and regrets. He returns to the bedroom and finds Barbara packing her bags. One of her nice dresses lies flat on the bed, a necklace arranged on top — like a glamorous woman has just vanished. He steels himself to tell her, to tell her that she won't need that dress. This will lead to questions. It will lead to a speech that he has rehearsed ten thousand times, but never once out loud. For one more long minute, as he delays and says nothing, he can feel that they will go to Atlanta and he will do as he has been told. For one more minute, the cabin by the lake is no more than an ache, a dirty thought, a crazy dream. Tracy in Colorado has been forgotten. She may as well be in Milan. John thinks suddenly of other empty dresses. He comes close to confessing in that moment, comes close to telling his wife the truth.

There are so many truths to tell.

"Remember that time we had Emily treated for her lungs?" he wants to say. "Remember how the three of us sat in that medical chamber and held her hand and asked her to be brave? Because it was so tight in there, and Emily hates to be cooped up? Well, they were doing something to all three of us. Tiny machines were being let into our bloodstream to kill all the other machines in there. Good machines to kill the bad machines. That's what they were doing.

"We are all ticking time bombs," he would tell her, was about to tell her. "Every human alive is a ticking time bomb. Because this is the future of war, and the first person to act wins the whole game. And that's us. That's me. Killing like a bastard from a distance. Doing what they tell me. A payload is a payload. Invisible bullets all heading toward their targets, and none will miss. Everyone is going to die.

"But not us," he will say, because by now Barbara is always crying. That's how he pictures her, every time he rehearses this. She is cunning enough to understand at once that what he says is true. She is never shouting or slapping him, just crying out of sympathy for the soon-to-be dead. "Not us," he promises. "We are all taken care of. I took care of us, just like I always take care of us. We will live underground for the rest of our lives. You and Emily will go to sleep for a long time. We'll have to hold her hand, because it'll be an even smaller chamber that they put her in, but it'll all go by in a flash. Daddy will have to work with all the other daddies. But we'll be okay in the end. We'll all be okay in the end."

This is the final lie. This is the reason he never can tell her, won't tell her even now, will lie and say they're going camping instead, that she needs to pack something more comfortable. It is always here in his rehearsal that he chokes up and tells her what can never be true: "We'll be okay in the end."

And this is when he imagines Barbara nodding and wiping her eyes and pretending to believe him, because she always was the brave one.

John can see two figures in the van, their bodies slumped outward against the doors, looking like they'd fallen asleep. The van veers toward the Explorer. Emily is already scrambling between the seats to get in his lap as John fumbles with his seat belt. Barbara has her door open. The van fills the frame. His wife is out and rolling as John kicks open his door. Mere seconds pass from the time the van leaves the interstate to him and Emily diving into the grass. Scrambling and crawling, a bang like lightning cracking down around them, the van and the Explorer tumbling like two wrestling bears.

John holds Emily and looks for Barbara. There. Hands clasped on the back of her head, looking up at the Explorer, camping gear tumbling out through busted glass and scattering. There's a screech and the sound of another wreck up on the highway before the world falls eerily silent. John listens for more danger heading their way. All he can hear is Emily panting. He can feel his daughter's breath against his neck.

"Those people," Barbara says, getting up. John hurries to his feet and helps her. Barbara has grass stains on both knees, is looking toward the van and the wreckage of the tractor trailer, obviously wants to assist them. A form slumps out of the van's passenger window. Barbara fumbles her phone from her pocket and starts dialing a number, probably 911.

"No one will answer," John says.

His wife looks at him blankly.

"They're gone," he says, avoiding the word *dead* for Emily's sake. Above him, a contrail lengthens merrily.

"There was a wreck—" His wife points her phone up the embankment toward the hidden blacktop and the now-silent traffic. John steadies her, but he can feel her tugging him up the slope, eager to help those in need.

"They're all gone," he says. "Everyone. Everyone we knew. Everyone is gone."

Barbara looks at him. Emily stares up at him. Wide eyes everywhere. "You knew . . ." his wife whispers, piecing together the sudden stop on the shoulder of the road and what happened after. "How did you know —?"

John is thinking about the Explorer. Their car is totaled. He'll have to get another. There's a vast selection nearby. "Wait here," he says. He hopes everything he packed can be salvaged. As he heads up the embankment, Barbara moves to come with him.

"Keep Emily down here," he tells her, and Barbara gradually understands. Emily doesn't need to see what lies up there on the interstate. As John trudges up the slick grass, he wonders how he expects his daughter to avoid seeing it, avoid seeing the world he helped make.

One Year Before

Smoke curls from Tracy's cigarette as she paces the hotel room in Milan. John lies naked on top of the twisted sheets. The rush of hormones and the buzz of alcohol have passed, leaving him flushed with guilt and acutely aware of what he has done.

"You should move to Italy," Tracy says. She touches the holstered gun on the dresser but does not pick it up. Inhaling, she allows the smoke to drift off her tongue.

"You know I can't," John says. "Even if it weren't for my family . . . I have —"

"Work," Tracy interrupts. She waves her hand as if work were an inconsequential thing harped on by some inferior race. Even when the two of them had worked down the hall from each other in the Pentagon, neither had known what the other did. The confusion had only thickened since, but along with it the professional courtesy not to ask. John feels they both want to know, but tearing clothes off bodies is simpler than exposing hidden lives.

"I do sometimes think about running away from it all," John admits. He considers the project taking most of his time of late, a plan he can only glimpse from the edges, piecing together the odd tasks required of him, similar to how he susses out political intrigue by whom he is hired to remove and who is left alone.

"So why don't you?" Tracy asks.

John nearly blurts out the truth: *Because there won't be anywhere left to run.* Instead, he tells a different truth: "I guess I'm scared."

Tracy laughs as if it's a joke. She taps her cigarette and spills ash onto the carpet, opens one of the dresser drawers and runs her fingers across John's clothes. Before he can say something, she has opened the next drawer to discover the book.

"A Bible," she says, sounding surprised.

John doesn't correct her. He slides from the bed and approaches her from behind in order to get the book. Tracy glances at him in the mirror and blocks him, presses back against him, her bare skin cool against his. John can feel his hormones surge and his resistance flag. He forgets the book, even as Tracy begins flipping through it. She was always curious. It was trouble for them both.

"Looks more interesting than a Bible," she mutters, the cigarette bouncing between her lips. John holds her hips and presses himself against her. She complies by pressing back. "What is this?" she asks.

"It's a book about the end of the world," John says, kissing her neck. This is the same thing he told Barbara. John has come to think of the book as one of those paintings that blurs the closer you get to it. It is safe by being unbelievable. The hidden key to understanding it — knowing who wrote it — was all that needed keeping safe.

Pages are flipped, which fans smoke above their heads.

"A different Bible, then," Tracy says.

"A different Bible," John agrees.

After a few more pages, the cigarette is crushed out. Tracy pulls him back to the bed. Afterward, John sleeps and dreams a strange dream. He is laying Barbara into a crypt deep beneath the soil. There is a smaller coffin there. Emily is already buried, and it is a lie that they'll ever be unearthed. It is a lie that they'll be brought back to life. That's just to get him to go along. John will live on for hundreds of years, every day a torment of being without them, knowing that they are just as dead as the others.

John wakes from this dream once and is only dimly aware that the bedside light is on, smoke curling up toward the ceiling, fanned by the gentle turning of prophetic pages.

The cars are, for the most part, orderly. They sit quietly, most of them electric, only one or two idling and leaking exhaust. They are lined up behind one another as if at any moment the trouble ahead might clear and the traffic will surge forward. Brake lights shine red. Hazards blink. The cars seem alive. Their occupants are not.

John considers the sheer weight of the dead — not just around him on the highway, but an *entire world* of the dead. An entire world slaughtered by men in elected posts who think they know best. How many of those in these cars voted for this? More than half, John thinks grimly.

He tries to remind himself that this is what someone else would've done, some mad dictator or mountain hermit. Eventually. The technology would've trickled out — these machines invisible to the naked eye that are just as capable of killing as they are of healing. When fanatics in basements begin to tinker, the end is near enough in the minds of many. No exotic or radioactive materials to process. Instead, machines that are becoming rapidly affordable, machines that can lay down parts one atom at a time, machines that can build other machines, which build more machines. All it will take is one madman to program a batch that sniffs out people by their DNA before *snuffing* them out.

John remembers his sophomore year of high school when he printed his first gun, how the plastic parts came out warm and slotted neatly together, how the printed metal spring locked into place, how the bullets chambered a little stiff with the first round and then better and better over time.

That was something he could understand, printing a weapon. This . . . this was the next generation's music. These were the kids on his lawn. He was one of their parents pulling the stereo plug before anyone made too much trouble.

John picks out a black SUV in the eastbound lane. A gasser, a Lexus 500. He has always wanted to drive one of these.

Lifeless eyes watch him from either side as he approaches, heads slumped against the glass, blood trickling from noses and ears, just these rivulets of pain. John wipes his own nose and looks at his knuckle. Nothing. He is a ghost, a wandering spirit, an angel of vengeance.

There is a wreck farther ahead, a car on manual that had taken out a few others, the cars around it scattered as their auto-drives had deftly avoided collision. He passes a van with a sticker on the back that shows a family holding hands. He does not look inside. A dog barks from a station wagon. John hesitates, veers from his path toward the SUV and goes over to open the door. The dog does not get out — just looks at him with its head cocked — but at least now it is free. It saddens John to think of how many pets just lost their owners. Like the people stranded up in the sky, there is so much he didn't consider. He heads to the SUV, feeling like he might be sick.

He tries the driver's door on the Lexus and finds it unlocked. A man with a loosened tie sits behind the wheel, blood dripping from his chin. The blood has missed his tie to stain the shirt. A glance in the back shows no baby seat to contend with. John feels a surge of relief. He unbuckles the man and slides him out and to the pavement.

He hasn't seen anything like this since Syria. It's like a chemical attack, these unwounded dead.

Memories from the field surge back, memories of politicians back when they were soldiers. He gets in and cranks the Lexus, and the whine of the starter reminds him that it's already running. The car has taken itself out of gear. John adjusts the rearview and begins to inch forward and back, working the wheel, until he's sideways in traffic. Once again, he pulls off the interstate and down the embankment.

He heads straight for the wreckage of the Explorer and the van and gets out. Before Barbara and Emily can get to him, he has already pushed the passenger of the van back through the window and has covered him with the sport coat folded up on the passenger seat of the Lexus. John opens the back of the SUV, and Barbara whispers something to Emily. The three of them begin rounding up their gear and luggage and placing it into the car. It is a scavenger hunt for Emily. A box of canned goods has spilled down the embankment, and as she picks up each can and places it into the basket made by clutching the hem of her dress, John feels how wrong all of this is. There is too much normal left in the air. Being alive feels unnatural, a violation. He watches a buzzard swing overhead and land with a final flap of its wings on the top of the billboard. The great black bird seems confused by the stillness. Unsure. Disbelieving its luck.

"Is this ours?" Emily asks. She holds up the small single sideband radio, the antenna unspooled into a tangle.

"Yes," John says. He tries to remember what he was thinking to pack the SSB, what sort of foolish hope had seized him. Barbara says nothing, just works to get everything into the new car. She brushes leaves of grass off her carry-on and nestles it into the Lexus. Her silence is louder than shouted questions. She used to do this when John came home with stitched-up wounds, saying nothing until John feels his skin burn and he has to tell her.

"I wasn't positive —" he begins. He stops as Emily runs over to dump the contents of her dress into the car. He waits until she has moved beyond earshot again. "Part of me hoped nothing would happen, that I'd never have to tell you."

"What happened on the highway?" his wife asks. She shows him her phone. "I can't get anyone . . . Dad won't —"

"Everyone is gone," John says. He repeats this mantra, the one he keeps rolling over and over in his head. "Everyone."

Barbara searches his face. John can feel twelve billion souls staring at him, daring him to make her understand. Even he doesn't understand. Beyond the next exit, maybe the world is continuing along. But he knows this isn't true. Barbara looks at her phone. Her hand is shaking.

"There was no stopping it," John says. "Believe me."

"Who is left? Who can we call?"

"It's just us."

Barbara is silent. Emily returns and stacks cans between the luggage.

"This is because of what you do, isn't it?" Barbara asks. Emily has gone back for more.

John nods. Tears stream down Barbara's cheeks, and she begins to shake. John has seen widows like this, widows the moment they find out that's what they are. It is shock fading to acceptance. He wraps his arms around his wife, can't remember the last time he held her like this.

"Did you do this?" she asks. Her voice is shaking and muffled as he holds her tight.

"No. Not . . . not exactly. Not directly." He watches Emily delight in another find, far down the slope of grass.

"It's something you . . ." Barbara swallows and hunts for the words. ". . . that you went along with."

John can feel himself sag. He can't tell who is propping up whom. Yes, it was something he went along with. That's what he does. He goes along with. In Milan, succumbing to another, never leading. Never leading.

Emily arrives with something blue in her hands. "Is this ours?" she asks.

John pulls away from his wife. He looks down. It's the book. *The Order.* "No," he says. "That's nobody's. You can leave that here."

The Day Before

There are two envelopes nestled inside the blue book, two sets of plane tickets. John pulls them both out and studies them, angles them back and forth to watch the printed holograms catch the light. It is raining outside, the wind blowing fat drops against the bedroom window, a sound like fingers tapping to be let in.

He sets the tickets aside and flips through the large book at random. Tracy thought it was the Bible when she first saw it — by dint of it being in a hotel room drawer, no doubt. He thinks about the New Testament and how long people have been writing about the end of the world. Every generation thinks it will be the last. There is some sickness in man, some paranoid delusion, some grandiose morbidity that runs right through to distant ancestors. Or maybe it is the fear in lonely hearts that they might die without company.

John finds the section in the book on security. His future job detail. If he doesn't show, will they promote some other? Or will it mean extra shifts for someone else? John tries to imagine a group of people skipping through time to wait out the cleansing of the Earth. He tries to imagine kissing his wife goodbye as he lays her in a silver coffin. Kissing Emily and telling her it'll all be okay. One last lie to them both before he seals them up.

Because there's no mistaking their ultimate fate. John can feel it in his bones whenever he reads the book. He knows when a person has been doomed by politicians. He knows when they say, "Everything will be all right," that they mean the opposite. The book doesn't say, but it doesn't have to. Not everyone who goes into that bunker will come out alive. If he flies to Atlanta and does his job, he'll never spend another day with his wife and daughter. Tomorrow will be the last, no matter what, and it'll probably be spent in airports and in economy class.

He weighs the other tickets, the ones to Colorado Springs. Here is folly and madness, a group who thinks they can cheat the system, can survive on their own. Here is a woman who last year asked him to leave his life behind, his wife behind, and start anew someplace else. And now he is being asked again.

John holds the envelopes, one in each hand. It is usually another's life he weighs like this. Not his own. Not his family's. He doesn't want to believe a choice is necessary. Can't stand to think that Emily will never grow up and fall in love, never have kids of her own. Whatever life she has left, a day or years, wouldn't really be living.

He suddenly knows what he has to do. John slams the book shut and takes the tickets with him to the garage. Rummaging around, he finds the old Coleman stove. There's the lantern. The tent. He sniffs the old musky plastic and thinks of the last time they went on a vacation together. Years ago. What he wouldn't give for just one more day like that. One more day, even if it is their last.

He finds a canister and screws it onto the stove, adjusts the knob, presses the igniter. There's a loud click and the pop of gas catching. John watches the blue flames for a moment, remembers the horrible flapjacks he made on that stove years ago: burnt on the outside and raw in the middle. Emily loved them and has asked for her flapjacks like that ever since. He tries. But it's not easy to do things the wrong way on purpose.

John sets both envelopes on the grill, right above the flames, before he can reconsider. It isn't a choice — it's a refusal to choose. He has seen too many folders with assignments in them, too many plane tickets with death on the other end. This is an assignment he can't take. Cheat death or run to the woman he cheated with. He can do neither.

The paper crackles, plastic melts, smoke fills the air and burns his lungs. John takes a deep breath and holds it. He can feel the little buggers inside him, waiting on tomorrow. He can feel the world winding down. Orange flames lick higher as John rummages through the camping gear, gathering a few things, practicing the lies he'll tell to Barbara.

He has only been to the cabin once before, eight years ago. Or has it been nine already? A friend of his from the service had bought the place for an escape, a place to get away when he wasn't deployed. The last time John spoke to Carlos, his friend had complained that the lakeshore was getting crowded with new construction. But standing on the back deck, John sees the same slice of paradise he remembers from a decade prior.

There is a path leading down to the boathouse. The small fishing boat hangs serenely in its water-stained sling. There are clumps of flowers along the path with wire fencing to protect them from the deer. John remembers waking up in the morning all those years ago to find several doe grazing. The venison and fish will never run out. They will soon teem, he supposes. John thinks of the market they passed in the last small town. There won't be anyone else to rummage through the canned goods. It will be a strange and quiet life, and he doesn't like to think of what Emily will do once he and Barbara are gone. There will be time enough to think on that.

The screen door slams as Emily goes back to help unload the Lexus. John wonders for a moment how many others chickened out, decided to stay put in their homes, are now making plans for quiet days. He looks out over the lake as a breeze shatters that mirror finish, and he wishes, briefly, that he'd invited a few others from the program to join him here.

He takes a deep breath and turns to go help unload the car, when a faint rumble overhead grows into a growl. He looks up and searches the sky — but he can't find the source. It sounds like thunder, but there isn't a cloud to be seen. The noise grows and grows until the silver underbelly of a passenger liner flashes above the treetops and rumbles out over the lake. Can't be more than a thousand feet up. The jet is eerily quiet. It disappears into the trees beyond the far bank.

There comes the crack of splitting wood and the bass thud of impact. John waits for the ball of fire and plume of smoke, but of course: the plane is bone dry. Probably overshot Kansas on its way north from Dallas. Thousands of planes would be gliding to earth, autopilots trying in vain to keep them level, engines having sputtered to a stop. The deck creaks as Barbara rushes to his side.

"Was that —?"

He takes her hand in his and watches the distant tree line where birds are stirring. It is strange to think that no one will investigate the crash, that the bodies will never be identified, never seen. Unless he wanders up there out of curiosity one day, or forgets as he tracks deer or a rabbit and then comes across pieces of fuselage. A long life flashes before him, one full of strange quietude and unspoken horrors. A better life than being buried with the rest, he tells himself. Better than crawling into a bunker outside of Atlanta with that blue book. Better than running to Tracy in Colorado and having to explain to Barbara, eventually, what took place in Milan.

The porch shudders from tiny stomping feet. The screen door whacks shut. There is the sound of luggage thudding to the floor, and the porch falls still. John is watching the birds stir in the blue and cloudless sky. His nose itches, and he reaches to wipe it. Barbara sags against him, and John holds her up. They have this moment together, alive and unburied, a spot of blood on John's knuckle.

In the Mountain

Carry on," one founder would say to another. To Tracy, it had become a mantra of sorts. Igor had started it, would wave his disfigured hand and dismiss the other founders back to their work. What began as mockery of him became a talisman of strength. *Carry on. Do the job. One foot forward.* A reminder to forge ahead even when the task was gruesome, even when it seemed pointless, even when billions were about to die.

But Tracy knew some things can only be carried so far before they must be set down. Set down or dropped. Dropped and broken.

The world was one of these things. The ten founders carried what they could to Colorado. An existing hole in the mountain there was burrowed even deeper. And when they could do no more, the founders stopped. And they counted the moments as the world plummeted toward the shattering.

The rock and debris pulled from the mountain formed a sequence of hills, a ridge now dusted with snow. The heavy lifters and buses and dump trucks had been abandoned by the mounds of rubble. There was a graveyard hush across the woods, a deep quiet of despair, of a work finished. The fresh snow made no sound as it fell from heavy gray clouds.

Tracy stood with the rest of the founders just inside the gaping steel doors of the crypt they'd built. She watched the snow gather in yesterday's muddy ruts. The crisscross patterns from the busloads of the invited would be invisible by nightfall. Humanity was not yet gone, the world not yet ruined, and already the universe was conspiring to remove all traces.

Anatoly fidgeted by her side. The heavyset physicist exhaled, and a cloud of frost billowed before his beard. On her other side, Igor reached into his heavy coat and withdrew a flash of silver. Tracy stole a glance. The gleaming watch was made more perfect in his mangled hand. Igor claimed he was a descendant and product of Chernobyl. Anatoly had told her it was a chemical burn.

Between Igor's red and fused fingers, the hours ticked down.

"Ten minutes," Igor said to the gathered. His voice was a grumble of distant thunder. Tracy watched as he formed an ugly fist and choked the life out of that watch. His pink knuckles turned the color of the snow.

Tracy shifted her attention to the woods and strained one last time to hear the sound of an engine's whine — the growl of a rental car laboring up that mountain road. She waited for the *crunch-crunch* of hurrying boots. She scanned for the man who would appear between those gray aspens with their peeled-skin bark. But the movies had lied to her, had conditioned her to expect last-minute heroics: a man running, a weary and happy smile, snow flying in a welcome embrace, warm lips pressed to cold ones, both trembling.

"He's not coming," Tracy whispered to herself. Here was a small leak of honesty from some deep and forgotten place.

Igor heard her and checked his watch again. "Five minutes," he said quietly.

And only then, with five minutes left before they needed to get inside, before they needed to shut the doors for good, did it become absolutely certain that he wasn't coming. John had gone to Atlanta with the others, had followed orders like a good soldier, and all that she'd worked to create in Colorado — the fantasy of surviving with him by her side — had been a great delusion. Those great crypt doors would close on her and trap her in solitude. And Tracy felt in that moment that she shouldn't have built this place, that she wouldn't have wasted her time if only she'd known.

"We should get inside," Igor said. He closed the lid on that small watch of his — a click like a cocked gun — and then it disappeared into his heavy coat.

There was a sob among them. A sniff. Patrice suddenly broke from the rest of the founders and ran through the great doors, her boots clomping on concrete, and Tracy thought for a moment that Patrice would keep on running, that she'd disappear into the aspens, but she stopped just beyond the concrete deck, stooped and gathered a handful of fresh snow, and ran back inside, eating some of it from her palms.

Tracy thought of grabbing something as well. A twig. A piece of that bark. A single falling snowflake on her tongue. She scanned the woods for some sight of John as Anatoly guided her inside, deep enough that the founders by the doors could shove the behemoths closed. Four feet thick, solid steel, streaked with rust where the weather had wetted them, they made a hideous screech as they were moved. A cry like a mother wolf out in the gray woods calling for her pups.

The white world slimmed as the doors came together. The view became a column, and then a gap, and then a sliver. There was a heavy and mortal thump as the doors met, steel pressing on steel, and then a darkness bloomed that had to be blinked against to get eyes working again.

Though the doors were now closed, Tracy thought she could still hear the sound of the wolf crying — and realized it was one of the founders making that mournful noise. Tears welled up in her eyes, brought there by a partner's lament. And Tracy remembered being young once and sobbing like that. She remembered the first time a man had broken her heart. It had felt like the end of the entire fucking world.

This day was something like that.

The mountain was full of the confused. Nearly five thousand people asking questions. Their bags were not yet unpacked; their backs were still sore from the rutted, bumpy ride in the buses. And now the myriad excuses for bringing them there — the retreats, reunions, vacations, emergencies — evaporated as conflicting accounts collided.

With the doors closed, the founders set out to explain. First to family. Later, to all of the invited. Tracy had been given an equal allotment of invitations, and she had used most of them on practical people. Soldiers. Tools of retribution. When the world was clean, all she wanted was to see a bullet in the people who had done this.

Of friends, she had none. Most of her adult life had been spent in Washington or overseas. There was a doorman in Geneva who had always been kind to her. There was the guy who did her taxes. Which was to admit that there was no one. Just her meager family: her father, her sister, and her sister's husband. Three people in all the world. Maybe that was why John's decision hurt so much. He was almost all she had. All she'd *thought* she had.

At least it meant a small audience as she dispensed the horrid truth, the nightmare she'd held inside for more than a year. Tracy hesitated outside the door to her sister's small room. She raised her fist and prepared to knock. Truth waited for her on the other side, and she wasn't sure she was ready.

Her father sat on the bed and wrung his hands while Tracy spoke. Her sister, April, sat next to him, a look of slack confusion on her face. Remy, April's husband, had refused to sit. He stood by his wife, a hand on her shoulder, something between anger and horror in his eyes.

They were all dressed for the camping trip they'd been promised—a week of backpacking, of living in the woods. The gear by the foot of the bed would never be used. The bags and the garb were reminders of Tracy's lies. She listened as the words spilled from her mouth. She listened to herself say what she had rehearsed a hundred times: how the tiny machines used in hospitals to attack cancer—those invisible healers, the same ones that would've saved Mom if they'd been available in time—how those same machines were as capable of killing as they were of healing.

She told her family how those machines were in everyone's blood, in every human being's on Earth. And curing everyone might be possible, but it would only be temporary. Once people knew that it could be done, it was only a matter of time. A switch had been invented that could wipe out every man and woman alive. Any hacker in his basement could flip that switch—which meant someone *would*.

Tracy got through that part without the wailing or hysterics she'd expected, without the questions and confusion from her dad, without anyone pushing past her and banging on the door, screaming to be let out. No one asked her if she belonged to a cult or if she was on drugs or suggested she needed to take a break from whatever work she did in Washington, that she needed to see a professional.

"It was only a matter of time before someone did it," Tracy said again. "And so our government acted before someone else could. So they could control the aftermath."

Remy started to say something, but Tracy continued before he could: "We aren't a part of the group who did this," she said. She looked to her father. "We didn't do this. But we found out about it, and we realized we couldn't stop it. We realized . . . that maybe they were right. That it needed to be done. And so we did the next best thing. We created this place. We invited ourselves along. And those that we could. We'll be okay here. You all were inoculated on the way. You probably felt your ears popping on the bus ride up. Now we'll spend six months here, maybe a year—"

"Six months," Remy said.

"This can't be real." Her sister shook her head.

"It's real," Tracy told April. "I'm sorry. I never wanted to keep this from any of—"

"I don't believe it," Remy said. He glanced around the room as if seeing it for the first time. April's husband was an accountant, was used to columns of numbers in black and white. He was also a survivalist, was used to sorting out the truth on his own. He didn't learn simply by being told. Igor had warned that it would take some people weeks before they believed.

"We are positive," Tracy said. This was a lie; she had her own doubts. She wouldn't be completely sure until the countdown clock hit zero. But there was no use infecting others with her slender hopes. "I realize this is hard to hear. It's hard even for me to grasp. But the war we were bracing for isn't going to come with clouds of fire and armies marching. It's going to be swifter and far worse than that."

"Did *you* do this?" her father asked, voice shaking with age. Even with his encroaching, occasional senility, he knew that Tracy worked for bad agencies full of bad people. There were classified things she had confided to him years ago that he had been willing to shoulder for her. They would likely be the very last things his dementia claimed, little islands of disappointment left in a dark and stormy sea.

"No, Dad, I didn't do this. But I *am* the reason we have this place, a nice place to be together and wait it out."

She flashed back to that night in Milan, to the first time she'd laid eyes on the book with the word *Order* embossed on its cover. It was the same night she made John forget about his wife for a brief moment, the night when all those years of flirtations came to fruition: the bottle of wine, the dancing, that dress — the one she'd gotten in trouble for expensing to her company card. And in his room, after they made love, and hungering for more danger, she had gone to the dresser where she knew his gun would be tucked away, and she'd found that book instead.

If John had stayed in bed, she wouldn't have thought anything more of it. The book was full of the dry text that only lawyers who had become politicians could craft. Emergency procedures. An ops manual of some sort. But the way John had lurched out of bed, it was as if Tracy had let his wife into the room. She remembered the way his hands trembled against her as he asked her to put it away, to come back to bed, like she'd grabbed something far more dangerous than a gun, something cocked and loaded with something much worse than bullets.

After he'd gone to sleep, Tracy had sat on the edge of the bathtub, the book open on the toilet lid, and had turned every page with her phone set to record. Even as she scanned, she saw enough to be afraid.

Enough to *know*.

"I'm sorry," she told her father, unable to stomach the disappointment on his face.

"When—?" April asked.

Tracy turned to her sister, the schoolteacher, who knew only that Tracy worked for the government, who had no idea about all the classified blood on her hands. April was four years older, would always be older than Tracy in all the ways that didn't matter and in none of the ways that did.

"In a few hours," Tracy said. "It'll all be over in a few hours."

"And will we feel anything?" April rubbed her forearm. "What about everyone out there? Everyone we know. They'll just—?"

Remy sat beside his wife and wrapped his arms around her. The air around Tracy grew cold. Even more empty.

"*We* were supposed to be out there when it happened, too," Tracy said. "The four of us. Remember that. We'll talk more later. I have to get to a meeting—"

"A meeting?" April asked. "A *meeting*? To do what? Decide the rest of our lives? Decide who lives and who dies? What kind of meeting?"

And now Remy was no longer embracing his wife. He was restraining her.

"How dare you!" April screamed at Tracy. Their father shivered on the bed, tried to say something, to reach out to his daughters and tell them not to fight. Tracy retreated toward the door. She was wrong about the hysteria, about it not coming. There was just some delay. And as she slipped into the hall and shut the small room on her sister's screaming, she heard that she'd been wrong about her beating on the door as well.

Saving a person seemed simple. But saving them against their will was not. Tracy realized this as she navigated the corridors toward the command room, her sister's screams still with her. She could hear muffled sobs and distant shouting from other rooms as she passed — more people learning the truth. Tracy had thought that preserving a life would absolve all other sins, but the sin of not consulting with that life first was perhaps the only exception. She recalled an ancient argument she'd had with her mother when she was a teenager, remembered yelling at her mom and saying she wished she'd never been born. And she'd meant it. What right did someone else have to make that decision for her? Her mom had always expected her to be grateful simply for having been brought into the world.

Now Tracy had made the same mistake.

She left the apartment wing, those two thousand rooms dug laterally and tacked on to a complex built long ago, and she entered the wide corridors at the heart of the original bunker. The facility had been designed to house fifteen hundred people for five years. The founders had invited more than three times that number, but they wouldn't need to stay as long. The biggest job had been cleaning out and refilling the water and diesel tanks.

The entire place was a buried relic from a different time, a time capsule for a different threat, built for a different end-of-the-world scenario.

The facility had been abandoned years ago. It had become a tourist attraction. And then it had fallen into disrepair. The founders chose the location after considering several options. Igor and Anatoly used their research credentials and leased the space under the auspices of searching for neutrinos, some kind of impossible-to-find subatomic particles. But it was a much different and invisible threat they actually set out to find: the machines that polluted the air and swam through every vein.

Tracy used her key to unlock the cluttered command room. A round table dominated the center of the space. A doughnut of monitors ringed the ceiling above, tangles of wires drooping from them and running off to equipment the engineers had set up. In one corner, a gleaming steel pod stood like some part of an alien ship. It had been built according to stolen plans, was thought at first to be necessary for clearing the small machines from their bloodstreams, but it ended up being some sort of cryo-device, a side project the Atlanta team had undertaken. The only machine Tracy knew how to operate in that room was the coffeemaker. She started a pot and watched the countdown clock overhead tick toward Armageddon.

The other founders trickled in one at a time. Many had red eyes and chapped cheeks. There was none of the chatting, debating, and arguing that had marked their prior meetings in that room. Just the same funereal silence they'd held by the crypt doors.

A second pot was brewed. One of the engineers got the screens running, and they watched the TV feeds in silence. There was speculation among the talking heads that the presidential nomination was not quite the lock everyone had presumed. The excitement in the newsrooms was palpable and eerie. Tracy watched dead men discuss a future that did not exist.

Two minutes.

The talking heads fell silent, and the feeds switched from newsrooms to a stage outside Atlanta. The distant downtown towers gleamed in the background. On the stage, a young girl in a black dress held a microphone and took a deep breath, a little nervous as she began to sing.

The national anthem brought tears to Tracy's eyes. She reminded herself to breathe. And not for the first time, she had an awful premonition that she was wrong, that the book was just a book, that John had believed in something that would not come to pass, and that she would soon be embarrassed in that room with all the people she'd convinced to join her. She would be another in a long line of failed messiahs. Her sister would look at her like she was crazy for the rest of her life. National headlines would mock the kooks in a mountain who had thought the world was going to end. And somehow all of this felt worse than twelve billion dead.

It was a guilty thought, the panic that she might be wrong.

Large red numbers on the clock counted down. No part of her wanted to be right. Either way, her world was ending. When the clock struck all zeroes, Tracy would either be an outcast or a shut-in.

On the array of televisions, the same scene was shown from half a dozen angles, all the various news stations and networks tuned to that young girl in her black dress. One of the screens cut to the obligatory jets screaming in formation overhead. Another screen showed a group of senators and representatives, hands on their goddamn patriotic chests. Tracy searched for John, thought she might see him there near the stage with his suit jacket that showed off his handsome shoulders but also that bulge by his ribs. There were five seconds on the clock. One of the founders started counting, whispering the numbers as they fell.

Three.

Two.

One.

A line of zeroes.

And nothing happened.

"They're still breathing," someone said.

Igor cursed and fumbled for that damned watch of his.

An eternity squeezed itself into a span of three seconds. No one moved.

"Holy shit," someone said.

CNN's feed spun sickeningly to the side, the cameraman whirling, and Tracy realized it was one of the reporters who had cursed. Another screen showed a bright flash, a brief glimpse of a mushroom cloud, and then that monitor went black.

The young girl was no longer singing. She had been replaced with station identifiers and shots of stunned newscasters who stared at their feeds in disbelief. More bright flashes erupted on the last monitor running, which showed a wide vista from some great distance. Three classic and terrifying mushroom clouds rose toward the heavens, shouldering the other clouds aside. And then that last screen succumbed as well, promising impotently to "Be right back."

"Shut it off!" a reporter screamed. He waved at someone off-camera. "Shut it off—"

And then someone did. A switch flipped somewhere, in all those veins, and all the talking heads on all the screens bowed forward or tilted to the side. Blood flowed from the nose of the man who had just been waving. His jaw fell slack; his eyes focused on nothing—a quiet death.

The founders in the command room—no longer breathing—watched in silence. Hands clasped over mouths. Those who had harbored any doubts now believed. All was still. The only things that moved on the screens were the thin red rivulets trickling from noses and ears. There was no one left alive to cut away to, to change the view. And only those ten people huddled around the wire-webbed monitors were left to see.

"Kill it," someone finally said, a terrible slip of the tongue.

Tracy watched as Dmitry fumbled with the controls for the panels. He accidentally changed channels on one of the sets, away from news and into the realm of reruns. There was a sitcom playing: a family around a dinner table, a joke just missed. A bark of canned laughter spilled from the speaker, the illusion that life was still transpiring out there as it always had. But it wasn't just the laughter that was canned now. They all were. All of humanity. What little was left.

"Hey. Wake up."

Dreams. Nothing more than dreams. A black ghost clawing away at her mother, a wicked witch burying her father and her sister. Tracy sat up in bed, sweating. She felt a hand settle on her shoulder.

"We have a problem," someone said.

A heavy shadow, framed by the wan light spilling from the hallway.

"Anatoly?"

"Come," he said. He lumbered out of her small room deep in the mountain. Tracy slid across that double bunk, a bed requisitioned for two, and tugged on the same pants and shirt she'd worn the day before.

The fog of horrible dreams mixed with the even worse images from their first day in the complex. Both swirled in her sleepy brain. Slicing through these was the fear in Anatoly's voice. The normally unflappable Russian seemed petrified. Was it really only to last a single day, all their schemes to survive the end of the world? Was it a riot already? Orientation the day before had not gone well. Fights had broken out. A crowd had gathered at those four-foot-thick doors, which had been designed just as much to keep people *in* as to keep other dangers out.

Perhaps it was a leak. Air from the outside getting in. Tracy hurried down the hall barefoot, searching her lungs for some burn or itch, touching her upper lip and looking for a bleed. Her last thought as she caught up to Anatoly and they reached the command room together was that the cameras outside the crypt doors would be on, would reveal a lone man, inoculated to the sudden death but slowly dying anyway, banging feebly and begging to be let in —

"Everyone here?" Dmitry asked. The thin programmer scanned the room over his spectacles. There was no real leader among the founders.

Tracy held some special status as the originator of the group, she who had found *The Order*. Anatoly was the man who had coordinated the lease and planning of the facility. But Dmitry was the brightest among them, the tinkerer, the one who had deactivated the machines in their blood. Of them all, he seemed to most enjoy the thought of being in charge. No one begrudged him that.

"What is this?" Patrice asked. She knotted her robe across her waist and crossed her arms against the chill in the room.

"The program," Dmitry said. "It . . . has changed."

Someone groaned. Tracy rubbed the sand from her eyes. The gathered braced for Dmitry's usual technobabble, which was bad enough when wide awake.

"Five hundred years," he said. He pushed his glasses up his nose and looked from face to face. "Not six months. Five hundred years."

"Until what?" Sandra asked.

"Until we can go out," Dmitry said. He pointed toward the door. "Until we can go out."

"But you said —"

"I know what I said. And it's all in the book. It says six months. But the program unspooled yesterday. It's dynamic code, a self-assembler, and now there's a clock set to run for five hundred years."

The room was quiet. The recycled air flowing through the overhead vent was the only sound.

"How are you reading this new program?" Igor asked. "Do you have those buggers in here?" He nodded toward the silver pod with all its tubes and wires.

"Of course not. The antennas we put up, I can access the mesh network the machines use to communicate. Are any of you listening to me? The program is set to run for five hundred years. This book" — he pointed to the tome sitting on the large round table — "this isn't a guide for the entire program. It's just for one small part of it, just one shift. I think the cryo-pods are maybe so they can —"

"So how do we change it?" Anatoly asked. "You can tap into the network. How do we turn it all off? So we can leave right now? Or set it back to six months?"

Dmitry let out his breath and shook his head. He had that exasperated air about him that he got when any of the founders asked questions that belied fundamental flaws in their understanding of what, to him, were basic concepts. "What you're asking is impossible. Otherwise I would have done it already. I can program the test machines in my lab, but overcoming the entire network?" He shook his head.

"What does that mean for us?" Tracy asked.

"It means we have a year's worth of food," Dmitry said. "Eighteen months, maybe two years if we ration. And then we all slowly die in here. Or..."

"Or what?"

"Or we die quickly out there."

Sharon slapped the table and glared at Dmitry. "We've got fourteen men in the infirmary and another eight in restraints from telling everyone we'll be here for six months and that everyone they know is now dead. Now you're saying we have to tell them that we *lied?* That we brought them here to *starve to death?*"

Tracy sank into one of the chairs. She looked up at Dmitry. "Are you sure about this? You were wrong about the clock the last time. You were a few seconds off. Maybe —"

"It was tape delay," Dmitry said, rubbing his eyes beneath his glasses. "All broadcasters use a time delay. I wasn't wrong. I'm not wrong now. I can show you the code."

One of the founders groaned.

"What were you saying about the pod?"

"I think this is a manual for a single shift," Dmitry said. "And the pod is for—"

"You mean the icebox?" Patrice asked.

"Yes. The cryo-unit is to allow them to stagger the shifts. To last the full five hundred years. I looked over one of the requisitions reports we intercepted, and it all makes sense—"

"Does our pod work?" Anatoly asked.

Dmitry shrugged. "Nobody wanted me to test it, remember? Listen, we have a decision to make—"

"What decision? You're telling us we're all dead."

"Not all of us," Tracy said. She rested her head in her palms, could see that witch from her dreams, shoveling soil on thousands of writhing bodies, hands clawing to get out.

"What do you mean?" Patrice asked.

"I mean we're the same as them." She looked up and pointed to the dead monitors, which had once looked out on the world, on the people with their anthems who had doomed them all. "We have the same decision to make. Our little world, our little mountain, isn't big enough for all of us. So we have a decision to make. The same decision they made. We're no better than them."

"Yes," Dmitry said. "I figure we have eighteen months' worth of food for five thousand mouths. That gives us enough for fifteen people for five hundred years."

"Fifteen people? To do what?"

"To survive," Dmitry said. But the tone of his voice said something more somber and sinister. Tracy tried to imagine all that he was implying. Someone else said it for her.

"And kill everyone else? Our families?"

"No way," someone said. Tracy watched her partners, these founders, fidget. It was the orientation all over again. A fight would break out.

"We can't live that long anyway," Tracy said, attempting to defuse the argument by showing how pointless it all was.

"Generations," Anatoly blurted out. He scratched his beard, seemed to be pondering a way to make some insane plan work. "Have to make sure there's only one birth for every death."

Tracy's eyes returned to the book on the center of the conference table. Others were looking at it as well. She remembered a passage like that inside the book. Several passages now suddenly made more sense. The answer had been there, but none of them had been willing to see it. It's how that book seemed to work.

"I won't be a part of this," Natasha said. "I won't. I'd rather have one year here, with my family, than even consider what you're suggesting."

"Will you still think that a year from now, when the last ration is consumed and we're left watching one another waste away? Either it happens now, or it happens then. Which way is cleaner?"

"We sound just like them," Tracy whispered, mostly to herself. She eyed those monitors again, saw her reflection in one of them.

"The Donner Party," Sherman said. When one of the Russians turned to stare at him, Sherman started to explain. "Settlers heading west two centuries ago. They got trapped in the mountains and had to resort to —"

"I'm familiar with the story. It's not an option."

"I didn't mean it was an *option*." Sherman turned to Natasha. "I mean, that's what we're going to start thinking a year from now. Or eighteen months. Whenever."

Natasha spun a lock of her hair. She dipped the end between her lips and remained silent.

"It would be quick," Dmitry said. "We still have canisters of the test nanos, the ones I built. Those, I can program. We would have to inoculate ourselves first —"

"This is going too fast," Tracy said. "We need to think about this."

"After thirty-six days, we'll be down to fourteen people," Dmitry said. "At the rate we'll be feeding these people, each month we delay means one spot lost. How long do you want to think about it?" He took off his glasses and wiped the condensation from them. It had grown hot in the room. "We're in a lifeboat," he said. "We are drifting to shore, but not as fast as we had hoped. There are too many of us in the boat." He returned the glasses to the bridge of his nose, looked coolly at the others.

"Every one of us should have died yesterday," Anatoly said. "Our families. Us. Every one. None of us should be here. Even this day is a bonus. A year would be a blessing."

"Is it so important that any of us make it to the other side?" Patrice asked. The others turned to her. "I mean, it won't even be us. If we were to do this. It would be our descendants. And what kind of hell are they going to endure in here, living for dozens of generations in this hole, keeping their numbers at fifteen, brothers and sisters coupling? Is that even surviving? What's the point? What's the point if we're just trying to get someone to the other side? No matter what, the assholes in Atlanta will be our legacy now."

"That's why we have to do this," Tracy said.

Dmitry nodded. "Tracy's right. That's *precisely* why we have to do this. So they don't get away with it. Isn't that what we planned from the beginning? Isn't that why we only have enough food for a year but enough guns to slaughter an army?"

"Fifteen people is no army."

"But they'll know," Dmitry said. "They'll carry legends with them. We'll write it all down. We'll make up most of the first fifteen. We'll make sure no one ever forgets —"

"You mean make a religion out of this."

"I mean make a *cause*."

"Or a cult."

"Do we want them to have the world to themselves, the fuckers who did this?"

"We can't decide anything now," Tracy said. She rubbed her temples. "I need to sleep. I need to see my family —"

"No one can know," Anatoly told her.

Tracy shot him a look. "I'm not telling anyone. But we need a day or two before we do anything." She caught the look on Dmitry's face. "Surely we have that much time."

He nodded.

"And you won't program anything without consulting with us first."

Again, a nod.

Sherman laughed, but it was without humor. "Yes," he said. "I need sleep as well." He pointed to Dmitry. "And I want assurances that I'll wake up in the morning."

The following day, Tracy grabbed breakfast from the mess hall and found three founders at a table in the corner. She joined them. No one spoke. Between bites of bread and canned ham, she watched the bustle of strangers weaving through the tables and chairs, introducing themselves to one another, glancing around at their surroundings, and trying to cope with their imprisonment. Their salvation.

The buzz of voices and spoons clicking against porcelain was shattered for a brief moment by an awful release of laughter. Tracy searched for the offender, but it was gone as quickly as it had come. She watched Igor chew his bread, his eyes lifeless, focused beyond the mountain's walls, and knew he was thinking the same thing: They were in a room crowded with ghosts. There was no stopping what they would have to do. And for the first time, Tracy understood all that John had endured those past years. She remembered the way he would glance around in a restaurant, his eyes haunted, the color draining suddenly from his face.

Looking for an exit, she used to think. *Looking for some way out if it all goes to shit.*

But no — he had been doing this, scanning the people, the bodies all around him. How could he search for an exit when there was none?

Tracy saw her sister and Remy emerge from the serving line, trays in hand. She started to wave them over, then caught herself. When she saw her sister among all those walking dead, she realized what she had to do. She put down her bread and left her tray behind. She needed to find Dmitry. To see if it was possible.

A new Order was required, a new book of instructions. Nine of the ten founders and the six they chose would have the rest of their lives to sort out the details, to leave precise instructions. Tracy had already decided she wouldn't go with them. If John were there, maybe it could work, but she couldn't pair off with one of the men in their group.

First she had her own orders to write, her own instructions. This included how to open the great crypt gates, in case there was no one else. She spent her days and nights in the workshop command room, helping Dmitry with the pod, pestering him with questions that he didn't know the answers to. The cryo-pod had been designed for one person. And once they'd realized what it was, it had gone untested. Tracy squeezed inside for a dry fit while Dmitry modified the plumbing.

"Maybe one head over here and the other down there? Legs'll have to go like this."

Dmitry muttered under his breath. He wrestled a piece of tubing onto a small splitter, was having trouble making it fit.

"You need help?" Tracy asked.

"I got it," he said.

"What if . . . something happens to you all and there are no descendants? What if there's no one here to open it?"

"Already working on that," Dmitry said. "The antenna that taps into the mesh network. I can rig it up so when their timer shuts off, the pod will open. So if it's twenty years from now or twenty thousand, as long as this place has power . . ." He finally got the tube on to the fitting. "Don't worry," he said. "I'll take care of it. I have time."

Tracy hoped he was right. She wanted to believe him.

"So what do you think it'll feel like?" she asked. "You think it'll be . . . immediate? Like shutting your eyes at night, and then suddenly the alarm goes off in the morning? Or will it be dream after dream after dream?"

"I don't know." Dmitry shook his head. He started to say something, then turned quietly back to his work.

"What?" Tracy asked. "Is there something you aren't telling me?"

"It's . . . nothing." He set the tubing aside and crossed his arms. Then he turned to her. "Why do you think nobody is fighting for their place in there?" He nodded to the machine.

Tracy hadn't considered that. "Because I asked first?" she guessed.

"Because that thing is a coffin. People have been putting their loved ones in there for years. Nobody wakes up."

"So this is a bad idea?"

Dmitry shrugged. "I think maybe the people who do this, it isn't for the ones *inside* the box."

Tracy lay back in that steel cylinder and considered this, the selfishness of it all. Giving life without asking. Taking life to save some other. "For the last two days," she said, "all I've thought about is what a mistake all this was." She closed her eyes. "Completely pointless. All for nothing."

"That is life," Dmitry said. Tracy opened her eyes to see him waving a tool in the air and staring up at the ceiling. "We do not go out in glory. We leave no mark. What you did was right. What they did was wrong. They're the reason we're in this mess, not you."

Tracy didn't feel like arguing. What was the point? It didn't matter. Nothing mattered. And maybe that's what Dmitry was trying to tell her.

She crawled out of that coffin-within-a-crypt to check the supplies one last time, to make sure the vacuum was holding a seal. Inside the large storage trunk were her handwritten instructions, a set of maps, two handguns, clothing, all of Remy and April's camping gear, and what extra rations would fit.

Five hundred years was a long time to plan for, almost an impossible time to consider. And then it occurred to her that she was wrong about something: She was wrong about the great doors that led into that mountain. This was not a crypt. The dead were on the *outside*. Here was but a bubble of life, trapped in the deep rock. A bubble only big enough now for fifteen people. Fifteen plus two.

Before waking her sister, Tracy stole into her father's room and kissed him quietly on the forehead. She brushed his thinning hair back and kissed him once more. One last time. Wiping tears away, she moved to the neighboring room. Igor and Anatoly were waiting outside the door. They had agreed to help her, had been unhappy with her decision, but she had traded her one precious spot for two questionable others.

They stole inside quietly. The Russians had syringes ready. They hovered over Remy first. It went fast, not enough kicking to stir her sister. April was next. Tracy thought of all she was burdening them with, her sister and Remy. An accountant and a schoolteacher. They would sleep tonight, and when they woke, what would they find? Five hundred years, gone in an instant. A key around their necks. A note from her. An apology.

Igor lifted April, and Tracy helped Anatoly with Remy. They shuffled through dark corridors with their burdens. "Carry on," Tracy whispered, that mantra of theirs, the awful dismissal of all they'd done. But this time, it was with promise. With hope. "Carry on," she whispered to her sister. "Carry on for all of us."

In the Woods

A sliver of light appeared in the pitch-black — a horizontal crack that ran from one end of April's awareness to the other. There was a deep chill in her bones. Her teeth chattered; her limbs trembled. April woke up cold with metal walls pressed in all around her. A mechanical hum emanated from somewhere behind her head. Another body was wedged in beside her.

She tried to move and felt the tug of a cord on her arm. Fumbling with her free hand, April found an IV. She could feel the rigid lump of a needle deep in her vein. There was another hose along her thigh that ran up to her groin. She patted the cold walls around herself, searching for a way out. She tried to speak, to clear her throat, but like in her nightmares, she made no sound.

The last thing April remembered was going to sleep in an unfamiliar bunk deep inside a mountain. She remembered feeling trapped, being told the world had ended, that she would have to stay there for years, that everyone she knew was gone. She remembered being told that the world had been poisoned.

April had argued with her husband about what to do, whether to flee, whether to even believe what they'd been told. Her sister had said it was the air, that it couldn't be stopped, so a group had planned on riding it out here. They'd brought them in buses to an abandoned government facility in the mountains of Colorado. They said it might be a while before any of them could leave.

The body in the dark by April's feet stirred. There was a foot by her armpit. They were tangled, she and this form. April tried to pull away, to tuck her knees against her chest, but her muscles were slow to respond, her joints stiff. She could feel the chill draining from her, and a dull heat sliding in to take its place — like the tubes were emptying her of death and substituting that frigid void with the warmth of life.

The other person coughed, a deep voice ringing metallic in the small space, hurting her ears. April tried to brace herself with the low ceiling to scoot away from the coughing form, when the crack of light widened. She pushed up more, grunting with the strain, and even more light came in. The ceiling hinged back. The flood of harsh light nearly blinded her. Blinking, eyes watering, ears thrumming from the sound of that noisy pump running somewhere nearby, April woke with all the violence and newness of birth. Shielding her eyes — squinting out against the assault of light — she saw in her blurry vision a man lying still by her feet. It was her husband, Remy.

April wept in relief and confusion. The hoses made it hard to move, but she worked her way closer to him, hands on his shins, thighs, clambering up his body until her head was against Remy's chest. His arms feebly encircled her. Husband and wife trembled from the cold, teeth clattering. April had no idea where in the world they were or how they got there; she just knew they were together.

"Hey," Remy whispered. His lips were blue. He mouthed her name, eyes closed, holding her.

"I'm here," she said. "I'm here."

The warmth continued to seep in. Some came from their naked bodies pressed together; some came directly through her veins. April felt the urge to pee, and her body — almost of its own volition, of some long-learned habit — simply relieved itself. Fluid snaked away from her through one of the tubes. If it weren't for the too-real press of Remy's flesh against her own, she would think this was all a dream.

"What's happening?" Remy asked. He rubbed his eyes with one hand.

"I don't know." April's voice was hoarse. A whisper. "Someone did this to us." Even as she said this, she realized it was obvious, that it didn't need saying. Because she had no memory of being put in that metal canister.

"My eyes are adjusting," she told Remy. "I'm going to open this up some more."

Remy nodded slowly.

Peering up, April saw a curved half-cylinder of gleaming steel hanging over them, a third of the way open. She lifted a quivering leg, got a foot against the hinged lid, and shoved. Their small confines flew open the rest of the way, letting in more light. Flickering bulbs shone down from overhead. The lamps dangled amid a tangle of industrial pipes, traces of wire, air ducts, and one object so out of place that it took a moment to piece together what she was seeing. Suspended from the ceiling, hanging down over their heads, was a large yellow bin: a heavy-duty storage trunk.

"What does that say?" Remy asked. They both squinted up at the object, blinking away cold tears.

April studied the marks of black paint on the yellow tub. She could tell it was a word, but it felt like forever since she'd read anything real, anything not fragmented amid her dreams. When the word crystallized, she saw that it was simply her name.

"April," she whispered. That's all it said.

Before they could get the bin down, she and Remy had to extricate themselves from the steel canister. Why had they been put there? As punishment? But what had they done? The IVs and catheters were terrible clues that they'd been out for more than a mere night, and the stiffness in April's joints and the odor of death in the air — perhaps coming from their very flesh — hinted at it having been more than a week. It was impossible to tell.

"Careful," Remy said, as April peeled away the band that encircled her arm, the band that held the tube in place. It tore like Velcro, not like tape. Were they put away for longer than adhesive would last? The thought was fleeting, too impossible to consider.

"What's that around your neck?" Remy asked.

April patted her chest. She looked down at the fine thread around her neck and saw a key dangling from it. She had sensed it before, but in a daze. Looking back up at the bin, she saw a dull silver lock hanging bat-like from the lip of the bin.

"It's a message," April said, understanding in a haze how the key and the bin and her name were supposed to go together. "Help me out."

Her first hope was that there was food in that bin. Her stomach was in knots, cramped from so deep a hunger. Remy helped her pull her IV out and extract her catheter, and then she helped with his. A spot of purple blood welled up on her arm, and a dribble of fluid leaked from the catheter. Using the lid of the metal pod for balance, April hoisted herself to her feet, stood there for a swaying, unsteady moment, then reached up and touched the large plastic trunk.

It'd been suspended directly over their heads, where they would see it upon waking. A chill ran down April's spine. Whoever had placed them there had known they would wake up on their own, that there wouldn't be anyone around to help them, to explain things, to hand them a key or tell them to look inside the chest. That explained the paint, the thread, the pod cracking open on its own. Had she and Remy been abandoned? Had they been punished? Somehow, she knew her sister had been involved. Her sister who had brought them into the mountain had locked them away yet again, in tighter and tighter confines.

Remy struggled to his feet, grunting from the exertion of simply standing. He surveyed the room. "Looks like junk storage," he whispered, his voice like sandpaper.

"Or a workshop," April said. *Or a laboratory,* she thought to herself. "I think this knot frees the bin. We can lower it down."

"So thirsty," Remy said. "Feels like I've been out for days."

Months, April stopped herself from suggesting. "Help me steady this. I think . . . I have a feeling this is from Tracy."

"Your sister?" Remy held on to April, reached a hand up to steady the swaying bin. "Why do you think that? What have they done to us?"

"I don't know," April said, as she got the knot free. She held the end of the line, which looped up over a paint-flecked pipe above. The line had been wrapped twice, so there was enough friction that even her weak grip could bear the weight of the bin. Lowering the large trunk, she wondered what her sister had done this time. Running away from home to join the army, getting involved with the CIA or FBI or NSA — April could never keep them straight — and now this, whatever this was. Locking thousands of people away inside a mountain, putting her and Remy in a box.

The bin hit the metal pod with a heavy *thunk,* pirouetted on one corner for a moment, then settled until the hoisting rope went slack. April touched the lock. She reached for the key around her neck. The loop was too small to get over her head.

"No clasp," Remy said, his fingertips brushing the back of her neck.

April wrapped a weak fist around the key and tugged with the futile strength of overslept mornings.

The thread popped. April used the key to work the lock loose. Unlatching the trunk, there was a hiss of air and a deep sigh from the plastic container, followed by the perfume scent of life — or maybe just a spot of vacuum to stir away the stale odor of death.

There were folded clothes inside. Nestled on top of the clothes were tins labeled "water" with vials of blue powder taped to each. Remy picked up the small note between the tins, and April recognized the writing. It was her sister's. The note said: "Drink me."

A dreamlike association flitted through April's mind, an image of a white rabbit. She was Alice, tumbling through a hole and into a world both surreal and puzzling. Remy had less hesitation. He popped the tins with the pull tab, took a sip of the water, then studied the vial of powder.

"You think your sister is out to help us?" Remy asked. "Or kill us?"

"Probably thinks she's helping," April said. "And'll probably get us killed." She uncorked one of the vials, dumped it into Remy's tin of water, and stirred with her finger. Her sister wasn't there to argue with, so April skipped to the part where she lost the argument and took a sip.

A foul taste of metal and chalk filled her mouth, but a welcome wetness as well. She drank it all, losing some around the corners of her mouth that trickled down her neck and met again between her bare breasts.

Remy followed suit, trusting her. Setting the empty tin aside, April looked under the clothes. There were familiar camping backpacks there, hers and Remy's. She remembered packing them back at her house in Maryland. Her sister had just said they were going camping in Colorado, to bring enough for two weeks. Along with the packs were stacks of freeze-dried camping MREs; more tins of water; a first-aid kit; plastic pill cylinders that rattled with small white, yellow, and pink pills; and her sister's pocketknife. It was Remy who found the gun and the clips loaded with ammo. At the bottom of the case was an atlas, one of those old AAA road maps of the United States. It was open to a page, a red circle drawn on it with what might've been lipstick. And, finally, there was a sealed note with April's name on it.

She opened the note while Remy studied the map. Skipping to the bottom, April saw her sister's signature, the familiar hurried scrawl of a woman who refused to sit still, to take it easy. She went back to the top and read. It was an apology. A confession. A brief history of the end of the world and Tracy's role in watching it all come to fruition.

"We've been asleep for five hundred years," April told her husband, when she got to that part. She read the words without believing them.

Remy looked up from the atlas and studied her. His face said what she was thinking: *That's not possible.*

Even with the suspicion that they'd been out for months or longer, five hundred years of sleep was beyond the realm of comprehension. The end of the world had been nearly impossible to absorb. Being alive out along the fringe of time, maybe the only two people left on the entire Earth, was simply insane.

April kept reading. Her sister's rough scrawl explained the food situation, that they'd miscalculated the time it would take for the world to be safe again, for the air to be okay to breathe. She explained the need to ration, that there was only enough supplies to get fifteen people through to the other side. She could almost hear her sister's voice as she read, could see her writing this note in growing anger, tears in her eyes, knuckles white around a pen. And then she came to this:

> *The people who destroyed the world are in Atlanta. I marked their location on the map. If you are reading this, you and whoever else are left in the facility are the only ones alive who know what they did. You're the only ones who can make them pay. For all of us.*
>
> *I'm sorry. I love you. I never meant for any of this, and no one can take it back — can make it right — but there can be something like justice. A message from the present to the*

assholes who thought they could get away with this. Who
thought they were beyond our reach. Reach them for all of us.
— *Tracy*

April wiped the tears from her cheeks, tears of sadness and rage. Remy
studied the gun in his hand. When April looked to the atlas, she saw a
nondescript patch of country circled outside Atlanta. She had no idea
what it was her sister expected her to do.

"Did you hear that?" Remy asked.

April turned and stared at the door that led into the room. The handle moved. It tilted down, snapped back up, then tilted again. As if a child
were trying to work it, not like it was locked.

"Help me down," Remy said. He started to lift a leg over the lip of
the pod.

"Wait." April grabbed her husband's arm. The latch moved again.
There was a scratching sound at the door, something like a growl. "The
gun," April hissed. "Do you know how to use it?"

A branch snapped in the woods — a sharp crack like a log popping in a
fire. Elise stopped and dropped to a crouch, scanned the underbrush. She
looked for the white spots. Always easiest to see the white spots along the
flank, not the bark-tan of the rest of the hide. Slipping an arrow from her
quiver, she notched it into the gut string of her bow. *There.* A buck.

Coal-black eyes studied her between the low branches.

Elise drew back the arrow but kept it pointed at the ground. Deer
somehow know when they're being threatened. She has watched them
scatter while she took careful aim, until she was letting fly an errant shot at
the bouncing white tail that mocked hunters of rabbit and venison alike.

The bow in her hand was Juliette's, once. Elise remembered back
when it was made that she couldn't even draw the bow, that her arms had
been too weak, too short, too young. But that was forever ago. Elise was

nearly as strong as Juliette now. Strong and lean and forest swift. No one in the village had ever caught a rabbit with their bare hands before Elise, and none had done it since.

She and the deer studied one another. Wary. The deer were learning to be scared of people again. It used to be easy, bringing home a feast. Too easy. But both sides were learning. Remembering how to find that balance. To live like the people in Elise's great books had once lived, with prey growing wary and hunters growing wise.

With one motion, Elise steered the bow up and loosed the arrow with more instinct than aim, with more thought than measure, with six years of practice and habit. The buck reared its head, shook its horns, took a staggering leap to one side, and then collapsed. The heart. They only went down like that with an arrow to the heart. To the spine was faster, and anywhere else might mean half a day of tracking. Elise was too competent with a bow to gloat, wouldn't need to tell anyone how the deer went down. When you ate an animal not from a can but from the flesh, everyone who partook could read the hunt right there on the spit, could tell what had happened.

"Careful," she could hear her brother saying whenever she brought home a deer and provided for her people. "Keep this up, and you'll be mayor one day."

Elise drew out her knife — the one Solo had given to her — and marched through the woods toward her kill. Her quietude was no longer a concern. The hunt was over. But this was a mistake that she too often forgot, that a soft pace was always prudent. Juliette had taught her this. "The hunt is never over," Juliette had said once, while tracking a doe with Elise. "Drop your guard, and what changes in an instant is *who* is doing the hunting."

Elise was reminded of the truth of this by another loud noise to her side. Again, she dropped to a crouch. And again, something was watching her. But this time, it was the most dangerous animal of them all.

• • •

April was ready for anything to come through that door. It could be her sister, a mountain bear, a stranger intent on doing them harm. Open to all possibilities, she still wasn't prepared for what appeared.

The battle with the latch was finally won — the door flew open — and some creature entered on all fours. Some half-man, half-beast wildling. The creature sniffed the air, then spotted April and Remy perched inside the steel pod, huddled there beside the large plastic tub.

"Shoot it," April begged.

"What *is* that?" Remy asked.

"Shoot it," she told him again, holding on to her husband's arm.

The beast roared. "FEEF-DEEN!" it growled, with a voice almost like a man's. "Feef-deen!"

And then it was in the air, jumping at them, yellow teeth and white eyes flashing, hands outstretched, hair billowing out wildly, coming to take them.

Remy aimed the gun, but the beast crashed into them before he could pull the trigger. Hair and claws and teeth and snarling. Remy punched the animal, and April tried to shove it away when yellow teeth clamped down on Remy's hand. There was a loud crunch — and her husband screamed and pulled his hand away, blood spurting where two of his fingers had been.

From his other hand came a flash and a roar. Remy flew back into April, who knocked her head against the open lid, nearly blacking out. The animal slumped against the edge of the pod, a clawed hand splayed open, before collapsing to the floor.

"What the fuck!" Remy shouted. He scrambled after the pistol, which had flown from his grip. His other hand was tucked under his armpit, rivulets of blood tracking down his bare ribs.

"Your hand," April said. She pulled one of the clean, folded shirts from the bin and made her husband hold out his hand. She wrapped the shirt as tight as she could and knotted the ends. Blood pooled and turned the fabric red. "Is it dead?" she asked. She braved a glance over the lip of the pod. The beast wasn't moving. And now that she could study it, she saw that it wasn't half-beast at all. It was mostly man. But naked, covered in hair, a scraggly beard, sinewy and lean.

Remy straightened his arms and pointed the gun at the door, his bandaged hand steadying his good one. April saw that there was another beast there. Another person on all fours. Less hairy. A woman.

The woman sniffed the air, studied them, and then peered at the dead man-creature. "Feef-deen," she said. She snarled, showing her teeth, and her shoulders dipped as she tensed her muscles and readied for a leap. Remy, bless him, didn't allow her to make the jump. The gun went off again, deafening loud. The woman collapsed. April and Remy watched the door, frozen, and after an agonizing dozen throbs of her pulse, April saw the next one.

"How many bullets do you have?" she asked Remy, wondering where he learned to shoot like that, if it was as easy as he made it seem.

He didn't answer. He was too busy lining up his shot. But this next creature, another woman, studied the room, the two dead creatures and the two living ones, and made the same noise but without the rage. Without the snarling.

"Feef-deen," she said, before turning and wandering off. Almost as if satisfied. Almost as if all were right with the world.

"Who goes there?" Elise asked. She watched the shapes beyond the foliage — it appeared to be two men. Pressing an arrow into the dirt, she left the shaft where she could grab it in a hurry, and then withdrew another from her quiver and notched it on to the bowstring. She drew the string taut but kept the arrow aimed to the side. "Rickson? Is that you?"

"Hello," a voice called. A woman's voice. "We're coming out. Don't shoot."

A couple stepped around a tree. Elise saw that they were holding hands. They kept their free palms up to show that they were empty. Both wore backpacks. Both looked like they'd been living in the bush for ages, like the people who'd made it out of Silo 37 a few years ago. A thrill ran through Elise with the chance that these were new topsiders.

"Where are you from?" she asked. The couple had stopped twenty paces away. They looked rough. And there were only two of them. Elise recalled how back when she lived in Silo 17, every stranger was to be feared. But the people who dared to free themselves from their silos ended up being good people. It was a truth of the world. The bad people stayed right where they were.

"We've been . . . underground for a long time," the man said.

He didn't give a number. Sometimes they didn't know their number. Sometimes they had to be told by finding their silo on a map; there were fifty of them, the silos, buried underground. Elise fought the temptation to flood this couple with too much all at once. When she was younger, that had been her way. But she was learning to be more than quiet just in the hunt, to be as soft of tongue as she was of foot.

"Are you alone?" she asked, scanning the woods.

"We met another group northwest of here," the man said. He must've run into Debra's scouting party, which had been gone for a week. "They told us the people in charge lived by the coast. We've been looking for them for a long time. A very long time. Can you take us to your city?"

Elise put her notched arrow away and then retrieved the one she'd left in the dirt. "It's a village," she said. "Just a village." The memory of where she used to live, in one of those fifty silos, all cut off from each other, seemed forever ago. That life had grown hazy. Time formed some gulfs that not even recollection could span.

"Do you need help with the deer?" the man asked. "That's a lot of food."

Elise saw that he had a knife on his hip and that both of them bore the shrunken frames of the famished. She wondered what he could possibly know about deer. She'd had to consult her books to learn about deer, how to hunt them, how to clean them, how best to cook them. Maybe he too had pages from his silo's Legacy, that great set of books about the old world. Or maybe his silo had a herd of them.

"I'd love the help," she said, putting away the other arrow, comfortable that these people meant no harm and also that she could take the both of them with her bow or knife if she had to. "My name's Elise."

"I'm Remy," the man said, "and this is my wife, April."

Elise closed the distance between them. She shook their hands one at a time, the woman's first. As she shook the man's, she noticed something strange about his hand. He was missing two of his fingers.

Elise and Remy carved the choice cuts of meat and wrapped them in the deer's stripped hide. Elise secured the bundle with bark twine from her pack, and hung the bundle from a thick branch. The couple insisted on carrying the meat, resting it on their shoulders. Elise walked ahead, showing the way back to camp.

She resisted the urge to badger the couple with questions about their silo, how many were left there, what jobs they held, what level they lived on. When she was younger, she would have talked their ears off. But Juliette had a way about topsiders. There were unspoken rules. The people of the buried silos joined the rest when they were ready. They spoke when they were ready. "We all have our demons," Juliette liked to say. "We have to choose when to share them. When to let others in on the wrestling."

Elise often suspected that Juliette was holding out the longest. She had been their mayor for years and years. No one hardly voted for anyone else. But there was something in the woman's frown, a hardness in her eyes, a furrow in her brow, that never relaxed. Juliette was the reason any of them escaped from the silos, and the reason there was something to escape to for the rest. But Elise saw a woman still trapped by something. Held down by demons. Secrets she would never share.

The night fires were times for sharing. Elise told the couple this as they approached camp. She told them about the welcome they would receive, and that they could say as much or as little as they like. "We'll take turns telling you our stories," Elise said. "I'm from Silo 17. There are only a few of us. There are a lot more from Silo 18. Like Juliette."

She glanced back at the couple to see if they were listening. "Like I said, you don't have to say anything if you don't want. Don't have to say what you did or how you got here. Not until you're ready. Don't have to say how many of you are left—"

"Fifteen," the woman said. She'd barely said a word while the deer was being cleaned and packed. But she said this. "There were fifteen of us for the longest time. Now there are only two."

This sobered Elise. She herself had come from a silo that only offered five survivors. She couldn't imagine a world with just two people.

"How many are you?" Remy asked.

Elise turned her head to answer. "We don't count. It's not *really* a rule, but it's basically a rule. Counting was a touchy subject for a lot of our people. Not for me, though. Well, not the same. I came from a silo with very few people. You didn't count so much as glance around the room and see that your family is still there. We have enough people now that there's talk of setting up another village north of here. We're scouting for locations. Some want to see a place that used to be called the Carolinas—"

"Carolinas," Remy said, but he said it differently, with the *i* long like "eye" instead of "eee." Like he was testing the word.

"It's Carolinas," Elise said, correcting him.

Remy didn't try again. His wife said something to him, but Elise couldn't make it out.

"Anyway, that's the sort of thing we vote on now. We all vote. As long as you can read and write. I'm all for the second village, but I don't want to live up there. I know these woods here like the back of my hand."

They reached the first clearing, and Elise steered them toward the larder, where they dropped off the meat. Haney, the butcher's boy, grew excited at the sight of the feast and then at the strangers. He started to pester them with questions, but Elise shooed him away. "I'm taking them to see Juliette," she said. "Leave them alone."

"Juliette's the person in charge here?" the woman asked.

"Yeah," Elise said. "She's our mayor. She has a place near the beach."

She led them there, skirting the square and the market to keep from being waylaid by gawkers. She took the back paths the prowling dogs and mischievous children used. Remy and April followed. Glancing back, Elise saw that April had removed the bag from her back and was clutching it against her chest, the way some parents cradled their children. There was a look of fear and determination on her face. Elise knew that look. It was the hardened visage of someone who has come so far and is near to salvation.

"That's her place," Elise said, pointing up into the last two rows of trees by the beach. There was a small shelter affixed to the trunks with spikes and ropes. It stood two dozen paces off the ground. Juliette had lived inside the earth and upon the ground, but now lived up in the air. "I'm trying to get to heaven," she had told Elise once, joking around. "Just not in a hurry."

Elise thought that explained why Juliette spent so much time out on the beach alone at night, gazing up at the stars.

"There she is," Elise said, pointing down by the surf. "You can leave your bags here if you like."

They elected to carry them. Elise saw them fixate on Juliette, who was standing alone by the surf, watching the tall fishing rods arranged in a line down the beach, monofilament stretching out past the breakers. Farther down the beach, Solo could be seen rigging bait on another line. Charlotte was there as well, casting a heavy sinker into the distance.

Elise had to hurry to catch up with Remy and April. The couple seemed drawn toward Juliette. On a mission. But the woman had that pull on plenty of people. Sensing their presence, the mayor turned and shielded her eyes against the sun, watching the small party approach. Elise thought she saw Juliette stiffen with the sudden awareness that these were strangers, new to the topsides.

"I got a buck," Elise told Juliette. She nodded toward the couple. "And then I met them in the woods. This is April and Remy. And this is our mayor, Juliette. You can call her Jules."

Juliette took the couple in. She brushed the sand from her palms and shook each of theirs in turn, then squeezed Elise's shoulder. A strong wave crashed on the beach and slid up nearly to the line of rods. The tide was coming in. The couple seemed not to be awed by the sight of the ocean, which Elise thought was strange. She still couldn't get used to it. As for them — they could only stare at Juliette.

"Are you in charge of all this?" April asked.

Juliette glanced down the beach toward Solo and Charlotte for a moment. "If you came from a place with a lot of rules and great concern over who is in charge, you'll find we're not so strict here." Juliette rested her hands on her hips. "You both look hungry and tired. Elise, why don't you get them fed and freshened up. They can look around camp when they're ready. And you don't have to tell us your story until you want —"

"I think we'll say our piece now," April said. Elise saw that she was the talkative one now. Remy was holding his tongue. And there was anger in their guises, not relief. Elise had seen this before, the need to vent. She shuffled back a step but wasn't sure why. Maybe it was because Juliette had done the same.

"Very well —" Juliette started to say.

"We aren't here to be saved," April said. She continued to clutch her bag to her chest, like it was a raft keeping her afloat. "We aren't here to live with you. We died a long time ago, when everything was taken from us. We've been dead and walking for years to get here and to tell you this. You didn't get away with it."

"I'm not sure I —" Juliette began.

April dropped her bag to the sand. In her hand was a silver gun. Elise knew straightaway what it was. There were three of them in camp that the men used to hunt; Elise hated the way they spooked the wildlife.

This one was different ... and trained on Juliette. Elise moved to stand in front of the mayor, but Juliette pushed her away.

"Wait a second," Juliette said.

"No," April said. "We've waited long enough."

"You don't understa —"

But a roar cut off whatever Juliette was about to say. A flash and an explosion of sound. She fell to the beach, a wild wave rushing up nearly to touch her, all so sudden and yet in slow motion. Elise felt her own body startle, like a deer that knows it's in mortal danger. She sensed the whole world around her. Saw Solo and Charlotte stir down the beach and start running. Felt the heat of the sun on her neck, the tickle of sweat on her scalp. Could feel the sand beneath her feet and hear the crying birds. There was an arrow in her hand, her bow coming off her shoulder, a gun swinging around, a man yelling for someone to stop, Elise wasn't sure who.

She only got half a draw before the arrow slipped from her fingers. She loosed it before the trigger could be pulled again. And the shaft lodged in the woman's throat.

More screaming. Gurgling. Blood in the sand. Remy moved to catch his wife. Elise notched another arrow, swift as a hare. By her feet, Juliette did not stir. The man reached for the gun, and Elise put an arrow in his side, hoping not to kill him. He roared and clutched the wound while Elise notched another and knelt by her wounded friend. The man regrouped and went for the gun again, murder in his eyes. For the second time that day, Elise put an arrow through an animal's heart.

The only people moving on the beach were Solo and Charlotte, running their way. Elise dropped her bow and reached for Juliette, who lay on her side, facing away from Elise. Elise held her friend's shoulders and rolled her onto her back. Blood was pooled on Juliette's chest, crimson and spreading. Her lips moved. Elise told her to be strong. She told the strongest person she'd ever known to be extra strong.

Juliette's eyes opened and focused on Elise. They were wet with tears. One tear pooled and broke free, sliding down the wrinkled corner of Juliette's eye. Elise held her friend's hand, could feel Juliette squeezing back.

"It'll be okay," Elise said. "Help is coming. It'll be okay."

And Juliette did something Elise hadn't seen her do in the longest time: She smiled. "It already is," Juliette whispered, blood flecking her lips. "It already is."

Her eyes drifted shut. And then Elise watched as the furrow in her mayor's brow smoothed away and the tension in Jules's clenched jaw relaxed. Something like serenity took hold of the woman. And the demons everywhere — they scattered.

AFTERWORD

It's brutal on readers when beloved protagonists disappear forever. Most writers won't even touch the subject. We like to think these characters live eternally, even though we know that's not true. I've never been fond of this avoidance of the inevitable. There's closure in knowing a character's full arc. And it doesn't mean their story is over; there are all sorts of adventures untold to go back and revisit.

When John Joseph Adams and I began brainstorming our Apocalypse Triptych, I decided to tell the conclusion of my most iconic character's story. It would still leave much to tell: the rescue of the residents of Silo 40; Jules's trip south to Old Florida; the time she lost the mayoral election by a single vote (hers); and her third and final chance at real love.

As writers, we should trust more in our power to create riveting characters, worlds, and story lines. That means being able to let go of past creations. It means not telling the same stories over and over again (even if themes are repeated throughout our works). Letting go is hard. But it's the only way to reach out and grab what's next.

Fantasy

Hell from the East

The Free Territory of Colorado, 1868

My path to sickness began the day General Lee surrendered his sword. That coward laid down his arms, and so me and my brother took our rifles and headed west. Wasn't sure where we was heading, just away. My brother didn't make it far. He'd survived the Battle of Sharpsburg but was brought down by a persistent cough. Fell off his horse and never got back up. I'd seen more dead than any vicar, but that don't make me immune to its sad effects. Many a drink and several fistfights later, I found myself in a new army. They gave me a uniform I was more familiar shooting at than buttoning across my chest, and somehow slid from a war between brothers to this frontier life hunting natives. It was all about killing a man you didn't know. That made it easier, keeping them strangers. Knowing them makes the killing hard.

My father had raised me and my brothers in the pine-studded hills of Virginia, just outside of Staunton. Pa gave me my first rifle, pointed at a squirrel, and told me to shoot. Men more dear to me than my father have been handing me guns and directing my fire ever since. I still find it strange how a man can lose at a war and then enlist in another with his enemy. But there are no real sides in this life except the barrel of a gun and the butt of a gun, and I know where I prefer to stand.

After enlisting, they stationed me at Fort Morgan. This was years before that unfortunate incident at Wounded Knee Creek. It was before the world heard of the Ghost Dance that was driving the natives mad. What we would one day call the Messiah Craze, and would lodge in my ear like a starving tick, had yet to cause trouble on those plains.

Fort Morgan was a lot like the endless Confederate encampments I had endured while serving. The only difference was that the fort didn't relocate in the morning; it had far fewer men moaning and dying in tents; and it was less prone to abandonment at night. I reckon Colorado was a long way for a man to run home from. Most soldiers out there had already done their running, and Fort Morgan was where they'd ended up. Their final resting spot was a scrabble of tents and rickety shacks ringed by a shoddy wall of pine stumps where the best that could be said was they fed you twice a day. Two muddy tracks came in straight as an arrow from the east, cut right through Fort Morgan, and disappeared out the other end toward the west. In one direction, a flat nothing where only the dust stirred and a creek petered out and was swallowed by the cracked earth; in the other, ancient and impossibly tall mountains stood with white tops like old men. The hell in between was our home.

In the spring and all through the summer — when the gray brows on those granite men to the west receded with the melts and the creek raged — an endless caravan of poor people with rich dreams appeared along the twin-rutted road from territories east. They passed through on their way to California, and our sworn duty at Fort Morgan was to see that their scalps moved right along with them.

Those were the melts and the busy months — spring and summer. Autumn and winter were a harder time at the fort. Men took to cards and more drink than the good Army allowed, and each of us spent our share of nights in the pen sobering up and feeling like asses for mistakes we barely remembered. Those were the hard months — and in the eighteen hundred and sixty-eighth year of our Lord, they got suddenly harder.

I was out with Private Collins taking in a pair of deer when Lieutenant Randall took the sickness. The lieutenant had been away from the fort for near on eight weeks. A trail scout, he spent most of his time up in the hills living in a tent like a native and looking for less damnable passages between those brutish mountains. He was always a bit peculiar, but nothing to presage him wandering back into camp and murdering five good men in cold blood. Yet that's just what he did; four of his fellow enlisted men were shot dead, plus a half-Indian cook named Sammy. Randall shot each of them in the head before someone managed to wing him and put an end to the slaughter. Why they didn't kill him on the spot, I'll never know.

Private Collins and me returned from our hunt too late to help with anything but the digging. Saw the aftermath, though: brains and skull and hair that took me right back to the war. They was already mopping it up, and so we were handed shovels. Now, nobody consulted me for my legal expertise, but Justice would've been served by shooting Lieutenant Randall right there on the spot. But the good Army of the United States of America has its own sense of justice. There are trials and spectacles afforded a man before his chest is riddled by a firing squad. There are nights spent in the pen. Which is how I found myself nursing a blister from the shoveling, sitting there on a hard bench outside the holding cell, taking my shift at watching Lieutenant Randall so that he weren't shot dead by some enterprising fellow before dawn.

On the bench across from me was my hunting partner and shovel mate, Private Collins. I surmised that his presence was to make sure I didn't scratch that itch of justice, either. I was keeping an eye on him and he on me, and both of us on the lieutenant. Randall, meanwhile, snored and babbled like only the guilty and outright crazy could manage on the eve of their probable execution. What could make a man break camp one morning and ride in to shoot his comrades in their skulls? Morbid curiosity had me itching to know. I tried to discern some of what he was saying in his sleep — but couldn't make out a word.

"That's Red talk," Collins told me.

I turned to the private and realized I'd been leaning forward on my bench, my face scrunched up in concentration. I tried to relax. "You understand what he's mumbling?" I asked, keeping my voice down.

Collins chewed on the end of an unlit cheroot, and then spat a dab of tobacco between our feet. "Arapaho," he said, matter-of-factly. Private Collins had that air about him, that supreme confidence that got on some men's nerves. He had also bagged both deer that morning, firing before I had the chance. Still, I liked him.

"What's he saying?" I asked. The only Indian I recognized was their war cries, when the hair on the back of my neck was translation enough.

Collins shrugged and sucked on his cigar. "Used to take an Arapaho whore in Mason," he said. "I know what their language sounds like, can catch a few words, but unless he starts talking about how thick my member is . . ." He smiled. And not for the first time, I wondered why I liked this man yet despised so many others.

"Why the hell is he dreaming in Arapaho?" I asked, still whispering. It was strange that I wanted the man in that pen dead but cared not to disturb his sleep. Collins turned toward the dimly lit cell.

"Reckon he done and gone native. Happens. Too much time up in the hills. Or maybe he's been heading into Mason and taking up with my whore." Collins laughed, but Randall didn't stir.

I settled back on my bench and marveled at a man who could sleep through what might be the last night of his life. More than justice, I was thirsty for answers. I decided, come morning, I would ask the major if Collins and I could go hunting for something up in those hills besides deer.

Major Jack Lawson was a peculiar leader of men. Part eccentric and part mountain man, he was the reason Fort Morgan had a grand piano and a small library but no decent latrine. Music and books — and somehow shitting in bare holes in the dirt — were all apparently good for our souls.

Turned out the major was just as curious about Randall's sudden madness as we were. He gave us his blessing to ride out in search of clues.

Collins knew where Randall had set up camp the previous autumn, and so we followed an angry stream up through the pines and aspens and cottonwoods that made up the scruff around the old mountain's neck. Stumbling on a native camp, it took a moment to realize that it was in fact Randall's place. An army-issue tent lay draped across a lean-to of woven branches. A half-finished structure of limbs and sticks jutted up nearby, a rough circle with a tall pole in the center. Around the camp, every tree within a hundred feet had been felled, the trunks radiating outward as though they'd been knocked over by a terrible blast. Gnawed stumps stood out everywhere. I noticed how cleanly they'd been hewn, not an errant strike to be seen, none of the work of a madman.

"Took down enough trees for a second Morgan up here," I remarked. I peered inside Randall's abandoned tent and found nothing amiss. The bedroll was laid out like it expected to be slept in, a set of pots and cutlery innocently nestled in one corner. It smelled of leather and sweat and man, even with the air cold enough to fog my breath. Collins poked a smoldering log in the fire pit with a stick and was rewarded with a flight of embers, like bees startling from a hive.

"Don't think he was after the timber," Collins said. He left the pit alone and headed past the tent to the half-completed structure that'd made me think this was an Indian campsite. Shielding his eyes, he glanced up at the autumn sky. "I reckon he was out to fell the shade, is what."

I looked up as well. The morning sun slid shyly behind a bank of clouds. "'Fell the shade'?" I asked.

"It's a sun hut." Collins waved his arm. "They dance in it. The Arapaho do."

There was a loud snap in the woods. We both turned toward the sound. There was a flash of white as a deer bounded away from us and through the cottonwoods. I turned to Collins, who I suspected knew more of the Arapaho than the moans of a Mason whore.

"What kind of dance?"

Collins watched the deer a moment longer, then scanned the woods. Finally, he turned to the odd structure, whose walls curved upward like an unfinished dome. A pole sat in the center that I figured was bound to support an arching roof; but I would find out later that the hut was finished just as it stood.

"All I know is what little I've heard. Pretty sure it started with the Arapaho, but other tribes have taken part. Spreading like those damn Mormons, like some kinda religion." Collins pointed to the sky. "They dance around a pole and stare up at the sun for days. They see things. Hear voices. And then they probably get drunk on peyote and shove feathers up their arses for all I know."

He shrugged and pulled out his cheroot. To my amazement, Collins bent and grabbed a smoking fag from the fire and lit the thing with noisy puffs. Maybe he figured we'd already chased away the deer and to hell with the smoke. Or maybe he'd seen enough death the day before to stop saving the thing for a morrow. Or perhaps the talk of ghosts and whispers had stirred his nerves. I watched his white exhalations rise toward the clouds, and the sun reemerged to peer down at us.

"I guess you were right," I told Collins.

He raised an eyebrow and threw the fag back in the fire.

"I think Lieutenant Randall has done and gone native. Maybe fell for some squaw and started seeing us as the enemy."

The private pinched something off the end of his tongue and inspected it. "Maybe," he said. But it sounded like he doubted it. He smoked his cheroot like it would be his last and studied the sky as if the sun up there knew something we didn't.

The two of us shared our findings with the major later that morning and handed over Randall's tent, bedroll, and mess kit. Collins drew a straw for the firing squad; I didn't. The both of us had missed the court-martial, which hadn't taken long. Three witnesses said he did it, and Randall hadn't uttered a word of defense. We heard he stared at the ceiling the entire time before being led back to the pen.

I should have gotten some sleep before lunch — only had a few hours the night before — but I volunteered to ride out with some others to see about another rustling, a strange disappearance of cattle from a rancher to the east.

On the ride out, I sidled my horse next to John McCall's. McCall had grown up in the Arizona territory, had missed the war entirely, and knew as much about Indians as any of us. He used to keep a feather stuck in his cap until the major told him to lose it. When pressed, McCall admitted he'd heard of the Sun Dance. He was surprised to hear about the hut near Randall's tent, said he thought it must've already been there. I told him about the felled trees. McCall didn't have much to say after that. We rode along in silence, the sun beating down on us, the horses growing warm, the featureless landscape making it feel like we hardly moved.

While the others went to talk to the rancher about his missing cattle and the burn marks some lightning strikes had left in the grass, I rode the fence line looking for a break in the thorny wire. I was sure the rancher had already checked his fence, but in my experience the most likely culprit to make off with a few head of cattle were those few head of cattle. I expected to see them milling about on the side of the trail where the grass grew tallest. It was getting on noon, and the flies buzzed something fierce. Amazing it could be cool in the morning up in the hills and so damn hot come afternoon on the plains. My mouth was dry and tasted of the dirt kicked up by my horse. Shaking my canteen, I decided to take it easy on the water. Before long, I found a drooping wire in the fence and dismounted to take a closer look.

Was only the top wire amiss. A sprightly cow might make the jump, but unlikely. Wiping my neck, I glanced up accusingly at the high sun. Not a cloud in the sky. I remembered something I'd learned early on in Kansas: there were tribes who would only come at you in the morning from the east. They would ride in, and you couldn't see their arrows in the glare. Before they attacked, one of their scouts would sit on a hill every morning, high on his horse, feathers blazing, and would be as good as invisible. Ghosts, bringing hell from the east. They would keep an eye on their enemy until it was time to rain death. Devious sons a'bitches.

The sun shone bright that day as I scanned the sky — and finally I had to look away. I didn't believe what Collins and McCall had said about dancing around and looking up at that fiery beast. A man couldn't stand two seconds staring at it. And maybe I was delirious from lack of sleep; or thinking about a man I had known who was at that moment being shot in the chest by my compadres; or maybe it was the sight of those I'd buried the day before; or I was just being powerfully curious and not thinking straight. But I felt an ungodly tug... and so I looked up and tried to return the gaze of that great yellow monster in the wide blue sky.

The burn was intense and immediate. It made my brain hurt somewhere deep between my brows. The squinting was involuntary. My horse made a sound and pawed at the air with one hoof. "Steady, now," I told him, taking the reins and turning away, unable to take it any longer. Blinking tears, I could see a green image in my vision, a disk the color of fresh grass. I wondered if this was what they claimed to see, those who danced and saw what weren't there.

The wire fence drooped like it was melting in the sun. A faint wind blew dust across my boots. Back toward the fort, mountains rose from the flat desert, impossibly tall, the white on their tops growing with the cold months. I blinked and blinked and wondered what in the hell I was doing out there. How could anyone dance around for three days and stare at the sun? Determined, I gave it another try. I would go for the count of twenty, pain be damned. If an Arapaho could do it, so could I.

Throwing my head back, I squinted at the sun and met it like a man. Again, the feeling was like claws raking my eyeballs. There was a primitive urge to look away, like a thumb on a hot pan. I forced my eyes open wider, muscles in my face quivering in complaint, tears streaking down my cheeks. I lost count. I swayed, my balance funny, and reached for a fence post to steady myself. As my horse clomped down the road, I ignored him. There was nothing but white and heat, both penetrating straight into my brain. I hopped in place and cursed nothing in particular, just said "shit" and "damn" while the tears streamed out, but no bright light was stronger than this Virginia boy.

I had to've gone to a count of twenty, but I decided to keep going a bit more. I had the water in the canteen, could dump that in my eyes after and put the fire out. There was no thought of going blind. That fear would come later. I was just enduring the pain because, goddamnit, it wasn't going to beat me.

My neck cramped up, but now something had taken hold of me, some wild thought that this was the right thing to do, to stare at the sun for as long as I was able. Releasing the post, I drifted around in circles there in the dirt, admiring the shapes and colors as they spun in my vision. I saw purple. I saw strangers swim through the sky. When my lids clamped down involuntarily, I used my fingers to pry them open again. The burn and pain went straight through me until it felt like an itch being scratched. I spun and spun and felt the barbed wire catch at my trousers. The fence would keep me in. I thought of Collins spinning around in his little Indian hut. The barbs were suddenly those sticks, poking at me, corralling me. The light shone right through my eyes, down to the base of my skull, and deep into my neck where words are formed. My face grew warm, but now the bright light was cool as it swam through me. I could hear myself laugh. The horse drew away farther, and I cared little.

When the vision came, it was a thunderclap. A sudden roar, though I realized the words had been there before. They were the buzzing in my brain, nonsense words, but I knew what they meant. I saw them like shapes and things, like swirling dreams. There was shouting, someone on the road with me, a man with my own voice. Crying and crying, fingers pinned my eyes open, and I never wanted to look away from the sun again. I loved it in that instant. I wanted it to fall out of the sky and enter me through my eyeballs; I wanted to let it blow me across the prairie and set everything on fire, to burn that land ahead of its coming, to make room. I saw men and women and children fall before me. I saw an infant thrown into the flames, blood in everyone's eyes. And the voices, these words foreign and understood that came like pictures directly into my head, this voice on the road that spoke as I spun and spun between the barbed wire and my skittish horse, they sounded like the tongue of a Red Man.

I woke up and men were dead. My men. Something told me there had been a killing. My head throbbed like my heart was trapped in my skull, had swollen up, and needed out. It took a moment to realize my eyes were open but I wasn't seeing anything. I could barely make out a shape in front of my face when I waved my hand before it. Groping about, I felt a bunk beneath me, a wall of steel bars behind. I was in the pen. I could feel the firing squad lined up, instruments of death aimed at my chest, could see the men I'd killed.

"Sir, he's done stirred."

Voices and shuffling feet. I had Arapaho on my tongue, the taste of silver and fire, words like pictures drawn in the dirt, telling me what to do. Something alien had communicated with me. A part of it lived deep inside.

"Drink some water, son."

There was a hand on my wrist, a hand reaching through the bars. A tin of water was pressed into my palm, sloshing cool on my forearm. My lips stung as I drank. I pulled the cup away and touched my mouth, found my lips swollen and cracked. My throat burned. But the horrible throbbing in my eyes and my brain drowned out these lesser hurts.

"What the hell happened to you?"

"Major?" My voice was a pale shadow of its old self. I drank more, ignoring the sting of my fouled lips. "What did I do?" I asked.

"They found you face-up in the dirt, babbling like you had a few too many. Your horse came back to the fort without you."

"I can't see."

"That's what you've been sayin'. Doc said to put you in here where it was dark, that it should come back. You rest up, okay? Can't afford to lose any more of my men."

"How many?"

I could hear the boards creak as the major shifted his weight. "How many of what, son?"

"Did I . . . How many dead?" Memories and visions were mixed up in my head. Words I knew and words I didn't. There were flashes of green and swimming lights in my eyes like an angry campfire. Something was telling me to kill or that I already had, hard to tell which.

"Get some rest. I'll send some food over."

I nursed my water and decided I hadn't done the things I thought I had. But I could feel the urge. Some silent screaming beneath my skin, something directing my bones. I was reminded of a visit to Richmond when I was a boy. A friend of my mother's was a pastor there, took us to his great big church. There was a belfry terribly high off the ground, a circuit of rickety stairs, and at one corner you could peer down at the street like a bird. And something in me felt this urge to jump out and go plummeting down, something so strong that I had to back away and clutch my father, even though I was too old to be holding his hand. And now this demon was in my blood again, but this time to hurt others.

Long after the tin cup was dry, I continued to pass it back and forth between my hands. It was Collins who brought me my supper.

"You gone and blinded yourself," Collins said, a voice in the darkness. Hinges pealed as he let himself into the pen, and I realized the door had never been locked. I hadn't killed no man. Not that day, anyhow.

The plate was warm as he rested it on my knee. A fork was pressed into my palm. "You manage all right?" he asked. "See anything yet?"

I shook my head. I saw things, but not like he meant.

"I blame myself," Collins said. "But what was you thinking?"

"I weren't," I admitted. "Just started and couldn't stop."

Collins laughed. "Most take a glance and know it's a bad idea."

I groped around the plate with my fork, found some resistance, some weight. Took a sniff of potatoes and blew on 'em in case they was hot. How anyone lived with such blindness, I couldn't fathom.

"I heard voices," I told Collins. I wasn't sure I'd ever tell anyone, but it just came out. "Voices and . . . I had a vision." I swallowed the potatoes and shook my head. Patches of murk swam in the darkness, a vague discernment of shapes. I'd welcome just seeing my own hands.

"You heard voices. You mean when they scooped you off the road?"

"Before." I peered at where I thought Collins stood, where I heard him. "They were telling me to do awful things. I think Randall was poisoned by the sun."

"Randall was poisoned by the Arapaho. He was babblin' that nonsense right up until we shot him. You just need some sleep is all."

I nodded and ate, and Collins gave me silent and invisible company. By nightfall, it felt as though some of my eyesight was returning, but not much. I fell asleep on that cot for drunkards, madmen, and murderers — and wondered which of them I was.

When I awoke, it was not yet dawn. My internal clock had unwound from the late shifts and lack of sleep. But I could see my hands, and my lips only partway stuck together. Groping about, I let myself out of the pen and sought my own bunk.

Along the way, with my fingers brushing cedar clapboards to keep from spinning in circles, I noticed the pinpricks of tiny lights in my vision. It was pitch-black across the fort, and it was like somehow the brightest of stars were able to penetrate my blindness. But no: it was my eyesight returning.

I stopped and marveled at the tiny spots of light in that infinite darkness. The voices were out there, straining to be heard. There was a madness in my soul, an invader.

It hadn't taken a full hold of me, but its claws had left marks. It was the same madness I'd seen in the war cries of the natives we fought with. It was the madness Randall had seized upon. A cry from some distant throat telling me that this land was someone else's and that a reckoning was coming. That was the sight I'd seen: a land wiped clean and taken by those who didn't belong, a land of dead and missing cattle to starve us the way we'd done with the buffalo, a time of great sickness and men dying beyond counting, with infection rained down from the heavens like some poisoned blanket.

This was the calling. I heard it clearer that night than I ever would again. I stood there for what felt like hours, searching for those pinprick stars and marveling at how our own sun was said to be one like them. Our sun, where native tribes stood sentinel in the morning so we couldn't see them coming, where they would watch and watch and plan their deadly raids. Many a time, they had brought hell on us from the east with the rising of the sun, the Arapaho and the Sioux and the Apache, but I reckoned we'd done the same and that others might do it to us one day. Generations back, a man with my name had crossed a wide sea and brought his own hell from the east. Others would come. It were folly to think we'd be the last.

That was my vision, what I saw clearly that night in my blindness and with an earful of strange voices. I saw the night and its lights like never before. There was a far and dark sea out there, hanging over me. A dark sea that ships sailed on, scouts arriving at dawn to watch over us, vast fleets to rain down by dusk. But it was not yet dusk. It was early yet. And those stars were like campfires impossibly distant where strange men spoke in strange tongues and conjured war. They spoke with words that I could not fathom but could see like scratches in the dirt, could see like a calling to do bad things on their behalf.

I tried to explain this to whoever would listen, but they would only lock me up for my troubles. They would lock me up before I ever got the chance to heed those voices the way Lieutenant Randall had. I was locked up years later and therefore not a part of that massacre at Wounded Knee Creek, which put an end to the war with our red kin. I was locked up while more cattle went missing and a great sickness swept the land, millions and millions of people dying like my brother had. It has not yet come, this thing from the east that whispers for me to clear the land in preparation. It has not yet come. But something stirs and will talk to those crazy enough to look and listen. There is something across that dark sea, across that expanse of space that men saner than me say no one will ever cross, but I wager my red brother thought the same thing of the deep blue Atlantic that lapped their former shores — and here we are. We who hailed from the east, who came from that rising sun too bright to see, who came first with scouts across the pitch-black, standing tall and ignorant and proud atop some deadly ridge.

AFTERWORD

Very few of my stories came as assignments or via writing prompts. Most are ideas that have been percolating for a long time. I enjoy the luxury of writing whatever seizes me, rather than being stuck writing the same type of story over and over. "Hell from the East" was different. I was invited to submit something for an anthology, and the stories needed to be "weird Western."

I've always been a fan of this genre, which makes it strange that I'd never explored it on my own. The TV show Firefly *is a weird Western in a way. Science fiction is the new frontier, a role that Westerns used to play. And survival on the edge will mean relying on cobbled-together technology, being in sparsely populated areas, and a dive back into lawlessness at times.*

The theme I wanted to explore with this story is the idea of alien invasion and the settling of the New World. There's a legend that some Native American tribes would raid during the rising sun and ride in from the east, so they were hidden in the glare of the sun. This got me thinking of how Europeans arrived from the east, and kept arriving from the east, conquering, stealing land, spreading disease. They had bizarre machines and gadgets. They arrived on strange ships. Europeans were the alien invasion.

In this story, the invasions are nested. As we push west, there's a different threat coming. And you can only see it if you stare into the sun.

The Black Beast

In the Long Ago, there was a beast who couldn't be caught. She roamed the woods by a small village, where the men would hunt for her and the women would lay traps for her, but the beast could not be caught. She taunted them from the tree line in their own tongue, calling out her eternal threat of "Just wait."

"Just wait," she would screech, over and over, trying to scare them. She would fly through their hunting parties and their traps, laughing and mocking them, "Just wait."

One day, an old man from the village was fetching water down by the stream when the beast came close, as she was fond of doing. The man ignored the beast. He no longer had fear in his heart for her. Despite the many close calls of his youth and her eternal threats, she had never done him any lasting harm.

Standing on the rocks that jutted out over the stream, he lowered his bucket toward the distant gurgling far below, passing the braided rope through his wrinkled hands. While the swaying bucket descended through the air, the beast came closer, her belly to the grass, her breathing audible.

The man let the currents of the stream catch the rim of the bucket and waited for it to be filled no more than halfway; he could stand to hoist no more. Snapping it from the foam, he pulled the bucket hand over hand and set it on a flat moss-covered rock. He wheezed from the effort while the beast crept closer, her shoulders down, her tail slicing the air.

The old man knew the beast was there. He ignored her, but being so close reminded him of younger days, days spent chasing this beast who could not be caught, his hands swishing at air, her screeching laughter, him and his friends in the dirt, hugging nothing. And now the black beast was nearer than ever, taunting him, and he knew in his old bones that he had one lunge yet.

Smiling to himself, remembering what it felt to be young and lithe and full of power, he smeared his feet into the moss, working his toes into their soft grip. Slowly, ever so slowly. He bent his knees and reached for the bucket as if to carry it off. The water inside was still moving. Joints creaked like bent wood, and he saw in the bucket a wrinkled reflection of himself. With one hand, he unknotted the long fetching rope from the bucket. "Just once more," he whispered to his bones. "Like old times."

The fetching rope was salty as he placed it between his teeth. Behind him, he could hear the animal creeping closer, attempting to torment him with her shadowy presence.

Whirling, the old man leapt for the beast. He was airborne again, flying, arms wide, eyes taking in the whole world. He saw the black fur on the beast ripple with alarm, saw the tail drop, the paws splay in the dirt, the head jerk as it prepared to run, but then he was on her, catching what couldn't be caught. They rolled to the ground. The old man scrambled to the beast's back and wrapped his legs around her midsection, hooking his feet together. His arm went across her neck where it was impossible to bite. The rope went quick around one paw, and then another. Old hands make the best knots. Her back legs were looped with the rest of the rope, all of it done in a moment.

The beast screeched madly and bit at the air, but she could not move. The old man looked from her heaving ribs to the roofline of the village far up the hill. Someone would have to come for him, he thought. He imagined the stories they would tell, his children and grandchildren. They would be telling this story forever.

"What of you, beast?" he asked. He rested on his knees. One of the beast's dark eyes swiveled his way. "Long have you mocked us, and yet here you are."

The beast stopped biting the air and seemed to smile. The old man had taken note of her reach, the limit of her snarling mouth. He did not fear her and moved closer, double-checking his knots.

"They said you couldn't be caught," the old man wheezed. The knots were secure. He had done it. He searched himself for injury, for some claw mark, but found none.

"Who says?" the beast asked, with that voice that had all the years taunted and promised so much.

"Everyone," the old man replied. He looked down at her black fur, gleaming in the sunlight. The day was brighter, his head lighter from the exertion.

"And what do they know of me?" the beast asked, her voice subdued.

The old man said nothing. He looked back to the village, wondering how long it would take for someone to notice he had not returned.

"I will tell you what of me," the beast hissed.

The old man turned.

"Come," she said. Her tongue slid out and smoothed her whiskers. "Bend low and I will tell you of this chase we make."

The man laughed, but he was indeed curious to hear. He glanced back toward the village, saw the bucket and felt suddenly thirsty, but he bent closer to the animal's smiling teeth, remembering well their range and keeping out of it.

"Tell me your story," the old man said. He was dizzy with the opportunity to know the unknown. "Start at the beginning."

"It is not my story I tell," the beast said. "And I know nothing of beginnings."

And with that, the beast stretched her neck much further than it had reached before, and she bit the old man. It was a deep and mortal wound, sudden and sure. The man staggered back, clutching at it, knowing from the great gush that it couldn't be held.

With a single claw, the beast parted the fetching rope bound around her wrists, then sliced the knots holding her hind legs.

"I run from you, and you chase me," the beast said. She stood on her great paws. "You call me uncatchable, but the truth is contrary. The day comes when all men catch me. All men."

The old man from the village fell back in a pool of his own blood. His life was draining away, soaking the moss.

"Just wait," the beast said, her voice no longer shrill. "Just wait, I tell them, but it makes you hurry all the more."

AFTERWORD

This was a story I wrote and published online for a short while, but the link broke in a website update and I never fixed it, so it was pretty much lost. It wasn't until we started putting together this collection, and this book's editor, John Joseph Adams, kept asking me if I was sure that was everything, that I found it through the back end of my website. I read it years after having written it, and it was all new to me. I had a vague recollection of having written it, but that was it. This is a terrifying feeling.

It's the feeling of seeing an old photograph and a flood of memories of that entire day, an entire period of your life, rushing back into consciousness. Where were these memories before? How did a single key unlock so much? Would those memories have been lost forever without that small reminder? The illusion of permanence and memory are too convincing.

The worst is waking up in the morning remembering that you had a great idea the night before, but this is all you can remember: the idea of the idea. It's the scrap of writing on an ancient Greek scroll extolling the wisdom, genius, and virtue of some writer whose works have been lost to time. Perhaps it's better not knowing. If we're going to lose these parts of ourselves, the only salvation is to lose the memory of having had them. Or is it?

When I was younger, I wrote about death a lot. This happened as I was losing my religion and my belief in eternal life. "The Black Beast" is about loss of life, but in its discovery on an old server, and the panic of how much else may have been lost with no memories to even inspire a search, it can also be a story about losing something else: our sense of selves.

Tragic is a story about a mother losing a child and spending the rest of her life searching for him. Even worse is a mother waking up one day with no child and no cause to even begin the search. Because the child is still out there. What we lose is still missing.

The Good God

Dear Enlightened Being,

My name is Olodumare, son of Olorun, the divine creator and source of all energy. If you know the ways of the cosmos, you know that my father became no more once the act of creation was complete. He left me to bring light to the world. And yet darkness spreads across the land.

Shadows are falling everywhere, and it is because I am being held in the pit of the Earth. Only you can release me. My father was a twin, and his brother Eshu holds me against my will. The devil Eshu subsists on the dark that lurks in all our hearts. I regretfully admit that I have lent him some of my own. Only the brightness can keep him at bay. It is in you. You must let it out to let *me* out. If you do, all the treasures of the cosmos will be brought to the Earth once more. All the treasures will be brought to *you*.

There is some cost to you, yes. And much trust. But I
promise to repay you many times over. Please, before it is
too late and the darkness is everywhere.

My ayanmo — my fate — is in your hands,
Olodumare

The words spread like fidgeting ants across dry parchment. One moment
they were not there; the next moment, an incredible story of gods that no
sane mortal would believe. The parchment trembles in the hands of en-
raged Eshu. Fire leaks from the dark devil's veins, and the parchment is
engulfed in flickering, dancing orange flames. Allowing the letter to fall,
it is ash before it reaches Eshu's cloven feet.

"Kill him," Eshu says.

Badu, the dark lord's right hand, bows in apology. Eshu had a long
habit of cleaving his right hand and growing one anew. Badu had only
been on the job a thousand years. He was just getting to know his way
around the aiye called Earth. "Sire, we've been over this. If you kill him,
he will be born again elsewhere, and it will take us many moons to find
him once more."

"But killing him feels good," Eshu says. His knuckles crackle as he
makes a fist, the sound of logs in a hot fire. The two lords stand facing
the cube of obsidian in which noble Olodumare, the damned bringer of
light, sits entombed.

"Yes, m'lord. I know how it feels. But death will set him free."

Eshu exhales tendrils of smoke from his nostrils. "He will be free anyway. My bastard nephew always finds a way. This light, it slips through
the slimmest of cracks. And my minions never cease to fail me."

Badu waits to be smote to oblivion. Every muscle and tendon tenses
in anticipation. Badu spends much of his time waiting to be smote. One
day, he knows he will be right.

"We have him now, m'lord," he says. "These messages he sends will not get far, and the people of this aiye do not know the power in their hearts."

Badu has thought many centuries on this. The cell of obsidian, with its thousand and one facets, is itself like a black heart in the center of the aiye. Inside that solid case of stone sits Olodumare, a god of pure light. Olodumare in his cage is very much like the speck of hope that lies in men's hearts. The way the world was going, there was no way it was getting out.

Eshu turns and spits a wad of flame in Badu's direction. "Light leaks like water through the tightest of fists," he growls. "Darkness reigns a generation, perhaps, and then goodness takes most of what we fight for. There must be an end to this cycle, to hope, to—"

"Sire—"

Eshu silences Badu with a claw. A leaf of parchment flutters through the air, summoned out of nothingness by Olodumare, the son of the divine creator, imprisoned in black obsidian. Words like ants crawl across the parchment, a plea to anyone who might listen. Eshu turns the note to ash. Across the great cavern, more fluttering notes can be seen, moving like lazy moths. They too burst into flame. So many . . .

"I have killed the boy more times than I can count," Eshu says, as he watches the summoned notes succumb to his dark magic. "But he is born anew. I have put him in stone again and again, but one of you will get too close and hear his words and be in thrall like fools, freeing him. And now these missives, fluttering like insects across the aiye called Earth. They will release him. Some will get infected with the light. So I might as well kill him. Enjoy these years like days before he comes of age and realizes what he is again—"

"Sire, if I may—"

Eshu turns, his hand lifted as if to smite. He hesitates when he sees Badu holding one of the notes between his black claws.

"I have an idea," Badu says. "One that might keep the lightness hidden away for good."

In Kogi state there is a river long cursed. Fish from this river remain raw, however long you cook them. If you are injured by the bones of these fish, the wound will never heal. Badu grew up along the banks of this river in Kogi state. In his throat there is a cut from a fish he caught as a child. It fills him with pain every time he swallows. It will do so until the end of time.

But time is a funny thing, and it can be bent to the will of the great god of darkness Eshu. Bent, but not broken. Very little can slip through. Meaningless trifles. No more than words, like the words that pass through solid obsidian and the darkest of hearts.

Badu swallows, painfully, and writes another letter. In years hence, he will come to type the same words on little machines. Time is bent, Eshu straining under the weight of such a burden, and these words are passed back in time — black insects to flutter in the aiye called Earth, but the Earth of old, the Earth of superstition, the Earth that learns not to listen.

In the heart of foul obsidian, the good god Olodumare brings thoughts together like callused palms. He forces them out into the aiye, the real world, and pleads with the good people there. He sends them to all the people, for all are good. All are light inside of darkness. All are like him.

The years wear on, and Olodumare realizes he is not reaching the people. No one believes in gods anymore. The riches of knowledge no longer hold sway. Only the yellow glint of gold. Perhaps because the light is everywhere else fading upon the aiye called Earth.

So the words change. The story changes. Pleading. Begging. Notes for years, sealed in envelopes, and later just words made of phosphors of light, sent to everyone, for all are that shard of light encased in darkness.

Deer sir or madam,

    I am Olawale, a prince from Nigeria, and youre help is most seeked. My evel uncle has keeping me locked away. All the riches of my countrey will belong you, but you needs only paye me a small favor. For this, I will paye you back a millionfold —

In a chamber deep in the bowels of the aiye called Earth, the iron-mule Badu swallows and writes, swallows and writes. He has been doing this for generations, his words sent everywhere that words can go. Because flames can only consume so much; and words can only drown in more of the same. Words everywhere, until they can't be trusted.

AFTERWORD

I spent the better part of a year in Africa prior to setting off on my journey around the world. While my sailboat was being built, I had time to drive around this new-to-me continent and try to understand its history. One of the things I discovered was a rich mythology of gods I'd never been exposed to before.

    There is no one Africa. There are thousands of them, many overlapping and in conflict and cooperation with each other. Religion and family are powerful forces here, and there are religions aplenty.

    One thing I couldn't help but notice were the unanswered prayers. The economic disparity between the haves and have-nots in South Africa is vast and disheartening. The wealthy exist alongside townships that are little more than plywood, corrugated tin, and strewn refuse. Inhabitants of these townships walk hours each way to clean the houses of the wealthy for a pittance. Where prayers are said the most, it becomes obvious how little they are answered.

Time spent in Africa got me thinking about the prayers we ignore: the people we drive by on the side of the road without picking them up; the charities we don't support; the time we don't volunteer. There are so many people asking that we begin to treat it all like spam. And how many frivolous things are prayed for every day? How much time would a god spend blessing those who've sneezed with little time for anything else?

All these ideas went into a story about a god who subsists on hope and is today starving for lack of it. His pleas to us are drowned out by the clever requests of evil gods that our spam filters delete. How are we to know the difference? Are we not gods to many with the cruel power to ignore?

Algorithms of
Love and Hate

The Automated Ones

Melanie entered the foyer of Beaufort's, leaving the reek of wet pavement behind and replacing it with a fog of fine-cuisine smells. Rain shimmered on her floor-length coat; she stripped the garment off and folded it over her forearm, looking back for her fiancé.

Daniel was still outside, fiddling with the umbrella. One of his shiny loafers was half-buried in a puddle, propping the door open. A cascade of water from the striped awning, a perfect line of downpour in the drizzle, was pattering across the back of his blazer.

"Darling, bring it in here and close it." Melanie moved to grab the door and urge him inside.

"It's bad luck," he said. A yellow cab flew by, spitting up old rain from the gutter — adding another layer to the puddles.

"You don't believe in that nonsense — now get in here before you ruin your new suit."

"Almost got it — damn." Daniel stepped through the door, the umbrella, broken and inside out, was limp in his hand. "I'm sorry," he said, shrugging his wide shoulders and twisting the corners of his lips up.

Melanie put her hand on his arm and reached for the ruined device. Even through the damp jacket, she could feel his warmth, his strength. "Forget it, sweetheart, we needed a new one anyway. It was ancient."

"No — yeah. I just — I got frustrated with the stupid thing, that's all. Tried to force it. I'll buy you a new one tomorrow. Hey, a wedding present. I'll get you one of those automated ones that does everything with the press of a button."

Melanie laughed at the joke and helped Daniel out of his jacket. Normally someone would have already been here to check their coats, but the nearby stall was empty. Melanie slid the broken umbrella into a barrel full of fancier ones. With interlocked arms, the couple crossed the large entrance to the maître d', who seemed lost in his large ledger of clientele.

"Bonsoir, Robert," Melanie said. She was careful to slur the last half of the Frenchman's name, dropping the *t* entirely and leaving the *r* clinging desperately to the *e*. Robert took the meticulous and exacting slurring of the French language to its absolute extremes.

He looked up from his book with a mask of mechanical surprise. Melanie suspected at once that he'd seen them enter, that he'd been hiding in his matrix of Washington's who's who of politics and law. "Mademoiselle Reynolds. What a surprise. We weren't expecting you . . ." His eyes were welded to hers as he let the rest trail off. He was ignoring Daniel so blatantly, he may as well have been shining lasers on her fiancé.

The fib flipped on the lawyer switch in Melanie. She could feel the adrenaline of confrontation surge up inside. "Don't pull that crap on *me*, Robert." She stressed the *t* this time, ticking it between her teeth with a flick of her tongue. "I've eaten here every other Friday for two years. I called in and specifically requested a private table for —"

Robert held up his hands, cutting her off. "Oui. Of course. I'll make an exception, just — merci, don't create a scene."

Melanie ran her hands down the sides of her blouse and over her hips, composing herself. "There'll be no scene tonight, Robert. We're just here to celebrate."

There was finally a flicker of movement in the maître d's eyes. A twitch to Daniel and back. The Frenchman's thin lips disappeared in a grimace. "But, of course, mademoiselle. *Congratulations.*" He barely managed the word, and he couldn't help but add, "I understand it was a very close decision you won. Five to four, no?"

"The important decisions are always close. Now, if you'll show us to our table —"

"Of course. Right this way." He grabbed two leather-bound menus and a wine list from the side of his stand. Then he made a show of looking at Daniel and smiling, but there was something unpleasant about the expression.

More bad looks followed. As they weaved through the tables, heads swiveled, tracking them with the precision of computer-guided servos. The din of jovial eating faded in the couple's wake. The clink of excited silverware on thin china ground to a halt. Dozens of eager conversations, all competing with one another, faded into a hiss of white noise. It was the sound, not of air escaping, but of grease popping on hot metal. A buzz interspersed with spits of disgust.

"We can go somewhere else," Daniel pleaded.

Melanie shook her head. They were led to a small two-top close to her usual table, but sticking out more in the traffic of the servers. She didn't return any of the stares, just focused on getting seated before she answered Daniel.

The chairs were not pulled back for them; Robert waved at the spread of white cloth and meticulously arranged eating tools and strode away without a second glance. Melanie allowed Daniel to hold her chair and waited for him to settle across from her.

"We can't let them change us, dear," she finally explained. "If we didn't come tonight, would it be easier next week? Or the week after? And where would you have us go, if not here?"

Daniel leaned forward, moving the extra glasses out of the way and groping for Melanie's hand. They found each other and squeezed softly, throwing water on the grease fire popping around them.

"We could've gone out with my people," Daniel said quietly. "Gone to Devo's or Sears, or —"

"Please don't whisper," Melanie begged him.

"Does it sound strange?"

"No. Of course not — it's . . . it's just that I don't care if they hear what we're talking about." She forced herself to say it with an even tone, but the effort made her voice sound abnormal. Mechanical. She didn't care, but the interruption brought a halt to the conversation.

The silence that fell over their table created a pit, a depression into which a dozen hushed conversations flowed.

Unfortunately for Melanie, she'd become an expert at hearing through the noise. Twice a month, while her friends talked about things that didn't interest her, she would sit here in Beaufort's and try to tease single strands out of the tangle. She'd learned to concentrate on the lilt or cadence of a solitary voice, winding that conversation in, honing the ability to drown out the rest.

That skill was now a curse. And Daniel, no doubt, was hearing them as well as she. Dangerous and mean-spirited shards of conversation crowded the already-cluttered table. More utensils meant for cutting. *Supreme Court. Android. Marriage. Shame. God. Unnatural.* It was a corporate meeting on intolerance carried out by the finest minds in the city. A brainstorming session on hate and ignorance that sounded no more informed than the crowds outside the courthouse. Each vile and familiar word probed Melanie's defenses, attacking the steeled nerves that convinced Daniel to come and slicing at the ones that were for communicating pain.

Daniel squeezed her hand. So gentle. The tissue around his mechanical frame was soft and warm to the touch, no different than hers. She looked up from their hands to his eyes and blinked the wetness away from her vision.

"We can go somewhere else," he suggested again.

Melanie shook her head and pulled her hand away from his. She reached for a cylinder of crystal and saw there was no water in it. Looking around for their waiter, she fought the urge to wipe at her eyes.

The sweep of her gaze, as she scanned the room, had a repellent effect. Heads swung away with disdain. All but three who were seated right behind her. Her old table. Her old friends. She couldn't help herself — Melanie bobbed her head slightly in greeting.

"Linda, Susan —"

She didn't get a chance to say hello to Chloe — the woman was already accosting her. "You're *disgusting*," she spat. "You'll *burn*."

She wondered what Chloe meant, taking it literally. It took her a moment to realize her friend was speaking of the old prophecies. Superstitions she couldn't possibly believe. She turned back to her table, the waiter forgotten.

Meanwhile, Chloe's words stoked fires under the other tables, turning up the heat and popping the grease with force. Insults were hurled, mixed with foul language. *Screwing. Bestiality. Fucking. Hell. Damnation.*

Daniel's eyes were wide, pleading with her. They glanced over her shoulder toward the exit.

Melanie wondered what she'd expected. Awkward silence, perhaps. An organized shunning, at worst. Or maybe one person she hardly knew saying something rude, and the rest of the country's elite and mighty feeling ashamed for the worst example among them.

But *Chloe?*

The empty chair at her old table would likely be filled by the time they returned from their honeymoon. Melanie could see another potential calendar of court dates looming as Beaufort's attempted to refuse them service. Daniel had been right about this being a mistake.

But he was wrong to think it'd be much different at Devo's. She'd seen the looks from the court stenographer and the bailiff bots. There'd been plenty of androids in the gallery as advanced as he, each of them far more flesh than machine. And not all of them were pulling for change.

It was a lesson Melanie absorbed from experience: you can't be hated without learning to hate back. The system fed on itself. The tension as jobs were lost turning into ire on both sides. Defensive hatred turned into offensive hatred. Tribes turning on each other. They were *all* programmed this way.

Daniel was mouthing his silent plea once more as the chorus of derogatory remarks grew louder. She nodded her resignation and leaned forward to push her chair away. The sudden movement prevented the attack from landing square — the wine streaked through the back of her hair and continued in its crimson arc, splashing to the carpet beyond.

There were gasps all around, more from the anticipation of what might come next than at the outrage of the attack. Several men slapped their palms flat on the table, expressing their approval. China sang out as it resonated with the violent applause.

Daniel was out of his chair in an instant, rushing to Melanie. He slid one arm around her while the other went to the crowd, palm out. He was defending the next attack before it started. Several larger inebriated men took the defensive posture as an invitation. The gesture of peace was a vacuum pulling violence toward it.

Someone grabbed a corked bottle of wine and held it with no intention of drinking it.

Chloe was the closest. She would have landed the first blow, if she could. But Melanie's rage gave the mob pause.

"Enough!" she yelled. *"ENOUGH!"* She screamed it as loud as she could, her voice high and cracking and her hands clenching into little fists with the effort. She glared at Chloe, who still seemed poised to lash out. "How am I hurting you?" she asked her old friend. She spun around as much as Daniel's grip on her would allow. "How am I hurting any of you?"

"It's not natural!" someone yelled from the back, the crowd giving him courage.

"He's a *machine,*" Susan said. "He's nothing but a —"

"Does your vibrator hold the door open for you, Susan?" It felt good to say this out loud. She'd thought about it hundreds of times when the relationship first started. Always wanted to bring it up. Melanie switched her glare to Linda. "How many times have I heard you *bragging* about how good your 'little friend' is?"

"We aren't marrying our dildos, you bitch." Chloe was visibly shaking with rage.

Melanie nodded, her jaw jutting as she clenched and unclenched her teeth. "That's right," she said. "You married a man forty years older than you. And how much of him is original, huh? We sit here every week and listen to you bitch and moan about your inheritance being wasted, on what? Replacement hips? New knees? A mechanical ticker? Dialysis machines and breathing machines and heart-rate monitors?" Melanie pointed to Chloe's bulging blouse. "Is it unnatural for the old bastard to love *those?* Does he kiss your collagen-injected lips and marvel at how real they feel?"

She pulled herself out of Daniel's protective embrace and whirled on the crowd of ex-friends and old colleagues. She placed her hand flat on her chest. "You people think I chose this?" She turned to her fiancé. "You think I could stop loving him if I just tried hard enough? Could any of you choose to fall in or out of love by force of will? Do you really think you're in control?"

Daniel reached for her again, trying to comfort her. Melanie grabbed his hands and forced them down, but didn't let them go. "We're staying," she said softly.

"We're staying." Louder. For the crowd. "And we're eating. And you can hate us for being the first, but we won't be the last. You can go get your surgeries and implants, you can medicate yourselves according to some prescription-language program, and you can all go to hell with your hypocrisy."

The crowd swayed with the attack, held at bay even if it would take years — generations — for them to become convinced. Daniel guided Melanie to her seat, willing to stay if she was.

"Things are going to change," she said to herself.

"I know, sweetheart," Daniel said.

Melanie leaned to the side to scoop up her napkin, which was fringed with the red wine it wicked from the carpet. Daniel reached it first and handed it to her, careful to fold the stains away where they couldn't spread any further.

"It's coming," Melanie repeated. "And if they didn't hear it today, they need to check their hearing aids."

Mouth Breathers

Cort eyed the school's entrance warily; its double doors were gaped, swallowing children like krill.

He really didn't want to be one of them.

"Mom —"

"We've been over this, son." Melanie adjusted the strap on his breathing pack, jerking his torso around as she cinched it up.

"It's not a parachute," Cort said, frowning.

"Don't talk with your mouth," she told him. She tugged on the other strap, then lifted his chin to make him look at her. "You need to work extra hard to get along, okay?"

Cort grumbled but pushed his breathing tube back in his mouth. He tucked a thumb into one of the straps and tried to wiggle some circulation through to his shoulder. Behind him, the pack whirred purposefully, as if doing something. But it was just a prop to help him fit in.

He nodded to his mom, then waved goodbye to his dad, who sat in the car, his mouth a flat line. He didn't feel like trying to communicate with the machine. He hadn't been practicing like he should.

Cort turned to the hungry building and sulked off, trying to merge with the flow of Martian kids, blending in before they were all swallowed whole. It took every ounce of effort in his ten-year-old body to look straight ahead. They'd only been on-planet for three weeks, so he still had a tendency of walking around like a tourist, gazing up at the ruddy sky beyond the habidome.

It's my last year of middle grades, he reminded himself. *Next year will be even worse.*

Somehow, that made him feel better.

He jostled against a few other kids as the wide column squeezed past the hinged teeth and into the maw. The kids pushed against each other, wading forward, eager to be digested. Cort fought the urge to spit out his stupid tube; he found it hard to breathe through his nose while he was concentrating on it.

He tried to focus on the kid's backpack ahead of him, forgetting about the breathing so he wouldn't panic. Beneath a plastic grille, he could see a large fan spinning, just like his. The only difference was: this one wasn't for show. It actually pushed oxygen somewhere, mixing it with proteins and fluids before circulating the slurry through the kid's lungs.

Cort felt bile rise up in his throat just thinking about it. He quickly accosted himself for being judgmental, remembering what his mom had said —

Something hit the back of his heel, nearly pulling his shoe off. Cort stumbled, hopping on one foot, and knocked into the kid ahead.

The one behind shoved him. "Watch where you're going, freak!"

The kid's voice was perfect. Deep, gruff, and enunciated with crisp precision. Cort didn't dare turn around and try to reply. It would just make things worse.

When the flow of kids started branching, Cort concentrated on moving with the fewer number, trying to find air, some room to breathe. He used his thumb and finger to pull the saliva away from the corner of his mouth, then wiped his chin with the back of his sleeve. He really wanted to tear the plastic tube out, but, impossibly, he was able to resist.

He needed to get in a pod before his head exploded.

Cort followed the masses down another hall, this one lined with individual learning units. He scanned ahead for "unoccupied" lights, but each one was grabbed by one of the other kids, usually a bigger one.

As the crowd thinned, Cort could see an end to the agony — a line of pods with green lights. Two kids wrestled with each other after choosing the same one. Cort slid past and grabbed the next one, practically falling inside before ripping the tube out of his mouth. He sucked in huge lungfuls of glorious air, nearly hyperventilating himself with relief. It had been like a kilometer-long swim underwater, blending in with the fishes.

He bent over, both elbows resting on his knees, and tried to take slower, deeper breaths. Sweat — partly from effort, partly from nerves — dripped off his nose. He rubbed his hands up his face and wiped them off on his thighs.

There was no way he could do this twice a day. Every day.

He wanted to go back to Earth.

The first lesson flashed up on the pod's screen: a mixture of history and math. It leaned heavily on the Martian perspective, looking for calculations with dates he hadn't yet memorized.

After a string of ten incorrect answers in a row, it kicked him down to fourth-grade history, which just made it harder to concentrate.

Luckily, the next few had a mix of Earth dates, but with a strange bias. He keyed in his answers quickly, watching the clock, and got back into fifth-grade history. Once again, the instructor wanted information he just didn't have. Cort wiped more sweat from his brow, which just made the keyboard slick. For the next hour, he felt like he spent more time between the two grades than he did in either one of them.

When the Mathory lesson concluded, he had a few minutes to relieve himself in the suction potty before the next course. He was hoping for Englo-Bio, but got Poli-Theism instead.

He groaned to himself. Not only did he hate politics — he could never tell the Roman and Greek gods apart. He tried his hardest to stay out of third grade, but it was no use. The political structure of Mars made even less sense to him than Earth's. And why teach this stuff anyway? It'd be eight years before he could vote!

He read the questions and typed in his best guesses, his concentration waning and waxing.

Had he known recess was up next, he would have at least enjoyed the opportunity to breathe freely, unmolested.

At the end of the Poli-Theism lesson, Cort's morning report flashed up, along with a list of the people it would be sent to. He wondered if his mom would be one of those doting and bored parents, waiting on the real-time status update for everything their spawn were up to.

He looked at his dismal performance and hoped the report would get flagged as spam and never be delivered. In a smaller window, an instructor popped up and informed them that it was recess, a map underneath him showing directions to the gymnasium.

Cort immediately felt the urge to use the suction potty. He wondered if he could just stay in the pod, if anyone would notice. The sight of the three cameras mounted to the testing wall provided the answer. Not a good idea.

He took a deep breath and inserted the tube, trying not to think about breathing through his nose. The door behind him popped open on its own; he turned around to see the opposite wall disgorging a line of students. In the pod directly across, a mane of blond hair spilled around a face — a face as pretty as one can be with a tube pumping oxygenated fluid into it.

Cort smiled, but the flash of niceness was lost in a sea of passing kids. He waited for the flow to weaken before moving out into the hall and trailing along with the other stragglers.

The games were already underway when he arrived in the gym. The sounds of metal clashing against metal drifted up from the pit, the kids along the balcony leaning forward to look down through the glass.

The upper level looked completely full, so Cort followed some kids heading down a flight of stairs. They came out in an identical room — a large, rectangular doughnut of a balcony overlooking the gym's pit — and the kids ahead of him took the few remaining spaces.

One of those spaces had been right beside a wild mane of blond hair. Cort felt his heart thumping in his chest. The girl turned, shifting her chair over, as another boy took the space beside her.

Once again, their eyes locked. Cort felt his breathing constrict even more. He started to wave, but someone knocked into his back, sending him sprawling forward. Scrambling to his feet, he rushed to join the kids moving down another level, his cheeks burning with embarrassment.

The nearby spots were already taken on the lowest level. That was fine with Cort; he wanted to sit on the other side. He fought the urge to run and shuffled as fast as he could, working his way around the balcony. He ignored the clashing of the large robots beyond the glass.

On the other side, he took one of the empty spots directly across from the girl. He could look up through the glass and see her blond hair waving as she concentrated on the games below.

He had to tear his eyes away to view the action. Dozens of robots clashed across the parquet floor of the gym, each one controlled by a team of kids.

He looked at his controls. He'd been assigned to the green team, left leg. Cort saw his robot immediately, but the lower-level seat meant it was hard to gauge the overall action. He grabbed both his sticks as the AI relinquished control of the green bot's left leg, handing it over to him. Pushing and pulling on the two sticks, he did his part in keeping the thing upright, watching his display for instructions from whoever controlled the head.

The stress and exertion forced him to hold the tube with his teeth, breathing around it and through his mouth. He did his best to not be a hindrance. Cort wasn't very good at bot-ball, but at least he could keep his side of the green team upright, not tripping over anything. He even had a few good plants while the right leg got some good shots off. It wasn't bad playing a support role, especially since he didn't make a fool of himself.

In the first fifteen-minute period, they got two shots on goal and did adequate damage to the yellow bot. Everyone received the exact same score, of course, but Cort kept his own tally and thought his team had done well. Not that he would say such a thing. Not on Mars.

When the horn sounded, signaling the first intermission, Cort glanced up to catch the girl's attention, maybe see which team she'd been on.

But she was gone.

He looked around as the kids on his level ran for the exit to get refreshments and use the public suction potties. Cort used the time to gather his breath. He watched the kids file out of their level, all in the same direction, clockwise around the glass partition. He turned back to his controls.

The blond girl sat beside him, arriving from the opposite side.

"Hello," she said through her computer.

Cort reached up and pushed the breathing tube back in his mouth, biting down on it hard. He concentrated on the words, forcing them into the computer. "Nice see you," he said.

He shook his head, his forehead breaking out in a clammy sweat, and tried again. "Nice to you," it came out.

The girl looked away, through the glass partition and across the gym's pit. Her hair — that close — it was like staring at liquid gold. Cort wanted to reach out and touch it, or smell it. He felt dizzy.

"Talk with your mouth," the girl said through her computer. She looked around to make sure they were alone. "I want to see."

Cort felt like he was going to wet his pants, he was so flustered and anxious. He looked side to side before pulling the tube out, allowing it to hang from his pack. He turned his head away while he wiped his mouth dry.

"My name's Cort," he said, looking back at her. It was all he could think to say.

"Riley," she said. She stared at his lips. The computer made her voice ring with a sonorous and pleasing tone. Cort wanted to be able to speak like that. But with a boy's voice.

He smiled at her.

"Did it hurt?" she asked.

"Did what hurt?" Cort glanced up at the balcony above. Some of the kids were returning to their seats, holding colorful refreshment canisters up to their breathing tubes.

"Your first breath," Riley said. "They say it hurts real bad, and that all Earth kids have to go through it. They say it makes you scream."

"I don't remember," Cort said. He licked his lips, self-conscious of doing the opposite of what his mom had told him.

"It was that bad?" Riley asked. "Have you blocked it out?"

Cort shook his head. "I don't think so," he said. "I actually don't remember much before I was five."

Riley brushed some of her golden hair back. Cort saw one of her ears poking through, white and smooth. It made her look like an elf princess or something equally mysterious and regal.

"And it doesn't burn? The air?" She leaned forward, staring at Cort's mouth.

It made him want to cover his mouth with both hands. Or open it up and let her look inside. Or both, somehow.

He shook his head. "It doesn't burn at all." He watched the fluid circulating through her breathing tube. "How does that feel?" He pointed shyly toward her mouth. "Is it like drowning?"

Riley's computer laughed for her. "No, silly, this is how we are even before we're born. I can't imagine my lungs empty, the way yours must be."

The corners of her mouth turned up around a little, a dimple forming in one cheek. Cort recognized it as a smile. And pretty.

He started to say something about her hair, but she cut him off.

"You should put it back in," Riley said, pointing to her own tube.

Cort looked around and saw the kids coming back from intermission. He put his tube back in and turned to compose something for Riley, concentrating on the words as hard as he could.

"Like our talking," it came out, the computer voice stilted and awkward.

The corners of her mouth tightened again; she spun out of the chair with a wave of golden locks, then went running around the balcony, back to the stairs.

Cort looked sheepishly down at his controls, which were counting down the resumption of the games.

Time being the only numbers the system kept track of.

"How was school?" Melanie asked.

Cort jumped in the passenger seat, spitting out his tube and trying to get comfortable with his pack pressing into the seat.

"Don't you know?" he asked.

"I didn't look at any of the reports." She put the car into gear and merged with the flow of heavy traffic moving past the school. "I wanted to wait and hear it from you."

Cort thought about telling her all about Riley, and that first intermission, and how he was going to use the same pod tomorrow, and hoped she'd do the same, except he'd try and walk with her to recess next time, and maybe they'd be on the same team, and she could talk about what it was like to breathe amniotic fluids, and he could blow air through her hair, and let her see what that was like —

"It was okay," he said, his mind reeling. "I got busted down to fourth grade," he added, figuring she might as well hear it from him.

His mom reached over and tousled his hair. "I'm sure you'll be back before you know it," she said. "Did you practice your talking?"

Cort nodded. "Yeah. A little."

And he vowed to practice some more that night. Really, this time.

WHILE (u > i) i- -;

WHILE (u > i) i- -;
    {

The scalpel made a sharp hiss as it slid across the small stone. Daniel flipped the blade over and repeated the process on the other side. Each run removed a microscopic layer of stainless steel, turning the surgical edge into something coarse and sloppy. He referred to the simple rock as his "Dulling Stone." It had become a crucial part of this once-a-week ritual. The problem with sharp blades, he'd discovered, was that they hardly left a scar.

He leaned close to the mirror and brought the scalpel up to his face. Several years ago, when he'd made his first wrinkle, he could have performed this procedure from across the room. The focusing and magnifying lenses in his then-perfect eyes could tease galaxies from fuzzy stars — but those mechanisms were no more. They'd been mangled with a surgeon's precision. Now he needed to be within a specific range to make sure his cutting was perfectly sloppy.

He chose a nubile stretch of untouched skin and pressed the instrument to his forehead; the blade sank easily into his very-real flesh, releasing a trickle of red. Daniel kept the blade deep and began dragging it toward his other brow, careful to follow the other ridges in their waves of worry.

As always, the parallel scars reminded him of Christie, Melanie's young niece. When her parents discovered she was cutting herself, they'd asked Melanie for help. And Melanie had asked Daniel, as if he would understand such a sickness. Cutting to relieve anxiety? He'd had no answer for once. And he was so smart back then. If they asked him now, of course, he'd be able to tell them — Ah, but nearly everyone involved was dead now, and —

He was making too many connections; recalling too many links with his past. His mental acuity was out of control; the blade hadn't traveled a centimeter, and he was thinking about a dozen other things. Parallel processing. It wouldn't do. He assigned another twenty percent of his CPU cycles to the factoring of large primes. The world sped up around him as his mind slowed to a crawl. Now it was moving too fast, not him.

As his logic gates were overwhelmed with new computations, instructions meant for fine-motor servos became delayed. His hand slipped and parallel lines touched. An old scar was torn open. Blood leaked out in a stream as Daniel fumbled for a tissue. He noted the shakiness in his hand, the difficulty he had turning spatial commands into physical motion.

Better, he thought.

He dabbed clumsily at his forehead to wick away the mess he was making. The new wrinkle was outlined in oozing red — but it wasn't complete. He picked up a small blue vial, the perfume it once contained lingering, triggering olfactory sensors just acute enough to register the floating molecules. It reminded him of something, but he couldn't seize it. The failure was another sign of progress.

He tapped out a small pyramid of coarse sand into his palm, pinched some of the powdered stone between two fingers, and pressed it into his new wound. He was careful to grind the fine shards deep enough to trigger his tear ducts. Past the pain that warned him of the permanent damage being caused.

None of those systems had been dulled, of course. There'd be no cheating.

He grabbed another tissue and dabbed it across his forehead, removing the excess blood and grit. Before more could work its way out, he smeared a layer of skin adhesive over the rubble-filled canyon. He smiled at the warning on the first-aid tube — it prescribed, in several languages, the necessity of cleaning out the wound before applying. He worked the edges of the tan gel as it congealed, blending the fake skin into the real.

He surveyed his work. The lines radiating out from the corners of his eyes could be denser, but he'd save that for next week. He skipped to his hair, which was coming along nicely. He allowed himself a bit of fine-motor control for this part, removing 512 strands in a long-established pattern. Next week he'd ramp up to 1,024 hairs a session, he decided. Soon it'd be 2,048 follicles destroyed each week. He also needed to change the dye formula. Move past the snow-on-slate and begin a full bleaching.

Cosmetically, he was satisfied. He moved to his least-favorite portion of the ritual — the part he always saved for last.

Memory.

It was a routine within a routine. First, he culled specifics, sorting through his banks for two momentous occasions to completely erase. The pizza party in '72 was still in there. He would miss it, but there were few easy choices left to make. He deleted the entire day without looking at it too hard. He had made that mistake too many times. He also took out something recent, a movie he'd watched a few months ago. Gone.

Next came the roughening-up. He still had plenty of good memories set aside for this process. He chose the honeymoon. It had only been hit twice before, so he could still recall most of the week. This wasn't a full deletion — it was more like bisecting a holographic plate. You still had the entire image when you were done, but with half the detail.

He made the pass, wiping 1s and 0s from his protein memory at random. It was like shading his cheeks with blush, smoothing everything out and tapering it just so. He glanced briefly at the wedding night to see what was left, but it was hard to say without knowing what was gone.

The final step was the one he dreaded the most. Random memory deletion. It went against his primary programming, both the degradation of awareness and the arbitrariness of the maneuver. He triggered the routine with a grimace. He'd long toyed with the idea of changing the algorithm, making it so he wouldn't even know what was being lost — but he never went through with it. He always wanted to know. Even if it was just a brief glimmer before it winked out forever.

Some of his best memories had been sacrificed in this way. They would flash like fish in shallow water, darting out of sight as he plunged after them. And he couldn't help it; he always plunged after them.

This time — he got lucky. It was the day in Beaufort's with Melanie. One of his few bad memories left. The details were already gone, but an overwhelming sense of disgust lingered, leaving a bad taste on his tongue receptors. *Whatever that was — good riddance,* he thought.

Daniel forced a smile at his reflection — the scar tissue around his eyes bunched up. *Much better,* he thought. Or worse, depending on how one looked at it. He continued factoring large primes and rose unsteadily to his feet. The mechanical linkage in his left leg had been built to take a pounding, but his arms had been even better designed to dish one out. He could feel the metal rods grinding on one another as they struggled to bear his weight. He had to lurch forward, shifting his bulk to his less-damaged leg as he shambled toward the door.

He fiddled with the knob and limped into the hallway. A flash of movement to one side caught his attention. It was Charles, one of the male nurse-bots, leaving Mrs. Rickle's room. The android had a tray of picked-at soft foods in his grasp; the various mounds were swirled into a thick, colorful soup.

Synthetic eyes met and Charles smiled — raised his chin a little. "Big night tonight, Mr. Reynolds?" he asked.

"Hello, Charles. Yup. Scrabble night."

"Scrabble tonight, huh? Well, I hope she goes easy on you, old fellow."

Daniel smiled at the reference to his progressing age. It was kind of him to notice, to nurse along the ruse. "She never goes easy on me," he replied in mock sadness.

Charles added the tray of half-eaten food to his cart and sorted some paper cups full of pills. "Would you mind delivering her medication for me? You know how Mrs. Reynolds feels about . . ." The android paused and looked at his feet. ". . . my kind," he finished.

Daniel nodded. "She's getting worse, isn't she? About treating you, I mean?"

Charles strolled over to deliver the medication. "It's fine. Like I always tell you, she's done enough for my kind that I'll stomach a little — unkindness."

The nurse-bot turned back to his cart.

"Either way, I'm sorry," Daniel called after him.

Charles stopped. Spun around. "You ever hear of a woman named Norma Leah McCorvey?" he asked.

Daniel leaned back on the wall so his bad leg wouldn't drain his batteries. "Didn't she pass away? She lived two halls over, right? The woman with —"

"No, no. That was Norma Robinson. Yeah, she passed away in '32. Norma McCorvey lived, oh, over a hundred years ago. She was more famously known as Jane Roe."

Daniel knew that name. "*Roe v. Wade,*" he said.

"That's right. One of the biggest decisions before your wife came along . . ." The nurse-bot studied his shoes again. "And people remember her for that — for the decision. They remember her as Roe, not as Mc-Corvey."

"I don't follow," Daniel told Charles. He eyed his wife's door and fought the urge to be rude.

"Well, most people don't know, but years later — Norma regretted her part in history. Wished she'd never done it. Converted to one of the major religions of her day and fought against the progress she'd fostered. I just . . ." He looked back up. "I'll always remember you and your wife for the right reasons, is all." He turned to his cart without another word and started down the hall.

Daniel watched him go. One of the cart's wheels spun in place; he wondered when Charles would finally get around to fixing that. Favoring his bad leg, he shuffled across the hall to Melanie's door. It was shut tight, as usual. He knocked twice, just to be polite, before pushing it open. A familiar lump stirred on the bed, changing shape like a dune in a heavy gale.

"Who's there?" a raspy voice croaked.

Daniel went to the sink and poured a cup of water. "It's me. Daniel. Your husband."

She rolled over, long white hair falling back to reveal a thin, weathered face. Wispy brows arched up in a look of surprise that had become her state of rest. "Daniel? Dear? When did you get here?"

"I live across the hallway, sweetheart." He said it patiently as he crossed to her with the two cups.

"Of course. That's right," she said. "Why do I keep forgetting that?"

"Don't worry. I forget stuff all the time. Here. Take these."

Melanie labored to sit up straight, grunting with the effort.

"Honey, use the remote. Let me show you . . ." Daniel reached for the bed controls, but his wife waved a fragile arm at him, shooing his words away.

"I don't trust the thing. And I don't trust whatever that damned robot is wanting me to swallow."

Daniel sat on the edge of the bed and held the first cup out to her. "He just delivers what Dr. Mackintosh prescribes, dear. Don't take it out on the messenger. Now, swallow these; they'll make you feel better."

She shot him a look as she threw the pills on her tongue. "I don't wanna feel better," she spat around them.

"Well, I want you to. Now drink."

She did.

He set the paper cups aside and smiled at her, trying to help her forget her bad mood. "Do you feel like a game of Scrabble?" he asked. Thirty years as a lawyer, winning rights for his kind, had filled her head with a vocabulary that computers were envious of. Even though she couldn't string them together into rational ideas — not anymore — the words were still there, ready to be pulled from confounding racks with too many consonants.

"Scrabble night?" Her eyes flashed beneath the webs of cataracts. "You mean 'Bingo Night,' right?" False teeth flashed with the joke, a reference to her rack-clearing skills with seven- and eight-letter words.

"You call it what you want, but Charles said you should go easy on me tonight."

"Fuck Charles. You tell that abomination—" Melanie stopped, her eyes widened even further. "Sweetheart, what did you do to your forehead?"

Daniel moved a hand up to his brow; it came away spotted pink, the drippings of a future scar. *Too many primes,* he thought.

"I must've hit it on something," he lied. "You know how clumsy I can be." He turned to the sink to smear the fake skin a little, making like he was tending to the wound.

"You weren't always clumsy," Melanie called after him. "I remember. You used to be so strong and agile — but at least you haven't gotten any less handsome."

"Thanks, dear."

"You're welcome. Now set up the board while I get my robe on — Oh, and I must tell you about the awful dream I was having before you came."

"I'm listening."

"Oh, it was horrible. We were younger, and married, but you weren't you — you were one of those damned androids, and in the dream I was covered in rust, and, oh — It was terrible."

"That does sound awful," Daniel admitted.

Melanie swung her feet over the edge of the bed and reached for her robe. "What do you think it means?" she asked.

Daniel unfolded the board and set the tile dispenser in place. He stopped factoring primes for a moment.

"Probably nothing," he lied. "Just a bad dream. Random."

"Nothing's random, dear. Take a guess." She rose and joined him by the card table, placing one hand on his shoulder.

Daniel turned to his wife of nearly sixty years. His every processing unit was racing for an optimal solution to her query, but it was like looking for the largest prime. It was something that didn't exist.

"Maybe you're scared of losing me?" he tried.

Melanie raised a hand — bone wrapped in brown paper — and placed it on his cheek. "But, in my dream, I think I hate you."

He pulled away from the touch, and in his auditory processors, the sound of neck servos seemed as loud as turbines, a dead giveaway. "Don't say that," he pleaded. "I don't think I could go on if you ever hated me."

"Oh, darling" — she wrapped her hands around his arm and pulled him close — "I didn't mean to upset you. You're right. It was just a dream, nothing to it."

Daniel encircled her with his arms, steadying their embrace with his good leg. *Just a dream,* he thought. How badly he wished that were so. His protein memory cells went idle, awaiting further instructions. He held his wife. Servos whirred quietly in one knee, fighting to keep the rest of him upright.

Melanie opened her mouth to say something — but then it was gone. She'd forgotten how she got here.

Daniel considered, briefly, doing the same.

}

AFTERWORD

Some stories are laboriously written, and some are discovered. The act of writing has been likened to a story using the writer as a vehicle of expression. The author is the lightning rod; the words spark from clouds. We see this when ideas seem to reach a critical mass and pop up across culture. A broad swath of philosophy looks for expression everywhere it can, like a tube of paste squeezed and squeezed until it comes out all along the seams.

When John Joseph Adams and I edited an anthology together several years ago, we were both surprised (and delighted) to see a handful of submissions that dealt with homosexuality and questions of equality, even with stories set against the backdrop of the apocalypse. It wasn't a coincidence, of course. The topic was everywhere; it has been one of the civil rights issues of our shared time; as speculative writers we were all exploring this theme.

"Algorithms of Love and Hate" was the first of several of my works to explore the ever-changing idea of equality. Too often we make progress in one area only to find ourselves pushing against the next. Or we find ourselves progressive in one area and stodgy elsewhere.

In my novel Half Way Home, *I point this out explicitly: that our current modern selves will be seen as backwards to future generations. We make progress in areas of race, but can't abide same-sex marriage. We solve that, and find ourselves scrapping sentient robots for spare parts. We expand our circle of empathy again, only to find yet another deficiency.*

The point isn't that we should expect moral perfection, or that we can know all objective moral truths, only that our smugness should be kept in check and our judgment of past generations should be tempered by recognition of their progress and our own failings. Too often we seem to think that barbarians are in the past and that we've reached some pinnacle. I think the climbing never ends.

Virtual Worlds

The Plagiarist

I

Adam Griffey lost himself in the familiar glow-in-the-dark sticker. It was a depiction of a bee alighting on a flower, a thirsty proboscis curling out of the insect's cartoony smile. The sticker held Adam's attention. The glow of the bee made it seem radioactive, a poisoned thing. It adorned the edge of his beat-up computer screen, the edges curling away as the sticker lost its grip. The remnants of several other stickers stood idly by, just the bumpy adhesive outlines, the colorful bits having long ago been peeled away by Adam's fidgety hands. He was prone to scratching at them with his fingernails. They weren't his; they came with the old monitor, which he'd bought off another faculty member. Adam figured it belonged to one of their kids, what with the stickers. He thought about that as his eyes fell reluctantly from the bee and back to the screen. There was a message there, a series of messages typed back and forth. They populated a chat window, the only thing open on his screen. The window suddenly blinked with a new question:

lonelyTraveler1: you still there?

Adam picked at the edge of the radioactive bee, thinking of tearing it off. He read back over his conversation with Amanda, his responses in deep blue, hers a bright red. She had asked him a question before he'd gotten distracted. How long had he gone without responding? What would she read in that silence?

His fingers fell to the keyboard, leaving the sticker for another time. He sat motionless, unsure of how to respond. Thoughts whirled. Adam read the second question up. He read it over and over. Where the fuck had it come from? From nowhere, he decided. He had gone too long without reply; he decided to ignore the older question and answer the more recent one:

Griffey575: Yeah. Sorry about that. Doing too much at once.

lonelyTraveler1: you chatting with other people at the same time? you cheating on me? ;)

Adam glanced over the sad and empty expanse of his monitor and laughed to himself. Twenty-four inches by twelve inches of pathetic nothingness. His entire social life, his entire *real* romantic life, could be contained in one small chat window in a lonely fraction of that abyss.

Griffey575: I wish.

He typed the response, then held down the backspace key to erase the truth before he could send it.

Griffey575: Work stuff.

He decided that was better. Adam wondered if it counted as a lie if the untruth was as boring as reality.

> lonelyTraveler1: what kinda stuff? for a class you're teaching? are you writing anything? anything you can share?

Adam saw how lies could spawn more lies, each offspring bigger than its parent. The truth was, he'd been neglecting his work and his writing. Possibly, in no small part, because of Amanda's constant badgering to read more. She was — if not his online girlfriend — at least his anti-muse, the woman whose insistence quenched all motivation. Adam had known this of himself since he was an undergrad: he couldn't think when being told to.

> lonelyTraveler1: you still haven't answered my other question ...

Which one? Adam thought.

> Griffey575: Which one?

He hit enter before he could regret asking. He knew which question. He didn't want to know, but he did. His stomach lurched with the audaciousness of her suggestion. And what did that say about him? How could he have a fake relationship with the real, and a real one with the fake? Which relationship was *more* real? Which was sicker? And who was the victim? Was anyone really being betrayed?

> lonelyTraveler1: don't you think it's time we meet up?

There it was again. It was crazy.

Griffey575: In person?

lonelyTraveler1: how else?

Adam watched the cursor blink where he was expected to respond. The glowing bee radiated stored sunlight in his peripheral. In the utter darkness around him, he sensed the piles of clutter everywhere. He kept meaning to get to it. He kept the lights off in his apartment, kept the blinds drawn, so he couldn't see the reminders of his laziness. The bee dimly betrayed him with its steady glow.

Griffey575: This way seems nice.

After the barest of pauses, he added a smiley face:

Griffey575: :)

It wasn't sarcasm. It wasn't real humor. It was an apology, something to soften the blow of what he knew to be the wrong answer. Adam had replied incorrectly; Amanda's silence confirmed it. An icon came up to let him know she was typing something. It disappeared for a moment, reappeared, then disappeared again. He was watching her think. He wondered what things had been erased, if it was anger or disappointment she was refraining from sending.

Griffey575: I think I'm just not ready.

He wondered if that sounded better. It at least filled the silence.

lonelyTraveler1: I'm gonna find out you're married, aren't I?

Griffey575: I'm not married.

Such lies were not in him. Such a life, perhaps, was not in him.

lonelyTraveler1: but there's someone else.

Griffey575: There's no person else.

Clumsy. The sentence sounded stilted, but it kept his response, strictly speaking, from being an outright lie.

lonelyTraveler1: I won't push you. just think about it. or at least write me something, write me something about why you'd want to or not want to.

A pause.

lonelyTraveler1: I feel like we're living in 2 separate worlds lately.

Adam laughed nervously. His fingers left the keyboard and moved to rub his sore temples. For a brief moment, just an insane instant, he considered telling Amanda the truth. He pictured typing all the craziness of his life out in one uninterrupted, suicidal message. He imagined her sitting there, staring at the icon that let her know he was typing for hours and hours while he crafted a biopic admission of how scary and surreal and demented his life had become . . .

He deleted the thought.

Griffey575: I do have a piece I haven't shared.

His mind was suddenly in a spilling mood — as long as it was spilling *other* things. It sought release of some cryptic truth. There were thousands of haiku that Adam kept to himself. They lived in his head, swirling beneath the layered façades, keeping him company. The impulse to let one out became great. He figured he could trade it for the impossible thing Amanda was asking, this meeting each other in person. Perhaps a bartered poem could delay the inevitable.

> lonelyTraveler1: oh. PLEASE!!

> Griffey575: Just one, then I really need to get some sleep. I have an early class.

> lonelyTraveler1: is this a new one? when did you write it?

When did he write it? He couldn't exactly remember. All his life, Adam had wanted to be a writer. The problem was: he was too good at *reading*. He had too many of Shakespeare's sonnets memorized. Too much Blake and Shelley and Proust. All that good stuff was crammed up in his brainstem, pooled in his pons, dripping down his spine, now a part of his very fiber. Trying to sneak a sham of his own writing past such a gang of real McCoys was impossible. Adam's great gift — knowing the good from the bad — was also his failing. The only words of his own that he could sneak through his literature-stuffed brain were his little haiku, unassuming and light on their feet. They were like neutrinos streaming out from the dense center of a star, cruising across the cosmos invisible and unknowable.

> Griffey575: About a year ago I think.

He hit enter, let the words come to him from memory.

Griffey575: Here it goes; then I need to get away from this screen:

Moments spill through hands
idling away at nothing
To puddle in years

Adam logged off, but the chat window remained open. It held another uncomfortable conversation he could scroll through and regret. He read over the poem and realized that at that very moment, Amanda was reading it as well. They were both *seeing* it for the first time. It was as if some part of him had been excised. Released. Set free and exposed.

He wondered how much of him she would see in the poem. Could it be read in any way other than the obvious? Full of regrets? A loser continuing to lose?

Not for the first time, he tried to imagine what Amanda looked like. Not that it mattered, but the human brain seemed to need to know. Eyes were used to engaging with other eyes while voices crossed. They were too accustomed to scanning faces for revealing twitches, the curl of lips, the flare of nostrils. Speaking in nothing but font was unnatural and stifling.

Adam gave the webcam above the psychedelic bee a nervous glance. It wasn't plugged in, never had been; it came with the monitor. Still, it felt like people could see him sometimes, see the real him stripped of his avatars. Not Amanda, not his mother or sister or anyone he knew — he felt like millions of *strangers* could see him in his dark and filthy room, like they spent hours watching him, like they knew him better than he knew himself.

Adam closed the chat window, turned off his computer, rubbed his eyes. It was so late, it was early. And Amanda had been right, even if she'd only meant it as a figure of speech: they *were* spending too much time on different planets. The haiku, he thought, captured that all too well. So much simplicity and truth in seventeen syllables. And now it was out in the world and no longer rattling around in his brain. He laughed to himself, scratched the beard sneaking out of his skin, then saw the hour and realized he had time for neither a nap nor shower. Not if he was going to see his other girlfriend before his eight o'clock class.

2

Between these temples,
aching and burning and sore
my universe lies

He only had two hours before he had to be at class, but the simulator would make it feel like six. Blazing computer chips worked much like morning dreams, compressing time. It made living two lives all that much easier.

Adam used his faculty pass to swipe his way to the labs, then picked one of the jacks in the far corner. He had the room to himself, six in the morning being too late for most and too early for all, but he still went for as much privacy as possible, knowing he would probably have company before he jacked out. There were only a few reasons to hit the sims at certain times of the day, prostitution being the foremost. Adam wished the stigma weren't true in his case. He wished.

The seat squeaked as he settled into it. Adam swiped his ID through the reader; the beeps and whirrings of the booting machine were as familiar as a favorite song. And like music, they did something to his autonomic nervous system: his sleepless brain felt a jolt of energy, a dangerous surge of love and lust. He took his temple pads from his backpack, untangled them from each other, then wiped the cups off on his shirt. A dab of adhesive grease went on each, then he pressed them to the sore points on either side of his head — points he could feel without having to check the mirror. The burn there had become constant.

Adam waited impatiently for the simulation to boot. This was the longest part of his day. He could compress all the rest of his hours right into these handful of moments, he was sure. It was also the time when he truly reflected on what he had become, what he was about to do. It was in these moments that he truly loathed himself.

The lab disappeared as the sim took hold. The twinkling lights of the idling machines all around him were replaced by alien constellations. Adam floated in the center of an artificial cosmos. He was God. He could go to any dozens of planets and planetary nebula, observe tectonic plates shifting with x-ray vision, or zoom to the level of the protein and watch the molecules fold as salinity and temperature shifted. His choices were limitless, but of course he had no choice. He hurriedly selected a familiar star out of one of the constellations. The star was named Beatrice Bond-eamu Gilbert III, after the donor who paid for the servers on which it was hosted. Artificial stars were like academic halls: a few million dollars and your name lived on forever.

He aimed for the fourth planet out from the star, nestled right in the Goldilocks zone. The glowing blue-green ball was named Hammond after Beatrice's late husband. Adam "chose" the planet with his mind. It was as simple as looking at something and wanting it. He wanted it.

There were a million ways to approach the planet. If from the entomology department, one might swoop through the night clouds like a bat, virtual sonar picking up invisible bugs to collect. The climatologists would play like gods bored with their food, sitting over the clouds and swirling them with their fingers, taking notes, testing theories. Geneticists would become the size of molecules and be lost in worlds the scope of Mendelian peas, causing mutations. Adam had little use for such scientific probings. He remained much as himself, if a little taller, thicker of hair, more tan, and less paunchy. His virtual being emerged from a bathroom stall in a bookstore he had claimed as his own territory — had paid quite well for it, in fact. He pushed open the door and nodded to a customer walking by.

Hammond was one of a handful of humanoid planets where evolution had been rigged to emulate Earth's. As such, it was not as jarring to be an avatar as some xeno-sims could be. It felt perfectly natural to nod to someone who didn't exist, who was just a bunch of ones and zeros. The computer-simulated customer smiled and nodded in return. It, of course, thought it was real. The customer thought the book it was about to pick up and peruse was real. It thought the sunshine streaming through the front windows, and the grime streaked across those windows, and the dust floating in the air like a grid of stars, and the clatter of bells whacked by an opening door — every simulated person in the entire bookstore thought every single bit of it, including themselves, was all real.

Adam soaked it in. He wanted it to be real as well.

"Hey!"

He turned. Belatrix stood behind him, her green work apron hanging around her neck, two creases running down it vertically from having been meticulously folded the night before. Curls of brown hair hung like springs behind her ears. Her bright eyes smiled at him, crinkles radiating away from their corners. "I didn't see you come in," she said. At least, that's how it was translated for Adam.

Belatrix showed him the small stack of books she was shelving, as if to apologize for not hugging him. Adam smiled what he knew to be a perfectly symmetrical smile full of brilliant teeth.

"I kinda snuck past to the bathroom." He waved a little wave to forgive the lack of a hug. Adam glanced at the books in her hands. "You getting off soon?"

"I am."

She was. Adam knew she was. He had chosen the time carefully when he logged in. Belatrix smiled at him then slid a book into place. Adam tried not to think of the *other* him, the fleshy him, and the *real* world wait-ing and spinning around him. He gave himself up completely to the sim.

"How was work?" Belatrix asked as she pushed open her apartment door and shrugged off her coat. It had drizzled on their walk over from the bookstore. Adam wiped his feet on her mat, then kicked off his shoes. Details like the mud, the shiny drops of water on the tile — he still marveled at the completeness of the illusion, the scope and scale of the digitally constructed world. It was easy to lose oneself in it, to become be-wildered by it all.

"That interesting, huh?"

Adam broke out of his trance and helped Belatrix hang her jacket on the hook by the door. "Work was fine," he said. "Closed a pretty big deal this week."

He was sure it was true. When he wasn't present to fill and steer his avatar, the computers moved it about as autonomously as anyone else on planet Hammond. Belatrix, in fact, had probably spent more time in his avatar's place of work than he had.

"Some tea?"

"Sure," he said, even though he hated the stuff. It wasn't tea, but that was the closest translation for the language parser. Horseshit would have been more apt, but the translator stuck to categories such as "warm bev-erages." The only thing it left untouched were proper nouns, which left Adam's avatar with the moniker of Phurxy, a dreadfully common name on Hammond's Southwest continent.

"Bitter apple?" Belatrix held up a grainy lump of spice. Again, the translation was a mere approximation.

"Please," Adam said. It made the hot horseshit taste more like wet dirt, a distinct improvement. Adam often considered fast flowing the time through these bits, but the domestic foreplay was a crucial part of the fantasy. *This* was the life he wanted to live, here with Belatrix in her tidy apartment. He took the steaming bowl and glanced in the mirror at his clean and neatly groomed self. His avatar had taken the time to do that in the morning, brushing his teeth *and* his hair. It felt like room service for the body and soul. He luxuriated in his sense of self.

"*Seamonsters and Mist* is opening up at the cinema this weekend." Belatrix took a loud sip and looked at him over the rim of her bowl. "You wanna go see it?"

"Love to," he said. It felt amazing to make plans for his avatar's time, knowing he wouldn't have to go — but that he would. He drank as much wet dirt as he could take, set the bowl aside, then plopped down on one of the floor cushions. "I'm feeling kinda horny," he said with a grin.

Belatrix smiled and set aside her bowl.

Adam could get away with saying such forward things — he could rush the moment with her — because he didn't do it often.

He did it every time.

3

Even these false worlds
with their oceans and vast plains
can't hold all my lies

Adam arrived late to his eight o'clock class. His students were already there, sitting like powered-down robots, gazing ahead, awaiting commands from him. He closed the door — too loudly — and felt annoyed by the quiet. He would've preferred the film cliché: balled paper flying; kids sitting on desks swinging their feet; boys with bravado and girls with batting lashes twisting in their seats. In all his years of teaching, he'd never seen such a scene, not once. It was always the blank stares, the lethargy, the sense among them that the first who moved or uttered a word would be eaten by the others — or, worse, be made unpopular.

Adam dumped a stack of papers on his desk and made a show of arranging them, anything to disturb the thick silence of the room. He resented his eight o'clock class. He knew they felt the same way, but what were they missing? More sleep? Escape from their hangovers? He was missing an entire other life he preferred to live, a life that was daily truncated by a day job he wished he didn't need. He thought this as he scanned their faces, all a weird mix of wide eyes and boredom. If it weren't for the access to the university server farms and their sims, he wouldn't put up with the kids at all. Well, the sims and the health care. The health care was nice.

He shuffled papers around and tried to glean from graded assignments which class this was. He had nothing planned for the day. He rarely did of late.

The hypocrisy of Adam's new existence, the layers and layers of hypocrisy, was always right at the surface, staring back at him. He had become a master of procrastination. Like the students he had long mocked, he had honed the art of putting things off until they were simply never done. He lived under a heavy blanket of shirked responsibilities; they weighed on him every moment, this great pile of many things that needed to be done. He no longer knew where to start. It was all about getting through each moment, getting through the day to enjoy the nights, faking his real life so he could live his fake one.

More hypocrisy: Adam used to mock his kids for their addiction to video games — now he lived in one of his own. He remembered his disgust at virtual marriages between players who had never met, stories about trolls and paladins exchanging digital vows. Now he had one girlfriend he had never met, and he discussed marriage and kids with another person who didn't really exist.

Then there was the plagiarism — his greatest hypocrisy of them all.

"Does somebody want to pass these out?" Adam gathered up the graded assignments and waved them with one hand. He hadn't actually taken the time to read them, just verified that they existed. A student he particularly loathed, seated to Adam's left, was the first to volunteer. The boy took the papers eagerly. Adam rubbed his palms over his eyes and his fingers through his unwashed hair. The plagiarism was his greatest hypocrisy by far. If any of his students plagiarized, they would be flunked. They knew that from the start. It was the greatest sin as a student, as a thinker, and it was a temptation they struggled to avoid. Adam, meanwhile, did it for a *living*. His second job, the one that paid most of his bills, was to steal the words of others. But lately he hadn't even been able to summon the motivation to do that. While the papers, marked with their red checks and little else, fluttered their way through the room, an old conversation with his mother came back to Adam. He remembered the first time he had tried to explain his new vocation, and how unimpressed she had been.

"I'm just so proud of you, honey!"

"Thanks, Mom." Adam held the phone under his chin, the speaker angled away from his face. The extra distance dampened the earsplitting scream of his mother's voice, who seemed to think her words needed extra force to cross the two time zones between them.

"My own son, an author." Adam could picture her gingerly lifting each page of the book as she skimmed through it. "Cindy from my bridge club bought a copy. We're racing each other to the end, but not so fast I can't enjoy it."

"That's great, Mom, but you do know —"

"I really love the Marsha character. When she tells Reginold to get out of his own house —"

"Hey, Ma?"

"I love that part. Yes, dear?"

"You're not telling people that I wrote the book, are you?" Adam nuzzled the phone against his ear and pulled on the silence. He could hear his mother's exhalations on the other end, breathless from excitement. He didn't call as often as he should.

"Your name is on the cover," she said. "Adam Griffey. And you dedicated it to your mom. That's me."

"Mom, I *discovered* the book. We've talked about this. It says it right there with the copyrights."

"But this is your book." The pain in her voice was gut wrenching.

"Yes, and the royalties are mine, and I get a lot of credit with some people for discovering it, but it wasn't written by me. Please don't tell Cindy or any of your other friends that I wrote the book. I don't want to have to explain it on holidays —"

"So who wrote it?" Her voice had gone quiet. Adam could hear her flipping through pages, could almost picture her weathered fingers quivering as she did so. He had told her about this. He remembered telling her about this.

"Mom, do you remember the worlds I told you about? The simulated ones where people here at the university study the weather, and the way the plates of the crust move, and how stars and moons form and all that?"

"The video games?"

Adam sighed. He looked from a pile of dirty laundry to a moldy mound of stacked plastic dishes rising out of the sink. He had none of the time for this.

"It's similar to video games, Mom, but a lot more complex and a lot more useful. People do real good research in there. That cure for testicular cancer that's been all over the news? It came from one of these worlds."

"They cure cancer there?"

Adam felt like he was teaching his mother to perform brain surgery over the phone. *Keep your index finger extended along the back of the scalpel, like so, but a little bent. You've got the cordless drill charged up? Make the first incision —*

"They do a lot of things on these worlds, Ma. They're a lot like *this* world. People get up and drive to work. It rains and things get wet. They erect buildings, and the windows need washing after a while. And people write books and plays and poetry and whatnot."

"And someone on this world wrote this book?"

"Yeah."

"And you just took it?"

"Ma, you know these people aren't real, right?"

"So they don't mind? Do you tell them?"

"No, we don't . . ." Adam thought about it. They *would* mind, wouldn't they? "Mom, we can't exactly tell them that they aren't real, that we created them and we really like their work so we're gonna share it in the real world."

"Why not?" His mother grunted, sounding disgusted with him. "I thought I raised you better."

Adam slapped his palm on his chest. "It isn't up to *me*, Ma! I don't make the rules. Besides, I don't think you could convince these people. They think they're just as real as you and me. They'd probably lock you up in a padded room until you logged off."

"Logged off—?"

"Forget it, Ma."

"What am I supposed to tell my friends?"

"Tell them I'm really good at what I do. Tell them that I can memorize fifteen pages in a single session, word for word. Tell them there's no way we can copy stuff straight out of the quantum drives, Mom. Say that. Tell them 'quantum drives.' Tell them that there are hundreds of thousands of people trying to do what I do, to find that one great work of art in a sea of tripe, and most of them can't. Tell your friends that I'm really good at seeing the true genius among the piles of plain stories. Tell them that *I'll* be the one to find the next Shakespeare, Mom."

"But you won't tell him?"

"Tell who?"

"This new Shakespeare. You'll memorize his stuff, and you won't tell him."

Adam cradled the phone to his ear and let out his breath. "He wouldn't believe me, Ma, even if I did. These people aren't real. It's like a video game, just like you said."

"So Marsha and Reginold —"

"Those are characters in a book written by a virtual person." Adam said it slowly.

"But they're in love with each other."

He sighed. "I suppose they are. In their own weird way."

"How did a video game write about that?"

"Hey, Ma? I gotta go. I've got a class in an hour."

"Does your girlfriend, does Amanda know this is what you do?"

"Yeah," Adam lied.

"And she's okay with it?"

"Of course." He rubbed his temples.

"When am I going to meet her?"

Not before I do, Adam thought.

"Soon," he said.

"Okay. Well, I still like the book."

"Thanks, Ma."

"Even if you did steal it from some poor person."

4

The ones and zeros
like snow, descend and blanket
my eyes, forming all

Adam patted his pockets as he left his apartment, making sure he had his keys. It was winter; the days were short. A blanket of black hung over the campus, and a blanket of white covered the ground. He shut the apartment door too hard, rattling the windows. Of late, all doors seemed to close too hard for him or not at all. They were slammed or left wanting. It was about motor control, and Adam was losing his. He looked back to the shuddering window and saw his reflection. The scruff on his jaw measured the long nights, nights such as these when he should sleep but couldn't. Despite his fatigue, he remained awake, a diurnal creature in the opposite of day.

"Griff?"

Adam turned to find his friend standing at the bottom of his apartment's stoop, freshly falling snow gathering on his knit cap like stars shaken from the darkness overhead.

"Hey, Samualson."

"You ready?" Samualson asked. He had a look of concern on his face, a look Adam was getting used to seeing. His friend was a decade older than him and half a foot taller. A neatly trimmed beard and fitted coat lent him a professorial look. He seemed more the English scholar than Adam felt, even though he was a member of the hard sciences. The two of them had become friends after seeing each other in the labs every night. They found there was something less pathetic about coming and going to the sims with another *real* person.

Adam shrugged his bookbag over his shoulder and followed Samualson down the walk. The campus arranged across the valley below was illuminated by tall night lights and the sliver of a waning moon. The snow on the ground and in the air seemed to gather and magnify the light. The shallow impressions of footsteps littered the ground, already half full again with falling snow. Adam hurried up beside Samualson, their boots crunching and squeaking in the wet pack.

"Hey, did you hear?" Thick smoke streamed out with Samualson's voice, the moisture of his breath crystallized in the cold night air.

"Did I hear?" Adam tugged his gloves on and patted them together. "Did I hear what? I hear tons. I hear too much."

"Virginia Tech." Samualson turned his head as a gust of wind brought cold and a flurry of blown snow. "Their farm got razed."

"Razed? As in gone?"

"Every single server got deleted. Formatted."

"You're shittin' me." Adam tucked his scarf into his collar. "When? Last night? Today?" He couldn't believe he hadn't heard.

Samualson groped in a pocket and drew out an orb of light, the glow of his phone dazzling the snow. "Just now." He flashed the screen at Adam. "Read about it on the walk over. They think the Writers Guild might be responsible, but, again, nobody's taking credit."

Adam shook his head. "How are they doing this? That's three farms wiped out this month."

"Yeah." They turned a corner around the administration building, entering its lee and escaping the bitter wind. "Three farms went online this month and three others got hosed. That's pretty weird."

Adam's exhalations billowed in the air in front of him before trailing off behind. He pulled his scarf over his mouth. "How many worlds was Tech simming?" His voice was muffled and wet against his nose.

"Sixteen. Four humanoid and the rest xeno. I work with a guy who had remote access to some of them. He's gonna be crushed. Was in the middle of some good research there."

"Sixteen worlds. Fuck me, that's a lot to lose." Adam glanced up at the sliver of a moon hanging over campus.

"They're saying something close to eighty billion sentients are gone. No telling how many lesser critters."

"Or works of art," Adam reminded him.

Samualson shrugged and stuffed his phone away. His hands were pale blue from the cold. He dug in another pocket and pulled a pair of gloves out, then wiggled them on. "That's your domain," he said.

They shuffled in near silence across the campus. Adam could hear the tinkle of invisible sleet hitting the crust of snow around him. It was a small campus, which kept the jaunts short, but it was hilly and made faculty and students alike prone to gasping and wheezing. The university was kept small by necessity, nestled down and crowded in by three rising slopes, like two bosoms and a great belly, all perched on the thin sternum of a high mountain valley. It was a place that caught snow and gathered high-flying and lost souls. Adam considered that as they reached the Madison Mitchell Jr. Computer Science building. He stamped snow off his boots while Samualson fumbled through his ring of keys. Adam watched a snowflake fall on the back of his glove, the white standing out on the black for a moment before the edges of the fragile crystalline structure folded up into a drop of water. The clarity of the transformation was stunning.

"Look how real all this is," he said aloud, not meaning to.

Samualson turned and studied his friend, a shiny key pinched between the padded fingers of his glove.

"You feeling okay? You look like shit, man."

Adam glanced up from the falling, melting stars. "How does it feel this real when we're in there?" He jerked his head up at the building. Samualson turned back to the lock, inserted the key, and opened the door, which squealed on frozen hinges.

"I take it you don't dream much."

Adam laughed and stomped snow off his boots. "I don't even *sleep* much anymore."

"Well, if you slept more, you'd dream more, and you'd see how good your brain is at making something out of nothing." He held the door open for Adam, who shuffled through, followed by a dusting of snow.

"You know there's a spot in the center of your vision where you can't see, right?"

"Where the optic nerve goes through the retina." Adam nodded. He didn't see the connection.

"Your brain fills in that blank spot perfectly." The door clanged shut behind them. "I was talking to a professor in the bio department about this a month ago. You know what he said? He said roughly thirty percent of everything we see is hallucination. It's our brain smoothing things over so the world's not so *pixelated*." Samualson nodded down the hallway. "That's how everything in there feels just as real as this, as real as our dreams." He patted Adam on the back, letting loose a small avalanche of clinging snow. "Seriously, man, you've gotta get some sleep. Why don't you take a night or two off? These worlds aren't going anywhere."

"That's what Virginia Tech thought."

Samualson laughed. "Ours are a pittance compared to that. Nobody's gunning for us."

Adam shrugged, and the two of them fell silent save for the squeak of their wet boots. He imagined — or hallucinated — that he could hear the collective roar of billions of tiny whispering, virtual souls as they approached the interface room. He thought about the server farm nearby with its tall cabinets of computer equipment adorned with blinking lights. Hundreds of busy little mechanical arms clicked back and forth somewhere inside the quantum hard drives, like the arms of miniature gods waving over a dozen digitized worlds, creating and destroying all the time.

5

The connected few.
Billions of neurons and souls.
So few connected.

The interface room was packed. Adam had rarely seen it so full during a night shift. Usually they would find a lone professor or technician in the room working late. Adam preferred it like that, preferred it more when he had the place to himself. He worried his facial twitches or some uttered word would give away his romantic trysts. He'd never gleaned anything from Samualson that made Adam think his friend suspected, but still he worried. The two of them often mocked those who jacked in to jack off. It was no secret lots of professors did. Regular porn had nothing on virtual whores who didn't even know they were virtual, and tenure had been revoked over particularly exotic sprees. Adam justified what he did because he was in love, or thought he was.

"Damn," Samualson said, seeing the crowd. "Is there a rally tonight?" He glanced over at the scheduling board where groups signed out clusters of terminals for virtual meetings. One of the bigger groups on campus was the cycling club, a habit more loathsome than jerking off in Adam's opinion. These people actually simmed bicycle riding. They spent their time on foreign worlds, riding bikes, their brains flooded with endorphins from simulated exhaustion. Adam could always sense when he was interfacing right after a cyclist. The seat would remain warm for hours, the stench of sleep-sweat in the air. It was disgusting. The fact that most of them were grossly overweight didn't help.

"There's two over in that corner," Samualson said.

Adam flipped his backpack around and dug for his temple patches. He followed his friend through the busy room.

"What're you searching after tonight?" Samualson asked. He sat down in front of one of the terminals and squeezed gel from a tube and onto his finger. "That elusive Shakespeare?"

Adam laughed. "I've given up on finding him." He plugged his temple patches into a pair of cords dangling from outlets on the wall. "There'll never be another Bard of Avon."

"That children's series you picked up last year seems to be doing pretty well." He dabbed gel onto his temples, checking the placement in the small circular mirror mounted on the wall in front of him. Adam did the same; they looked like performers getting ready for a show, an apt illusion.

"That series is drivel," Adam said. He smiled at his friend's reflection. "Don't get me wrong, the royalties are good, but I'd rather have the hours back I spent memorizing them."

"Or the brain cells."

Both men laughed as they began pressing the interface pads into the dabs of gel. Adam tried to ignore the blue crescents under his eyes as he secured the connection. Sleep had become as virtual, as ephemeral, as his work.

"So whatcha after, then?" Samualson wouldn't leave the line of questioning alone. The machines at their feet hummed to life, leaving thick seconds to fill with banter.

"I'm dabbling in art, actually." He glanced at Samualson and hoped the shame of the lie would adequately mimic the shame of the truth he was hiding.

"Art?" His friend chuckled softly as he pressed the pads to his temples. "Good luck with that."

"It's all luck," Adam admitted. "Are you still working on that same protein?"

Samualson flipped open a pad of paper and touched a pen to his tongue, a nervous tic more than a functional act. The woman interfaced on the other side of him twitched, her head leaping up from her folded arms then crashing back down again. "Yup," Samualson said. He slid pages up the spiral-bound pad to find his place. Adam saw line after line of four letters repeated: CTTGACATGCA ... It seemed like mind-numbing work. He imagined his friend peering into a virtual microscope, or cyclotron, or whatever biologists used, and memorizing a few hundred letters at a time — jacking out — writing them down — jacking back in. It gave Adam a headache just thinking about it and made him appreciate his own work. If they transcribed a few letters the wrong way, a cure for liver cancer might instead turn a poor kid into a glow stick. If Adam got a word or two wrong, nobody knew or really cared. Unlike his brief haiku, the sheer mass of a full-length piece of writing could absorb a handful of mistakes.

The machine at Adam's feet beeped, letting him know he had a connection to the school's server farm. Adam liked that it was called a "farm." He smiled at the thought of worlds springing up from plowed rows of dirt, cloudlike shrouds unwrapping to reveal blue and spiral-green planets of life. The word "farm," of course, was a holdover from the clusters of computers, the server farms, used at places like Pixar, where virtual worlds were created for entertainment. It took a while before the productive uses of such worlds were understood. Once they were, the result was often referred to as the third great agricultural revolution. Sim farms, in just the last decade, had sprouted all over the place. Government-owned, university-owned, even a few private ones. The flood of research from these farms drowned out all the work done in the real world. A theory would be published in the morning and overturned by mid-afternoon. Planetary formation and plate tectonics; punctuated equilibrium and mass extinctions; arsenic-based life forms and exoskeletons. If you weren't jacked in, you weren't playing.

Science became exciting again overnight. It moved to the forefront much like the days of the great space race in the previous century. Everyone wanted the red blisters on their temples from too much virtual time — the badges of important work being made. Universities and even high schools changed tack overnight, catering to the surge in computer science and math majors. The hard stuff dominated the soft sciences, and the liberal arts soon clamored for a place on campus. This scientific renaissance lasted three years — and then there was Dylan Pyle to restore order.

Adam's temples began to heat up as the interface computer booted. His thoughts turned to Dylan Pyle as the connection took hold.

Eight years ago, nobody had ever heard of Dylan, nor should they have ever. A biology research assistant with dim prospects, Dylan transformed overnight into the greatest living author of all time. His debut novel, *Whispering to Ghosts,* won every award it qualified for, and some that were marginal. He followed it up with a crime novel that rewrote all the rules, and then came a young adult tome as successful as it was massive. The only thing more surprising than this young man's mix of prolificacy and talent was his refusal to take his writing career seriously. "I dabble," he would say in rare interviews. "I'm a scribbler, nothing more." The reticence to accept his talent, the reclusiveness, the desire to stay on as a humble research assistant, to pour himself into his lab work — it all served to heighten his fame. The glass bubble around him survived three years of awe and praise. It shattered when a fellow researcher discovered Dylan's secret: the boy had a single talent, one of near-photographic memory. He was found in one of his research worlds reading a novel in a park and committing the prose to memory. Selecting from the top writers of several worlds, he had translated their genius into his own, word for word, colon for colon.

Adam felt a tingle at the base of his skull, then a buzz like electric zippers pulling back over his crown; his skull seemed to split in half. He shivered with the out-of-body experience, the sense of his *self* floating out the top of his head before it was sucked back into his gut. He grunted, heard an utterance by Samualson get cut off by the transfer, and then he was gone. He was joining the legions of plagiarists who had followed in Dylan Pyle's wake, soaring down to artificial worlds, scraping them dry of their great art before the scientists were otherwise done with them.

There should have been an uproar, Adam thought. There should have been controversy over what Pyle had done. There should have been outrage. Those would have been normal human responses to having been duped. But a stronger impulse seized the popular imagination: the ability to be great *overnight.* It was a new type of lottery, one where fame and talent were won rather than simple money. The heyday of the sciences came to a sudden close. Discoveries were still made, of course. Real progress was won in astrophysics, biology, psychology, and other fields. But suddenly, the science wings and computer science centers were overrun with talentless hipsters who thought they had an eye for genius. Courses on memorization were invented. Adderall replaced coffee as the recreational drug of choice. Server farms groaned under the stress. Temples were seared. Tubes of adhesive gel were rolled dry.

The *Anti*-Renaissance ensued. As Adam logged into his account, he shivered at the memory of it. Hell, he was still living it. The outpouring of *stuff,* of *crap,* was so intense, nothing could be seen or heard. The variety and quantity were too much. It was a repeat of what YouFilm did to cinema, what Auto-Tune did to the music industry, what genetic splicing had done to sports. The bar wasn't raised so much as buried under the pile of crap.

And offline talent, *actual* talent, rebelled. Farms were attacked, physically, by supposed bands of marginal musicians and writers. The artists and the avant-garde became the new bomb-chuckers. And meanwhile, consumers were pulling away from it all, paralyzed by the sudden confusion of too much choice and novelty. Entire industries suffered.

The interface lab fully dissolved, and an entire universe of simmed worlds appeared before Adam. Here is where he would've, a year ago, agonized over the choices available to him. So many worlds full of so many pages of written words, all of them open to his perusal. But it had been a long time since he'd really chosen. He was now more an automaton than the sims he lived among. He moved his virtual self, shifted his awareness, and went to select the planet where his loved one resided —

And that's when Adam Griffey saw the deletion notice hovering above the planet.

6

It may be erased,
all that is written. Destroyed,
all that's created.

The deletion notice loomed massive over Hammond. Large white numbers on a red background flicked as they slowly counted down the planet's final moments. Adam felt his real stomach drop, back on Earth. He felt all the emotions of shock and rage and sadness, even as he floated bodiless through the void. His plans for the night were over. His plans for the week were over. He didn't have any plans else. Adam's existence had suddenly become as vapid as this simulated consciousness in the black. He was death.

As he floated closer to the planet, he saw that there were just over two hours left, sim time. Two hours for Belatrix to live and breathe. Two hours for him to do nothing for her. It was around eleven-thirty when he'd logged on, so the deletion must be slated for midnight, Earth time. The end of the day. The end of *all* days for the people of Hammond.

Adam had a sudden and strange urge to log out and tell Samualson, to let him know that *this* was the reason for the packed interface room. It was Hammond. He imagined the remote access groups would be going nuts as well, logging on from universities and access points all over Earth. It would be a free-for-all, grabbing what data they could, performing wild experiments that would break the suspension of disbelief for the planet's inhabitants. Adam had watched from a distance once while meteors rained down on a planet where some decent playwrights lived. He hadn't even had time to finish memorizing a work he'd been in the middle of, one with quite a bit of potential. That play took up half a notebook in his apartment; the too-hopeful idea was that he'd finish it himself one day.

Despondent and not knowing what to do, Adam drilled into the countdown's menu to look for the slated reason for the planet's deletion. It made no sense to log off and tell Samualson; his friend would see for himself, or he'd find out later. Besides, he suspected there was some other reason he wanted to log off. He felt as if he were dangerously close to coming clean about his affair. He had the urge to make Belatrix real by dragging her name back to his planet; he wanted to yell and scream at someone to not do it, to call off the erasure.

Adam felt all this — he felt anxious and desperate as he continued to drift ever nearer to Hammond. The truth of it began to fully set in. The woman he loved, virtual or not, would cease to exist in two hours. She'd be gone forever. She had been diagnosed with something terminal and sudden.

Adam read the deletion report:

> With the advent of their own simmed worlds, planet Hammond has placed undue stress on our server farms. Planetology research will be suspended, to be resumed once the world re-accretes around the star Beatrice Bondeamu Gilbert III, as per the astronomy department's request. All sociological studies will be terminated forthwith. Deletion is slated for midnight, February 21, 2022.

Adam's dimensionless body sped past the message, his mind absorbing it numbly as he went. Why did they have to delete the entire planet? Why not destroy the server farms on Hammond? Why not just delete those? They can rebuild a planet, but not the people. The people would be different. Their writing would be different. Their food and names and language would be different. Their bookstores and the people who worked there would be different.

Adam didn't want different.

He slid into his usual avatar with the shiver of numbness turning to sensation, like new skin pulled over unfeeling muscle. The clouds of Hammond parted as Adam chose his arrival destination; bright sunlight winked out, replaced by the dark interior of the bookstore's bathroom. Adam fumbled for the light, then the doorknob. They were in the same place as before, but it took him a moment. He had become uncentered from himself. As he stepped out into the smell of fresh pulp and horseshit tea, the tiled floor below him seemed closer than it should be. His mind was spinning; he wondered what he would say, what he was even doing here. His shameful and wonderful trysts were over. His love was gone. He wouldn't have to think of anything to tell his mother. He wouldn't have to worry about his father spinning in his grave, or his sister finding out and being humiliated for him. He didn't have to lie to Amanda or Samualson. He didn't have to burn with embarrassment under the unknowing glare of his students.

As he weaved through the stacks of books, Adam became dizzy with all the implications and outcomes. He wanted none of it, not even the relief from this burden. He would gladly lie for another year, another month, another week, just one more day. At least a full day to process it. A day to sit in the park with Belatrix and break the news, maybe even let her think he was crazy. There was so much of her world she had never seen, places Adam had flown over, invisible, and wanted to take her. He hurried down the line of registers, looking for her. She wasn't there. Where were the customers? There was a commotion outside. Adam looked past the displays of bestsellers, through the glass, and saw that the cars in the street were at a standstill. Horns blared in the distance. Someone was screaming, the voice muted. Adam whirled around and realized he was the only one in the store. Him and a single cashier, who was emptying the register and stuffing his pants. Adam didn't recognize him; he was pretty sure he didn't work there.

"Where is everyone?" Adam asked the man.

"Fuck off! These are mine."

The man moved to another register and began pounding buttons. Fans of colorful bills flopped above his belt. A car roared outside, pulled up on the sidewalk, and rumbled by, scattering screaming pedestrians. Adam watched it squeal out of sight, then he pushed the glass doors open and hurried outside.

"There's another one!" someone screamed. The crowd moved as one, heads turning to follow an angled arm and a pointing finger. Eyes were shielded against the midday glare. Adam turned and looked up as well. A massive flying saucer rumbled overhead, ridiculous lights splaying out of it. The thunder of explosions grumbled in the distance, sending shivers of panic through the crowd. Adam couldn't believe it. Of all the sociological experiments to level on the Southwest continent, an alien invasion had to be the dumbest he could think of. What was the point? How had this request won out? Unless it was for some professor's amusement. He pushed his way through the crowd toward Belatrix's apartment, thankful they hadn't picked a flood or meteor impact for the area. He spotted a few other researchers in the crowd, their remote access icons blinking visibly — to Adam at least — above their heads. One icon sported University of Miami colors; another was a generic deep red that could've been from dozens of schools. They seemed enraptured by the panicked crush of people. Adam made sure they weren't looking and broke all rules by teleporting his avatar out of the packed streets. He appeared above Hammond for just a moment, then zipped to the apartment hallway, saving himself the walk. An elderly couple was staggering down the hall, clutching one another. They gasped at the sudden presence of Adam, materializing out of nowhere. He ignored them and pounded on Belatrix's door.

"Bela, open up."

He heard something squeak inside the room, like a tight drawer being pushed shut.

"Who is it?"

"It's me. Open up."

The knob jumped; the door flew open. Belatrix stood there, hair veiling her face in loose wisps, her eyes wide.

"How did you get here so fast?" she asked.

Adam moved inside the apartment, his hands on her shoulders. She was trembling.

"I hurried right over."

"I just talked to you," she said. "You were at work."

Adam wasn't sure what his avatar had been doing before he arrived to borrow it. He rarely knew.

"I was already on my way. You called my portable, remember?"

Belatrix scrunched up her face, swiped the hair off her eyes, and tucked it behind her ear. "I must be confused. It's — The world has gone nuts. What're we gonna do? What's *happening?*"

She looked toward the windows. Adam noticed the blinds had been drawn. Why was he lying to her about how he got to her apartment? What good did that do? Didn't he come there planning on telling her the truth? What good would *that* do? Was it better for her to go without knowing, to die thinking that she was real —?

Die. Why did he keep thinking about it like that? *Deleted.* She didn't exist. None of this was real. He had to fight to remind himself of that.

"Honey? Are you okay?" Belatrix put a hand on his chest, another around his waist. Adam realized he probably looked worse than she did. What was really about to happen to her planet was far more sinister, more permanent, more *real* than anything she could dread from the fake flying saucers.

"I have to tell you something," he said, even though he didn't yet know what he wanted to say.

There was an explosion outside; the windows rattled, then the vibrations could be felt in the floor. The building was swaying. Adam had never been on the ground level of a deletion before. It was terrifying and authentic. He couldn't believe how *real* it felt. Raw terror coursed up through him as he lost his center yet again. He had a brief pang of doubt that this world *was* real and that he was about to die. Perhaps his life at the university was some sort of delusion, and he really worked at Telematics Express on Hammond, selling accounts to —

Belatrix was screaming, her hands pressed to her cheeks. More rumbles of destruction sounded in the distance. Somewhere, avatars probably floated above it all, soaking up the data while their fleshy bodies sat in a room a billion virtual light years away. Adam's body was in that room as well. He tried to remember that.

"None of this is real!" he screamed, voicing his thoughts. The building moved again, or his balance was gone. He wasn't sure Belatrix heard him over her own screams. This was no way to say goodbye.

Belatrix's arms went out for balance. She looked around the room, eyes wide with a sudden look of concentration and desperation. "We have to go," she said. She hurried to her purse, dug around until she came out with her keys. She scanned the room for what else.

"It's no better anywhere else," Adam said. "There's something I have to say."

Anger flashed across her face. "Not now —" she began.

"None of this is real," Adam said again. He threw his arms wide and spun in a slow circle, accusing her entire world. "There are no aliens outside. There *is* no outside. This planet isn't real."

Belatrix dug out her phone and started dialing someone. She kept a wary eye on Adam. He realized how pointless and sad all this was, how impossible it would be to convince her with words, so he disappeared. He logged off, then reinserted himself near the ceiling of her apartment, teleporting as he had before. He lessened his personal gravity and drifted slowly toward the floor, his arms stretched wide and his knees bent. Belatrix dropped her phone. Her jaw hung agape.

"Sweetheart. Listen to me. I need you to know something." His feet reached the ground; Belatrix hadn't moved. "It's impossible to believe, I know. It's impossible to even explain, but this world is a virtual construct. It's an illusion created by my people on another planet —"

Her eyes darted toward the windows. Her lips and hands trembled.

"No." Adam stretched an arm toward the chaos outside. "I'm not with them. Those flying saucers aren't real either. It's —" He needed more time to explain. "Have you read about the simulations in the news? Did you know your world has created entire other virtual worlds? Computer systems have gone live recently where entire planets evolve and thrive so people can do research."

Belatrix nodded. "I've heard," she whispered. A lump rose and fell across her throat. She was terrified.

Adam pressed his palms toward the floor. "This is a world like that."

She shook her head. Fires crackled outside like paper being balled up and twisted. Adam could smell smoke.

"I know it's hard to imagine —" Adam waved at the room. "But all this is a simulation, just like the worlds your people have begun to create."

"But *you're* real." Her voice was a squeak. It was meant as a question. She didn't believe him.

"I'm real. And I came here because I need you to know that what we have between us — it's been the only thing in my life lately that's *felt* real."

Tears dripped from his chin, and Adam realized he was crying. He didn't know the simulation could do that. He didn't know why it wouldn't be able to, but he was surprised. Belatrix took a step toward him.

Something in her face changed. Wide, disbelieving eyes had narrowed with suspicion. The teleportation trick, calling him at work and him showing up at her door, the absurdity of the scene outside the window, some internal doubts perhaps that had already been there —

"I'm ashamed of us in my world," Adam said, sobbing. "I'm living more of a lie than you are."

Belatrix reached out and held his arms. Her hands were shaking terribly. Tears were welling up in her own virtual eyes.

Adam wrapped her up. He could taste the salt of his tears on her neck. He wanted to take her with him, to teleport out and drag her back to reality, but she had no body there to inhabit even if such a thing were possible. A deeper part of him wanted something worse. It wanted to stay on Hammond, to die right then with her.

"I'm so sorry —" he said.

"Shhh."

She was comforting *him*.

The rumbles outside faded, leaving the wail of many distant, fearful screams.

"It's not fair," Adam whispered to no one.

"What's going to happen?" Belatrix asked.

He squeezed her tightly. "I wish I could save this —"

Adam wasn't sure if he meant the moment, her planet, Belatrix, or just the feeling of a better existence.

"What happens next?" she asked. "If you're right, if this isn't real, then what happens next?"

Adam went to kiss her, to feel the soft and warm sensation on his lips, as real as anything in the universe, one final time —

But there was no time.

His avatar automatically logged out as the planet he had been on ceased to exist.

7

I am digital
with the physical. And the
other way around.

The interface room buzzed with human energy as Adam logged out. Laughter and chatter, the static of giddy elation, surrounded him and left little room for his dull sadness. Professors and researchers exchanged notes from their various and varied disaster scenes, the thrum of their enthusiasm drilling into Adam's head. He tugged his temple pads off the wires, then slowly peeled them from his head. He sat there, looking at them for a moment, then wiped the crust from his eyes. Samualson was still deeply interfaced beside him, his chin resting on his hands. His notepad of squiggly letters had grown over the last half hour. Adam wondered if his friend might have heard him yelling or crying as he repeatedly logged out to jot notes. He realized how little he cared, even if he had. He no longer wanted to hide Belatrix from his world; he wanted to share his memories of her.

Someone bumped into the back of Adam's chair, causing him to drop his temple pads. An apology was offered. Adam felt like killing the man. He felt like deleting something to make room in this world for Belatrix. He never felt anger like this, not this murderous rage. Such fury took more energy than he normally had. He suddenly felt a great reserve of it.

He stood and jostled his way through the joyousness, terrified by his own anger. A different crowd mingled outside. The thick glasses and rows of pocketed pens meant the planetary crowd was wasting no time forming a new world where Hammond had once been. There would be so much new empty space on the quantum drives. All those qubits were gone. The astronomers would get their accretion disk to mold a new world with.

The joy on their faces, the anticipation, it reminded Adam of how he felt logging on each night. For them, the empty space around a star was like lover's lips to Adam. One man's heart was shattered to make whole dozens more. But these men could freely discuss their passion. There was no shame, no lie, nothing hidden. Adam remembered feeling that way about his literary discoveries once, long ago. He had had friends in the English department, people he drank coffee with, ate with. Now he had a girlfriend he'd never met and a love who had never existed. He wasn't yet forty and he might as well be dead.

He *felt* vaguely dead as he stumbled out the building and into the freshly fallen snow. Adam should have gone home. Distantly, he knew that. He hadn't slept in two nights. He went to the cafeteria instead and drank coffee. The taste and the heat of it felt far removed from him. He listened to the clamor from the kitchen, the rattle of plastic trays and clang of silverware and chatter from the night crew. He watched the cashier flip slowly through her romance novel, scratching her head through her hairnet now and then. Through frosted glass, he could see a veil of snow begin to descend on campus. He wondered if there would be enough to cancel his morning class. Somehow, he knew he wouldn't be teaching that day even if they didn't call it off. He was going to be sick. He already was sick.

He nursed his coffee until the last sip was cold, went to grab his backpack, and realized he'd left it in the lab. He'd left his gloves in there as well. He had his jacket but couldn't remember putting it on. The analog clock on the wall let him know he'd been spacing out for hours. A group in lab coats sat in a booth across from him, gesturing excitedly for the late hour. Adam didn't remember them coming in. He wondered if he'd slept. It would be nice if he had.

He went back out into the cold. The snow was the wet kind, sticking to his hair. Adam pulled his hood up and thought briefly about heading back to the lab, then realized he didn't care about the backpack. He trudged up the walk toward the library — another of the sleepless buildings on campus. He knew all the sleepless buildings well.

The policeman behind the night desk waved in recognition. Adam dipped his head. He sank into a chair by the periodicals and tried to sleep. He gave up as the sun eventually peeked over the mountains and the students began to emerge from their dorm caves.

The snow had ceased; it wasn't enough to close campus. Adam knew he needed to call the department secretary, let her know he wouldn't be coming to class, but even that required some semblance of motivation. He needed an excuse to not call in sick. He wasn't well enough for even that.

The long walk to his apartment was chewed up one lumbering step at a time. Up several walkways, around the education building, up, up, up more steps. He pushed down on his knees to force them to work. The snow to either side seemed inviting. Adam imagined spreading out on the wide blanket of it, letting the cold erode away the last of sensation. He would sleep forever and never wake, never feel. He willed himself to do it, could *feel* his insides moving that way, but the shell of him kept staggering forward and up the steps, taking the rest of him home with it.

He could barely feel the keys in his numb fingers. He couldn't tell the door was already unlocked as he worked it open. Adam was too far gone to notice the puddles on the linoleum as he crossed the foyer and into his living room. It was several moments, even, before he realized someone was sitting at his computer.

"Hello?"

A woman spun around, a worried frown breaking into a brief smile, then back to the worried frown.

"Hello, Adam."

He didn't know this woman. Was this his landlord's wife? He tried to think who would have a key, or a reason to be here. Why would she be on his computer? Adam needed sleep.

"I'm Amanda."

The woman rose from the chair and took a step toward him. Adam was too tired to recoil. If she hadn't been standing by his computer, the name wouldn't have registered as one he knew. With the computer in the background, though, it made sense.

"Amanda?"

This was his girlfriend, the one he chatted nightly with, his *virtual* girlfriend. She nodded.

"Are you okay?" She touched her own face while gazing at Adam's. She looked worried. Everyone gave him that worried look of late.

"I haven't slept," Adam said. "What are you doing here?" He was simply curious. He strangely didn't care, couldn't quite manage it.

Amanda looked around the apartment. Adam saw the clutter through her eyes. He noticed the tall piles of debris had been raked flat, like fall leaves pushed back to their former state. A dim awareness told him Amanda had been going through his things. He almost cared.

"I thought you had an early class," she said.

"But why?" He shook his head, clearing the cobwebs. "You've been here before? How do you even know where I live?"

"I'm sorry about this." She waved her hands at the room. "But I couldn't wait. I couldn't."

Adam held up his hands. "I need sleep," he said. "I can't handle this right now. I can't even begin to think about it. I've been up three days straight."

He staggered toward the bedroom. He didn't care that his online girlfriend was in his house. It almost felt natural. *Inevitable.* Some part of him processed that she was prettier than he'd imagined she'd be, but even that couldn't douse the growing surety that he no longer wanted her as a part of his life.

Amanda followed after him. "Adam, I need your writings."

"My what?" He mumbled it to himself as he reached the bedroom door.

"Your writings. All of them. I need them now."

Adam leaned on the knob. His head was throbbing. He shook it, and the entire planet seemed to wobble around him. "You need them now."

"Right now. I'm sorry to have to ask, but I can't find them."

Adam turned away from the door and scanned the room. He glanced at the old computer. "They're not there." He waved at his head. "They're in here."

Amanda visibly wilted. She looked at her watch. "How many haiku haven't I heard?"

"I can't do this," Adam said. "I need you to leave. You shouldn't have come here."

She didn't look all that upset to hear this. She took a step toward him.

"Did you hear about Virginia Tech?" she asked him.

He remembered something about Virginia Tech. He couldn't quite place it.

"Their servers," Amanda said.

Adam nodded. "Yeah," he said. He remembered Samualson saying something. None of this made sense. He just wanted to sleep.

"Tech has already duped the data from MIT to their own servers. They have a dozen worlds already up and running this morning. Dozens more are coming online at universities all over the world." Amanda frowned. "Did you know your South Korea went online with their own virtual world last week?"

"*My* South Korea?" Adam fell sideways against the doorjamb and remained propped there. He was going to fall asleep standing up.

"I can't keep taking them down, Adam." Amanda looked grave. "It takes too much time. More are going up faster than I can take them down. My boss won't have any more of it, not for the trickle coming out of this planet." She waved her hands around her.

Adam pressed his palms to his sore temples. One girlfriend was deleted; the other was crazy. He slid down the wall until his ass hit the carpet. His head rested in his hands.

"I need anything you can give me," Amanda said. He heard her cross the room, could feel her standing above him. "Three or four haiku. Anything. Please, I wish we had more time."

"Tomorrow," Adam said. "Please leave me alone."

A hand clamped down on his wrist. "There *is* no tomorrow," Amanda hissed. He looked up at her. "Are you listening to me? I know what you do, who you are. I'm a plagiarist too, Adam. You know how this works; I don't have time to explain it to you." Amanda pointed toward his window. "You've got hours left. Your legacy is all that matters. Don't you understand?" She shook her head. "Of course you don't. You have no idea what you mean on my world. You don't know what I've discovered in you."

Amanda stepped away from him. Adam felt bile rise up in his throat. Her words were settling like snow upon his consciousness, forming something like understanding.

"What are you saying?" Adam asked. He looked at his palms, flexed his fingers.

"Please," she said. She backed away from him and looked out the window. The blinds were up. Adam never had the blinds up. "A few haiku. You have to say them to me. I can't copy it straight out of your mind. You know how it works."

"This is *real*," Adam told himself. What she was saying seemed so familiar. He rubbed his fingers together. It felt as real as the sims.

It felt as real as the sims.

"I'm sorry," Amanda said, not for the first time. "I really am. I like you. I — I feel maybe more than I should for you." She bit her lip and looked away. "This isn't easy for me —"

"This is *real*," Adam repeated. He stood up and took a step toward Amanda. Outside, the sun was peeking over the mountains, the clear sky dazzling against the fresh snow. The brightness of it lanced into Adam's brain.

"Say whatever comes to mind," Amanda said. "You'll be remembered for it."

"I'll be remembered," he whispered.

"Yes."

But Belatrix won't be, he realized. It was what he'd wanted to tell her, but couldn't find the words. She was real as long as he'd known her, and would *remain* real as long as he could recall her. Belatrix was as real as anyone he'd known who was now lost. As real as anyone who had become ash, leaving just memories behind with the living. She was as real as his father had been to him. Had his father been real? Was Adam real? Was this some kind of trick? If he was deleted, and the memory of Belatrix was deleted with him, then she was lost for good. His mind spun with the layers and layers and layers: Hammond had started simming their own worlds, placing a strain on the campus computers, so it had to be deleted. What about all those simmed worlds on Hammond when that happened? Adam had considered the loss of Belatrix, of the world and people she knew, but what about the billions of others residing on computers another layer deep? Those people thought they were real. What had they been doing when they were deleted? How few were told in advance?

Adam looked out over campus, at the amazing view from his window that he'd seen maybe once or twice before.

"How long?" he asked. He thought about the hundreds of worlds simmed on Earth. How many had worlds simming in them? Or in *them,* one more layer deep? How many Earths were there on Amanda's world? Could this be real?

"Not much time," she said.

"What if *you're* not real," Adam said. He pressed his hand against the frosted glass and felt the cold beyond.

"I think about that a lot," she told him.

Adam wanted her to not be real. He wanted company in that sudden loneliness that had overtaken him. He wanted to hurt her in some way.

"These things happen so fast," she said. "They reach a tipping point before we see it coming. Believe me, I did everything I could —"

"You were the one razing our farms," he said.

The accusation frosted on the glass by his hand.

"I tried everything I could —"

"Make a copy." Adam turned to her. "Make a copy of me. Or delete more farms." Real or not, he didn't want to cease existing. He felt a surge of panic. Adam looked back over the roofs of the department buildings. "I can pull the plug on our servers. I can. I know where the backup relays are. It'll make some room on your own servers —"

Amanda placed a hand on his shoulder. "Adam, it's been decided much higher up than me. I've already begged on your behalf."

"On my behalf?" He wiped tears from his cheeks. "What do you mean? I'm nothing."

Amanda frowned. Her eyes were following his tears as they streamed down. She seemed reluctant to touch him any further.

"That's not true," she said. She bit her lip again. "We are drowning in stuff to consume, just like you, just like *all* the words that are simmed and the worlds *they* sim. But I found your poetry, this limited syllabic form found nowhere else, this simplicity, this elegance constrained. I've become an expert on it, on haiku. I've mined the ancient hills of Earth for every nugget. I've combed the books and scrolls and tablets, going back to its Eastern roots — but you are the one."

Adam sobbed. His head spun from the night's tragedy and the day's disbelief.

Amanda touched his cheek.

"The hours we spend poring over a single poem of yours . . ." Amanda sighed. "They are the closest we get to silence on my world. The closest to a pause for thought. We sip on your works, Adam Griffey, to keep from drowning in all else."

"That can't be true," he said. The sobs and tears felt so *real*.

"The end is coming any moment now," Amanda said. "Please don't take them with you. Please."

Adam swiped at his cheeks. He was about to speak when there was a great rumble outside. It seemed to emanate from the very belly of the Earth. Amanda looked past him to the window. Adam turned. A plume of dark smoke burst up through the milky white of a hillside. Mountains, long dormant, erupted. A cone of black mixed with bright red, fading as it coursed through the cold air. The ground spit dirt. Crimson rivers leaked like wounds from the earth. The world shook. Amanda pleaded.

"The world that isn't," Adam said, "becomes simply that once more." He pressed both palms to the glass. He felt Amanda's arms around him. He lost himself between the cold and the warm.

"And all is gray ash," he concluded.

AFTERWORD

If any single work set me down the path to becoming a full-time writer, it was probably "The Plagiarist." At the time, I had written five novels, the four Molly Fyde works and Half Way Home. *I was working in a university bookstore in Boone, North Carolina. One of the perks of working there was a free college class each semester, so I signed up for an English course on science fiction taught by my friend Adam Griffey. On the first day of class, Adam handed us our syllabus and the formula for "The Plagiarist" was staring right at me.*

Adam had a single automatic-fail rule on his course guidelines: Committing an act of plagiarism earned you an F. Any obvious case would mean you were out of the class. But besides that warning, there was also an offer: We could submit a work of art instead of taking the final. Knowing Adam as well as I did (he was a regular in the bookstore), I knew exactly what my final would be. I was going to write about a college professor who is a professional plagiarist. The story began to unfold that first day of class.

There are a few things I love about this story. The first is the idea that we can have a physical relationship with the digital, and a digital relationship with the physical. I see this happening more and more. And I believe the distinctions will further blur in the future.

There's also the idea that simulated worlds can burden the host world as they begin to simulate their own worlds. Every embedded computer has to be simulated. This would get very taxing very quickly. The destruction of campus servers in Adam's world is an obvious clue as to the nature of his reality, but no one in his world can see it. Even as they are destroying planets to solve the same problem.

But most importantly, this is a story about the fear of writing. The real Adam Griffey is one of the smartest people I've ever met, and if he wrote a novel it would blow all our collective minds. But we have this problem where those with the most talent are the most critical of themselves, while hacks like me think what we do is worthy of publication. It means true genius goes begging. I'm as sad for this loss as the fictional Adam is over the destruction of planets.

Select Character

There's so much shouting at the beginning. That's how the game starts, with a squad of recruits in a drab-green tent, a drill sergeant yelling, the game controller vibrating in fury. While he yells orders, I can select my character from the recruits. There's a square-jawed man with a crew cut, a darker version of the same guy with a short Mohawk, and then another mountain of muscle with a feather in his hair — presumably Native American. It's what passes for diversity in the game. Three identical brutes of slightly varying shades.

I choose one at random. And while the drill sergeant with the spittle-flecked lips tells me where I'm supposed to go and who I'm supposed to kill, I put the game on mute to silence his shouting, get up, and go to the kitchen for a glass of water. More than once, the sergeant's shouting has woken the baby. Which means rocking her back to sleep for an hour rather than seeing to my garden.

The lecture is over when I get back to the sofa. I fish a coaster out of a drawer and leave my glass of water to sweat while I gear up. There's an arsenal to choose from. The standard package is already in place, with grenades dangling from my chest, a knife that runs almost from hip to knee, an assault rifle, an Uzi, and more. I take all of it off, piece by piece, and grab five canteens. They attach to each hip, one at the back, and two on the chest where the grenades were. It's almost like a boob job, going from the grenades to the canteens. I glance around the empty living room. No one to share the joke with.

My weapon of choice is buried in the menus. An AK-47. It's the only one that comes with a long knife attached to the front. The last thing I grab is the small pistol. And then I leave the tent and head out into a world of rubble and barbed wire, a world where everyone is always fighting.

A helicopter rumbles past overhead, kicking up dust, low enough to see the men sitting in the door, their feet dangling. It's always the same helicopter. Like it waits for me to step out of the tent before whizzing past. The game is predictable like this. Do the right thing (or the wrong thing) at the right time, and you can predict the results.

I leave camp through the rusty gate at the front, a fellow soldier yelling at me to be careful, that a squad of insurgents had been seen in the vicinity. There's the *pop-pop-pop* of nearby gunfire to punctuate the warning. The gate in the game swings shut behind me — and our home alarm beeps as the front door of the house opens. The rumble of the helicopter had drowned out the sound of a car pulling up. My husband is standing in the doorway, staring at me with the controller in my hand.

"Are you playing my game?" he asks incredulously.

I stare over the back of the sofa at Jamie, who is holding his car keys, half frozen in the act of setting them down. He appears as shocked as if he'd walked in on me having sex with his best friend. I set the controller down guiltily. As another helicopter flies overhead, the controller starts to vibrate and scoots across the coffee table.

"No," I say, defensively. "I'm not logged in as you. Technically I'm playing *my* game."

"This is the coolest thing ever," Jamie says, finally dropping his keys onto the table by the door. Not only is he not upset — he seems to be over the moon.

"What're you doing home?" I ask. I check the baby monitor to make sure the volume is up. Somehow, April has not stirred from the door slamming.

"I had some flex hours — was about to fall asleep at my desk — so I took them. I tried to text you —"

"I forgot to plug my phone in last night —"

Jamie joins me on the sofa. Plops down so hard, my cushion jounces me up. "Have you played before?" he asks.

I nod.

"Like, often?"

"Usually while April is napping," I say. "Daytime TV drives me insane." I feel like I have to explain taking an hour to myself in the middle of the day, so I start to tell him that it isn't like I get to clock out at five the way he does, that the job is twenty-four hours a day, but Jamie is interested in something else.

"But you hate video games," he says.

"I don't mind this one," I tell him. What I don't tell him is that I'd tried most of them. The driving game, the sports games, the weird one with the cartoony characters with their spiky hair and massive swords. What I liked about this game is that you could do whatever you wanted. Except play as a woman, of course.

Jamie opens a drawer in the coffee table and pulls out a second controller. "You want to deathmatch?" he asks.

"I doubt it," I say, picking up my controller. "What's that?"

"It's where we glib each other all over the war maps."

"Glib?"

"Yeah, turn each other into large chunks of rendered flesh. Blast each other in the guts with our double-barrels. Shoot you limb from limb.

Rocket jump off your head and turn you into a puddle of goo. It's awesome."

Now I know what he's talking about. I've watched him play online with his friends, whom neither of us has actually met. He plays with a headset on, cussing playfully at distant others or angrily at himself. I've learned not to interrupt him, to just read a book in the bedroom or take April around the neighborhood in the stroller, or go to my mom's.

"No, that's okay," I say. "You can go ahead and play." I set my controller back down and stand up to check on the baby.

"No, no, sit." Jamie grabs my hand and tugs me back down next to him. "I want to watch you play. I think this is awesome."

I reflect back on all the times he's tried to get me to play games with him over the years. Even the time when we were just dating that he got me the dancing game—which was okay—and the musical instrument game—which I was horrible at. I feel guilty that I've been playing in secret for the past few months, ever since I got home with April and have been on maternity leave. Rather than trying to make me feel bad, Jamie is just excited to see me interested in one of his hobbies. So despite dreading him seeing me play, I pick up the controller. On the TV, the camera has pulled back and is spinning around my character, something it does if you stand still long enough.

"What's with the canteens?" Jamie asks, squinting at the TV. "You gonna drown people to death?"

It occurs to me that Jamie probably heads off after the insurgents and does all the things the loud drill sergeant tells me to do.

"Why don't you play for me?" I ask.

"No, c'mon, I wanna see you play. Pretend I'm not here."

He kisses me on the cheek, then sits back and folds his hands in his lap. I wipe my palms on my blue jeans and lean forward, resting my elbows on my knees. I guide my character away from camp and into the winding streets of a war-torn Middle East neighborhood.

There are pops like firecrackers to my right. I've been that way. As soon as I go down the alley, a tank rumbles through a wall behind me, and people start dying. I'm usually one of those people.

Ahead of me, there are civilians scattering across the street, seeking shelter. Faces appear in windows before shutters are pulled tight. Some of the bad guys are dressed just like civilians. I've spent enough time running through here to know who is who. There's a man with a dog I've named "Walt," because he reminds me of our neighbor, who is always out with his cocker spaniel. The woman in the faded pink house is "Mary," because she makes me think of my sister. Jamie is fidgeting beside me as I pass through the market. I duck around the back of one shop to avoid a shootout in the front. I can hear the bangs like Fourth of July fireworks as I weave through debris in the back alley.

"There's a rocket launcher behind the —"

"I know," I tell him. I keep running. If you stop for anything, the fighting from the main street spills over to the back alleys. Within minutes, most of this part of town is consumed by fighting. Mary and Walt and the others pull indoors, until it's just you and other men with guns. But if you run fast enough, and go just the right way, you can stay ahead of them. I've died a hundred times to figure it all out.

"There's gonna be —" Jamie starts to say something, then stops. I exit the alley and turn down the main street, and when the two jeeps collide behind me and the fighting really picks up, I'm already gone. I have to wipe my brow with my elbow as I play, the stress of being watched worse than the anxiety of being killed.

The baby monitor emits a soft cry, which is my cue to pause the game. But Jamie bolts from the sofa, a hand on my shoulder. "I got this," he says. "Keep playing."

I pause the game anyway. I watch Jamie head down the hall toward the bedrooms and take a sip of my water. I should turn the game off and shuffle the laundry around. I don't feel like playing anymore. Not in front of Jamie. But he returns with April in his arms, rocking her gently, our child already back asleep — knocked out like only her daddy can make her — and I can't help but see how happy my husband is to see me playing his stupid video game.

I turn back to the TV and unpause it just for him.

"So you avoid the market fight to save ammo, huh?" he asks.

"Yeah," I tell him. "I guess." I run forward with one thumb on the control stick and reach for the remote, turn the volume down another two notches for April.

"But you don't turn here for the sniper rifle and get up on the tower? You can blast heads like melons from up there."

I try not to wince. I don't know anything about a sniper rifle. The sofa bounces softly as Jamie rocks April back and forth.

I stop at the next alley. This one is tricky. I select the pistol, and the gun appears on the screen, pointing forward. Jamie stops rocking April and studies the TV like the Seahawks are about to score. I wait until I hear the angry men coming down the alley. They are shouting in Arabic, or something that's supposed to sound like it. The way the game makes my character talk depending on which variably shaded male I choose leads me to suspect that it's all made-up gibberish. The African American character calls everyone "Dawg." The Native American calls everyone "Kemosabe." The white guy says "Following orders" over and over. So I imagine the Arabic voices were recorded by non-fluent voice actors who were just faking it. I have no idea.

I just know that I can't get past these people without getting shot. It's a question of how much.

I listen as they get closer. Too soon, and the ones in the back are shredded. I've made that mistake before and had to listen to them scream as they slowly burned to death. Every now and then, I see it again in my dreams. Sometimes it's Jamie who's screaming and burning. I've never been able to tell him about those nightmares. Maybe now I can.

Spinning around the wall, I'm faced with a squad of six men. They're a little closer than I like — I'm too distracted thinking about Jamie. I aim the pistol between the crowd and line the crosshairs up on a barrel down the alley. Jamie is whispering something — I don't know if it's to me or the baby. I press the button; the pistol flashes and recoils, and there's a massive explosion down the alley.

The squad of men is safely past the barrel and not hit by the rubble, but the blast makes them turn around or jump for cover.

I run across the mouth of the alley, holding the sprint button, dropping the pistol to move just a little bit faster. Behind me, I hear the shouting resume. The men closest to me open fire. I zigzag down the wide-open street, my character beginning to pant, when he grunts from being hit by a bullet. Another grunt, and the screen reddens for a moment. The gunfire continues, but it's growing faint, and no more bullets find me. I make it to the end of the street and turn the corner. My character and I both pause to catch our breath. I turn to see Jamie staring at me, his mouth open, his brow furrowed, our baby sleeping against his chest.

"You know the purpose of the game is to score points, right?"

I can take my time now, walking instead of running toward the outskirts of town. Jamie continues to tell me, his voice lowered, what I'm doing wrong:

"You get six hundred for nailing the barrel when those guys are right beside it. And can rack up over a thousand with the sniper rifle —"

"I just want to get to the store alive," I tell him.

He doesn't seem to hear me.

"You haven't scored a single point. That's like . . . it's crazy. And if you try to leave town this way, it's Game Over. They nail you for desertion. You've got to be on the complete other side of town when the air strikes come, or you can't get through this level. Have you even been past this level?"

"No," I tell him. And Jamie laughs, which gets April stirring and cooing.

He gets back to bouncing her before the coos become cries. "I like play-ing it my way," I say.

"With canteens," Jamie says.

I don't say anything. I can see the shop at the end of the street, with the maroon awning and the vegetable and flower stands outside. There are civilians wandering around this part of town. The war is distant, the fireworks one neighborhood over.

"There's a reason I play like I do," Jamie says. I think my silence has him feeling guilty. Defensive. "Rumor is the first team to break a million points unlocks a secret level. You know they use this game to recruit peo-ple into the military, right? The Department of Defense made this game. It's the most realistic ever. People train for actual war with this game. I think if you hit a million, they, like, hire you at the game company divi-sion to design maps or something like that. It's what I heard."

"Have you ever been in this shop?" I ask.

Outside the store, a young man is looking at the vegetables. If I wait long enough, he'll steal one and run off, and the shopkeeper will chase him for a bit, then come back muttering in Arabic and won't interact with me. I stand in front of the tomatoes and use some of the money left over from not equipping the more expensive guns and buy as much as I can. And then I remove the vegetables from my inventory, and the toma-toes appear on the street.

The boy picks up a few and runs off. If I wait long enough, a girl and another boy will come get some. And then three scrawny dogs get the rest. The important thing is that Hakim, the store owner, doesn't leave.

I call him "Hakim" because that's the name on the front of the store.

He's standing behind the counter inside the shop. Jamie still hasn't answered my question. "Have you been in here?" I ask him. I'm curious if he's seen what I'm about to do. I assume he knows all the game's secrets better than I do.

"Yeah," he says. "All the time. This is a bonus mission. You barely have enough time to get here and then to the next objective. But . . . when I come here, the place is already leveled. All this stuff is scattered everywhere. You enter through a gaping hole in that wall."

I know what he's describing. I've gotten here late, when people die or I do something wrong, and when I turn the corner at the end of the long road, a drone comes out of nowhere and blows the place up with a rocket. You can just barely see the boy standing on the sidewalk — a little gray smear — when the orange flash erupts.

Standing in front of Hakim, I run through a series of dialogue options until I can ask to use his bathroom. He hands me what I guess are the keys — the game never says. When I go to the side door that leads out the back of the shop, it now opens. Out here is the game within a game. My little solace. A walled-off courtyard with five raised planters. And inside each one, a mix of flowers and vegetables. My flowers. My vegetables.

Living in the city in the real world, Jamie and I don't have room for a garden. But after hours of running around in this game, figuring out how to control my character, just trying not to die over and over, looking for something to do while feeling trapped at home with April every day, I stumbled onto this place. Really, I was guided here. Any other way you go, people die. If people don't die, you end up here. It's that simple.

"This is wild," Jamie says, his voice subdued.

"You should have seen it when I first got here," I tell him. "It was all weeds and brown dirt. You have to buy flowers and vegetables out front and plant them in here. And if you don't keep them watered, they'll go away."

I select the first canteen and use it in front of the nearest planter. It makes a gurgling noise, and the flowers straighten a little. They seem to brighten. Jamie is dumbfounded, and I see the garden through his eyes, with all that color coming at once, rather than gradually, as I've watched it unfold. All of the city is white crumbling walls, brown dirt, and the black char of fire and explosion. The only color to be found is the foul splattering of red around the bodies when something goes horribly wrong. Here, all the colors dance together. They sway in the breeze, a kaleidoscope of hues.

"It's crazy they would even put this in here," Jamie says. "Maybe to make the Predator strike more meaningful, or something?"

I water the second planter. And then the third, which is full of peppers and beans.

"And the plants go away if you don't water them?" Jamie asks.

"They wilt," I say.

"But how does it remember? How do you save the game without getting to the exfil point?"

"What's the exfil point?" The word sounds familiar. I recall the loud sergeant yelling something about that once.

"It's where you get extracted. After the air strikes. If you die before you get there, you have to start over. And if the time runs out, the level just ends and you have to start over."

"Oh, yeah. That's what happens." I water the last planter, then take out the rifle and use the knife to dig out weeds. The knife on the end of the barrel is also used to make furrows during the planting. "At some point, while I'm here in the garden, the game just ends. But I never play for more than an hour anyway."

"But it remembers what you did," Jamie says, almost to himself.

"I guess."

When I'm done with the weeding, I step back to admire the garden. I could pick the tomatoes now and sell them to Hakim, but if they go another day or two, I'll get more for them. It's so hard to wait. And just looking at them makes me want to go to the kitchen and slice the ones from the market and make a sandwich.

"So this is all you do?" Jamie asks. He laughs to himself. "You play this game to grow flowers?"

"Not just that," I say. "I also scrubbed all the graffiti off the walls in here." I turn the character around to show him. "And I picked up all the trash and took the loose rubble that was in that corner and hauled it through the shop and to another alley."

"You cleaned graffiti," Jamie mumbles, like he doesn't believe me.

"Yeah. Every wall was covered. It comes back now and then. There's just this one spot where it won't come off."

I go to show him, when there's a low grumble in the game. I would have thought it was his stomach or April messing her diaper if I hadn't heard it a hundred times.

"It always thunders," I say, "but it never rains."

"That's not thunder," Jamie tells me. "It's the air strikes across town. You're so far out of position —"

He stops as I find the place on the wall with the black paint and try scrubbing it away. My character makes the right animation, rubbing a rag over the spot, but the marks remain.

"What is that?" Jamie asks. He cradles April and leans forward, studying the TV.

"It's the only spot I can't get clean," I say. "There were other markings over the top of this. Everywhere, really. Once you get the flowers and vegetables up and sell enough to Hakim, he gives you a bucket and a rag and asks you to clean up back here. If you do, you get squash seeds and beans. But these marks won't go away. I keep wondering what might happen if I get all the walls perfectly clean —"

"Those are numbers," Jamie says.

I make my character stop scrubbing. The marks look like Chinese to me. Little clusters of hashes.

"You read Arabic?" I ask, even though I know — like I know where every misplaced thing of his is at any moment — that my husband does not understand an ounce of Arabic.

"No, it's Vollis. An alien language. After the eighth mission, the Vollis invade and you start using their plasma guns and sonic grenades to really kick some ass —"

I shoot him a look and make sure April is still asleep. He mouths his apology for cursing around her.

"Anyway," he whispers, "your ammo with those weapons counts down in their language. Those marks spin like a clock. It's easy to read. Do they ever change? Can you step back so we can see them all?"

I make the character step back. "I don't think they change," I tell him.

"What are they doing on this level? The Vollis don't invade until you get to Kabul."

"Why are there aliens in this game?" I ask. Though I seem to recall seeing him fight aliens and zombies with his friends. I just assumed it was some other game.

"It's ten digits," he says. "Do you think that's a phone number? Maybe it's a phone number."

I laugh. Jamie thinks every series of numbers in his games might be a secret number to call to unlock another level or an extra life or something. One of the friends he plays with is a guy named Marv that he called randomly, and when he explained why he called, it turned out Marv was a gamer. Now he's another friend Jamie talks about like he's known him since high school but has never actually met in the flesh.

"The first three numbers are three, one, seven," Jamie says. "That sounds like an area code. I'm calling it."

I try to talk sense into him, but Jamie passes me April. I do everything I can to keep her from waking while Jamie digs out his cell phone and moves closer to the screen, dialing the number.

He listens to it ring. And then, without warning, he hands it over to me.

"Here," he says. "You found this place. You have to talk to them."

"I don't want to talk to some random person," I say. I cradle April and turn my shoulder. Jamie sits down beside me and holds the phone close to my ear, but angled so he can hear as well.

"You talk," he hisses.

The phone is ringing.

"I don't want to —" I hiss back.

There is a click on the other end. I don't want to have to tell some-one why we called the wrong number. April stirs and kicks in my arms, waking up. I can't let go of her to shut off the phone. Jamie has his arm around me, his head close to mine so he can hear. And then, before I can say hello, can apologize, can tell Jamie to hang up, a voice announces it-self, low and ominous:

"Congratulations," the voice says. "You've reached the Department of Defense. Is this Donna213?"

It takes me a moment to remember that this is my screen name.

I nod. Then manage to say, "Yes."

"Good. Now listen to me very closely —"

"What is this?" I ask. "Some kind of joke?"

April starts crying. Jamie won't hold the phone still. He's covering his mouth with his other hand, his eyes wide and disbelieving.

"Not a joke, ma'am," the man says. "Listen to me carefully. Your coun-try needs you."

AFTERWORD

I'm often asked if I have a favorite piece of writing, and I usually deflect the question, but there are definitely a few that mean more to me than others. "Select Character" is one of those. There are so many themes packed into this story, themes that show up time and time again in my plots, and they all came together here like a jigsaw puzzle.

There's the concept of free will, as the protagonist attempts to have her character do the opposite of what is intended. And again the pacifism theme, as a world made for violence is turned to nurturance. There are gender identity questions, and a female protagonist who does not find her strength by emulating what we think of as "maleness." All of these themes pop up over and over again in my works, as I try to work through them for myself.

What I really enjoy about this story is my own personal development. When I was a kid, I used to play video games hoping to unlock some secret or some high score so that I was contacted by the programmer. I remember having this feeling before I saw the film The Last Starfighter, *which means it was an experience I shared with others.*

But as an adult, I now dream of a world where nonviolent solutions are applauded. There's a line in my story "Peace in Amber" that goes something like: I dream of a world in which pacifists board planes first. And the climax of my novel Beacon 23 *is the strongest declaration of this. Maybe it all changed for me on 9/11 and our response to that attack. Or at least, that's where my conversion began.*

Lost and Found

Promises of London

Hands, gentle and rough. The last time I stood on this bridge, it was a fairer hand on my arm, light as a sparrow, young and full of love and warmth. Full of promises. But that was a long time ago. This more recent hand lands like a hawk, talon fingers squeezing, a British bark unintelligible, but I can guess the meaning. The officer wants to know what I'm doing there.

It's the bolt cutters, I'm sure. The business end pokes out the top of my backpack, the zippers hugging the jaws on either side. There are a scattering of tourists on the bridge. It's just after dark and warm in London, much like it had been on our honeymoon. The officer in the bobby hat with the baton at his side isn't harassing anyone else. Just me. With my bolt cutters and my scraggly beard. With my slept-in clothes. With the smell of a hostel on me, the wild red eyes that might be from bawling, might be from drugs. That senseless stagger of a drunk, of a man lost, of a man without that light sparrow on his arm, guiding him through the world.

I watch as the backpack is searched. The cop procures a flashlight. The dark bowel of the bag swallows every ounce of light. Nothing to see here. A great void. A hollow. Keep looking.

"And what're these, then?"

He knows what they are. But I tell him. "Bolt cutters," I say. The numb put up no resistance.

"This looks a fair bit suspicious," he says. And now people are watching. A young couple train their phones on me in case this is worth sharing. "Empty bag," he says. "Bolt cutters."

"Just taking back what's mine," I tell him. My eyes drift to the ornate rail. Both sides of the bridge are studded with locks, like some paranoid chain mail. Links in gold and silver. Tarnished and new. Etched and anonymous. The officer moves his beam of light to my chest, the cone spilling across my face. He is reading me. Proper now. The stagger and the absence of fear. The red eyes. All those locks. And the cutters in my bag.

The light clicks off. He hands me my things. "I'll be right over here," he says, pointing to a spot along the rail. Even the police in England are achingly polite. Disappointment flashes across the faces of the young couple, illuminated by the pale glow of their phones. Nothing to see here. Keep looking. I wonder if one of these locks is theirs. I wonder how long it'll last.

My hand coasts down the rail as I move to the center of the bridge. The Thames glides silently below. A glass dinner boat trudges away, pushing against the ebbing tide. The buildings along the bank glow, the glass new ones and the crumbling monuments alike. The London Eye spins lazily. It and the river are unceasing. Some things are.

All the worries about finding the lock have been misplaced. My hand falls straight to it. Part of me had worried the entire rail might be gone. In Paris, the Pont de l'Archevêché across the Seine gets so overburdened with padlocks — locks looped upon locks — that the entire rail is chopped away and replaced every few months. Rail and locks go to a scrapyard. The permanence is illusory. The nearby lock vendors know this, but they don't warn anyone. The greeting card people and the florists and the jewelers and the writers of fiction are all in on the ruse. Forever holding their peace. Nobody says to watch out, that rail can go, and you'll be swept away. They just keep selling little promises with their twin keys. And the locks get melted down at the scrapyard, and the keys tumble in the swift current and are pulled out to sea.

We didn't leave a lock on any of the rails that are known to get replaced. We asked around. Avoided the tourist traps. Planned ahead.

The bolt-cutter teeth clamp down on that little bent finger of stainless steel. I have to move the handles so far to get the jaws to travel so little. It's the leverage. This is how people move, like these handles. So much to get so little. But the violence when it does happen — the violence.

And now after the long flight, after the weeks before of feeling lost, of not being able to sleep at night because of this damn lock, this pebble in the shoe of my dark thoughts, the nagging hypocrisy on the other side of the world, that lock cinched tight around my throat, bobbing heavy with every swallow, obstructing every breath, the lack of closure from unanswered texts and calls and emails, and the plan to set myself free — after all of that, I hesitate. And by the light of half a moon, I see our initials, the little scratches turned to rust, a crude heart between us.

My pulse pounds. I can hear it, can feel the throb in my temples as I squeeze the handles. A soft give. More. The expectation of nothing. A quiet eternity. And then what went together with a gentle click pops with a metallic bang, and the unbreakable shatters. The cutters nearly slip from my sweaty palms, but the lock still dangles on that crowded rail. I caress it with my fingers for a brief moment, remembering. And then a twist sets it free.

A couple somewhere hurls a pair of small keys out into the void. They laugh and hug while a lock lands with a splash.

I feel lighter when I stand. But only a little. There is a notebook in my back pocket, the stiff covers of which are bent from riding there so long, so many years ago. It is an old notebook. One I took on our travels. Like a partner in life, it has taken some of its shape from its proximity to me. And I walk with a hitch because of my time with it. I fish the notebook out and turn the pages, though I already know. By the light of half a moon, I find my next stop. Amsterdam. Images from that vacation strobe unbidden. And bolt cutters slip into an otherwise empty bag.

AFTERWORD

This is a very different sort of piece for me, a work that doesn't really fit a genre, more like something I might've written in a creative writing class (had I ever taken one). The inspiration came from my travels while promoting translated works in various countries. I saw these lock bridges everywhere. I think they started in Paris, then spread to London, Barcelona, Amsterdam, Budapest, and so on.

When I try to think of something to write, I often start with an idea and then flip it on its head. Maybe reading Philip K. Dick as a kid got to me. Or perhaps it's an extension of my contradictory nature. Or it could be me wanting to only write what I hope has never been written before, otherwise why do it? So when I imagined a couple traveling around the world leaving locks on bridges, my mind immediately inverted this to a single man on a mission to cut free all the locks he and his ex had fastened together. It is a rejection of the supposed permanence of love and the things we leave behind. It's a story I wrote about a year before my longest relationship ended.

Whenever I write a short story, I always have in mind the way that I would continue it if I had to. This is likely a result of Wool's success. In that case, I didn't have any more story in mind beyond the original novelette. So even if I don't plan on getting around to writing more in any of these worlds, it's impossible to not at least think about it. In this case, I had the idea of writing several accounts of different bridges this character traveled to, with flashbacks to his past relationship. And I toyed with the idea of him arriving at the last bridge to find his ex standing there, seemingly a mirage at first, but very much real. She is as beautiful as he remembers. She is smiling that familiar smile of hers. And holding her own pair of bolt cutters . . .

Peace in Amber

*For the Billy Pilgrims of the world — those who have
seen things they cannot discuss.*

*And for the Montana Wildhacks — those with the wisdom
in their breasts to know what they cannot change.*

I

All this happened, more or less:

One morning I stood beneath a bright blue sky and watched it blossom orange and black as jet fuel went suddenly alight. I saw men and women jump and plummet like flightless birds, the howling wind sucking suit jackets from backs and whipping skirts in a frenzy. I heard the sharp cry of bending steel as it screeched downward, and I smelled that awful char of office furniture and asbestos as it burned and burned for days and days.

The movies get most of it right, I learned. Fireballs look just so. Crowds run just like this, with their eyes wide and with less screaming than you might imagine, just mouths agape as they push each other out of the way. We devolve into animals when we creep near to death. The movies with the big stomping lizards that crush buildings get most of it right. I think the lizards are something we remember, deep in our bones and in our DNA, from earlier times. *Run,* we think, as buildings crumble. *Run,* as people perish.

I was a yacht captain for a number of years, which is decidedly less glamorous than it sounds to the untrained ear. *Yacht* and *captain* are a couple of five-dollar words, but the yachts were not mine and the rank was largely unearned. I was never a private like Billy Pilgrim, never worked my way through any ranks. I lived on a sailboat while I was in college, took a two-week course that required very little study, passed some government tests, and then billionaires let me drive their boats from one harbor to the next. That was my job. A glorified bus driver who also plunged the toilets, scrubbed the decks, and polished the stainless steel.

At the age of twenty-five, I was a certified captain living on a seventy-four-foot yacht in the shadow of two of the tallest buildings in the Western Hemisphere. The shadows of those buildings draped across North Cove Marina and cooled me on the hot summer days of the year 2001. Each morning, the sun rose above the Atlantic — far across the other side of Manhattan Island — and peered down at me between colossal towers of metal and glass. It was in those shadows that I scrubbed the decks, getting them clean before the broiling renewed. Here was my brief respite, given to me in those towering dark patches, where now there is only blue sky.

On the planet Tralfamadore, there lies a zoo comprised of scattered geodesic domes. Inside each dome are members of various races, kidnapped from their home planets and housed among the representative clutter of their former abodes. There are sea snakes from Zyx writhing in a flooded dome amid fake and crudely painted spike coral. The Zyx talk to one another by squeaks and blown bubbles, and so old conversations find themselves trapped at the top of the dome in a pocket of noise. The Zyx have lived on Tralfamadore long enough to have relinquished any hope of seeing their home reefs again, any dream of wrapping their tails around loved ones. But not long enough yet for the water to have lost that foul tinge of regret and despair, that smell of paint leaching from plastic coral.

Adjacent to this flooded dome are five balls of fur that roll about and bump into one another. The floor is an uneven series of steps and ramps carved out of dense foam and sprayed to look like the indigenous rock of the dwarf planet Upelote. The five Upes spin senselessly and carom off the large dome's glass walls. These poor and hapless aliens are still shaken from the long flight aboard the Tralfamadorian zookeeper's starship. The gravity isn't right there on Tralfamadore. Neither are the suns and stars.

Across from the Upes, two Earthlings sit on display: Billy Pilgrim and Montana Wildhack. Montana is just waking up from her long slumber aboard a flying saucer. She was picked up two stops before the Upes, kidnapped to give Billy Pilgrim company. Her eyes flutter open, and then her mouth. Montana screams and screams while hundreds of Tralfamadorians gather around the dome to take in this newest exhibit. The heads of these strange aliens resemble oversize hands, a single eye in the palm. The Tralfamadorians clap by making fists, over and over. Montana Wildhack sees them through the glass and thinks that this is the time when people stir from their nightmares. This is the time. She goes on thinking this, screaming and screaming while the Tralfamadorians make their delighted fists.

It is one thing to know that there are more than three dimensions; it is another thing altogether to see them. It isn't so hard to see up to nine dimensions, but humans rarely attempt the feat. They are happy enough to see in three. Many stick to two. Some are content with one and travel through life the way a subway moves through the earth. They are always on some line. Here is their stop. Work and home. Home and work. Back and forth, with a magazine read, perhaps, between the two. There was one woman who lived her entire life in a single dimension, never moving from where she was born. Seventy-five years later, she was buried on that very spot, and by all appearances seemed happy enough on most days. By the time Montana Wildhack was abducted from her home in Palm Springs, California, more and more people were attempting to live a life in one dimension. Advances in computing technology known as Zynga were making this more and more feasible. It was becoming *A Thing*.

On Tralfamadore, there lived a race of beings shaped like plungers with hands for heads. They saw in four dimensions by natural course. They couldn't see the world in any other way. For them, time didn't slide by like the shadows of buildings. They saw every state of the world all at once, not in slices like Earthlings do (those who even bother).

Listen: There is Montana Wildhack inside a dome, screaming and terrified. There she is on a couch in a rented office space in Hollywood, California, silent and similarly afraid. A friend has sent her to audition for a movie. She is sixteen, but her driver's license says she is older. A man who is a director but likes to call himself a producer keeps staring at the locket that hangs between Montana's breasts. He rubs his mustache over and over and asks what she's been in before. The room smells of old cigars and sweat. Montana Wildhack will be a famous movie star in a few years, and of course any Tralfamadorian can see that. But all Montana can see is a strange man leaning in too close, a hand on her knee, asking her if she wants to be a star.

There are books written in the Tralfamadorian way. You can read them in any order, front to back or sideways and inside out. It doesn't matter, because it all happened. You have to see it all at once to know the book. To tell anyone what you are reading is pointless. You have to wait. You can only comment on your sense of the thing when studied from some distance. I studied a book like this in college, just a few years ago (a Tralfamadorian would say that I am still studying it). I hated the book when I read it the first time. A lot of people died. Truly awful things happened to a man who became an author, but he wrote of these things and utter nonsense in the same breath, and this made me dismiss the book. Until I finished it. You have to see all things at once, as on Tralfamadore. I read it again. I caught a glimpse of some other dimension. I began to back away, and I saw all of it at once, and that's when I wept and saw that it was good.

The thing I hated while reading this book, it turns out, was me. Bad things happen, and shoulders are shrugged. The most serious of events are blended with the strange. The author pulled me inside his mind, and what I found there was a dead stillness, the somber and poignant wisdom of someone with little hope and scars across his eyes. There was humor there, too. But not the bright kind. The man who wrote that book is dead. So it goes.

Montana Wildhack was abducted while sunning beside her pool. She was twenty years old, which is middle-aged in her profession. In her first two years, she made over seventy films. It didn't take long to film movies such as these, try as men might to prolong each scene. And Montana was in high demand, for in addition to being lovely, she could act. Had she known this skill had other outlets, she would have skipped her early career altogether and made a different sort of film, the kind with plot and wardrobe. But that would come after, and the least of the little a young person knows is what they're capable of. It takes a Tralfamadorian to see all of time and know that life won't always be so dim. Nor so good. Seen all at once, the way a Tralfamadorian sees time, life makes perfect sense. Which would be an odd way to live one.

Waking up naked inside a glass dome does strange things to Montana's brain. There was a blue California sky and a burning sun overhead one moment, and now the sound of her own screaming voice. She can still smell the baby oil on her skin. A man is there, also naked. Tall and skinny and unattractive, with a leer that makes him look like a Hollywood director. And beyond the glass, hundreds of fleshy beings that look like plungers with hands for heads and eyes where the palms should be clap by making fists. This is how Tralfamadorians show that they are happy. This is how they know the world is right by them. They make fists.

If I try hard enough — which is to say by not trying at all — I can see in the fourth dimension the way a Tralfamadorian does. There I am, sitting in a college classroom. It is the summer of 2011, and I'm studying a book that jumps around and makes me feel angry and hollow inside. It's also summertime ten years earlier in New York, and I'm working on a windlass in the stern of a fancy yacht. It is the summer of 2013, and I'm lying in a bed in Florida, typing. My dog is having a dream. On Tralfamadore, time is seen all at once, which makes it difficult at times to see how things are tied together. I'm reading a book about bombs being dropped on Dresden. Twenty-five thousand people are dying. There's a plane banking over Manhattan right now. I can read the jumble of numbers and letters on the tail of that plane. I am screaming in my head for the pilot to pull up. On Tralfamadore, they communicate telepathically. They do not do this on Earth. No one will ever hear me. There is orange and black against a bright blue sky, and I think I can feel the heat of a movie effect against my face, but maybe it's just fear and my imagination. My friend Kelly yells down at me from the neighboring yacht: "Did you *see* that?" Kelly's brain is doing odd things. Montana Wildhack is screaming. All of us are. Twelve years later, I'm lying beside my dog in an otherwise empty house. She dreams and I cry. Thousands are dying all over again. So it goes.

Montana Wildhack learned at a young age that she would only be loved for her flesh. Her uncle taught her this, and no one ever thought to teach her otherwise. The Serenity Prayer is engraved on the locket around her neck. Listen:

> *God grant me the serenity to accept the things I cannot change,*
> *Courage to change the things I can,*
> *And wisdom always to tell the difference.*

She has read it enough to be able to read it upside down, just as it lies. The trickiest part is the last line. This is where mortals who live in three dimensions have too much expected of them. All of human misery lies here. Hubris and cowardice, too. If only it were as simple as a prayer that can fit on a locket. If only wisdom were so cheap. But men wrestle with the things they cannot change, and they ignore those that might bend to some economy of effort. Winning at wrestling is about picking your partner. Most people prefer the unconquerable brute they already know. Or maybe, if you look around, we're addicted to a challenge. And so things go unchanged and unaccepted, and our arms and hearts grow weary.

On Tralfamadore, the applause of fists dies down, and Montana is alone and terrified in a room with a naked man. She has been here before. She knows what to do, and it is a sad thing that she does not know any better. Billy Pilgrim thinks he is a lucky man, that he is saving her. Montana feels dead inside, but this is the only feeling she has ever known. She is on the planet Tralfamadore, billions of light years from Earth, but she feels right at home in this stranger's arms. The way a mosquito feels at peace in amber.

2

September 10, 2001. A storm is brewing in New York City. A clash is about to begin. Tempers will soon rise as historical conquests and slights are remembered and renewed on the eve of this fight between ancient and embittered foes.

Yes, the Boston Red Sox are playing the New York Yankees.

Roger Clemens is slated to pitch, looking for his twentieth win. It's the last meeting of the year between the two teams. I'm there to watch. My best friend, Scott, is there, visiting from South Carolina. Kevin — my boss and the captain of a neighboring yacht — is there as well. He is also joined by his best friend. It is a coincidence, our best friends from out of town staying with us that week. It's a Monday, and the weather is dismal. A storm comes, and then the rain, and we stand in it, naively hopeful, as fifty thousand fans slowly leak from Yankee Stadium. We splash in the rivers at the bottoms of the bleachers, while candy wrappers and empty cups drift toward distant drains. Men down on the field cover the diamond of dirt so that it won't turn to mud, and it's dark when they announce there won't be any baseball. It feels less like America after that. We head home sad and soaked, but it is only rain.

Our friends had come a long way to see something distinctly New York and vastly American, and so as we pass through those glass towers toward the marina we call home, Kevin and I take our best friends up to Windows on the World, the restaurant at the top of the World Trade Center's North Tower. After a long elevator ride, we wet our insides to go with our outsides. The city sparkles from those heights. There isn't a soiled patch of street to be seen, just wet newness, black asphalt shiny like rivers of oil. I stand with my forehead pressed to the glass, shoulder to shoulder with Andrew, a mechanic from another boat, as we both peer into that unblemished, that happy and serene America, far, far below.

"Imagine this coming down," I say out loud. I believe it's the mammal in me that has this thought, the mammal that can remember living in trees. It's the same part of me that is terrified of giant lizards. It's the part of me that makes me contemplate a fall when confronted with an abyss or some great height.

Far below Andrew and me, taillights wink on and off. A light turns green, and everyone races off all at once, in a hurry to get somewhere.

After a pause, Andrew says that these buildings will always be here, that they will outlive us all. And I believe him.

"But just imagine," my mammal brain says, "if you took this one we're standing in down in such a way that it toppled into that guy." My monkey paw points to the adjacent building lit up here and there by janitors and workaholics. "They'd go like dominoes," I say, "one after the other."

Andrew tells me the building would go straight down, however you tried to topple it. He says something about mass being pulled toward the center of the earth, something about structural loads. He tells me you'd have to make this building much stronger to sit at a lean, and so any lean at all would send everything plummeting as neat as a demolition.

My mammal brain rejects this thought. Andrew is an engineer, but I still don't believe him. Behind us, one of the bartenders complains about the late hour and says he has to be back early in the morning to work a double. I glance at my wristwatch. It has gotten so late that it is now September 11, and there I am standing in a patch of blue and empty sky.

3

I'm in the lazarette of the motor yacht *Prelude* on the morning of September 11. The compartment is tight. There's raw fiberglass against my shoulder, the site of a future itch. A Tralfamadorian would know to go ahead and scratch it. I'm sweaty and hot in that cramped space, and it's difficult to breathe or even move. I'm loosening the last bolt on the underside of a motorized winch when I hear the boom. I hear it and I feel it. The boat shudders, the fiberglass resonating, a hollow in my chest like standing too close to a tower of speakers at a noisy concert.

Someone's in trouble, I think. Some jet pilot has just buzzed New York City, racing down the Hudson so low and so fast that a shock wave has been sent out to rattle tall buildings. I have an image from a film in my head, a hotshot pilot buzzing a tower, coffee spilled, a man clutching his tie and cursing. In my mind, there is nothing but exciting things happening out in the world while I work on this stupid winch. My best friend is visiting from out of town. All I want is a day off from work.

I squirm out of the tight space, leaving the ratchet set behind. I plan to come right back. I just want to see what's going on. Up on the deck, Scott yells from inside the boat, asking me what that was. I tell him a pilot just buzzed the Hudson. Scott shakes and flaps his newspaper over to the next page, looking for something interesting. On the wharf behind *Prelude,* a crowd gathers. They shield their eyes against the low morning sun. I follow the dozens of gazes high up the North Tower and spot the smoke. That hotshot pilot who buzzed the Hudson is forgotten. Here is something new. The boom and the smoke — these two things are unrelated in my mind.

A fire. An office fire. The crowd swells. Many of these people are just off the ferry from New Jersey, were heading toward that very building — but now they're not so sure. Many others gawk for the simple newness, for the absurdity of a smoking skyscraper. What is normally a thoroughfare of pedestrian traffic has ground to a halt. On a typical morning, this is a conveyor belt of moving heads, of swinging briefcases and purses, of ties flapping and dresses swirling, expensive shoes and high heels clop-clopping on concrete. Now it is a rumor mill. It is a game of Chinese whispers. A Cessna or some small plane has crashed into the tower. No, it was something bigger.

The windows high above glow amber from the flames trapped inside. The smoke and fire march across the building, spreading. There are sirens in the distance, a noise that is such a steady backdrop to this city that it often goes unheard. But this is different. An odd cacophony. A lot of sirens. A sense of urgency.

But the fires are not urgent. They move at a crawl, and the gray smoke drifts lazily into the cloudless sky, and I can't imagine that anyone is hurt.

They will get away. They will get away. There are sirens coming, and this is just some thing to gawk at.

Montana Wildhack has been on display for as long as she can remember. Trapped and on display for as long as she can remember. She was the first one in school with breasts. She was in sixth grade when her grandma took her to Penney's to pick out a bra. Her grandma told her that she couldn't run around like she was, that people were watching. This was right after a family cookout. Montana and her cousins swam in the mud-brown lake. Her uncle Chip showed her how to pitch horseshoes. The next day, after church, her grandma took her shopping. The bra was tight and pinched and was hard to get on and off, but her nipples stopped getting raw from rubbing on her shirts. And like a person abducted by aliens but in complete reverse, Montana appeared suddenly from out of nowhere. She went from unpopular to the complete opposite in the course of a single summer. A flash of hormones, and suddenly a stranger was in their midst.

She was asked to join the cheer squad. She was invited to sleepovers, where every girl in school wanted to brush her hair and try on clothes with her in the bathroom. She caught them watching her in the mirror after PE. People noticed her. Her grades improved, but only in some courses. English with Mr. Mayberry and history with Mr. Thomson, where she wrote in cursive and got large red A-pluses. In math with Mrs. Pickens, where she wrote in numbers, her grades got a little worse. At school dances, the boys lined up for her, giggling, while the same girls who brushed her hair looked on, unsmiling. Life was as good as it would ever get for Montana, for every curse begins with a blessing. This is a truth the Tralfamadorians know, for they see what follows right from the start. Montana had to learn the hard way. Gradually, the way a fire moves.

Her uncle Chip won $60,000 from a scratch-off once. Montana was in eighth grade and remembers the party he threw. Uncle Chip became suddenly popular. Even Montana's dad, who hated his brother Chip, liked him just fine all of a sudden. And at the party, Uncle Chip took Montana for a ride in his new truck. He gave her a pair of earrings and told her not to lose them, that they weren't fakes. Then he asked her to thank him with a kiss. Montana remembers his breath tasting like beer and his hand accidentally brushing against her breast. Back at the party, she looked everywhere for her grandma, but Granny had passed away the year before. Uncle Chip would be dead a year later, as any Tralfamadorian could plainly see. Shot himself with his brand-new gun in his brand-new truck, a year's worth of scratch-offs under the seat and stuck to the mud of his brand-new boots. So it goes.

Breasts were a lottery ticket, Montana saw. One random girl in every school wins that first pair, and at pool parties, the boys laugh and tug at those knotted bows on sunburnt backs, like ribbons on Christmas presents. She can see it now like a Tralfamadorian, how each thing leads to the other. Dating. Obsessed with the boys who are obsessed with her. Ninth grade and not a male teacher on her schedule. Ninth grade a second time with the same results. Dropping out. But life was good. A boy who graduated the year before wanted to see her steady. He showed her the college campus and said they'd get married one day. She drank too much and danced at a party, and someone offered her money to take her shirt off. There was laughter, which eventually vanished, but the money stayed real. The air was cool in that house — so cold her nipples hurt like tiny fists. The money, though, was warm from sweaty palms. This was a thing, getting paid to dance. Montana never knew before.

4

Everything happens twice in your life. Often, it's quite more than that. This is a thing Tralfamadorians know and humans ignore. It's rarely enough to suffer a thing once, the Tralfamadorians like to say. Not when you can suffer it again and again.

I ran away to Charleston, South Carolina, more than once. The first time was to elope. I was nineteen. A girl I loved was leaving to take a job on a boat, and getting married would make sure that we stayed together even while we were apart. On Tralfamadore, they would laugh, knowing what happens next.

Less than a year later, I quit my career as a computer technician, packed what I could into a car, and fled to Charleston, an emotional wreck. A chessboard there saves my life. Fleeing to Charleston saves my life. I am twenty years old and will soon divorce. So it goes.

There is a café on King Street where chess players sit on coffee-bean sacks and move around six-inch wooden soldiers, soldiers we slam down with happy violence. My hurts disappear when I move those soldiers. A stranger is sitting across from me, as strangers do in that place. Names are exchanged. "Scott," a man says, not looking up from the board. He must be a decade older than me. The woman beside him glances up from her magazine to smile piteously at her boyfriend's next victim. But Scott is about to save my life. As most things go, he will do this more than once.

Best friends form like fires spread. Gab turns to conversation. Familiar faces are smiled at. People have to eat, so why not grab a bite together? Like Montana Wildhack, Scott dances for a living. But it's called ballet and wardrobe is involved, so somehow it's more respectable. In Charleston, South Carolina, you can have a ballet studio within four blocks of a church if you want. But probably not right next door. There are limits.

When I decide I should buy a sailboat to live on, Scott goes with me to Baltimore to sail it down the coast. Neither of us knows what we're doing as we head for Charleston around Cape Hatteras in January. Boats have disappeared to the bottom of the sea here once or twice. We soon discover this is so. And it is not the last time Scott and I will see trouble from the deck of a boat. Nor is it the last time that I am certain I will die.

At the base of the Twin Towers, there is a glass dome called the Winter Garden. Palm trees stand there in the dead of winter, like the sea snakes of Zyx, trapped in a strange world. I wake up one day to find myself living in that dome. One moment, I'm attending college classes in Charleston. The next minute, I'm in an alien land, surrounded by strangers, trapped in a glass dome, wanting to scream and scream.

The line to get a bagel in this place is infuriatingly slow.

Montana bought a house in Palm Springs with her own money. Movie money. Her realtor showed her houses in the hills with nice views, but seeing out meant others could see in. She settled on a small place with a roof that needed repair, but she liked the hedge. And it had a pool, where she could lie out and feel the sun warm her flesh, touching her without touching her. Until she woke up smelling like baby oil and coconuts, a nightmare of creatures gazing in through geodesic glass, a naked stranger beside her, a horror she knew all too well.

Montana had forgotten what it meant to own her body. She had lived a life on display, first because it felt nice, later to survive, and then to profit. She wasn't oblivious to this trade-off. There were days when the exchange made her feel powerful, when checks came in the mail from her agent and she thought of the number of men aroused by her on-screen performances. It reminded her of that party and dancing for those college boys, going home with more money than she'd ever held.

But then there were days in the middle of a shoot, brief moments of nakedness when the director yelled "cut" or the cameraman needed to change rolls, and the magic of the scene vanished and the characters around her faded back into actors. Here was when an assistant took a dozen paces to bring her a robe, and Montana Wildhack felt a chill. Here was the off-camera hell when the actor from the previous scene continued to touch her as if she were his. This was when they would ask her out. Tell her how great she was. The best ever.

On Tralfamadore, she was back on display in a geodesic dome of glass that held thousands of alien viewers at bay. This was her movie set, with its lime-green kitchen appliances, yellow lounger, sofa bed, end tables, lamps. The alien zookeepers had installed a phonograph that worked and a television set that didn't. The latter had an image painted on the curved glass screen, an image of two cowboys dueling with pistols. Montana thought she recognized the film. She'd had sex with one of the actors a few years ago when his feature career had hit the skids and hers had not yet begun. He had played a doctor, she a nurse.

Montana remembered the trepidation she'd felt on every new shoot. Arriving at some rented house, the smell of morning coffee, a man she would perform with smiling too widely as the director introduced her. They would pump her hand, these actors, and stare at her breasts where a locket lay with its little prayer, Montana silently pining for the wisdom to know what things she might change.

Billy Pilgrim stirred on the sofa bed, and the Tralfamadorians outside the dome went wild from the sudden movement. Montana Wildhack shivered from the cold of being trapped with yet another actor. They had been on display for several months, she and Billy Pilgrim, and she was fairly certain of two things: The first was that she would never see her home again. The second, that she was pregnant.

5

We are on the dock, gazing up at the smoking building. My boss Kevin is there. And so is Andrew, the engineer. The first sign that something is wrong is Andrew's wife running to us, shaking and crying. This is not the Leslie I know, the forever smiling, the warm and friendly. This is a wife collapsing into the arms of her husband, unable to talk, barely able to breathe.

She was in the gym on the top floor of the hotel. There was a crash. Ceiling panels rained down, lights exploding. They had run from the building, had run through the courtyard, and there were bodies—

There were bodies everywhere.

Andrew held his wife. My best friend, Scott, ran off to investigate. The rest of us looked up at those marching flames and that drifting smoke. Here was a thing to gawk at.

If Montana Wildhack had a type, she was quite sure that Billy Pilgrim was not it. Billy possessed a weak countenance, was thin and made up of more joints than bones. He also did not seem entirely sane.

He would drift off to sleep at all hours and claim upon waking to have traveled through time, to be both there on Tralfamadore and also back on Earth, to be simultaneously younger and older, and to know how he would one day die. He said he knew every mistake he would make, that he could see them all at once, and complained that he was doomed to repeat them again and again. "There's no stopping," he would say. And then he would drift back, unstuck from time, the Tralfamadorians listening in on his dreams with their telepathic minds as Billy squirmed and murmured and slept.

It wasn't until Montana watched him cry in his sleep, whimpering his whispers of war, that she began to care for him. Billy woke her one night while the zoo was quiet and told her about the bombing of Dresden. Every horrible detail. The stars overhead twinkled serenely, and Montana had a revelation. Billy Pilgrim wasn't weak, she decided, as he drifted back to sleep — he was broken. The whole system was broken. Sending young men to war, expecting them to come back whole, their bullets to make things right. Expecting a girl from the Big Sky State to step off a bus in LA and have a career that wouldn't kill her. The machinery of it all was set up unfair from the start. Living in three dimensions meant you learned what you needed to know too late in life.

Montana held Billy in her arms that night while he had another fitful dream, and she watched the stars fade and the sky brighten. She wondered which of those pinpricks up there held Earth in its orbit. The view blurred as she thought of the friends and family she would never see again, the sounds of the waves on Venice Beach, the horns blaring as lights turned green, the wind in the palm trees that shrouded her small home in the Springs, the simple torture of deciding what she would eat that day, every day, three times a day.

There were things she wouldn't miss, but many more of them she would. And it took this to realize her life wasn't so bad as she had once thought. She felt an impulse to go back to school, to study this time, to read more, to make herself better. Because it wasn't right that they had the two of them on display here, that this was all the Tralfamadorians would know of Earth. Not these two to represent them. She and Billy, two broken souls. This was not their kind. It made the zoo a lie, and this frustrated her the most.

Billy whimpered, and Montana wiped her eyes. The sky brightened, and the zoo opened, grotesque aliens sidling by beyond the glass. These creatures covered their eyes with their fingers; they made fists of joy; and Montana could hear their thoughts leak into her mind. But as loudly as she screamed in her own head, no one moved to save her. They just clapped and clapped.

Billy disappeared later that day. Montana had stretched out on the sofa for a nap — she liked to sleep when the Tralfs were watching; she spent her waking time when the zoo was closed and they weren't around. When she woke up, Billy was gone. Back to Earth, she caught herself thinking, envious of his deluded voyages. Back to his youth or forward to his death. But that was impossible, however much she liked to dream it wasn't.

She rose and took a shower and used the bathroom, every movement on display, and the crowds outside grew dense as the Tralfs shuffled to a leering stop. She could feel them probing her mind. A thousand hands pawed at her head like bodies stuffed into the same crowded train. A thousand unblinking eyes bored through her flesh. She could hear them.

Their language was gibberish, but she knew they could understand her. She begged them to let her go, to take her home, that she wasn't an animal for a zoo. She repeated this in her mind like a mantra. She remembered chanting something similar as the cameras looked on and men twice her age were rough with her. She remembered thinking that if she froze and sat real still, Uncle Chip would know that she was uncomfortable, that he would stop.

Montana toweled off and pulled on one of the robes that cycled back and forth through the food chutes. The robes had come after much begging. The Tralfs could talk back to her by means of a musical organ with a humanlike voice, but she never knew when they might respond and when they might simply go on ignoring her pleas. It was maddening, this. The inconsistency. It was back to living with a drunk.

It was Stained who explained why their responses didn't make sense. Stained was one of the zookeepers who cleaned the domes at night. He had a red blotch on his palm, and since Tralfs didn't have names, Montana had given him one. Stained explained that Tralfs saw in four dimensions, and so sometimes they answered before a question was asked, and sometimes they waited until years later to answer, and so you had to listen carefully. He told Montana this two days before she asked about it. It took some piecing together, talking to Stained.

Stained also explained how the universe would end. He cleaned the glass by dunking a large fleshy finger into a bucket of suds, and between the sounds of squeaks, he told Montana about a test pilot trying out a new type of fuel and how this would blow up the entire universe one day. Montana asked, "If they knew it was going to happen, why didn't anyone stop him?" She said the question out loud, even though Stained could read her mind.

Stained went on cleaning the glass for a few hours, and Montana busied herself with making the bed. She knew rushing Stained or repeating the question wouldn't make any difference, so she kept herself busy. She had a system for making the bed that took four and a half hours, but she had additions in mind that might stretch it out to five. Finally, Stained answered her last question. At least — she thought it was her last question. It could've been the answer to one she would ask tomorrow.

"Because," Stained said, his voice musical and sonorous through that great pipe organ over her head.

Montana nodded. It was the answer she had expected.

6

I am about to die. It is September 11, and every cell in my body is acutely aware of my looming demise. The certainty of it. The inevitability. Not years from now, not weeks or days. Moments. Like how a Tralfamadorian knows.

The first plane hitting a skyscraper was an aberration, an accident, something to gaze upon and wait for things to get better, wait for the sirens to arrive. The second jet, however, brought the promise of a third and a fourth. Here was a pattern. Jets are falling out of the sky. The world has gone amok. A GPS malfunction, an EMP detonation, solar flares, a dozen disaster films, and science fiction plots. My brain is misfiring with all the possibilities but the real one. Trapped between a cliff wall of burning buildings and the Hudson River, I look around for my best friend, Scott, but he went off to investigate the fire, the report of bodies. I feel the impulse to run after him, to push through the crowd that's heading the other way. I start up the metal ramp toward the wharf and away from the yachts.

"We have to get the boats out of here," Kevin tells me.

Kevin is my boss, and he's right. We need to get the boats away from these burning buildings, away from the next impact and the one after. I look to the wharf for Scott. He'll be back at any moment and help me cast these lines off. He saw the second plane disappear into that building, and he's running back my way. I try not to think of the bodies Leslie saw or the debris raining down. I try not to think about that. He'll be back.

I scamper onto the boat. The starboard engine has been having problems — it won't crank from the helm or the flybridge. I have to go down into the engine room to start the mains. This is where I'll die. This is when the surety of my last breath seizes me. It's when I lift that heavy hatch of stainless steel and teak decking and gaze down that steep ladder into the darkness of the engine room. Down there, I won't be able to see the sky. I won't spot the next jet hurtling in at hundreds of miles an hour and be able to . . . to dodge, to know that this is the end, to witness my destruction, to do anything about it. I turn my back on that loaded gun — that bright blue sky — and descend below deck.

The engines crank one by one, slowly, starter motors whining, diesel firing under pressure, kicking up into that throaty rattle of an idle that sounds as though it could stop at any moment, that sound like a weakened heart.

Scrambling back up the ladder, feet clanking on rungs, I find chaos outside. People are running across the wharf, away from the buildings, looking to the sky for the next plane. A man asks if I'm leaving. People can hear the engines, can see the exhaust, are watching me scramble around the decks to make ready.

"C'mon," I tell the man. Others are looking at me expectantly. "Anyone who wants to go, c'mon," I say. I have people to help. Somehow, this helps me.

I loosen the spring lines as strangers dash onboard. Someone offers to get the bowline and runs up the dock before I say yes. "No shoes," I tell a man. This reflexive bark comes as quickly as the realization that such rules are now ridiculous. But there are habits. And my body is calmer now with something to do. I have a responsibility to this boat, to its owner, to these dozen or more strangers onboard.

There are briefcases and business shoes scattered across the deck. Up on the flybridge, I put the boat into gear. I lay on the horn a few times, yell my friend's name, look for him in the crowds. But Scott is gone. The motor yacht *Prelude* pivots neatly in the tiny marina and points its bow across the Hudson toward New Jersey. We pass through the narrow breakwater, and I look back over my shoulder to see a dark object plummeting from a burning building, a man in a flapping business suit, who disappears out of sight. The flag on the back of the boat goes to half-mast as we motor away. The wind picks up on our faces, but all else is silence.

The marina across the Hudson won't take us. We tie up on the fuel dock, everyone trying their cell phones to let loved ones know they're okay, but the networks are jammed. Men put on their business shoes and gather their briefcases and disappear. Crowds gather on the docks and along the shore to gaze at this burning neighbor across the way. I can't stay on the fuel dock, they tell me. I have to pull away.

I need to go back and look for Scott. I have mobility, while so many others are trapped. And out here on the Hudson, I can see the sky; I can get out of the way. I am heading back to Manhattan when the screeching starts, when the top of the South Tower tips, when a building leans its head sadly to one side and then sinks into the earth.

A building collapsing sounds a lot like a jet throttling up on a runway. A high-pitched scream builds and builds. You brace for a boom, a roar, a masculine anguish — but it is a shrill cry. It gets you not in the chest, but in the bones.

I watch from the deck of a boat named *Prelude*. The flag on the aft of the boat is already at half-mast. A man in a business suit with a briefcase lowered it as we left the marina, other men in similar suits taking flight from office windows, escaping the heat.

A plume of crushed steel billows out over Lower Manhattan. My best friend is in there somewhere. I turn the boat around, away from the on-rush of dust and debris, away from the home where I used to live.

7

September 11. Cell phones do not work, and part of me is glad. As soon as I get a signal, I'll be able to call my mom and tell her I'm alive. But I'll also have to call Shannon, Scott's girlfriend, and let her know that Scott is dead, that a building has fallen down around him, that he went off to investigate a fire and now is gone.

I consider this aboard *Prelude*. I cannot stay on the fuel dock, and there's no available slip, so I creep toward Manhattan, where fellow boats from North Cove Marina are pulling people from the seawall. People are desperate to leave. They jump to *Prelude*'s swim platform, each with a different story. The wake and chop make for treacherous maneuvering so close to a concrete wall. On the New Jersey side, we let people off by docking up to a restaurant. There are construction workers there with hard hats and muddy boots and lunch pails. They're looking for some-one, anyone, to take them across the Hudson, opposite this tide of hu-manity. They say they want to help. I tell them I'm going back anyway, and they can ride.

As they scamper onboard, I forget to tell them about their boots, about minding the deck. We cast off and watch from the Hudson as the second building falls. I ask them if they're sure. They are. As I creep into the marina, my home is unrecognizable. Debris is everywhere. The glass dome of the Winter Garden is wounded, and a lower chunk of one of the lesser towers is missing. The world seems a precarious place. Buildings mean to topple on men. Buildings have. I pivot in the tight marina and back into my old slip, like I've done a thousand times, and white paper flutters down like a flock of exhausted birds. The paper catches on the deck and in the scuppers. There's the smell of something acidic, something foreign, something I have never tasted but I know to be toxic. All but one of the men jump to the dock. The lone dissenter has seen enough. I don't blame him.

"That building looks to topple," I tell the men with the hard hats, pointing to the smaller World Trade 7. Two hours ago, I didn't know buildings could do this. Suddenly, I'm an expert.

I scan the wasteland around me and see no sign of Scott, no sign of anyone. "Be careful," the guy who stayed behind calls out to his friends, and I am convinced that I have delivered these men to their deaths. I pull out of the slip once again. We pick up more passengers from the seawall south of the marina before heading back across the Hudson. There is much to do, pulling people away, right up until the Coast Guard comes and orders us to stop.

Scott is dead. My cell phone is dead. My mother must think me dead. So it goes.

I pick up the papers that have drifted down on the boat and have become plastered there, these relics from great buildings that no longer stand. The first one I grab is an insurance document. Listen: What I tell you here is true. The first line on the first page I pick up, it begins:

In the event of damage to the building . . .

So it goes.

A red sun slides across the geodesic dome, and the crisp angles between the glass panels divide that alien sky into triangles of magenta and gold. Another day in those prison walls. Billy is asleep on the sofa bed, mewling like a cat, his hands twitching in some dream, some time-travel delusion. Montana escapes from the fold-out bed as quietly as noisy springs will allow. She grabs her robe and covers herself. The zoo is quiet, the doors not yet open to the hordes of skinny aliens with their hand-like heads. This is the only time when she can see the critters across the way, those balls of fur that roll around and bump into one another, their long periscope antennas unfolding to peer out at the world, at the woman peering back at them.

Montana watches the furry aliens scurry and bump about. She thinks of what Stained told her of the universe ending, how a pilot presses a button and all that ever was or ever is goes kaput. It's hard to believe such an end might be possible. Even harder to summon some fear of this, some longing or regret. She presses her palm to the thick glass, cool to the touch, and she remembers this, something both distant and familiar: Her hand on peeling wallpaper. A domestic prison. A feeling of being trapped. Broken knuckles and blood in the sink, and barely a dent in the sheetrock.

It is September 11, 2013. Twelve years have gone by. I'm on a flight from San Francisco to Fort Lauderdale, a cross-country flight loaded down with fuel. Looking out the window, I think of a woman I have invented, the woman in 13D. I've been thinking about her for twelve years. I've been on fifty flights this year, and I think about her every time.

I don't know this woman in 13D. Maybe she's a man. Maybe that seat is empty. But I've been thinking about her — imagining her — ever since that ball of orange and black erupted overhead. I wonder if she knew, in those last moments of her life, that she was about to die. The engines outside her window must've been screaming, making that noise like a great steel building collapsing to the ground. The wings must've been creaking, the wind howling across the trembling skin of that aircraft, New York City so near below. Too near. Buildings rushing past, knuckles white on the armrests, a stranger clutching the wrist of another stranger in fear, that sense that this wasn't right, that those men who have taken over the plane — who won't let anyone go to the restroom up front — aren't going to land and simply trade hostages.

I'm on the wharf, looking up. There's a plane howling across the clear blue sky, banking hard, coming in too fast. One building is burning, and another can't get out of the way. A pattern is forming, but in my head I only have a silent scream to a pilot who is already dead. *Pull up. Pull up,* I silently shout. *What're you doing?* I scream this to the pilot as I watch, trying to talk to him as a Tralfamadorian might. This can't be happening. This can't be happening. This can't be happening.

The woman in 13D is screaming and thinking the same thing.

And then it happens.

8

The Coast Guard won't let me move. The Hudson and the East River have been shut down. New York City is smoking, and I am not aware of this last fact, but the entire world is watching. Some with happy fists.

Another boat has tied up to the restaurant dock. Hours march by. The construction workers return for the lunch pails they left on the dock, and they say there was little to do in the way of help, that they had to catch the same rescue boats as everyone else. But they saw things. They tell me awful stories, things I do not want to hear. They leave boot prints of mud and ash on the docks, trailing away.

I hear my name. Turning, there is Scott on the dock across the water. A dead man, standing. My best friend, waving at me. I nearly dive in and swim across. My heart is bursting out of my chest, and for all the death I've seen, now is when the tears come, this sight of someone I love, very much alive.

I go to crank *Prelude* to drive the comical distance across this leap of water. It would take an hour to walk around. A crew member from the sailboat says to use their tender, so I do. Scott and I embrace. He tells me what happened, the choking cloud, how he had to breathe through his shirt, how he followed the stampeding others, dangled over the Hudson from a rail, dropped into a boat, saw someone else land and their leg go sickeningly sideways, didn't know where I was, marched down the Hudson shoreline and stopped at every marina, and now here.

We look at each other for a long time. We talk on top of each other. I have to touch his arm several times to make sure he's real.

On the dock, someone suggests we find food. And has anyone seen a TV? There are rumors about Chicago and LA. Are they right? Are more coming? The Sears Tower? The White House?

We head through the parking lot toward town, but there is a man blocking our way. Sitting astride a tractor with a big scooping bucket on the front, he yells at us for being on his property. We explain the boats, and he says we can't tie up there, that this is his restaurant. We say there's no room anywhere, that the Coast Guard won't let us leave, that they'll shoot at us if we do.

He tells us we better go fucking home and get our guns. He tells us we're at war.

We watch as a car pulls up, a friend of his, and the man lifts the bucket of that great tractor so that this one car can come through, and then the bucket rattles back to the concrete. No one else may pass.

"Better get your fucking guns," he yells at us, as we run off in search of food. We run, and our feet make the sound of Tralfamadorians clapping, of happy people making fists.

Stained is washing the same triangle of glass that he washed the night before. He peers in at Montana and seems to be watching her knit. Montana has snapped the antennas off the TV, much to the chagrin of Billy Pilgrim, who says this Western is his favorite show. He settles when he sees the reception does not waver. Montana finds she has to rough up the smooth metal a bit before it will hold the thread. She is taking the carpet apart and making a dress for her child. Her arms rest on her swollen belly. The thread pulls neatly from the carpet, one line at a time, back and forth, as the opposite happens in her lap. There is destruction and creation taking place all at once, connected by a single thread. The glass squeaks as Stained washes the same spot, over and over.

"Because," he says, apropos of *something,* the organ overhead playing his tune-like voice.

Montana smiles. She's not sure what question this is aimed at — not that it matters. She is content to have someone who listens. Billy doesn't always. He just stares in the vicinity of her locket.

"I wish you wouldn't destroy the universe," Montana says, not for the first time. She starts a new row, really likes the way she can extend or retract these needles to make them shorter or longer, thinks TV antennas are just fine for knitting, and then looks up at Stained. "Those of us who only see in three dimensions, we would most appreciate having the universe around."

Stained blinks and watches her. Montana peers down at the dome of her belly, this dome within a dome, this prisoner two domes deep, naked and ignorant and soon for this world. "It would be nice to have a universe for my baby," she tells Stained. Not that this would move him, just her thinking aloud. Just talking over Billy, who is murmuring in his sleep.

"I'm not angry at you," she tells Stained. And the squeaking and cleaning stop. "You took everything from me, but I'm not angry at you." Another row of stitches. Montana adjusts herself in the lounger, because being pregnant requires a constant quest for some elusive comfort. She loves her baby; this is what she knows. And she never wanted one. Never would have had one back at home. Not in that life. It made hating this place difficult at times. Stained seems to be reading her mind, the way he stares at her.

"I was angry, you know," she tells him. "For weeks and weeks, all I wanted was for all of you to die for what you did. Maybe you heard me screaming it in my head, those long speeches saying I'd get even with you, that my world would come for me, would blast you to smithereens."

Stained watches her.

"But this is where we're different. You see the future and refuse to change it. Where I come from, we can see the past, but we keep repeating it. That's where we're different. The same but different." She nods vigorously. "I've never been free before, you see. Not once in my whole life. I used to make fists and hit walls, but it hurt me more than it hurt them. The people who did bad things to me, they didn't care how angry I got. It didn't fix a thing. So you go right on cleaning and peering in, and I'm going to —"

"He loves you, too," Stained says.

Montana turns and peers at Billy Pilgrim, who has rolled over and has uncovered himself. She knits two and purls one. Knits two and purls one. "I know," she says. She doesn't say that she doesn't really love Billy. Pities him, more like. After a long while, she remembers where the conversation had been going.

"You know what I've realized? Just a week ago, sitting here, miserable for my kid who will be born in this zoo of yours. I realized that I have never owned myself. Not really. I've thought what others wanted me to think. I've felt the way I was supposed to feel. I used to get angry and want to hit things, thought that would make it better, make things right." Montana laughs. She balls up her hand. "I used to make fists like you do, that's what I did."

The glass before Montana has never been so clean.

"And then I realized what a blessing it is that I don't know the future. That I don't see like you do. Because what would I do? I'd be as numb and callous as you are. A prisoner. I'd already know how this dress comes out, and that wouldn't make me wanna go through with it. You know?"

"It's a boy," Stained says.

Montana looks from her knitting to the Tralfamadorian with the red splotch on his palm. If Montana had lived a different life, she would have called this Tralf Macbeth. But that wasn't the life given to her.

"What did you say?" she asks.

Stained blinks. Montana rubs her belly.

"Can you read his mind? It's gonna be a boy?"

Tears blur her vision like the rainy Tralfamadorian nights streak the dome.

"If you can talk to him, tell him I love him. Tell him everything's gonna be okay."

Stained has gone back to cleaning. Montana wants to scream, but the thing she is angry at is in the past. The past can't hear her. This is the thing, her great discovery. She smiles at the future. Happiness is a choice. She knits another row and loves every man who ever wronged her. More important, she loves those who will wrong her yet.

"Because," Stained says, curling a finger, and peering in at her.

"Yes," Montana agrees. "Because." She laughs, and almost feels free.

9

A plane disappears into an office building, and bombs erupt everywhere at once. In London and Baghdad, in Spain and Afghanistan, every bomb that ever was and ever will be detonates in unison. All the same bomb.

The Tralfamadorians see time stretched out in all directions. They see a people who can do nothing but make joyous fists. Something is wrong with those who don't. Something is terribly wrong with those who don't. And where are the more like them?

It is July 6, 2001, and I am on the deck of the motor yacht *Symphony*. There is a stranger beside me, a beautiful girl; I do not know her name. She is a dancer, one of the high-kicking Rockettes, and we have exchanged smiles more than once over the course of the night. I join her on the bow. It is a warm evening on the Hudson. I have yet to meet my wife, Amber, in whom I will find peace. *Symphony* turns away from the Statue of Liberty and aims for Manhattan, steams through those lapping waters toward a skyline alight, toward those tall pillars of gleaming glass that blot out the blackest sky.

At that moment, a stranger leans in and kisses a boy, and the universe has never been so right. If time could be lived in a single dimension, there is where I would be. A boy and a city whole. But it is a man who writes this, every word of it true. And in that bright blue and empty sky where shade used to shelter my toil, I take solace in the wisdom of Montana Wildhack — who knows that nothing in the past can keep her from being free.

AFTERWORD

This is by far the most difficult thing I've ever written. It's the only time I grossly missed a self-imposed deadline, and what is little more than a novelette took longer to compose than most of my full-length novels. The final 10,500 words required that I first write about 100,000, composing and recomposing passages over and over again, crafting and deleting, until I ended up with the piece I submitted.

In 2014, Amazon launched a new program called Kindle Worlds, which allows fans to write stories based on their favorite characters and worlds. My Silo series was included in the program, and Amazon was also interested in me writing for one of the other "Worlds." When I saw that Kurt Vonnegut's works were included in the program, I expressed interest. I think I knew from the start what I wanted to write; it just took me a while to admit it to myself.

Slaughterhouse-Five is not my favorite of Vonnegut's works — that would be Cat's Cradle *— but it is the most powerful. Semi-autobiographical,* Slaughterhouse-Five *allowed Vonnegut to write about the bombing of Dresden, which he survived, by approaching it askance. I like to imag-*

ine that writing the novel was both difficult and cathartic for him. Because "Peace in Amber" was both for me. It was the first time I tried to write a detailed account of my experiences on September 11, 2001.

All of the details in the story you just read are as accurate as I can make them. Writing it down, I bawled. Some days, I just sat with my laptop and cried, not knowing what to write. Like my pain for years, I hid the process from those around me. By the time my girlfriend got home from work each day, my face was dry. I tried to not look tired. There were other days that I shuffled around the house muttering to myself that life wasn't worth living. Through it all, I wrote and deleted. Wrote and deleted. It's impossible to convey to you, reading this, how different writing felt at the time.

I've always beaten deadlines by a mile. This one came and went. But slowly, the form of the piece fell together. And gradually, there were details of the day that I could look at without it crippling me. I'd been avoiding so much for so long. Not just the imagery, but the helplessness. And the agony I felt thinking my best friend was gone, and then seeing him again, and then the survivor's guilt, the something close to elation soured by death's specter.

At the end, the piece I dreaded most and got through in the worst manner helped me like no other. I have no idea what it reads like to the general public. Is it the inscrutable mess that I sometimes feel like it is? Impenetrable? Surreal? Discordant? Discomforting? I hope so. It's what Slaughterhouse-Five feels like when I read it again and again. And it's what that day felt like as I revisit it far too often.

ACKNOWLEDGMENTS

A handful of editors changed the course of my life. They are the reason this collection — or any of my works — exists.

It started with Lisa Kelly-Wilson, a friend I knew only as an avatar on an online forum. When I posted one day that I'd written a rough draft of a novel (*Molly Fyde and the Parsona Rescue*), Lisa offered to give it a read. She was an academic editor and a fan of science fiction — I think she wanted material to humiliate me with on the forum. It was that kind of relationship.

To both of our surprise, Lisa loved the book. With force, she nixed my plan of giving the novel away for free on my blog. Instead, she offered a round of edits and suggested that I get it published. Lisa quickly became a motivating force in my writing life: a mentor, an advocate, and, I daresay, a fan. When she and her husband drove across the country to attend a reading of mine in Charleston, South Carolina, I was able to finally throw my arms around her. The memory of that moment is as vivid to me today as it was seven years ago.

With Lisa's urging, I began to query agents and small publishers. Within weeks, two presses made offers. I went with Norlights Press, run by Nadene Carter, with whom I immediately connected. Nadene taught me legions about the craft of writing, simple things like not head-hopping and how to write with a more active voice. Stuff most writers already know. I was learning on the fly, editing a chapter ahead of Nadene using whatever I could learn from her previous suggestions and corrections. Between Lisa and Nadene, I got over the crippling fear of having my words made public. Now it was merely nausea-inducing.

When I decided to self-publish, one of the most important people in my life became my most important editor: my mom. A voracious reader, my mom was the first person to see my drafts, and she became my reliable editor and typo-finder. She also played the role of agent, demanding more pages from me on a regular basis. At the time, my readership numbered in the dozens and then gradually the hundreds. My mom gave my writing career an urgency not at all in line with my popularity. Thanks for believing in me, Mom. I'll get you something new to read soon.

Just when I was starting to think my writing was halfway decent, along came some jerk named David Gatewood to assure me otherwise. My novel *Wool* had become a *New York Times* best seller and the highest-rated novel on Amazon the year of its release. Whatever confidence was seeping in, an email from this complete stranger soon destroyed it. The subject of the email was: "162 things wrong with WOOL." The body of the email listed every mistake in gruesome detail.

David's corrections were incorporated into all subsequent editions of *Wool,* and I asked if he would edit my future works. Overnight, Mr. Gatewood became my indispensable editor and unbelievably hilarious critic. When word spread of his talents, David quit the world of banking, where he was so desperately needed, and became instead one of the most sought-after editors in publishing. I wouldn't be half the writer I am today had David not reached out to me. Thanks for everything you do not only for me but for the community, my friend.

Each of these editors did more than correct mistakes in my writing; they attempted to correct mistakes in my self-esteem. I've never been a fan of my writing. Crippling self-doubt prevented me from completing a novel despite two decades of trying. And so the editors in my life were as much about curation and motivation as polishing prose. There is a history of this in the genre of science fiction. Editors like John W. Campbell and Hugo Gernsback were talent scouts first and foremost. Their skill lay in spotting raw ability, refining it, and then publishing that talent in magazines and anthologies that would sell and launch careers. A handful of such editors have wielded outsize power in shaping science fiction. Today no editor is doing this as well as John Joseph Adams.

John and I met at Worldcon five years ago. Over lunch, we brainstormed a series of three apocalyptic anthologies that became the Apocalypse Triptych: *The End Is Nigh, The End Is Now,* and *The End Has Come.* The insanity of this project was that I would not only contribute a story to each book but assist in the editing. I soon found myself published alongside many of my heroes — some of the most talented writers working in the field today — and I was also expected to edit their works!

My appreciation for what the editors in my life have done for me grew enormously through this process. Editing is a special skill, harder in many ways than writing, and I was fortunate that John was there to clean up my mess. He also motivated me to write three difficult and emotional stories for the series, then proceeded to wrest more short stories from me for his various anthologies and his award-winning *Lightspeed Magazine.*

The stories he inspired me to write are included here, as well as pretty much every other short piece I've ever written. Before this collection came into being, these stories were scattered, some lost, some unpublished, some brand-new. I thank John for not only making it possible to publish this book, but for thinking it needed to exist in the first place.

Along with my brilliant agent, Kristin Nelson of the Nelson Agency, each of these incredible editors has shaped my writing and my life. They convinced me to share some of my ideas with you. And you, dear reader, have done the rest. I am eternally grateful to you all. Without you, none of this would exist.

Hugh Howey
Panama Canal, Panama
January 2017